HAVEN'T
KILLED
IN
YEARS

HAVEN'T
KILLED
IN
YEARS

AMY K. GREEN

BERKLEY
NEW YORK

BERKLEY
An imprint of Penguin Random House LLC
1745 Broadway, New York, NY 10019
penguinrandomhouse.com

Book design by George Towne
Interior art: Stack of vintage photos © Azure / Shutterstock

Library of Congress Cataloging-in-Publication Data

Names: Green, Amy K., author.
Title: Haven't killed in years / Amy K. Green.
Other titles: Have not killed in years
Description: New York: Berkley, 2025.
Identifiers: LCCN 2025006481 (print) | LCCN 2025006482 (ebook) |
ISBN 9780593953495 (hardcover) | ISBN 9780593953501 (ebook)
Subjects: LCGFT: Detective and mystery fiction. | Novels.
Classification: LCC PS3607.R4298 H38 2025 (print) |
LCC PS3607.R4298 (ebook) | DDC 813/.6—dc23/eng/20250327
LC record available at https://lccn.loc.gov/2025006481
LC ebook record available at https://lccn.loc.gov/2025006482

Printed in the United States of America
$PrintCode

The authorized representative in the EU for product safety and compliance is
Penguin Random House Ireland, Morrison Chambers, 32 Nassau Street,
Dublin D02 YH68, Ireland, https://eu-contact.penguin.ie.

HAVEN'T
KILLED
IN
YEARS

PART
ONE

ONE

— — — —

O N THE DAY MY mother was released from prison I stubbed my toe four times. Same toe. Four times. It was a statistical anomaly and, in hindsight, a warning that bad things were coming my way.

The first stubbing happened before I even left the apartment. I had eaten three caramel candies the night before and had to get aggressive with a bit of floss, disastrously so. I inspected my bloody gums in the mirror, looking like a total cannibal.

As I grabbed a square of toilet paper to wipe my mouth with, I kicked my toe into the base of the toilet head-on. It was only the beginning.

Two hours later it happened again. I was at Painting Pots, a place where I spent too much of my free time. It was primarily a do-it-yourself ceramics store where customers, mostly kids, painted already-sculpted pieces, but I hung in the back with the actual pottery wheels. It was an obsessive hobby that required the focus I craved. Long ago I'd accepted that I had enough bowls and vases, so now most sessions ended with a dramatic flattening of my creation, reclaiming all the clay I could.

I had a comfortable rapport with one of the employees, a guy named Porter who was only a few years out of high school. Nothing in life brought him more joy than calling me Thirsty Thirty anytime I interacted with a man, and that day was no exception.

I was standing over the sink, scrubbing between my fingers, running late for a meeting, when I sensed Porter entering my space.

"There you go, Gwen." He appeared over my shoulder, his bleach-blond coif grazing my temple and causing me to look up.

A frazzled man gripping the hands of two identical preschoolers stood at the front counter, the twins tugging his arms in opposing directions as he struggled to maintain his footing.

"Single dad," Porter whispered into my ear as I tore off a paper towel. I swatted him away in a continuous motion. "Thirty *and* thirsty," he said, countering my dismissal right on cue.

I smirked as I walked away, taking four steps before a graceless boy wielding a dripping paintbrush darted in front of me. I swerved out of the way and into the leg of one of the tables. Same toe.

"Fuck," I shouted, and the world froze. It wasn't a great place to swear. "Sorry," I said to the first mother I made eye contact with, and the earth started spinning again.

I managed to survive the next eleven hours at work without stubbing my toe. My feet were hurting, but that was from standing for hours, in heels, at an undergraduate career fair. Making small talk with college juniors worried about summer internships was, at times, even more painful.

After the event wrapped up, since I was still downtown, I agreed to meet Brian for a nightcap. Brian was a guy I had been on two previous dates with. On our second date, I had gotten my period unexpectedly, which announced itself with instant debilitating cramps that sent me to the bathroom a suspicious number of times before I was finally able to go home. I assumed this date would be an improvement.

Brian was all right. He was polite and clean-cut and I let him tell me things about his day. He was attractive enough, even if I was bored by the majority of our conversations. He was a safe choice.

We each had two drinks and then, even though it was Friday night, I pretended I had to be up early the next morning. I slipped my phone into my purse, hopped off my seat, and swung my foot directly into the vacant stool between us. Same toe.

I gripped the bar table, shifting my weight onto it. Brian slid off his stool to help me. One or both of our unplanned yet synchronized movements knocked over the glass holding the last half of his third dark beer—the third drink I had hinted was not necessary.

The brown liquid seeped into the sleeve of my cream sweater. Brian pawed a clump of cocktail napkins and patted at my sleeve while I bent over, clenching my body to stop the blood from flowing to my toe. Once he had successfully set the stain into the fibers under the guise of helping, he went in for a kiss.

"I just stubbed my toe," I reminded him, halting his advance.

The fourth and final assault was the most significant.

I lived on the second floor of a three-story house that had been renovated by Dr. Frankenstein. At one point, someone had converted the top two floors into one unit, then someone else had needed more income and chopped a third unit into the building. It was small and a real structural misstep, but the finishings looked high quality and the commute into Boston was manageable. Plus, the rent was low for a one-bedroom, and having a roommate wasn't really an option for someone like me.

A two-hundred-year-old woman, Mrs. Magnus, lived below me and a burned-out musician lived on top. They were great at staying out of my business and I was usually able to relax once I was locked tight inside. That feeling was more valuable to me than things like space for a queen mattress or an actual bedroom closet.

I got home from my date and pushed open the building's front door, kicking it over the thick carpet runner that always bunched in places, preventing the door from opening or closing properly. Then I traipsed up the flight of stairs, exhausted from having to take two trains to get back to my car, hunched over like the universe was forcing me to climb Mount Everest.

A small brown box awaited me on the landing outside my apartment. I slid my key into the lock and swung the door open before picking it up. There was no label. It wasn't even properly sealed; the flaps were folded into each other without any adhesive. Through the cracks, I could make out one of those Trader Joe's newspapers. I undid a flap and the rest fell open.

I lifted the newspaper and revealed my gift, a man's left arm—hairy, colorless, severed right below the elbow. Wedged between the thumb and forefinger of his stiff hand was a tiny note card, the kind that comes with a bouquet of flowers, which simply read *Hi, Marin.*

I threw the newspaper back on top of the arm and lunged into my apartment with it, slamming the door behind me and pivoting directly into my iron entryway table. Same exact toe.

TWO

- - - -

HERE WAS NO WAY it was a coincidence. Of all the days for a severed limb to show up on my doorstep, it had to be the same day my mother was released from prison. *Hi, Marin.* That was the real kicker. Someone knew the truth of who I was, and that person was keen on letting me know.

I stared at the box for almost an hour. I had to get rid of it. One would normally contact the authorities, but this was not a normal situation. I grabbed a brown paper grocery bag from under the sink and placed the box inside. Then I hooked the handles around my wrist and slid over to the drawer next to the fridge. After fumbling through a bunch of utensils, I found the salad tongs and threw them in the bag with the box.

The rational parts of my brain told me to destroy it—dissolve it in acid, feed it to wild animals, burn it in a barrel—but I was desperate to know who the arm belonged to. I didn't have a convenient friend at a DNA lab or within the FBI, so I would have to plant the arm somewhere and let the cops figure it out for me.

I drove my car to a side street half a mile from the Wellington train station and folded my hair up under a baseball hat. I considered throwing my hood over the hat, but honestly, if you were looking for someone suspicious, a dark-hooded night prowler would fit the bill. I took the train eleven stops to Mass Ave. It was the kind of area where you knew to stay out of other people's business. After walking a bit, I came across an alley that looked secluded enough. I did a quick scan for banks or convenience stores—anywhere that might have a surveillance system. With nothing to give me pause, I crouched next to a dumpster in the alley and opened the bag, using the salad tongs to remove the arm from the box and place it behind the dumpster. When the garbage truck came, someone would see it. That was the point.

The train ride back to Wellington station took about half an hour. I wanted very badly to go home and pretend everything was normal— make dinner, read, and fall asleep on the couch. The problem was, everything had changed. Somebody knew who I was, and said person had killed or at least severely maimed a man. More troubling, though, was that it was not something I had merely stumbled upon; I was being provoked.

- - - - -

I WAS BORN MARIN Marie Haggerty, but that wasn't a name I heard anymore. I was Gwen Tanner at the doctor's office and to telemarketers (the only people who ever used my full name) and Gwen to everyone else. I worked for a financial services company as an assistant in recruiting—a stable entry-level job that I was probably stuck in for the long haul. I had never been in a serious relationship but dated enough so as to not raise any flags. I wore colorful clothes from stores like the J.Crew outlet so that I didn't look dark and deranged. At any given time, I was overtired and slightly dehydrated, but from the outside, I looked like your standard almost-too-basic law-abiding woman approaching thirty. On the inside? Eh, not so much.

When I was nine years old, my father, Abel Haggerty, was convicted on eight counts of first-degree murder and I was ripped from my home without warning. He'd also had a good job and worn nice clothes; it was the easiest way to hide in plain sight.

There's no death penalty in the state of Massachusetts, and Abel Haggerty was currently serving a life sentence at Edgar Valley Prison in Barker, Massachusetts. On a map, he was close, but in reality, he might as well have been two thousand miles away.

My mother, on the other hand, had only been convicted of aiding and abetting. Her lawyer argued that my father had brainwashed and abused her, garnering Reanne Haggerty a reduced sentence and the chance for parole. The last time I'd seen my mother I was also nine, and I had planned on keeping it that way. Unfortunately for me, a human forearm had been delivered to my doorstep and my dear mother was the only lead I had.

THREE

—— —— —— —— —— —— ——

O F COURSE, I HAD been keeping tabs. Reanne Haggerty had been granted a divorce from my father while in prison, and years later had married a sad sack named Gustus Trent—prison-wedding style. No gold foil save-the-date for me.

I drove thirty-five minutes to the town of Saugus and parked outside Gustus's house. It needed a paint job and a deep clean—maybe one of those exterminator tents. I waited in my car for two hours before I saw my mother emerge, her long, frizzy hair half-auburn, half-gray. She looked old, a lot older than fifty-two—beauty credit to the Massachusetts Department of Correction. She held a cigarette between her chapped lips and followed her husband into an old Ford sedan under the carport.

I trailed them to the nearby Stop & Shop, where he parked crooked in a handicap spot. I parked like a decent human being farther down the same row and hustled into the store after them.

I waited until Reanne was alone, a couple of aisles in, staring at the section full of Hamburger Helper and Rice-A-Roni type things—

delicious chemicals with the ability to turn from powder to paste. The options must have been overwhelming compared to what she'd had to pick from twenty years ago.

"Hi, Mom," I said.

She released a box and spun toward me. She took in my face, then examined the aisle around us, concerned she was hallucinating. "Marin?"

Marin. It was unsettling hearing that name. More so than I'd ever considered. I nodded. *That's me, I guess.*

"Your hair's so dark," she said.

"I dye it."

"You look different. You're real grown up. As tall as me."

I wasn't looking to list all the changes that can happen to a person from ages nine to twenty-nine, so I cut to the chase. "Can you tell me if you've been talking to anyone about me?"

"What do ya mean?"

"I need to know. No one is supposed to know who I am or where I live."

"*I* don't know where you live, and honestly, I don't know if I could have even picked you out of a lineup."

"No one has been asking you anything about me? Even a small thing could be something."

"No." She considered it. "No, I haven't talked about you in a real long time. I mean . . ."

"What about your new husband?"

"What about him?" she asked.

"Where'd he even come from? Does he know about me?"

"I don't know. It was in the papers all those years ago. He might know about ya, but not from anything I said."

"Are you sure?" I pressed.

She struggled to process my intensity. "What's going on, Marin?"

There it was again. *Marin.* It felt like I'd swallowed a cactus. I started backing away, realizing I had been overconfident in how apathetic I could remain in her presence.

"Do you want to go get a coffee or something?" she asked.

"No," I said.

"I'd like to see ya again. If you wanted to."

"No," I said, taking three steps backward before turning and booking it out of there.

— — — —

I COLLAPSED INTO MY car and cranked up the music, attempting to drown out my thoughts, but it didn't work. It only made them louder to compensate. Seeing Reanne had been a bad plan. Useless. The only thing it did was open old wounds. I hated my mother more than anyone—even more than my serial killer father. He couldn't help himself. He liked killing people. He needed to kill people. Something was wrong with him; there were a lot of theories— borderline personality disorder, psychopathy, sociopathy, extreme narcissism, et cetera, et cetera. Plenty had diagnosed a more biblical than medical cause: EVIL.

My mother had no clinical excuse for keeping me there, in that house with him, all those years. She wasn't brainwashed or abused; I was sure that was all bogus. My father had made her feel important, chosen, and she'd thought it was exciting and made her better than other, ordinary people. It was only once they were caught and faced life in prison that she started to spin a different tale. My father never argued against it. He really did love her. He loved us both. We were his.

Talking to my father was going to be much more complicated. I couldn't very well show up and get my name on his visitor log, putting a connection between Gwen Tanner and Abel Haggerty on record. Not to mention, even the thought of talking to him released the equivalent of a paralytic gas into my brain. My mother might not have been brainwashed, but I certainly had been. I'd been young, but I had very vivid memories.

I remembered a night he took me into the city to go skating at the Frog Pond. It was freezing and I had to wear these big dopey mittens that slipped off anytime I put my hands down. He held my hand and we went around the rink maybe a hundred times. Afterward, we went to dinner and I ordered a strawberry milk shake and chicken fingers that I couldn't finish. We took an indirect route back to the car and I watched my father suffocate a homeless man with the plastic bag from my leftovers.

That's how it always was. It was never particularly premeditated. He would get a feeling or a message or a sign—whatever way he wanted to explain it to me in the moment—and then it would happen.

The homeless man sat against a concrete wall. He let us approach, didn't even flinch. When my father held out the bag, the man smiled, hoping for a warm meal. Instead, my father removed the Styrofoam container and handed it to me. The man was confused, but I was not; I knew what was happening.

In an instant, the plastic bag was over his head. My father yanked him to the ground so that he could drive his knee into the man's back, pinning him down while squeezing the bag closed. Eventually the man stopped struggling—a few errant spasms and then nothing. When it was done, my father handed me the bag and I put my chicken fingers back inside.

I had watched him kill so many times—more than what he was charged with, by the way. It wasn't upsetting or shocking. It was all

I knew and it had been happening since before I could form memo-ries. It was our little secret, because I was special too, like him. So fucked-up. I didn't know that then, but later in life I did a lot of reading and the message became pretty clear.

That's how I adapted—how, outside my father's grasp, I was able to learn more socially acceptable behaviors. From *Crime and Punish-ment* to *The Hunger Games*, murder was always a big, bad thing and it was supposed to take a real toll on you, even if you were the one who did it . . . on purpose. You weren't supposed to dust off your hands and go about your day. I mean, you're even supposed to feel things about a bunch of *trees* being killed in *The Lorax*. So it was pretty obvious that it didn't bother me like it should, but my indif-ference wasn't something I was proud of, just something I had to hide.

I couldn't go see my father; I didn't trust myself. I had a good thing going. I had a decent job and an apartment and a Roku TV. I didn't have much of a life—it was pretty boring, actually—but that was a necessity, and I had learned long ago to make the most of it; we were living in a television renaissance, after all.

The fact that my father was in prison, physically at least, meant he had not cut that arm off and he certainly had not brought it to my doorstep. He wasn't the one I needed to talk to; I needed to talk to whoever was talking to him.

I hatched a genius plan thanks to my new stepdaddy, Gustus Trent.

I opened my computer and searched **how to talk to prisoners**. It was that simple. The search returned a million websites for exactly that. With a few clicks I filtered the search options to men ages eigh-teen to forty at Edgar Valley. I did a quick scroll for the most attrac-tive, and there was my knight in shining armor, Connor Nettles.

Connor was twenty-six and serving ten years for armed robbery. It was the best dating site; they laid everything out right in the open for you. Connor was a Virgo who liked drawing and was training to be a mechanic. I wrote him an email making me sound like a dream come true and attached a picture from five years ago that accentuated my body and not my face.

Plan in motion. True love awaited.

FOUR

‒ ‒ ‒ ‒ ‒

B Y NIGHTFALL I FOUND myself back at Painting Pots. I'd attempted to stay quarantined at home, scrolling through the options on Netflix, but my increasing agitation was a warning I knew to respect. I needed a distraction and a dose of human interaction. If someone wanted to kill me, they could try it surrounded by hyperactive children.

The store ended up being a bit of a ghost town, but fortunately for me, Porter's essence could make an empty ballroom buzz. I allowed him to coax me away from the wheel and we sat cross-legged on top of one of the tables, painting Christmas ornaments that he pulled from the back of the stockroom. I was adding lightning bolts to a snowman for absolutely no reason. Porter was working diligently on a Santa head.

"My masterpiece." He presented it to me, cradling it in his hands. The Santa looked possessed. There was red paint dripping from his eyes and big red lips, the two reds bleeding together.

"That's beautiful," I said. "Not disturbing at all."

He turned the ornament back around to admire it. "It's an Expressionist piece."

"What does that even mean?"

"You wouldn't understand," he teased, blowing an errant strand of hair out of his face.

I smirked and went back to my bolts.

"I'm bored," he said, throwing down the demon Santa and lying back on the table. "Entertain me."

"You could clean the brushes." I tipped my head toward the overflowing sinks.

He crossed his eyes and held them that way until I reached over and flicked him on the bridge of his nose, freeing him to turn on his side, propping his head up with his elbow. "I'm going to a party tonight. Do you want to come?"

"No."

"You never say yes to anything," he protested.

"You never ask me to do something I would actually want to do. It's always some sort of house party that you, yourself, complain about being mostly high schoolers. It's creepy enough that you still go; someone my age is borderline criminal."

"What do you want to do? Get coffee? We talk here all the time. Why would we need to go talk at Starbucks?"

"Exactly," I said, and he rolled his eyes.

Porter had taken a gap year after high school, which was a fancy way of saying his parents had blown the small savings they had sending his older sister to two years of college before she dropped out. He'd told me that on a night much like this, when we were alone in the store and he had pulled a bottle of vodka from his bag. We drank too much and got too chatty. Well, he did. I knew better than that. People feel comfortable talking to me when I want them to. It was a skill I mastered in those crucial years after I was taken from my parents, left in a facility surrounded by children and teens with an array of poorly treated mental disorders.

Porter had told me his life story and admitted he feared that he was destined to be a townie instead of one of the pivotal voices of our generation. It seemed to unburden him and we became close-ish after that, as close as I would allow. His gap year had turned into two, and it was the only real friendship I had. I suspected it might be the same for him.

He lay back on the table, exhausted by the weight of the world. "What do you want to be when you grow up?" he asked.

"I am grown up."

"Garbage. We need to get out of here. Let's quit our jobs."

"I like my job," I said.

"You are literally the worst," he said. "Let me come over tonight. I'll bring drugs."

"That's the vaguest offer I've ever heard. I don't want you showing up with a handful of Tylenol PM." I laughed.

"Wait, can I really come over?"

"No."

"Fine, then, I'm going to that party, but it's your fault and I won't accept any judgment."

"Fine."

"I have to shower . . ." He waited. I had to offer. He was polite enough to never explicitly ask.

I looked at the clock. I was technically a customer, but at this point I was more like a volunteer. I had my own keys and often came in alone early in the morning to start the kiln in exchange for the opportunity to use the studio before I had to be at work. "I can lock up."

Porter grinned and rolled off the table. He was harmless—young and invincible. I considered him safe—the innate selfishness of his twenty-one-year-old brain preventing him from ever asking me too many personal questions. That was the quality I looked for most in a person.

I closed up a half hour later and grabbed a teriyaki chicken wrap from the sandwich shop next door. A marathon of this show about regrettable tattoos had premiered earlier that week—the perfect mind-numbing fodder. I ascended the set of stairs to my apartment, salivating over the scent of teriyaki emanating from the bag. I was going to house that thing like a python once I got inside and into my sweats. That was the plan anyway.

Sitting outside my door was another box.

FIVE

— — — —

I KICKED THE DOOR CLOSED behind me, dropping my chicken wrap on the entryway table. I needed to give my full attention to the box. It was another man's arm. They could have sent an ear or something this time. I guess there was an intended message: another left arm = different victim.

Who out there could possibly care enough to exert this much effort to get to me? Maybe it was my father, working through a proxy, letting me know he was disappointed in me. More likely, it was one of his sycophants. My head fell into my hands and I took a moment to sit on the couch.

Someone wanted to play games with me. Could I play? Of course. I had already made a move by disposing of the first arm, after all. The question wasn't *Could I play?* The question was *Could I stop?*

I pulled another grocery bag out from under the sink. At least I had found a use for my growing collection of disposable paper bags, because for the life of me, I couldn't remember to bring one to the store. The salad tongs from the other night were still on the counter, resting in the drying rack. I threw them in the bag with the box, then I dragged a chair over to the kitchen closet. On the top shelf I found a blonde wig from a Halloween party I'd attended a million years ago and I tucked my wavy, shoulder-length, brown-from-a-box hair under the wig. It was a cheap wig and I looked like I belonged in a comedy sketch. I added a winter beanie to cover the Disney princess bangs and it helped. Then I grabbed my teriyaki wrap and my severed arm and headed back to the Wellington station.

This was my second body part disposal, so I had to go farther in the same direction. I figured any other direction would create a radius around my apartment if someone put the pieces together. It was enough to convince me I was being smart about this. I rode the Orange Line all the way to the Forest Hills stop and put the arm into a mailbox on a deserted street corner.

On the train ride home, I was finally able to eat my chicken wrap, which was now cold and soggy. It left me with wet teriyaki fingers, which I cleaned to the best of my ability by rubbing against my jeans. My phone vibrated in my pocket and I reached for it, transferring specks of sauce onto my coat. It was an email—a message from Connor Nettles, my prison soulmate.

- - - - -

FINDING A PRISON BOYFRIEND was one of the easiest things I'd ever done. I sent three emails and Connor put me on his visitors list. Usually when I drove to work instead of taking the train, it was out of laziness—spinning my wheels to find a plausible excuse to expense the thirty-five-dollar parking garage. This time I drove so that I could leave at lunch and head straight to Edgar Valley. If I left by eleven it was only twelve dollars—what a bargain. It had been a long time since I'd taken a personal day, even a half day, but I couldn't wait until the weekend. I couldn't sit around waiting for more arms.

This was my first time at a prison, which was remarkable considering two-thirds of my family unit had lived in one. The process was reasonably invasive. They inspected the inside of my trunk, I went through two metal detectors, and I had my hands swabbed at one point for drug residue. I didn't have anything to hide other than my true identity, so I didn't protest. Eventually I passed inspection and made it to the waiting area.

The corrections officer working the desk looked like someone's lonely uncle, typing away on the computer. He was oblivious to my existence as I approached. Working in a prison, he should probably be more aware of his surroundings.

"Excuse me," I said.

"Yes?" He paused typing and peered up at me.

"Can I ask you something?" I crossed my arms on the counter, pushing my slightly-below-average-size boobs together, creating the appearance of perfectly adequate boobs. He just nodded, not into my tits. This would never happen to Erin Brockovich. "Some of the women over there were saying that Abel Haggerty is at this prison. Is that true?"

"You're not one of those freaks, are you?" he asked, pursing his lips.

"Um, no." I stood up off the counter, letting my boobs flop back to a comfortable distance away from each other. "I was only asking."

"The bad ones always attract the nutcases," he muttered.

"Does he get a lot of visitors?"

"Nah, he only has one guy on his list." He went back to typing. If I wasn't going away, he was at least going to multitask. "But the mail—you wouldn't believe the sick shit people send him. And us guards have to sit and read all of it."

"He only has one visitor?"

"Same guy, every Thursday. More loyal than the wives around here."

"What's his name?"

He paused typing again. "Nice try." His snide grin judged my whole existence.

"Right. It's not like the name would mean anything to me anyway." I let my eyes wander around the room to cap off our interaction.

He couldn't care less.

I left the waiting room and hustled across the parking lot to get back to my cell phone. I retrieved it from the glove compartment and sent Connor a message apologizing profusely for not making it and asking if I could pretty please visit on Thursday instead.

SIX

‐ ‐ ‐ ‐

CONNOR NETTLES HAD GIGANTIC pupils—it was jarring. I sat down across from him, a thick layer of glass between us. He reached out a tattooed arm and picked up the phone and I followed his example.

"Hi there," he said. "I'm glad you made it." He had loose tough-guy shoulders, and when he spoke, his head kind of shimmied back and forth.

"Yeah, me too." I reclined in my seat, trying to see people in my periphery—trying to find my father's visitor.

"Looking for something?" he asked.

"No, sorry. This is new for me. I've never visited a prison—" I stopped myself.

He smiled. "It's okay, you can say it. I'm a prisoner. I'm not a bad guy though."

I nodded like I cared whether he was Satan or Santa.

"Damn, you're beautiful," he said.

"Thanks," I mumbled as a new visitor entered the room and commanded my attention.

I watched him walk to his seat. He looked about my age with a healthy margin of error. He had messy brown hair, darker than mine, and he wore a crisp plaid shirt, untucked, with fitted gray jeans even though he was a little thick. He was a young man, there alone, holding a notebook—the only visitor thus far who showed any promise, but thanks to an angry woman holding a baby and a crying elderly lady between us, there was no way I was going to be able to eavesdrop.

"You don't have a boyfriend?" Connor reminded me he was still there.

I turned back, making contact with his big black eye holes. "No."

"I don't believe it. Maybe my luck isn't so bad after all."

"Look, I'm really sorry," I said. "You seem like a sweet guy, but I don't think I can do this."

Connor leaned back, unlucky after all. "Really? That's it?"

"Yeah, I'm sorry." I hung up the phone and offered a sideways aw-shucks smile. That was that. *I'll never forget you, Connor.*

I stood from my chair and everything slowed. The rapid-fire accusations from the woman next to me muted; the elderly lady's tears stuck in place against her cheeks. I watched the guy with the messy dark hair glance down as he listened intently through the phone. He turned his head a fraction and I caught his bright blue eyes and regular-sized pupils. Were those eyes sending me body parts? He didn't notice me as I approached, and once I could see what held his attention, I lost interest in him as well.

Behind a rat's nest of a beard was the leathery face of my father. I balled my hands into fists and clenched my teeth, resisting the urge to drift toward him. I managed to face forward, toward the exit, but

I caught him grinning. I caught him touching his ear. I caught him inhaling and exhaling once before I was past them and I couldn't see him anymore. Then I could only feel him.

— — — —

I BURST OUT INTO the parking lot. It was like my heart was being stabbed. Not figuratively—literally it felt like I was getting internal acupuncture. I hadn't seen the man in almost twenty years. He was old. I was old. Was he orchestrating this because I never visited him? I wouldn't blame him. Why didn't I ever visit him? I mean, I know— he was a serial killer. He did insane things like cut symbols into my side, along my rib cage, which were supposed to protect me from demons. Sometimes he wouldn't let my mother or me eat for days. Often he killed in front of me. But there were other things—deep experiences that bonded us.

I focused on the barbed wire looping itself along the top of the tall fence that surrounded me. I traced it with my eyes, counting each barb until I reached one hundred. I felt better. A person like me didn't become a functioning member of society without a few tried- and-true coping mechanisms.

I sat down on a cold metal bench and waited.

My vitals returned to normal, and forty-five minutes later the visitor came out. "Hey," I said, standing to intercept him.

He stutter-stepped, not expecting an interaction. "Hi?"

He was sizing me up. Did he recognize me? Did he look like a man just busted? Not really. He looked confused, and the longer I waited to say anything, the closer it resembled concern.

"Can I help you with something?" he asked.

"Sorry." I shook out my awkwardness. "I saw you in there. Was that Abel Haggerty you were visiting?"

"Yeah . . ."

"You know him?" I asked.

"Maybe. Why?"

"I don't know. It's interesting." This was not going smoothly, mostly on my part. I thought it would be obvious what to say once I met the visitor. We would have a showdown and I would be like *What's your problem? Quit dropping arms off at my door. I don't want to play this game with you.* But I couldn't get a read off this guy.

"Are you really interested?" he asked, slipping his hands into his pockets. He scanned the parking lot, and the shadiness factor skyrocketed.

I rubbed my lips together and let my eyes narrow. *Okay, you asshole, I'll bite,* I thought. I let the corner of my mouth curl up into the beginnings of a smile that said both *very interested* and *I will not hesitate to destroy you. Your move now, buddy. Tread lightly.*

From his pocket he produced a business card and handed it to me. "I run a tour out of Boston. Just started a few weeks ago. We go to all the crime scenes and his old house. It's the only one like it out there."

I looked down at the card I now found in my hand. On one side was the tour website and the guy's name and number, *Call Dominic.* On the other was a clip art van being driven by a cartoon devil with my father's signature beard. A tour. A tour guide. This was a fate worse than death.

SEVEN

— — — — —

HE ABEL HAGGERTY MURDER Tour left Sundays at eleven a.m. from a side street adjacent to the New England Aquarium. There had been no more arms, no announcements about the first two I'd planted, no nothing. While I'm sure the severed limbs had been intended to upset me, the waiting was proving to be far more agonizing.

My Sunday mornings were usually reserved for Painting Pots, but so was almost every other day, including yesterday and probably tomorrow. I had a slightly more pressing extracurricular activity for once.

I convinced Porter to call in sick so I could bring him along. I knew he would add a levity to the experience and keep me sane. I needed someone to carry the small talk. I needed to observe at first, not reveal too much. I could count on Porter to fill silences and keep the guy talking. Plus, this would buy me some time before Porter would start hounding me to go out with him again.

We walked past seven kiosks for other tours before I saw him.

Waiting between two generic city tours, he stood alone, holding a sign with the same ridiculous van-and-devil graphic, forcing an inviting smile on passing tourists.

We made eye contact and he lowered the sign. "Hey!" He waved.

"Do you know him?" asked Porter.

"I met him once."

"Twist." Porter elbowed me in the side. "Thirsty—"

"Don't say it!" I reciprocated with an elbow to his side.

Dominic ditched his sign against the curb as we approached.

"Hey," he repeated. "Sorry, I don't think you told me your name the other day."

"Gwen. Dominic, right?"

He smiled, extending his hand to mine. "Yeah." His fingers were icicles.

"I'm Porter." My accomplice inserted himself and Dominic dropped my hand for his. "Holy shit, your hands are cold."

"Oh, sorry." Dominic recoiled and rubbed his hand against his tight jeans. "I've been out here for a few hours trying to drum up business."

"And . . . ?" Porter made a scene of looking around for other customers.

"And I'm so glad you guys showed up." Dominic landed the setup. "Shall we go?"

"To the deathmobile." Porter pointed with fervor in no particular direction.

Dominic reached down for his sign, waiting for my answer.

"Let's do it," I said.

The black van was parked two blocks away in a loading zone.

"Shotgun," Porter yelled as he picked up his pace. His enthusiasm was exceeding expectations. He loved true crime podcasts and documentaries, but mostly the *Serial* and *Making a Murderer* type that were part of the zeitgeist. This was literally just a van in an alley, so the hullabaloo was a bit much.

Dominic opened the van door for me and I climbed onto the bench seat. Porter was already buckled in and ready. Dominic walked around the van and got into the driver's seat. He grabbed at his hair, jerking it up like he was styling it, but then just left it pointing in all directions. He adjusted the rearview mirror, wiggling it back and forth before returning it to its original position.

"Welcome to the Abel Haggerty Murder Tour," he began. "My name is Dominic and I will be your tour guide."

"We know," said Porter.

"The tour is a little over five hours. We will be visiting many of the crime scenes as well as the Haggerty home outside of Worcester."

"Worcester?" Porter lifted his sunglasses as he turned around to glare at me, apparently his enthusiasm knowing bounds and those bounds being the turnpike.

I shrugged like I'd had no idea we'd have to drive so far. How would Gwen Tanner know where Abel Haggerty had lived?

Dominic flipped open the center console and slid out two thin bound packets. He handed one to Porter and then turned to give me mine. "Here you go."

"What's this?" I asked.

"It's visuals to look at during the tour."

Porter started flipping through the pages.

"Hey," Dominic snapped. "No skipping ahead. Turn to page one."

He eased the van out onto the street as I turned the cover over to reveal page one as instructed. It was a staged family photo—the kind you get done at Sears. Of course, it was *my* family. I was a toddler with bouncy blonde pigtails, that shade of blonde that toddlers grow out of, and a chubby round face. I sat on my mother's lap, with a huge smile revealing my Tic Tac teeth. My father stood behind my mother with his hand on her shoulder, his beard much shorter and better maintained back then. They both stared directly at the same spot, slightly off-camera, neither one of them smiling. Honestly, it would have been better to set the mood for the tour if Dominic had cropped me out.

Once we turned out of the alley and onto a congested city street, Dominic started his script. "This is the Haggerty family in 1998. Abel; his wife, Reanne; and their daughter, Marin. You can see the evil behind their eyes."

"Not the kid," said Porter. "She's grinning so hard she's gonna shit her pants."

I laughed. They had no idea it was me. Well, Porter had no idea. My gut was telling me Dominic was just as clueless, but my brain told me not to buy it so easily.

"Fun fact," said Dominic. "Reanne Haggerty was just released from prison."

That was a fun fact. This is so fun. Let's talk more about me shitting my pants.

"Did she kill anyone?" Porter asked, not taking his eyes off the picture.

"The story is no," said Dominic.

The answer is no, I thought.

"But you think she did?" Porter inferred.

"I wonder how you stay with a man all those years, knowing what he was doing, helping him, if you weren't into it."

"Probably the sex," said Porter. "Can you imagine? Most men come home from work and are like, *I filed some files today*, and then they climb on top of their sad, clumsy wives and are like, *hump-hump-done*. This guy probably came home all like, *There's a body in the trunk, let's cut it up and get freaky.*"

"They actually didn't dismember any of the bodies," Dominic

corrected him—a little on the nose given the recent severed arms at my doorstep.

"You're missing my point," said Porter.

"How many people did he kill?" I asked from the back seat, eager to get off the topic of my parents having sex.

"Eight—that he was convicted for," said Dominic. "There's really no way to know. He didn't have a signature style. They were able to prove six without a doubt and then pinned a couple more unsolved murders on him."

"What do you think?" asked Porter.

"Oh man . . ." Dominic stalled as he considered his words. "It's hard to say. It's hard to know what's true and what a person wants you to think is true."

"Deep," teased Porter, and Dominic raised his eyebrows, playing into how coy he was attempting to be. I'm sure it was all theater, but that didn't leave me feeling any more patient about the whole thing.

I wanted to lunge forward, hook my arm around Dominic's neck, and demand he tell me everything he knew. *Wait*, my father's voice echoed in my brain. *Don't do the work for your enemy. Let him reveal himself. Let him pull his own trigger.*

It was another of my father's old adages. He had many, and most of them had found a way to stick with me all these years, popping into my head for one reason or another, usually accompanying a memory. This one in particular I remembered my father saying to me as were walking the halls of my elementary school, on our way to a meeting with my third-grade teacher, a man I despised, a man I wanted my father to do something about. (Not *that* something.)

We sat in a stuffy conference room in the school office as he complained to my father that I had *a real lip*. He rattled off examples and my father only stared at the man, uttering an occasional *mmm*.

The teacher's frustration grew to a point where I thought steam might shoot from his ears. Then my father finally spoke.

"What are you suggesting I do? Smack her?"

It was so unsettling to the teacher, making him realize that he, and only he, had become so angry and aggressive in a conversation about an eight-year-old girl. He turned on a dime, reduced the significance of my *lip*, and even apologized. I thought my father was so cool in that moment—an all-American hero. It was those times, away from anything sinister, when my dad knew just what to do and I was in awe. It had made *everything* about him more digestible.

Dominic slowed the van to a crawl. "Go ahead and turn the page."

"Whoa," exhaled Porter as he saw the next picture.

I followed suit and was blessed with the first of what would be many crime scene photos on this tour. A young woman in revealing clothing was sprawled across the pavement. There was dark red blood coming from her nose and mouth. Her lace top was slashed to pieces, soaked in the same red. She'd been brutally killed by my father—my supposed hero.

"This is Amanda Fallon, street name Fountain," said Dominic.

"She was a sex worker?" asked Porter.

"Likely, from what they could gather asking around. She lived on the streets. Not a lot of information beyond that. She was one of Abel's later victims. He killed her only two weeks before he was arrested."

"Allegedly," I said.

"No, this one's good. They found her missing earring in his house."

I looked closer at the photo. I remembered this one. The recent ones were easier to remember. "How many times was she stabbed?" I asked.

"Twelve," answered Dominic.

They were quick stabs and I knew the cadence. I counted the ticks in my head. *1-2-3-4-5-6-7-8-9-10-11-12.* I didn't like when he stabbed. It was never a quick killing. The stabs were quick, but the death was not. There was always a moment, some longer than others, when the victim would look at us, knowing they were dying. I didn't like when they looked at me. What did they expect me to do about it? Anyway, his gloves were drenched in blood. We threw them into the river on the way home. My dad was always having to buy new gloves. It was a shame Amazon Prime didn't exist back then.

— — — — —

A FEW HOURS AND several crime scenes later, we were pulling up in front of my old house. It was painted gray now, recent enough so as to not show any signs of deterioration. In my mind, no one would ever want to live in that house and it would just sit there, slowly dilapidating over time. I guess with housing prices the way they were, a little dark history was worth it for a nice discount.

Dominic parked the van in front. "Here it is, the Haggerty family home. Abel and Reanne lived here for eleven years before they moved to a larger home—the big house, get it?"

"That's awful," said Porter. "Don't do jokes. I don't think they're your thing."

"Be sure to put it on the comment card at the end of the tour," Dominic joked, ignoring the advice. "Now, turn to the next page and you'll see a picture of Abel and Reanne being led from the house."

I'd seen that picture before. It had been in a lot of papers. Once again, both of my parents stared blankly off-camera. They loved doing that. Such creeps.

"Can we go inside?" Porter asked our guide.

"No. People live in there."

"So what?" Porter opened the door and hopped out of the van.

Dominic cut the engine and we both raced to get out and follow Porter as he darted across the lawn toward the front porch.

"Stop," Dominic whisper-shouted. "It's trespassing."

Porter knocked on the front door, then turned back. "I'm knocking. It's not trespassing."

Dominic and I mounted the porch behind him with no choice but to wait and see if someone answered the door. Porter bounced a little as he waited. He was really into this, but I wasn't sure what he expected. It's not like the new homeowners had a shrine to Abel.

Minutes passed and Porter got antsy. He pushed through us and down the porch steps. I saw Dominic's shoulders relax, relieved to go back to the van, but he wasn't so lucky. Porter took off along the side of the house toward the backyard. Once again, we were chasing him.

The grass was greener, literally, and the patio furniture was better quality, but the trees were the same. There was one in particular with low branches that I had been able to reach and climb on for as long as I could remember. I stood still while Dominic followed Porter around, begging him to go back to the van. I closed my eyes and smelled my neighborhood. I crouched down and ran my hand over the grass. I remembered being there. It was still part of me.

"Gwen! Can you help me or what?" Dominic shouted from across the yard.

Porter was shimmying open a window. It broke my trance and I headed toward them.

"Porter, what are you doing?" I asked, not nearly as panicked as Dominic.

"I want to go in, don't you?"

"What do you think is going to be in there? Dead bodies?"

Porter slipped through the window, ignoring my shade. Dominic looked to me for help, but I wasn't offering any. Porter appeared again, opening the door for us, and then he dipped back into the house.

I stepped around Dominic and went inside. The back door led into the kitchen. It had a nice cream-patterned wallpaper now and a lot of shiny appliances, including one of those expensive KitchenAid mixers that people get as wedding gifts. We hadn't even had a toaster when I'd lived there.

I wandered into the hallway, where Porter stood perusing the framed family photos. "That's a different family," I said. "Stop being weird."

He didn't acknowledge my presence until a piercing beep ripped through the house—an alarm system that we had triggered.

"We have to go," Dominic shouted from the back door, and Porter finally agreed.

We raced out of the house and back to the van, Porter and me giggling, Dominic looking constipated. He cranked it into drive and we peeled out down the street, but at the stop sign, Dominic didn't turn toward the highway. He looped back into the neighborhood.

"Where are we going?" I asked.

"One more stop. Can't miss this one."

I knew where we were going—the Abbington house.

Dominic weaved the van through the neighborhood and eventually turned off on the small street the Abbingtons had lived on. They hadn't been rich by any means, but they had somehow ended up as the only house on this little lane due to zoning around the river and some rare bird that had moved into the trees along the bank in this particular bend. I remembered attending a town hall meeting about it with my parents; it had been only a few days after New Years, I'm not sure which one. Abel had killed a young woman that New Year's Eve. She was wearing a sparkly silver dress. I thought it was so pretty, but she was clearly freezing, waiting on the corner for a cab. My father offered her a ride—an attractive, smiling man with his little girl in the passenger seat—nothing an after-school special ever warned about. He snapped her neck and we left her body behind a college dining hall among the trash, twenty thousand free suspects.

All the way home, my father had told me how he'd saved her from an awful fate, how he'd been merciful in giving her a painless death when he'd snapped her neck. He had received a message, a sign that he should kill her—a sign that I could now understand was just opportunity. A vulnerable woman alone who could not fathom that a man would do something bad to her in front of his child.

"Abel's final crime . . ." Dominic announced as the house came into view. "And the one that got him caught—the murder of four members of the Abbington family. It wasn't like his other murders. He knew the victims. Cops searched his house and found evidence everywhere. He was arrested within days."

"Four people?" Porter asked as I stared out the window reminiscing.

"Yes, the parents, Phillip and Caroline. Their teenage son, Blake, and ten-year-old Cody."

"Who's the little girl?" Porter asked, studying the family portrait in the back of the packet, a portrait where the whole family had managed to look at the camera and smile.

"That's Elyse Abbington. She wasn't home."

"Lucky," said Porter.

"I don't know if she'd agree with you," argued Dominic. "Survivor guilt is real, man. There it is." He pointed across Porter's chest.

There it was, all right. It was abandoned, completely run-down, like I'd thought my house would be. I wondered if the rare birds might have taken up residence inside.

"Are you gonna stop?" asked Porter.

"Not a chance." Dominic hit the automatic lock button and Porter watched the latch on his own door click.

"Come on. Obviously no one is living in there," Porter protested.

Dominic slowed the van enough for us to get a good look but refused to stop. "Elyse Abbington still owns it. It was held in trust until she turned eighteen. She refuses to sell it, but refuses to do any maintenance. I think she likes watching it rot."

"I can't even see the backyard," Porter complained. "It says right here"—he tapped on the page—"Cody Abbington was killed in the backyard."

"Not happening." Dominic laughed and Porter flung the packet onto the dashboard in protest.

Cody Abbington was such a little asshole. It's bad karma to call a dead kid an asshole, but I was a kid too and he made my life miserable. Whenever we were alone, he would act like my best friend and then at school he would call me names and throw things at me to make the other kids laugh. When someone has serial killer parents, you shouldn't toy with their emotions like that.

I never should have told my father about Cody. If I had kept my mouth shut, he never would have gone to their house. Cody had almost survived. My father was inconsolable, manic, unrecognizable to me. He kept going to the hospital to finish it, my mother begging him not to—trying to convince him that it was too risky. It was seventy-two hours of hell—my father punishing her for questioning him, ignoring her, but ultimately failing to get into the boy's guarded hospital room.

It was my fault. That was when I got the X's. He said the demons had gotten to me—led me to corrupt our whole family, forced him to kill when he shouldn't have. He held me down, carving into my side, convincing me that it would fix everything. He had hit me before, dislocated my shoulder once, made me touch the stove a couple of times, but it was nothing like when I got the X's. It was the worst thing he ever did to me, but I deserved it.

Cody Abbington suffered a fatal seizure when doctors tried to wake him up a second time, but it was already too late for us. Cody had come to long enough the first time to give the cops the lead they needed. Five days after my father entered their home and two days after the cops stormed ours, Cody finally died.

If I hadn't told my dad about Cody, he never would have gone over there, and maybe he never would have been caught. My parents wouldn't have gone to prison and I wouldn't have become Gwen Tanner. It was a lot to deal with.

Sitting in traffic on the Massachusetts Turnpike for two hours wasn't a very climactic ending to the tour. Dominic and Porter went back and forth, gushing about Abel like he was a character and not a real person. I stayed silent for the most part and took it all in. I liked listening to them. I rarely let myself think of my father in the light that I really wanted to. He was crazy. He was brilliant. He was evil. He terrified me. He was the only person I had ever really connected with and his absence was something I felt every day.

We passed the remnants of an accident after the I-95 exit, and traffic finally started to move again. Dominic perked up in his seat. "This is maybe too forward, but do you guys want to come to a party?"

"Yes," Porter answered immediately.

Dominic looked at me in the rearview mirror. I didn't answer at first, prompting Porter to flip around in his seat and beg me with his face, ready to cash in on every time I'd rejected one of his invitations.

"Sure," I said. "Why not?"

EIGHT

I FOLLOWED BEHIND DOMINIC AND Porter toward a brick apartment building, wondering what I was doing. I was a little high from the walk down memory lane. My life now was structured, and I was coming to realize how much I was missing the rush. I'd gotten a taste of the rush when the arms arrived, and it intensified when I saw my father in prison. It was the rush I felt when we parked in front of my childhood home and it was the very same rush that I judged my mother for choosing over me.

The street echoed with muffled music from a handful of parties on that block alone—nothing says college neighborhood like parties on a Sunday night—and I wondered if Dominic might be a lot younger than I had assumed.

Once we entered the building, the others faded away and only the sounds of our party remained. We climbed the stairs to the fourth floor, the bass from the stereo beckoning us closer. My feet were heavy, but Porter was gliding up the stairs. Making new friends still seemed so attainable at his age.

Dominic turned back to me. "I have to warn you. This party might be a little weird."

"What does that mean?" I asked, staring up at him.

"We shall see." He smiled as he turned back and hustled up the stairs after Porter.

That was nice and ominous, but it was too late to back out now, even if I wanted to pretend that I wasn't suddenly very curious.

Dominic pounded on the door to apartment 7. It opened and the music poured out. A guy somewhere closer to my age than Porter's answered the door. He had one of those haircuts where the hair on top was long and I could see it was shaved underneath—thick, black, and slicked back in place. It was the exact opposite of Dominic's active hair, which was sticking out and positioned wherever he had last tugged it.

Dominic and our host exchanged a handshake-hug hybrid. "What's up, man?" the new guy asked. "I'm so glad you made it."

"I brought some friends. Hope that's okay."

"Of course, yeah . . ." He paused to look at us, like maybe the *of course* wasn't so unqualified. A smile slipped out for Porter, easily approved. For me he stared a bit longer, assessing how much of a square I appeared to be—not a great day for me to be wearing a peach cardigan and fake pearl earrings. "Please, come in," he finally said after a beat that probably felt longer to me than it actually was.

"This is Gwen . . . and Porter," said Dominic.

"I'm Jake. Dominic's stepbrother."

The guy seemed too cool for formal handshakes, and Porter and I both did awkward little waves as we stepped inside.

Thick curtains covered all the windows and the limited light came from a few shadeless lamps. The whole apartment had cheap laminate floors, scuffed to shit from a million different tenants. Jake led us toward an opening into the kitchen, where I could see a few people milling around the bar area.

"Help yourself." Jake nodded toward the alcohol. "I stole it all from work anyway."

Porter followed him into the kitchen, but I hovered at Dominic's side in the living room, where he surveyed the space for anyone worth talking to. I would describe the interior design as . . . posters? There were a lot of posters, some taped, some tacked to the wall. Posters of movies like *Scarface* and *Fight Club*, posters of mug shots like Charles Manson's and Ted Bundy's. There was no poster of Abel Haggerty, thankfully. My father had never really ascended to the commercial masses; he had more of a cult following—true freaks only, please. I blamed it on his branding, or lack thereof.

There were several doors off the living room and it was really anyone's guess how many people lived there. Three big couches with sheets thrown over them filled the space and it looked like a college flop house except there was a real thirties look to a lot of the faces in the room. No one noticed us walk in. One guy was flipping a switchblade open and shut, another yanked on a girl's ponytail until he could reach her lips, licking them—not kissing; licking like a dog. Not to be judgmental, but this was beginning to feel like a mistake. I counted the people to calm down. There were twelve people in the living room, plus the three in the kitchen, plus the stepbrother, plus Porter, plus Dominic. Eighteen people. The bathroom door opened—number nineteen stepped out.

It was another woman. We were the super-minority. There were only four of us out of nineteen. She had long, straight strawberry blonde hair and thick black eyeliner that said, *Don't talk to me.* I watched her, wondering which clique she would rejoin. She walked past the three couches to the window, pulling back the curtain and slipping out onto the fire escape. A minimalist tattoo of shrinking diamonds started at her neck and trailed down behind the swooping collar of her shirt. The curtain fell behind her and she was gone.

"Do you want a drink?" Dominic asked, and I stopped staring at the window.

"Sure, yeah, I'll come with you." I didn't see myself leaving his side anytime soon.

Porter was talking to Jake and the kitchen people like they were best friends for life and didn't seem too concerned with being my wingman anymore.

I removed my cardigan, leaving only a white tank top I would consider an undershirt in any other circumstance.

Dominic slid a bottle of Bombay Sapphire off the counter between two of the guys without disrupting their conversation. His eyes matched the blue of the bottle. He held it out to me as a question and I nodded. *Why not?*

He led me away from the bar, looking as eager for personal space as I was. "Did you enjoy the tour?" he asked as we sat down at the kitchen table. He poured the liquor into two shot glasses. Shots of gin—an unusual choice, hipster gone wrong, but it would get the job done.

"Honestly?" I asked.

"Yeah, honestly."

"I did," I admitted, but he could never know why or how much.

"Good." He beamed. "Tell all your friends."

He handed me my shot. We clinked the glasses together and threw them back. It burned as it went down my throat, craving to be mixed with tonic, a fire that said a buzz would be coming soon if I kept this up. I wanted to get him drunk. Then I would pick his brain, see what he'd talked to my father about, see if he would slip and reveal that he knew more than he was letting on. I had been so patient. My father would be proud.

"Another?" he asked.

"Sure," I said, letting him do all the work for me. "I can't tell you the last time I went to a house party like this."

"Do you spend most of your free time hanging out at prisons?" he asked.

"You're one to talk." I smiled. "You're the one hanging out with a serial killer. How do you even know him?"

"Kind of random actually. I was always interested in behavioral psychology. I tried minoring in it when I was in school. But anyway, a couple of years ago I started reading a lot, probably too much, about him. I went through a rough breakup and started writing him letters. Eventually he let me visit and now I've been going for almost a year. I guess we just hit it off."

I opened my mouth, but he cut me off.

"I know, it sounds insane. It's not like I thought writing to a serial killer would help me get over my ex-girlfriend. It was more like I was trying as many things as possible to distract me and that one stuck. I also tried golf, for the record."

He smiled and I laughed because he was attempting a joke, but I was more focused on how a malleable young man with a broken heart had fallen right into my father's lap. It was oddly convenient and maybe the whole story was a lie.

I brought my glass to my lips. I batted my eyelashes. So flirty, no ulterior motives here . . . "What's he like?"

He thought about it for a second, then slid his hands off the table and leaned back in his chair. "I feel like I should tell you something . . ."

I paused my eyelashes, leaving my eyes wide open.

"I'm not being presumptuous or anything . . ." He hesitated. "But given the context, it feels like a purposeful omission to not let you know that I recently got out of a serious relationship. I was engaged, actually."

"Okay . . ." I stalled.

"Just because . . . I said I first reached out to Abel Haggerty when I was going through a breakup, and now I'm going through one again, but that's not why I visit him," he insisted.

"What happened?" I asked. He had gone and changed the subject, and now I would have to dance back around to my real questions. Gwen Tanner would care about his failed engagement. At least I had some context clues to confirm he was old enough for me to be associating with him.

"Eh, you know. Got together right out of college. I can admit now that it probably started as a rebound for me. We followed what we thought were the right steps. Realized in time that it wasn't working. Not too interesting."

"Okay, robot," I teased.

He laughed.

That was easy. When people share something emotional with you, the sooner you get them to laugh, the faster you can move on. I didn't mean to be insensitive; it just felt more pressing to find out if he was chopping off men's arms than whether he was sad.

"What about you?" he asked.

"Not engaged," I teased again, but in a curt way that discouraged follow-up.

"Fair enough." He smiled. "So what do you do?"

Ugh, no, not the work small talk. I was losing control of the ship. "Human Capital Management. Helping recruit the best and brightest, then trying to keep them happy. I'm just an associate though. Basically I print things and then hand them out."

"Not very green." He grinned.

"Well, I also send a lot of emails."

Dominic laughed and I took the opportunity to pivot. "Needless to say, I wasn't at Edgar Valley for work."

"Yeah, I would assume they frown on criminal records."

"Definitely." I nodded. "I was visiting an old neighbor. In there for robbery. Nothing violent. I try to go a couple of times a year. He used to fix things in my apartment for free and I guess it feels like the right thing to do." A hundred percent bullshit, but a dead-end story without much intrigue, and I spewed it all out before he could form any questions.

"That's really nice of you. I don't think I'd be that nice."

"Your kindness is reserved for serial killers only, then?"

He laughed again, and just like that, we were back on course.

"What do you two talk about anyway?" I asked.

"Well, that's confidential," he said, and I glared at him. "What?" He grinned.

"You can tell me *something*. Be vague. You don't have to tell me where the bodies are buried." I took another sip. "I mean that figuratively, of course."

"Of course." He smirked. "We just talk."

"Too vague."

"He's helping me write a book."

"Like a biography?"

"Kind of. More about what makes Abel Haggerty tick."

"Are you trying to get into his head?" I was skeptical of the business plan here.

"I try. He tells me stories and I put myself there in that place. I think about what I would do and what would have to be different for me to do what he did. I want readers to be able to relate."

"And what would have to be different?"

"I haven't figured it out yet." He reached up and tugged at his hair.

"Tell me one of the stories," I said, absorbing his energy.

"Yeah?"

"Yeah . . ."

"Gwen!" Porter's hands landed on my shoulders and I jumped ten feet in the air.

"Oh my God, what?" I turned to look at him.

"Guess who's here."

"Who?" I asked. *This better be good.*

"Elyse Abbington—that girl from the family Abel Haggerty killed. Do you remember her?"

Of course I remembered her. What would really get this party started, though, was if she remembered me.

NINE

‑‑ ‑‑ ‑‑ ‑‑ ‑‑

LOOKED TO DOMINIC. WHY was Elyse Abbington there? What was happening? Was this a trap?

Dominic reached out and grabbed Porter's arm to settle him. "Hey, quiet."

"What?" Porter was not there to be scolded.

"She's a human being, you know," said Dominic, "not a sideshow attraction."

"Why is she here?" I asked, barely audible, ventriloquist style, struggling to move at all.

"Jake said she doesn't mind," Porter insisted. "She likes to talk about it."

"Jake's full of shit," said Dominic. "He's probably trying to cause a scene."

"How do you know her?" I asked with more volume, trying to put the pieces together without sounding accusatory.

"She's Jake's girlfriend. I think that's why the stuff about Abel

really struck a chord with me. You know, because I know her. It hits
so close to home."

Hitting close to home was right. She must be the girl I saw climbing out the window. There was a reason I had felt so compelled to
watch her.

The last time I'd seen Elyse Abbington, she was eight years old.
She was rail thin back then and always filthy. Her parents didn't pay
much attention to their kids and Elyse used to wander uninhibited
all over the neighborhood. No one wanted to play with her; she was
too little and always had snot all over her face. She was that kid.

"Will you introduce us?" Porter asked.

Dominic sized him up. "Are you going to play it cool?"

"Obviously," Porter said, brushing him off.

Dominic turned to me. "What do you think?"

"I'd like to meet her," I said, trying my best to *play it cool*.

Porter took hold of my arm and practically yanked it out of its
socket. "She's on the fire escape."

Porter lifted the curtain and heaved himself through the window
first. Dominic held his hand out for me and I used it to climb
through next.

She just sat there on one of the metal-grate steps. She wasn't filthy
anymore. Her nose was snot-free. She was beautiful and haunting
and dark—all of the things I wanted to be, but instead I was standing in my fake pearl earrings, holding my peach cardigan.

"Hey, Elyse," Dominic said as he followed through the window
behind me.

"You actually showed up," she said—her voice was different now,
of course. Part of me was expecting her to sound the same. She
would open her mouth and her shrill little eight-year-old voice would
spill out.

"Yeah, I needed to get you two off my back," he teased, shuffling in front of me. "These are my friends. The new friends *I am pro-actively making*," he accentuated for her benefit. "This is Porter . . ." Dominic gripped his shoulders and repositioned him to better reveal me. "And this is Gwen."

Porter lurched forward with his hand and Elyse hesitated a second before obliging him with a handshake.

"Awesome," said Porter, totally fanboying.

Dominic leaned over to assist Porter in letting go. I let him shield me from Elyse again. I wanted to see her without her seeing me.

From Dominic's shadow I looked up over his shoulder and found her eyes waiting for mine. Everything stopped again. Did she recognize me? Did she already know who I was? Was she the one leaving me gifts? She parted her lips and I realized my lips had parted too—maybe not visibly, but I could feel the separation. What was she going to say? What did she want? To kill me? To torture me? What if she wasn't involved at all and just recognized me from my face? *Stop looking at me.*

"Dominic took us on the tour today," said Porter, bringing sounds back to the world.

Elyse blinked and released me. She turned to Porter, probably feeling his eyes boring into her soul.

"It was really intense," he added.

"He does a good job," she said.

"Oh my God, have you done it?" Porter glowed.

She smiled politely. "No, I don't think it's for me."

Porter brought his hands to his face and rubbed his cheeks—the tactile sensation heightened by whatever he had ingested at the party so far. "This is so fucking cool. You were, like, there. What was it like?"

"Okay, buddy." Dominic took him by the shoulders. "Let's go sit down." He pulled Porter back toward the window against his will.

"What?" Porter begged for me to back him up. "I was just asking."

Go, I mouthed.

I could have followed them—taken my cue to exit—but I stayed. I walked to the edge of the balcony and leaned against the railing—staring out into the street.

"So what did you think of the tour?" she asked.

I turned back around to look at her; there was no longer a shadow to hide in. "It was . . . informative, I guess."

"I bet." She lifted a beer bottle to her lips and took a swig.

"Does it bother you?" I asked.

"What?"

"That Dominic does that."

"No, not really," she said. "It's nice someone is still thinking about it."

"Well, it's not exactly paying homage to the victims. Honestly, it kind of glorifies the killings."

She shrugged. "Gotta give the people what they want."

"You seem jaded."

She took another sip of her beer, drawing it out, exemplifying her jadedness. "I was eight. It's like it wasn't even me. Do you think you're the same person you were when you were that age?"

"I don't know." I waited for her to react. Was that a weighted question? Did this girl know we'd been children together?

She raised her eyebrows, then smiled, relaxing them. "How do you know Dominic?"

"I met him at— I ran into him and he convinced me to go on his tour. It was only Porter and me. Things got a little . . . comfortable, I would say, and then he invited us here."

"I swear he only does that tour to try to meet other freaks who want to talk about Abel Haggerty all day. No offense." She smirked.

"Aren't these *freaks* your friends?"

"I'm sitting alone on the fire escape, aren't I? They're more Jake's friends than mine. They only like me because my whole family was massacred. It makes me interesting."

I didn't really know how to respond. It did make her interesting, I supposed. Of course, I could have walked in there and stolen all her significance with one honest sentence, but I was only being petty. What she was saying was sad and I could tell it made her sad.

"They want to ask me all sorts of sick things," she continued, "but they don't want to scare me away, so it's like a dance."

"Why do you even hang out with them, then?" I asked.

"It can be intoxicating," she said. "How can I describe it so you'd understand?"

She thought about it, but I already understood. It was envy and obsession. To be obsessed over, to know something everyone else craved to understand, to hold it all inside while those around you salivated—it was our own special brand of celebrity.

"I get it," I said so she could stop thinking.

"A dead family is the best currency you can have around here." She smiled to prove it was a joke and that pity was unnecessary. "What about you? Where did you grow up?"

"Pennsylvania."

"Tell me about it." She gazed at me. What did she want me to say? She either knew the truth and was my super-stalker, or maybe she didn't and was hungry to digest my lies. She was hard to read.

"My parents died in a fire," I recited, a story I'd told a million times.

"Holy shit," she said. "I feel like an asshole now."

"Why?" I laughed. "You just said that was the best currency you can have around here."

"I'm used to being the most tragic one in the room, I guess."

The curtain was pulled back and we both turned to see Dominic in the window. "You might want to take Porter home. The guys have him in the kitchen chugging rum right from the bottle."

This was what I got for having a kid as a wingman. I rolled my eyes, but Porter was honestly doing me a favor. I needed time to process the reappearance of Elyse Abbington before I revealed too much.

"It was nice meeting you," she said as I moved toward the window.

"Yeah" was all I managed before leaving her there, alone on the fire escape—a fire escape my fake parents really could have used.

— — — — —

I SHOVED PORTER INTO the back of an UberX. He fell on his face and I reached in to turn his head to the side to prevent him from asphyxiating on the upholstery.

"He's not going to puke, is he?" asked the driver.

"No," I said, having no idea if it was the truth.

Dominic held the door open for me while I rearranged Porter. "Thanks again for coming on the tour and, you know, the rest of the night."

I wriggled the top half of my body back out of the car to bid him adieu. "It was fun." I hesitated a second to consider what Elyse had said about him and the fact that we had barely scratched the surface on what he was doing with Abel. "If you want someone to talk to about your book, you can call me."

"Really?" His eyes expanded. "What's your number?"

"I'll text it to you." I lowered into the back seat. "I still have your business card."

"Right, great. Okay, well, good night." We closed the door together, me pulling from the inside, him pushing from the street. It was a pleasant simpatico moment at a time when a potential cuckoo-nuts murderer was out to ruin my life.

－－－－

I DROPPED PORTER OFF and got back to my apartment a little after eleven. Of course, he had ended up barfing, so after I helped the pissed-off Uber driver scrub the back seat, he agreed to still bring me home if I gave him an extra forty dollars in cash. The car reeked, even from the front passenger seat with all the windows open, and I was pretty sure the driver was going to absolutely destroy my rating.

I collapsed onto the couch. What a day. I had so many new acquaintances—new acquaintances who were maybe psychopaths and killers.

I rolled onto my back and closed my eyes. There was a part of me that wanted to spend every free moment thinking about life and death. Why did people put so much work into something that could be taken away in an instant by anyone? I could have walked downstairs right then and slit the throat of Mrs. Magnus. I wasn't going to, but I could have.

I didn't let myself think like that very often. My job was 90 percent talking to people about their futures—career trajectories, advancement opportunities, compensation structures. It wasn't hard. I liked it. I was being paid to read people—see through the fake bullshit, find the best candidates, persuade them to take the job, and then let my boss take all the credit for hiring them.

Money, prestige, security—their wants were fundamental. I was under no illusion that I worked for Greenpeace or anything close to it. Still, it was my job to convince them I was invested in their futures and not that I could shove a letter opener into their jugular at any moment.

I had to numb those parts of my brain. I couldn't come home every night and think about killing people if I hoped to be normal—

a normal woman who worked in a high-rise downtown and went on occasional dates with guys like Brian.

People are nostalgic for things from their childhood. It didn't have to mean I was defective. Evil thoughts are not the same as evil actions, and bad children can be decent adults. That was the kind of thing I reminded myself of regularly, but it never stuck. I *was* defective, and all I could do to manage it was maintain a crafted isolation. As soon as I got this severed-arms situation under control, I would go back to the disciplined life I had created.

I nodded off to the image of Mrs. Magnus taking a bite of an English muffin with thick peanut butter, swallowing too soon, a chunk getting lodged in her throat. She gags, trying to breathe, finding no oxygen. Her hands move to her throat. *I'm choking, help me.* She drops to the floor. She knows she's done and at the last second, her hands fall from her neck.

A quiet scratching interrupted my slumber. At first I thought it was Mrs. Magnus's feral-ass cat, but the sound was more like shoes shuffling than that thing's nasty claws. The noise was right outside my door and I sat up in silence. The shuffling stopped and I held my breath. Then there were footsteps going down the stairs. *Oh no you don't, you fucker.* I jumped from the couch and raced to the door.

The hallway was empty, but at the bottom of the stairs the outside door was wide open. Barefoot, I flew down to the first floor and into the street. It was deserted. The only sound was the wind—no footsteps, no one running into a trash can, no barking dogs or car alarms. I spun around slowly like I was being mirrored by a guy with a Steadicam, capturing my bewilderment for the big screen. The theatrics dissipated once all I could focus on was how cold my feet were.

I returned to the house, pulling the front door closed. It stuck on the runner and I unleashed my fury, stomping the rug flat and slamming the door shut. They really needed to rip that thing up. I had a stalker, after all.

At the top of the stairs I realized I was right; someone had been outside my door. Written in big bloody letters was the word *LIAR*.

Of course, I *was* lying; everything about Gwen Tanner was a lie. Was there something I had done that day that was particularly triggering? A lie worse than any other?

I wiped my finger along the edge of the *R* and brought it to my nose. I sniffed it, then dabbed it on my lip. I swept my tongue over the substance. Corn syrup or something—not blood. I guess they'd run out of arms. I'd been waiting for their next move, but maybe they were waiting for mine. All it took was reuniting with Elyse Fucking Abbington to prompt another visit.

I brought over a sponge from the sink and scrubbed away the stupid message. I didn't like cleaning and I really didn't like being threatened. I could feel my blood pressure rising. My father always told me that we were not the type of people to mess with.

TEN

- - - -

THE COPS FOUND THE second arm, the one I left in the mailbox, first. No one noticed it until it was mixed in with all the other mail from the area, so they didn't even know which mailbox it had come from. Three days later, they made an ID. It belonged to Oswald Shields, a seventy-three-year-old former lawyer from Clinton, Massachusetts, but I already knew who Oswald Shields was. He had been *my* lawyer—nineteen years ago.

Having your name changed and your identity hidden requires a lot of paperwork—and then a lot of burying of said paperwork. My memory of Oswald was spotty at best. I'd only met him once or twice and remembered that he had a gross cough that sounded very wet. He had sideburns, I think.

After my parents were arrested, I was shipped off almost immediately to a distant relative I'd never known existed. I should have been a witness in the trials, but I never told a soul that I knew what my parents were doing—that I had been a part of it all.

I was allowed to pack a bag. I remembered that part because I'd wanted to fill it with Legos, but I only got to bring one stuffed dog and had to fill the rest with clothes and underwear. The man who made me put all the Legos back, even the microcopter that was so small it wouldn't have made a difference, was James—Detective James Calhoun, but I just called him James because I was nine and wasn't beholden to formalities. He was the only other person in the world who knew me as both Marin Haggerty and Gwen Tanner.

Learning the arm belonged to Oswald Shields confirmed that the arms weren't random props; the identities mattered. I didn't need to wait to hear from a forensic specialist to assume the other arm belonged to James Calhoun.

- - - - -

TWO DAYS LATER, THEY announced the second arm, elevating the story from a freaky blip to a serial incident. James Calhoun's identity was released the following day. Both men had still been alive when the arms were removed, and both were now missing. There was no mention of Abel Haggerty or how the men were connected. Even the dark bowels of the internet that had stumbled upon the story only suggested fantastical theories like mafia debts, sex cults, organ harvesting. In the real world, it was only a local story. One that most people would miss if they weren't looking, but it was out there and my stalker would know that I knew.

- - - - -

DOMINIC AND I HAD been texting quite a bit since the party, and that Saturday I invited him to join me at a bar downtown—then I didn't go.

I'd gotten enough clues about where he lived from texting with him about how walkable his neighborhood was, prompting him to tell me about the coffee shop at the end of his street. Thankfully, it wasn't one of a million local Dunkin' Donuts or I would still be out there looking for his place. I spotted his tour van parked in the driveway of a converted three-story house, like mine and most of the apartment options in Boston's outskirts. I arrived an hour before we were supposed to meet for drinks and waited for him to leave.

The front door was closed tight and in much better shape than my own. The mailboxes listed him and his roommate as apartment 2. Dominic lived with another stepbrother, Kevin, but Kevin had a job implementing IT systems around the country and was always out of town. Dominic had told me that in a way to make it seem like he basically had his own place, clearly self-conscious about it after moving out of the condo he'd shared with his fiancée.

I cut through the path between his building and the nearly identical one next to it. I had to turn sideways to slink through the tight spots caused by a broken washing machine and a couple of heavy-duty city trash cans.

Behind the house there was cheap white plastic patio furniture and a crusty firepit. I looked up to see the second- and third-floor balconies, one on top of the other. The balconies were self-enclosed and my only way up would be flying or climbing.

I yanked one of the garbage cans toward the back of the house, leaned it against the siding, and used one of the plastic chairs to climb on top. I could barely reach the bottom of the second-floor balcony. I sort of hopped and was able to grab two of the rail posts. I proceeded to hang there with my feet inches above the trash. My noodle arms and neglected abs were enough to lift my legs to about my waist, but there was no way they were getting my butt above my head. I let go and fell back onto the trash can. It wobbled as the top buckled slightly under my weight, and I lowered my center of gravity to balance.

I dropped to my knees and reached for the plastic chair, lifting it to my level. I flattened myself against the vinyl siding to make room atop the trash can for the chair. Then I did a delicate shimmy to slowly transfer my weight onto the seat. After a couple of close calls, I was on my knees, balancing on the chair on the trash can.

Calling upon the ten squats I had done three years ago, I used my thigh muscles to slowly rise to my feet. It was enough for me to grab the crossbar of the railing and swing my leg up. The rest was easy and I flipped my body onto the balcony.

Maroon curtains were drawn over the locked sliding glass door. What was not locked was the window to the right of the balcony. Not enough people lock their windows. Lazy landlords slap cheap coats of paint over the window frames without making an effort to avoid the latch, and layers harden on top of each other until eventually the latch won't budge. My father taught me that.

I leaned over and pressed my palms under the lip of the lower pane. A few tight jabs were enough to scoot the window up. I climbed onto the railing and slid my legs through the opening. Once there was more of my weight inside than out, I heaved off the balcony. It wasn't very graceful, but it was effective.

I slithered over a radiator in the bathroom until my feet hit the floor. It was a gross guy's bathroom, full of shaving residue, one bottle of all-in-one shampoo/body wash in the shower. There was some gel on the sink and I thought of Dominic compulsively grabbing at his hair all the time.

I walked into the living room and nothing appeared out of the ordinary—a little breakfast bar, a brown leather couch, a large flatscreen, clean other than a dirty coffee cup in the sink. No posters. Actual adults might have lived there.

The first bedroom I entered was dark and I hit the light switch. A picture of Dominic and a lady I assumed to be his mother told me it was his room and not Kevin's. The espresso-brown dresser and nightstands matched the headboard in what I imagined was a hasty four-pieces-for-eight-hundred-dollars furniture deal. There was a mismatched desk in the corner, with a stack of notebooks and his laptop. I took a seat, and while I waited for the laptop to boot up, I grabbed a notebook.

It was full of handwritten scribbles. I opened to a page at random. It was dated from right before Christmas. *Abel is in a good mood today. Doesn't want to talk about any killings. Wants to talk about the holiday. Not allowed to decorate.* How domestic. I flipped back to an earlier entry. *Elderly lady he saw in the park previous week. She had a bad leg. Too weak to fight. He snapped her neck. He had to do it. Came to him in a dream.*

A dream. I shook my head. My father had never desired to hone his narrative à la the Boston Strangler or the Wet Bandits. Every act, every story, every motive was different. The only through line was that it was necessary he do it, a mission that was communicated to him—only him, the chosen one. And someday, it would be my destiny to fulfill. That was a familiar part of the narrative, but only to me; it was never shared with anyone. As I skimmed through the entries, that detail appeared to be missing from these journals as well. My father had maintained at least this boundary with Dominic. Dominic wasn't that special. Not special like I was.

I scanned the pages for reference to Elyse or her family. The Abbington name popped up every twenty pages or so with brief notes. *He asked about Elyse again. It's almost every time now. Getting harder to distract him.*

I reached the end of my sporadic review of that notebook and went for another. It was older. *Reanne won't write back. Hasn't written since the divorce. Regrets it. Lonely. Doesn't get as many letters anymore. People are losing interest. Hopes the book will help.*

The laptop came alive and I put the notebooks back. His computer background was my father's mug shot. He used to be handsome, one of his assets, but one eye was slightly askew—the defect looked obvious now, but only in hindsight.

Assorted icons floated around the desktop, but in the top-right corner was a folder labeled **Abel Haggerty**. I opened it, revealing even more categories—**Background, Victim Profiles, Photos**, et cetera. I opened the **Background** folder, then a folder labeled **Family**, then finally one I knew would be there: **Marin Haggerty**.

I expected to find a treasure trove of information he shouldn't have. I expected pictures of me, current day, taken from the shadows: pictures at the movies photographed with night vision, pictures of me at Painting Pots taken from the parking lot through the big square windows, pictures of me in my home angled from his car below. That was the evidence I was looking for, but there was nothing.

There were a few pictures from my old elementary school, but I'd still been chubby then, with blonde hair and round glasses. There was a scanned report card from third grade that he'd gotten his hands on somehow, and a copy of my birth certificate. The only thing of note was a heavily redacted document with the few remaining words being the date my parents were arrested, a lot of pronouns and prepositions, three uses of the word *minor*, and the name of the detective filling it out—*James Calhoun*.

There was a noise at the apartment door before I could think anything through. The knob was rattling. I slammed the laptop shut and flew out of the chair toward the light switch. Cut to black.

The door creaked as it opened and a light crawled across the living room. I had no chance of getting back out the bathroom window. Footsteps. I slid into the closet and closed the door, leaving it slightly ajar because I couldn't risk the sound of it shutting.

Was someone else breaking in? This was *my* caper. Maybe it was the real stalker—stalking me, stalking Dominic. Or was it Kevin, not actually out of town? Boring and somehow the worse option. The footsteps were almost at the bedroom. I backed in between some hanging shirts and peered through the crack in the door.

Dominic walked into the room, pulling his sweater over his head. It wasn't a burglar; it was this asshole standing me up for the drinks that I was standing him up for and now I was stuck in his closet.

I stood in that closet for two hours while he made something in the skillet that smelled amazing and watched the second half of the Celtics game. Finally he got down to only his boxers, turned off the bedroom light, and climbed into bed. I waited another half an hour until all tossing and turning subsided. I cracked the closet door open a little farther and stuck my head out.

The whites of his eyes were all I could see in the darkness. He stared at me.

ELEVEN

TUMBLED OUT OF THE closet as Dominic sat up in his bed. "I was wondering when you were going to come out."

"What the fuck?" I said, tripping over a towel balled up on the floor.

"What the fuck yourself?" He reached over to turn on a bedside lamp.

I was totally busted and had no excuse. "How did you— Why didn't you meet me?" I rubbed at my forehead, hoping my brain would think of something smart to say.

"I saw you," he said. "I came back for a coat and saw you snooping around."

"So you just decided to mess with me?" I asked, somehow feeling justified to be pissed off.

He climbed out of the bed and walked toward me.

"You're clearly crazy," he said, stopping in front of me and crossing his arms. "So what kind of crazy are you?"

"Screw you. I did this to see if you were a psycho."

"And?"

"And I'm going to go," I said, turning away from him.

"Whoa, whoa, whoa." He grabbed my arm and I basically hissed at his fingers gripping my bicep. He pulled his hand back and tucked it under his other arm. I read it as an offer to keep his hands to himself going forward. He would be smart to realize that was what was best for him. "I think we should talk," he said. "Or I could call the cops. You did break into my apartment."

We sat together on his leather couch, leaning against opposite arms so that we could face each other. He had found a shirt and he tugged at his hair, *1-2-3*.

"I'm not really sure what to say," he said.

"You seem . . . excited," I said. "Are you getting off on this or something?"

"I am. Kind of," he admitted. "Not in a sexual way or anything, but I've never had a stalker before."

"I'm not stalking you. You can relax."

"Are you dangerous?" he asked.

"Oh my God, stop. Seriously. I get this looks bad, but you aren't going to be able to tick off any of your weird fetish boxes with me."

"Any of *my* weird fetish boxes?! You broke into my apartment, probably trying to steal my underwear."

"No one wants your nasty baggy boxers. You look like you're twelve years old," I spat back.

He glanced down, seemingly affected by my observation, but shook it off, remembering he had the upper hand in the situation. He sighed and tugged his hair again, *1-2-3*. "Tell me why you broke in, then."

"I wanted to see how obsessed you are with Abel Haggerty. I wanted to see if you were hiding anything." I was probably acting too casual for break-in behavior, especially if this guy was not playing the game I was. "I'm sorry," I said. "I was in a bad relationship once. It's made me paranoid, and probably a little impulsive."

He processed that before asking, "Are you afraid of me?"

I think he wanted the answer to be yes, but it was most certainly a no. I shook my head. "Are you afraid of *me?*"

"Should I be?" He tilted his head and gave me a little smile.

A silence took over that wasn't necessarily awkward, but it wasn't comfortable. My wheels were turning and so were his. He bit his lip and squinted at me, tentative to say something, but he got over it. "Have you ever seen a dead body?"

"No," I lied. Holy shit, was he about to pull out the rest of Oswald Shields's body from under the bed or something?

"Sometimes I go to the morgue," he explained.

"Why?" I asked, a bit disgusted—not because I thought it was disgusting that he went to the morgue but because that was his big bad-boy admission after I had already hyped him up in my head to be a murderer with the dead body of a man I knew under his bed.

"I do it to remind myself what it really is that Abel's talking about. It's different from hearing words or seeing pictures. When there's a dead body in front of you, it's real."

I could see how this would sound deep to someone else, but I had seen a lot of dead bodies and knew you didn't have to be so emo about it. "Do you want to be like him?" I asked. "Is that what this is about?"

"A killer? No." He shook his head, not offended. "I just . . . It feels like there's a key to life and death, and if I can figure it out, I can transcend it."

Oh God, his book was going to be awful. *Just write the facts with digestible prose, Dostoevsky* was what I wanted to say. "I think you're romanticizing" was what I said instead. "I don't think it's about transcending. I think it's about accepting. A person is only a thing and there are lots of things. In your own head, you think you are the shiniest, most unique thing out there, but you're not. Once you can understand that you're just another thing on this planet, you can accept it and it frees you."

He exhaled a little noise that said *wow* without actually having to say *wow*. "That's sad. Even if you're right, that's depressing. Do you really think like that? Do you think you're *free*?"

"I hope so," I said, knowing I wasn't free. I'd been in hiding since I was nine years old. I existed in a cage with a long list of rules. When I thought about it, it bummed me out. Stupid Dominic, making me think about these things. This was why I only dated Brians.

He was staring at me.

"What?" I asked.

He leaned across the couch and touched my cheek. He waited to see if I would hiss at him again, and when I didn't, he kissed me. I wasn't expecting the transition, but I went with it. So much for it not being sexual. It felt nice to be kissed by someone who was kind of a freak and who was attracted to the fact that I was probably one too. He had no idea though, really. He was hoping for the crazy ex-girlfriend type, but my crazy was way too severe to ever revolve around him. I couldn't let myself pretend it was anything else. I couldn't let anything cloud the serious mess I was in and how I was going to get out of it. I pushed him back enough to part our lips.

He sighed, biting his lip as he retreated, coming across more apologetic than disappointed. "Can I show you something?" he asked.

"Sure," I said, knowing better this time than to hope it was going to be a dead body.

- - - - -

"HAVE YOU HEARD ABOUT those arms they found?" Dominic asked as he brought his laptop back to the couch.

"No."

"They found a severed arm in the mail in Jamaica Plain and then a couple days ago they found another one near Northeastern. The second one was James Calhoun. Do you know who that is?"

"No."

He turned his laptop to show me a twenty-year-old picture of James from some newspaper article covering the arrest of my father. "He was the detective who caught Abel Haggerty." He waited for my reaction, but I wasn't ready to say anything.

"I know, it doesn't mean anything. This guy worked on hundreds of cases, but get this . . ." He turned the computer back around. "The other arm belongs to a man named Oswald Shields."

"And there's a connection?" My ignorance was easily digestible; Dominic was hungry to flex his knowledge of the situation.

"There is, but no one seems to have figured it out. Other than me, I mean." He grinned. "Oswald Shields was a lawyer—well, he used to be. He was disbarred around 2009 for falsifying some documents. Anyway, I went to Abel after they identified James Calhoun's arm and asked him if he'd ever heard of Oswald Shields and guess what? Oswald Shields had visited him while he was awaiting trial."

"Why?"

"Turns out Abel was working with James Calhoun to hide the kid, and Oswald was the lawyer Calhoun involved."

"What do you mean?"

"Remember I told you Abel and Reanne had a daughter? Marin? From the picture?"

"I remember."

"Abel wanted her buried." He shook his head "That was a poor choice of words. He didn't want the kid to be labeled a freak, you know, the daughter of notorious serial killers. So he begged Calhoun to help. Abel and Reanne signed away their parental rights. There's been no mention of Marin Haggerty since. They changed her name."

"To what?" I managed to ask without screaming.

"No idea. Calhoun refused to tell Abel. That was part of the deal. Abel tried a few times over the years to write to Oswald Shields, knowing he was a piece of shit who'd probably tell him, but the guy never responded."

Was this possible? I'd never thought much about the logistics. At the time I was nine. I did what I was told. I was keeping enough secrets; I couldn't worry about if other people were too. Would my father sign away his rights so easily? I'd always assumed he didn't have a choice. I guess I *was* a witness. I knew everything. Was it love or liability or some combination of both?

"And he just told you all of this?" I pressed Dominic.

"His entire gospel is his ability to read a person, and he knows he can trust me."

Ugh, his *gospel*. That's a way to put it. He never said *God*. Any ties to organized religion would dilute my father's perceived power. He liked to say *beings*, which was ridiculous; it sounded like aliens. That was why my father had to kill. He was told to kill those people, because way worse things would happen if he didn't. He insisted the signs would come to me too someday, but I had to be careful because I could be tricked.

In his mind, after the Abbingtons, he was proven right. That was where the *X*'s came in, carved down my side. They were small but deep, and somewhere in his twisted brain they would prevent impostors from getting into my head again. An insane logic from an insane man and I think just an excuse to permanently label my body as his, as if having his genes wasn't enough.

I knew what my father was doing with Dominic. He was telling him that he was the one Dominic was supposed to communicate with, only him, and that probably made Dominic rock-hard and dangerously loyal. If my father was orchestrating this business with the arms and the bloody messages, Dominic would be the one whose strings were being pulled.

"What about the police? Have they made the connection?" I asked.

"Far as I can tell, no. I mean, they assume two severed arms are connected, but I haven't seen anything that shows they've put it together. There's no obvious connection between Abel and Oswald Shields. You'd have to really know what you're looking for. The name wouldn't be in Abel's file—maybe the kid's, but those records are sealed. Don't tell me you think I should tell them. I can't do it. I swore to Abel."

"I don't think you should tell them. What's the fun in that?" I smiled, playing into his fantasies, motivated by self-preservation. The longer it took for the police and the media to focus in on my father, the better.

"Do you want to know what I think?" He paused rhetorically; I wasn't supposed to guess. It was for suspense. "I think Marin Haggerty is back."

TWELVE

MARIN HAGGERTY *WAS* BACK. Technically, Marin hadn't gone anywhere; she was just hiding behind Gwen Tanner. The problem wasn't Marin. The problem was someone else, and if it wasn't my father and/or Dominic, I had a pretty good idea who it was.

The next morning, I went straight to Somerville and parked outside the massive big-box home improvement store. I walked through the automatic sliding doors and was confronted by a seemingly endless supply of building materials I had no use for. I rejected three employees who asked me if I needed help before I made it into the garden center. It was a different vibe in there—natural light, bright colors, a wetness in the air.

I saw her emerge from behind a tall rack of hanging plants with names I could never hope to pronounce correctly. She pushed a cart loaded with—I took a guess—geraniums? Elyse's strawberry blonde hair was contained in a loose bun, but her eyeliner remained thick and off-putting. I turned my back to her and stared at a shelf of cacti.

I counted the first row over and over until I heard the wheels on her cart getting close.

"Can I help you find something?"

"Um . . ." I rotated to look at her. "Oh, hey . . . Elyse, right?" *What are the odds?!*

"Hi . . ." Her eyes widened, then she beamed, then she shifted her balance and subdued her aggressive smile. I noticed everything.

"I didn't know you worked here," I said, even though it was obvious from her Instagram if anyone cared to figure it out.

"I do. Are you looking for anything in particular?"

Yeah, proof it's you. "I was looking for something to brighten up my apartment a bit."

"Okay." She lifted her hand and scratched the back of her neck. I remembered her tattoo. "And you're thinking a cactus will do that?"

"Seems low maintenance."

"Low risk, low reward." She smiled.

"I'm not out to kill anything," I said like I was so clever.

"Jesus."

I shook my head. "Sorry, I didn't mean to be insensitive."

"Please. My skin is a little thicker than that." This time her eyes thinned when she smiled. "Follow me. I have something for you."

I nodded and she turned, leaving her cart. I stared at the diamond peeking out above her uniform shirt, the knot of her mandated apron covering half of it. She led me toward the front, past rows of pleasant smells, pinks and purples, even a couple of butterflies. The path was a walking cure for seasonal affective disorder and almost made me forget that I was there to try to rattle her—to read her—to look for signs of her derangement.

"Here," she said, stopping. "Orchids. They're colorful but subtle. Pretty easy to take care of. You just have to water them once in a while, but even if you kill them, I have it on good authority that they don't feel pain."

"Yeah? Okay," I said. I hadn't realized when I was originally crafting this plan that I would end up having to actually buy a plant.

She took one down from the shelf. "This one?"

"Sure."

She carried it to the register, where an older man greeted us, eager to make small talk, but Elyse stayed by my side, blocking his opportunity to strike up a conversation past "Hello."

I handed the man a crisp twenty-dollar bill that I'd taken out of the ATM for the fruit vendor near my office. I wasn't sure why it would matter, but in these cloak-and-dagger times, I didn't want to use a credit card.

"Did you make that yourself?" she joked.

"I wish."

The man handed me my change and opened his mouth to speak before Elyse cut him off. "Will I see you at Jake's tonight?"

"I wasn't invited," I said.

"I'm inviting you. Anytime after nine."

"Okay, then," I said. "Maybe."

- - - - -

I TOOK THE TRAIN to Jake's, a ten-minute walk from the Sutherland Road stop. I wore something more appropriate this time—a loose black sweater that hung off one of my shoulders. It was thin and I usually wore a tank top underneath, but these were edgy people and showing my bra in certain lights seemed a little edgy.

I was attending a party on my own like some sort of extrovert. Dominic was working—apparently the Abel Haggerty Tour didn't pay the bills. He taught GED night classes, which, I have to say, was much more charming than his entrepreneurial endeavors.

"Gwen," said Jake as he opened the door. "I didn't know you were coming."

"Elyse invited me. Is that okay?"

"Of course. Don't be silly. Come in. Come in." He closed the door and then ditched me, but I found a familiar face right away. "Porter?"

My little friend's eyes bulged and he open-mouth grinned at me. "Holy shit. Gwen, you animal!" He abandoned the drink he was making and ran over and wrapped his bony arms around me, lifting me off the ground and jostling me around.

"Okay, cowboy," I said, and he put me down. He looked different. I think he was wearing black eyeliner. And his clothes were black. We'd both opted for a little dress-up this time.

"What are you doing here?" I asked. I didn't like him here. This was Marin business. He was Gwen business.

"These are my people now."

"You just met them."

"So did you!" he argued. "What are *you* doing here?"

"I ran into Elyse and she told me to come by."

"Okay. Okay," he said, mulling it over.

"Is she here?" I asked.

"Yes, come." He snatched my hand and guided me into the living room.

A lot of semirecognizable faces and one very recognizable face occupied the couches. Everyone was immersed in some sort of group activity led by Jake, who had scurried back to his seat while Porter was assaulting me.

Elyse glanced up and I waved. She lifted her fingers off her knee and I started to step in her direction before Porter yanked me toward a vacant seat barely big enough for the both of us.

"Don't embarrass me," Porter whispered in my ear with love.

A coffee table anchored the group of people. On it was an array of drinks, ashtrays, shot glasses, a mug full of capsules, strips of cloth, and a knife—totally normal.

Jake grabbed the knife. "Who's next?"

Porter's hand shot into the air, almost hitting me in the face on its way up. Jake used the knife to motion him over and Porter dropped from the couch onto his knees. He crawled toward Jake, and as he came to a rest in front of him, Porter reached for the edge of his shirt, lifting it up and revealing his stomach.

I scanned the group, looking closer this time, and noticed several of the guys were touching their own stomachs, some brushing subtly past like a memory, others with their hands purposefully up their shirts. One guy, who I think I remembered from the last party, held a bloody piece of gauze in his hand. What the hell was this? An initiation? Or a cult ritual? A branding? I instinctively reached up and touched my side. I could feel the small raised marks from my father under my bra.

Jake braced one hand on Porter's shoulder so that he could steady himself. He took the knife to Porter's stomach and pressed down into his skin. "Five," he started, and the rest of the group joined in. "Four . . ." Jake moved the knife slowly across his stomach. "Three—"

"Okay!" Porter screamed, pushing Jake's arm away. The shirt dropped over the incision, but Jake was quick to yank it back up before any blood could get on it.

The group erupted in a mix of noises that sounded both congratulatory and unsatisfied. Jake put the knife down and grabbed a strip of cloth. He pressed it along the wound to stop the bleeding. "That's three," he said, taping down the gauze.

Porter reached for the bottle of rum on the coffee table as Jake cleaned the knife off with a Lysol wipe. It was kind of a vibe crusher seeing the same cleaning supplies they used at Painting Pots. He should have hidden the wipes in a skull or something.

Porter lifted the bottle to his mouth. Then everyone was counting again while he chugged. "One, twoooo . . ." Their rhythm slowed in sync for the last number, really drawing it out. "Three!"

Porter slammed down the bottle before crawling away—a couple of guys patted him on the back as he went by. He climbed up and plopped down next to me.

"This is a drinking game?" I whispered, as if it were beer pong or kings, where the better you were at the game, the less you were forced to chug—not the more you were sliced with a knife.

"Yeah," he scoffed. "Don't be judgy."

"Whatever would I be judging? Everything here seems on the up-and-up."

He threw me a side-eye before scooting forward in his seat to see who was next.

"Elyse?" Jake asked, lifting the knife again.

She nodded, then looked at me, almost for approval. I met her eyes, but tried my best not to say anything with my face. She stood and walked to him, dropping to her knees once she got there. She lifted her shirt, revealing several previous cuts in varying stages of healing. I could tell I was in her periphery and I gently tucked my hair behind my ear to let her know I wasn't bothered by what I was seeing.

"Shall we make this a little more interesting?" Jake asked her, and she adjusted, getting me out of her sight and giving him her full attention.

"Why not?" she said playfully—their way of flirting, I supposed.

He leaned in and kissed her on the forehead, his lips still on her as the knife touched her skin. "Ten . . ." he began, backing his face away so he could see what he was doing. "Nine, eight, seven . . ." they all chanted. Elyse didn't even flinch. "Six, five, four . . ." This game was combining my favorite things: counting and watching someone cause bodily harm. "Three, two, one!" Jake pulled back the knife and the group applauded her appropriately.

Elyse took a bandage off the table for herself and held it over her stomach as she returned to her seat.

"You're a cheap date, Elyse," Jake joked, again reaching for the Lysol wipes. "Next?"

"I'll go," I said, looking only at Elyse.

"Really?" he said. "Awesome."

I slid off the couch and did my own crawl to him.

"This is Gwen's first time," he told the group, as if this even registered on the spectrum of deranged things I had experienced in my life. He reached for the bottom of my shirt, ready to lift it for me, but I panicked and stopped him.

He grinned, thinking I was chickening out. The truth was, I had to be careful lifting my shirt, not wanting to expose that I had already been cut, much deeper than this tomfoolery. It would ruin the admiration these people were about to have for my pain tolerance.

I lifted my shirt myself, slowly. We made intense eye contact. That was part of it, I guessed—the anticipation building. I brought my shirt as high as my rib cage, holding it at the center like a tent, keeping my sides covered. I sucked in my exposed stomach from a place of insecurity, but quickly released it, knowing the more fat the knife found the better. I didn't want him accidentally slicing a tendon.

"Are you ready?" he asked.

I nodded and he put the knife to my skin. He hesitated again, waiting for me to change my mind. Everyone was silent, still. He put his other hand on my stomach to guide the knife. His thumb moved slightly, brushing my skin and trying to elicit a reaction. Realizing his parlor tricks weren't working, he finally pushed the knife down. "Five, four . . ."

It hurt. I won't pretend it didn't. I put my head down and looked over to Elyse—making obvious and piercing eye contact.

"Three, two, one!" Jake pulled the knife back and the sting amplified. The crowd cheered. How amazing it was to win the affections of this group of societal rejects. Maybe later they could prop me up on their shoulders and we could march to an animal shelter and kill some puppies. It could be any or all of these wackos who was messing with me—probably the one who had just sliced my stomach with a knife.

I crawled back to my seat after I let Jake bandage me. Porter grabbed my face and kissed me three times on the cheek. I could tell Elyse was watching me, but this time I didn't turn to her.

— — — — —

AFTER THE BONDING EXERCISE wrapped up, most of the group was experiencing the effects of the alcohol they had swallowed in defeat and I followed Elyse out onto the fire escape. She sat in her same spot, lighting a cigarette.

"How's your stomach?" she asked, pulling back the lighter and inhaling.

My brain was telling me to confront her. I liked her. I could tell her I understood that she was batshit crazy, but maybe she could channel it elsewhere and we could be friends. I wouldn't mind having a friend I could be honest with.

"Do you think it will scar?" I asked.

She shook her head as she blew out the smoke. "Jake tries not to cut too deep."

"How considerate," I remarked. "Do you do this sort of thing often?"

She offered me a drag of her cigarette, which I declined. "It's something to do. They're looking to escape. They like to get all fucked-up and think they're badasses."

"And you?"

"Everybody likes to do something they're good at."

"What's that?" I asked, leaning against the railing.

"Mind over matter." She brought the cigarette to her lips again. "You weren't so bad yourself."

"Why did you invite me here? I could have freaked out."

"I knew you wouldn't." She blew the smoke over her shoulder, her eyes leaving me to watch its trail.

"You must think you know me pretty well."

"Maybe."

"And maybe I know you," I said, waiting for her eyes to come back to mine.

"I doubt it." She grinned and I reciprocated.

Maybe this could be fun after all.

We stared out onto the street. College kids were everywhere, guys lugging cheap thirty-racks, girls moving in groups—still sober enough to make safe choices. Neither of us said anything, a surprisingly comfortable quiet given that we were, by most definitions, still strangers. I went numb for a moment, but the peace didn't last.

"Holy shit!" someone yelled from behind the curtain.

I clocked Elyse's reaction. She didn't seem interested, but a grumbling started inside the apartment that I couldn't ignore.

"I'm going to . . ." I pointed inside like I needed permission to leave.

"Yeah, yeah." She waved me off like I had disappointed her. She had a clear disdain for the things that brought excitement to the morbid people inside, her *friends*.

I would make it up to her later—prove I, too, was above it all because we were the real deal, not like these posers, but right now I wanted to know what all the fuss was about. I was only human.

－－－－－

I CLIMBED THROUGH THE window to find a bunch of the guys huddled around another of their kind who had gotten a laptop from somewhere. More were reading and scrolling on their phones. Jake was tearing up couch cushions looking for the remote. I found Porter in the second layer of people around the laptop.

"What's going on?" I said quietly so as to only draw his attention.

"They found one of the bodies. One of the arm guys."

"Which one?" I asked, like it mattered.

"Oswald Shields."

I sighed, actually relieved it wasn't James. I hadn't really known Oswald. "Where?"

"The river. By the science museum. Washed up on shore." The Charles River. I had gone with my father to dump many things in there, but never a body. He was not into disposing of bodies. He wanted people to see what he had done, and if he didn't, he made it look like an accident. He told me missing person cases were trouble for people like us. They let things linger, overlap, correlate.

The energy in the apartment was electric—a horde of dudes, euphoric from substances, horny for a dead body. It was like I was on the floor of some NSA facility the way they were all searching for information, shouting things out as they discovered them.

Did they suspect it had to do with my father like Dominic did? These were Dominic's friends and he was pretty adamant he was the only one who had figured out the connection to Oswald. It must have just been the body, confirmation of a murderer in their city, that was getting them all hot and bothered. It was gross fanaticism. I doubted any of these people had what it took to ever take matters into their own hands. They were the couch coaches of murder.

Or did that make them all the more likely? Obsession taking over like an addiction, the need to escalate to find the same high? In one breath I could convince myself there was no way it was one of these dudes. In the next I was sure it was.

I had to get out of there.

THIRTEEN

I T WAS GETTING HARDER to focus at work now that there was a body. Even though I wasn't surprised, the news still landed differently. Oswald had been shot in the head sometime after his arm was removed. That was all it said. That was a quick death. That was a hit, not a hobby. There was a reason to kill him and that reason was me.

The killing was eliciting a stronger reaction than a couple of arms, and I was struggling to dissociate. A game I was playing in the shadows was following me into the daylight. It would probably have been easier to manage if I'd had a decent night of sleep, but I was acting recklessly and had gone to a house party on a Sunday night even though Gwen Tanner had to be at work on Monday morning.

My office no longer felt immune to Marin Haggerty. The comfort I used to find in the high security of the building diminished once I started worrying my stalker might have the same laminated badge that I did. I stood up in my cubicle, like at that precise moment I would catch him or her across the bullpen, sawing through an elbow. All I saw were the tops of three heads and I sat back down.

Could it be someone I've worked with for years? I'd had two interviews before I got the job, but it had been Karen Gloss who'd pulled me in. I met her at one of those college mixers. *Did she seek me out?* I was the only person in the whole office with a patchwork degree from a community college. Maybe she was privy to my actual résumé? Karen was gossipy. Loose-lipped. I couldn't imagine she could keep even a small secret. Plus, she didn't sign my birthday card last year. There's no way that whoever was doing this to me would miss that opportunity. Obsession needs to be fed, even with crumbs.

Is a fresh face more likely? Their newfound proximity to me kicking off the chain of events? There were six new hires that quarter. *Which one would it be if I had to guess? Right now. Off the top of my head . . . Sam Nelson. Why? Why did I pick him?* It was that day in the elevator. He worked on the fifteenth floor, but he didn't get off there. He stayed on and got off on the seventeenth with me. *Why did he do that?*

Or what about Henry Fowler? He was a managing director and had no real obligation to attend more than two or three recruiting events a year, but he was always a little too eager to volunteer. *Why was he always showing up?* Meh, free alcohol and college girls. Thinking he was there to stalk me was giving Henry way too much credit.

This was paranoia. Plain and simple and probably the point. I closed my eyes and took a deep breath. Then I counted the keys across the top row of my keyboard. My father used to say that paranoia was the crutch of a feeble mind. There was little consistency with how his zealous statements were delivered to me. He could be holding my hand, my school backpack over his shoulder as he walked me home from the bus, mumbling. Or we could be in a stranger's home, a body behind him on the floor as he crouched down to my eye level, pinching my cheeks, drilling the words into me, neither of us daring to blink. "You cannot assume everyone is out to get you;

you *have to* assume they want something from you," he would say. "And their want is their weakness."

Paranoia is only noise, noise created by fear, fear driven by wants. It was hard to argue with my father's logic at the moment, since the more I wanted answers, the more paranoid I became. I had to fight the noise. It couldn't be *anyone*. Not really. That was weak thinking. It was an excuse for why I hadn't been able to figure it out.

This person wanted something from me.

Elyse Abbington was inviting me to knife parties. Dominic was desperate to find Marin Haggerty. Jake and his friends—stuck in a state of arrested development—were fixated on massacres and murderers. There had to be something there. But what?

My phone buzzed against my desk and I lifted it enough to stop the echoing rattle against the surface while I read the screen.

It was Dominic. C'mon—the timing! This was a joke, right?

"Hello?" I answered.

"Hey," he said. "How was last night? I heard you were at Jake's."

"It was good." I reached under my sweater, brushing the thin scab across my stomach. "They're an interesting group."

"You hear about the body?" he asked.

"Yeah, I bet you're excited about that." I was misplacing my residual disgust from the previous night.

"I wouldn't say it like that. Wondering if they'll find any evidence. I bet it will heat up the investigation now that there's a body."

"Is that a good thing?"

"Sure," he said. It was an odd response that didn't provide me much insight. "What are you doing today?" he transitioned.

"I'm at work. It's Monday."

"Can you leave?"

"Why?"

"For an adventure."

"What kind of adventure?" I'll admit, I enjoyed Dominic, but I didn't want to go on some forced mini-golf date because we had kissed.

"I'm going to Worcester to talk to James Calhoun's ex-wife."

"What?" I snorted. "Why?"

"I'm following a hunch."

"The Marin thing?" I tried to be dismissive.

"Yes, *the Marin thing*," he said, dismissing my dismissiveness.

I didn't know what scent he'd picked up, but I couldn't let him follow it without me. "I can take half a day. Can you wait until noon?"

"Really? Yes, for sure. I'll pick you up. Where's your office?"

"Financial district. I'll meet you at Post Office Square. The pointy side by the FedEx."

"That means nothing to me, but I assume it will once I get there."

"Yeah, call me if you don't see me."

"Okay, bye."

I hung up and pulled up the scheduling system, blocking out twelve to six as green **Out of the Office—Personal** before changing it to blue **Out of the Office—Meeting** just in case Karen or Sam or Henry had nefarious intentions after all. It's okay to be a little paranoid.

FOURTEEN

ELLEN CALHOUN LIVED IN a white ranch house with blue shutters seven miles from my childhood home. She answered the door in a lavender sweater set and the leftover body of someone who had birthed a gaggle of children many years ago.

"Hi, Ms. Calhoun, I'm Dominic. And this is my colleague, Gwen."

"Nice to meet you," she said, and I shook her flimsy Betty Crocker hand. "Come in."

We followed her inside. The decor was that of a woman who hadn't been with someone in a long time. That wasn't a criticism, simply an observation that her deepest design desires were left unchecked—so many florals, knickknacks, wallpapers.

Dominic and I sat on a pastel plaid couch while Ellen brought in a tray of iced tea. "You said on the phone that you're writing a book? Have you written anything I would know?" she asked as she handed him a glass.

"Probably not." He smiled, having written zero total books.

"That's okay," she said. "I don't read very much anymore." She took a seat across from us and rested her hands on her lap.

"Ellen—may I call you Ellen?" Dominic asked, and she nodded. "Has there been any news on James?"

She shook her head. "I know they found that other man. I know what that means, but they still won't tell me anything."

This had to be worse for her. It was pretty much a guarantee James was dead, but she was stuck living with the uncertainty. She needed a distraction—like a mold infestation or a hernia.

"I call the police station every day," she continued. "But they aren't very forthcoming. We've been divorced for twelve years after all."

"Right," he said.

"But we're still close. Neither one of us ever remarried."

"I know the Abel Haggerty case was a big one for James," said Dominic. "It couldn't have been easy for him, for both of you."

Ellen examined her nails for a beat and Dominic reached across and rested his fingertips on the edge of her knee. "Let me know if I ask anything too personal. We'll only talk about what you are comfortable with."

"No, it's all right," she said. "I don't mind talking about it. It sounds silly now, but I thought he was having an affair."

Dominic pulled his hand back, not anticipating that turn.

"It started when they arrested Abel Haggerty, and I know you want me to say something like that twisted man got in his head, but that wasn't it. James was actually in the best mood he'd been in in years. He was a hero. We would go out and people would come up and shake his hand, especially women. Then he started spending all day and night at *work*."

She tilted her head at me, the other woman in the room who would understand the connotations behind that. *I get it, girl.*

"At first," she continued, "it didn't seem strange to me. I mean, you have to do so much work when you make an arrest to ensure they can get a conviction. I'd gone through that with James many times."

"What was different this time?" he asked.

"I found a barrette in his car." She covered her face. "This feels like a lifetime ago." Her hands fell back to her lap. "We had a great marriage. I'd loved him almost my whole life, but when I saw that barrette, I thought of all those smiling women, and years of trust dissolved into suspicion. I went through everything. All of his pockets, his desk, whatever I could get my hands on, and do you know what I found?"

"What?" I said before I realized I was speaking.

"Nothing." She sighed. "I tried to let it go, but months later he told me he had to go out of town to New York for the weekend for work. How ridiculous. What local police detective goes out of state for the weekend for work? And he wouldn't tell me one single detail. Every time I asked, he completely shut me down. We'd been married for fourteen years and he never spoke to me like he did those days leading up to his *work* trip."

"So I let him go," she continued, "and when he came back, he went straight to bed and I went through his pockets and his car again." She paused, ashamed of her invasiveness. "There were receipts from East Buford, Pennsylvania. Meals for two. A hotel bill. Gas receipts. All crumpled up in a fast food bag I watched him burn in the backyard the next morning."

Crap. *I'd* spent eight years in East Buford, Pennsylvania. That trip had been when James brought me to that school. I'd stayed in that hotel. That was my barrette. I remembered when I lost it. My dad had given it to me. I didn't want to know where he'd gotten it from.

"I never told him what I found," she said. "I just kept it inside until it destroyed us. Once the boys were out of the house, there was nothing left to hold on to. I made him leave." A tear formed in the corner of her eye, but she was quick to wipe it away before it could get loose. "But enough about that. I doubt your book is about infidelity. You must think James's disappearance has something to do with Abel Haggerty."

"Frankly, ma'am, I hope not," said Dominic. "But it's best for now if we keep that suspicion between us. The police have a history of pinning things on Abel Haggerty and I would hate for them to jump to that conclusion without proper evidence. I don't want anything to affect finding James."

So smooth. An easy lie. I made a mental note.

- - - - -

AN HOUR LATER WE were back in the car. Dominic had picked Ellen's brain about every detail she remembered from the time, which wasn't much. It was clear my old friend James had kept all our secrets. I hoped this was the dead end I needed Dominic to hit.

"I knew it," he said as I closed my door.

"What?"

"James Calhoun hid Marin."

"What are you talking about?"

"There were only a few people with access to the kid after the arrest. He was the sappiest—had a handful of his own children, was a Little League coach, a real do-gooder."

"I'm not following."

"Somebody helped her disappear. There's nothing, no accessible information on her after the arrest. I know she was a minor and that stuff is all sealed, but she didn't walk out of the police station and take a bus to obscurity by herself. That just doesn't happen. I'll give you one guess who accompanied James Calhoun to Pennsylvania."

Eff off, Dominic, you intuitive asshole.

FIFTEEN

-- -- -- -- -- -- -- --

TRIED TO CHANGE THE subject to anything other than Marin Haggerty, but Dominic didn't have a lot of other interests. I got him to talk about TV shows for about fifteen minutes, but when I could tell he was getting antsy—too fixated on his new Marin theory—I turned up the radio.

He shot me a look. Maybe it was a little aggressive. Possibly rude. "I love this song," I yelled, hoping he had no follow-up questions about the title or the artist.

He politely waited until it finished before reaching over to turn down the volume. "What are you doing tonight? Want to come to dinner?"

"*Come* to dinner or *go* to dinner?" I asked. "*Come to dinner* sounds like an event."

"My stepsister, Megan, is in town for the night."

"Another stepsibling? No wonder you have attachment issues," I teased.

"Everyone has a date. Not that I'm saying it's a date . . . I just . . .

I'm not used to having to go to these things alone. Do you want to come or not?"

"Well, when you put it like that . . . Who is *everyone*?"

"Megan and her husband, Leo, and Jake and Elyse. That's it."

"What about Kevin?" I still hadn't met Kevin. It felt like a blind spot.

"No, Kevin's out of town. They aren't that close anyway. Not a lot of overlap there."

"This is very confusing."

"I know. Think of it like *The Brady Bunch* if *The Brady Bunch* recast most of the people every season. Megan was season two; Kevin was season five. My mom and I are the only ones in every season."

"That helps, actually."

"I know, I use it a lot. So is that a yes?"

"Fine." I wanted to see Elyse in a social setting outside those parties. I wanted to see all of them, actually. For research.

- - - - -

MEGAN WAS OLDER THAN our collective age range of mid-twenties to early thirties. She must have been a teenager when Dominic was a little boy. How they all preserved these temporary familial relationships over time was mind-boggling to someone like me.

Megan stood to give me a hug as we approached the table. Leo was more reserved, significantly shorter than his wife, which I noticed when he stood to shake my hand. Before we could take our seats, Jake and Elyse arrived and then we all did lots of hugging, everyone standing and scooting around in the tight space to get their arms around one another. For a beat I thought Megan was going to go for a second one, so I dipped into a chair.

I took the middle seat on the wall side. Megan landed across from me for a long night of eye contact, and Leo sat to her left. I assumed

Dominic would sit to my right, leaving the two seats on my left for Jake and Elyse, but when Elyse slid into the chair to my right first, it prompted a hushed but audible "Seriously?" from Jake.

Dominic took the seat to my left and Jake settled for the last seat to the right of Megan and the farthest point from his girlfriend.

"Let the siblings catch up," Elyse explained, looking for me to agree, so I nodded. I wasn't complaining.

There was a lot of standard group dinner talk. No one pulled out a knife to see how long someone could tolerate pain, so that was good. Smaller conversations broke out, the siblings talking about things the rest of us couldn't relate to, Leo sharing the issues they were having back home with their roof, Dominic checking in on me to make sure I was okay. Lots of talking and no chance for coded doublespeak with Elyse.

"So, Gwen, where are you from?" Megan asked out of nowhere, elbows on the table, chin resting in her hands.

It was a pretty standard question, but I went into a little panic. I honestly couldn't remember what I had told Dominic. Or Elyse. Had I told both of them I was from somewhere? I always told people I was from Pennsylvania, but that was with strangers and first dates, where Pennsylvania meant nothing. I wouldn't have told these two that, one actively trying to find out what happened to Marin Haggerty and the other possibly already knowing. See, this was why I didn't do things like this. It was too risky.

"All over New England, moved a lot," I said.

Elyse shot me a look. Clearly I had spun a different story to her. Maybe I did tell her Pennsylvania. So close, but so far from being New England. Panic geography.

"Military family?" Megan pressed.

"No."

Dominic read my curt response perfectly and sat up in his chair.

"Can you believe she lived all over New England and her dad never married Barbara?"

That elicited a laugh from the whole table. Barbara, his mother, the serial monogamist. It registered to me as a little off that Dominic referred to his mother as Barbara. It was as if he had adapted to being just another one of her stepchildren.

One person wasn't laughing. Elyse reached under the table and touched my thigh with her pinkie. I glanced down to where she was making contact and then rotated my head to look at her. She was making a subtle *You okay?* face and I was confused at first until I realized I had told her my parents died in a fire. *Ugh, and in Pennsylvania*, I now remembered. She was wondering if a joke about my dead dad marrying Dominic's mom had upset me.

I smiled and tapped her pinkie with my own, a sort of dismissal, and she took her hand back.

"How is Barbara?" Megan asked Dominic.

"She's holding on," he said. I waited for it and . . . his hand went to his hair, jerking it around, *1-2-3*. "We've got her settled into the house and the doctor has her on a new pain plan."

Apparently his mother was quite ill. I would have to ask him about that later. Or maybe not. Maybe it was one of those things he would share with me when he was ready. It explained his fascination with "transcending" death and I wondered if his half a semester in behavioral psychology was enough for him to realize that.

Megan reached across the table for his hand, the age difference giving her an unavoidable mothering quality. "She's comfortable though?" I was sure Megan would keep framing questions until she considered the answer to be a positive one.

"I think so," he said.

She gave his hand a little squeeze before pulling away. *Ugh, Megan, stop humanizing all these people. Is it you?* Were there any

murderer vibes under that purported softness? Leo might have a few
dead bodies in his basement, but probably not the ones I was looking
for. So many new people were popping up in my life, and with every
single one I had the same suspicions toward the timing of it all. I
didn't stop to consider that I was the one driving all these interactions.

The table had fallen silent. Megan had killed the mood by bringing up poor Barbara's health. I took an exaggerated sip of my drink.
Dominic scraped at his plate. Leo refolded his napkin in his lap. I
saw Jake look past me to Elyse. I turned to see her giving him
instructions with her face that I couldn't interpret, but he got the
message.

"Megan," Jake added a voice to the silence. "How was Key West?"

That was enough to get her going again and everyone properly
reset. Were all families like this?

- - - - -

IT WAS ONE OF those meals that just kept going. I had heard my
phone vibrate in my coat pocket behind me several times but didn't
want to be rude. When dessert was cleared and Megan ordered cof-
fees, I couldn't take it anymore and excused myself to the bathroom,
taking my phone with me.

It was Porter. Six missed calls, even more texts.

I sealed myself into a stall and sat on the toilet. The call rang
twice before I heard it click.

"Hey, what's going on?" I asked when he didn't say anything.

There was heavy breathing on the other end. "My dad kicked
me out."

"What are you talking about?" I whispered.

"Gwen . . ."

"Breathe."

"He thinks I tried to kill the fucking cat."

"Why?"

"I got home last night out of my mind. My sister's stupid cat followed me into the bathroom, and the next thing I knew, it was attacking me. I couldn't get it off, so I shoved it into the toilet. My sister woke up and freaked out. Told my dad I was trying to drown it. . . . No one believed me. Gwen, it was bad."

"Jesus," I exhaled, struggling to visualize what happened without defaulting to *Tom and Jerry.*

"I'm going to move in with the guys for a little while."

"No way," I said. "I don't think they're a good look for you."

"There aren't exactly options falling out of my ass," Porter said, his breath shorter, and I could tell he was on the move.

"You can stay with me tonight, okay?"

"Really?"

I squished my eyes closed. Was I really offering that? It was the least I could do. "I'm downtown, but I'm leaving right now." I opened my eyes and exhaled. "Meet me at my place."

"Okay."

"Okay," I said, and he hung up.

I stood so I could lower my pants to actually pee. I rested my phone on top of the toilet paper dispenser, but before I let go, it buzzed again. I flipped it over to see the screen. It was Brian. Ha. That guy. I had fallen very far from the Brians of the world. I rejected the call. *Sorry, Brian.*

— — — — —

PORTER BEAT ME HOME and was sitting on my front steps, hands clenched around the straps of his backpack. His head was shaved, his bleach-blond hair gone. He was shaky and jumped up as soon as he saw my car.

"Nice haircut," I said, walking toward him.

He didn't say anything at first, which was extremely out of character. There were scratches all over his arms, presumably from the cat, and he rocked back and forth.

"Are you on something?" I asked, continuing past him to open the front door, which I was still somehow surprised to see wasn't closed all the way.

"No." He shook his head. "This is an organic reaction to being totally fucked." He followed me inside like a lost little puppy.

"Second floor," I said so that he could keep going while I fixed the carpet. I couldn't handle his jittering next to me.

He stomped up the stairs while I forced the runner down with my foot.

"Whoa!" he exclaimed from the top of the stairs, his exaggerated steps halting. "What the fuck is this?"

SIXTEEN

_____

S _HIT._ THERE WAS SOMETHING outside my door. I sprinted up the
stairs. _Don't be a body. Don't be a body._

It wasn't a body, full or partial. It was another dripping red message across my front door. A question. _WHO'S NEXT?_

"What is this?" Porter asked.

"Nothing," I said, unlocking the door and pushing him inside.
"It's neighborhood punks."

"Yeah right. Neighborhood punks draw dicks; they don't write
cryptic messages in blood."

"It's corn syrup." I grabbed the sponge from the sink.

He hovered back by the door. "Next for what?"

"How should I know?" I grunted. "Grab the paper towels,
will you?"

He huffed but stomped off toward the kitchen when I ignored his
protest.

I closed the door once it was clean and took a fistful of dirty paper towels into the kitchen while Porter flopped down on the couch.

"I don't know why you won't tell me what's going on," he said. "It's sketchy."

"You're the cat killer," I yelled from the kitchen, eager to deflect.

"I wasn't trying to kill it," he moaned. "Is that what they think of me? Does my family think I'm a sociopath? That's what they say, right? People who kill animals are sociopaths."

"I thought you weren't trying to kill it," I reminded him.

"I know, but what if my sister hadn't woken up? What if I had held him in there for too long?"

I moved into the doorway so he could see me. "I guess we'll never know."

"Ugh," he grumbled. "You aren't helping."

I went to the couch and sat beside him so he could lean his head on my shoulder. I could tell he was craving comfort and for me to tell him he wasn't the next Jack the Ripper. "How do you feel now?" I asked.

"Like a total monster."

"See?" I said. "Sociopaths don't feel bad." I scratched his freshly buzzed scalp, a comfortable affection, my touchstone to humanity. "I have great news for you."

He looked up at me—doe-eyed, desperate.

"You're just a dumbass who needs to cool it on the party drugs."

Porter shook his head at me, a judgmental smile escaping—a familiar reaction to my nagging tendencies—and it was a moment of relief for both of us. He relaxed his head against the back of the couch before his phone lit up and he lurched forward to grab it.

"Who is it?" I asked.

"Eric."

"Who's Eric?"

"He's one of the guys. He's cool."

"Don't answer it," I said.

He silenced his phone and threw it down on the table, nuzzling back into my shoulder with a heavy sigh.

We were silent for a minute. If only it had stayed that way.

"I have to tell you something," said Porter. "I wrote a letter to Abel Haggerty."

I jerked away from him, forcing him to sit up before falling.

"It's not a big deal," he insisted. "He hasn't responded or any-thing."

"What did you say?" *God dammit, Porter.* I should never have brought him on that tour. This was my fault. He was clearly looking for a place to fit in, a group to belong to, and this was not the right one. It was dangerous for him and increasingly inconvenient for me.

"Nothing, really. I said that I was a friend of Elyse's. Dominic says he always asks about her. I want to see if he'll write back."

"And then what?"

"I don't know." He shrugged, not feeling any of the weight that I did about the revelation.

"You need a hobby or something," I jeered. "Not writing to serial killers or drowning cats."

"Helpful," he said, picking his phone back up and repositioning himself on the other side of the couch.

- - - - -

HE FELL ASLEEP AN hour later and I went into my bedroom. I had been too heavy-handed with the heat and now the air was stuffy. I wanted to open the window, but I knew what would happen. The breeze would cause noises. The blinds would slap against the win-dow. The curtain would drift against my dresser. Worst case, it would force my door open a crack. Each sound would jolt me awake, stopping my heart, forcing me to accept it was the end for me.

If I opened the door, it would dissipate the suction caused by the breeze, but I could never sleep with my bedroom door open, even with Porter on the couch. I'd basically be allowing some murderer or rapist to get all the way through my home and to my bedside before I finally woke up because his stomach grumbled or his breath was wheezy or he put his hand over my mouth. A closed door wouldn't stop him, but it would give me enough time to try to defend myself.

The silver lining was that I always thought like this. The fact that someone was out there killing people and frequenting my doorstep hadn't caused any significant escalation. I was trained for this. Something bad was always about to happen. I wanted to tell my brain *I told you so.*

It was almost easier now. It was tangible. There was less shame to the anxiety. I stared at the ceiling, running worst-case scenarios, my already-elevated body temperature rising. This was what all great minds did when trying to solve a problem. Do you think Albert Einstein or Sherlock Holmes slept easy?

There was a new message, a question that needed an answer: *WHO'S NEXT?*

Believing the people around me were involved kept me from having to worry they were in danger. Elyse, Dominic, Jake—they were all suspects. They had all been at the restaurant with me, but if one of them had hopped in a car the second after I left and drove straight to my apartment while I was on the train back to my car, they might have made it in time to write the message before Porter showed up. It was a tight window. Maybe the message was written on my door before dinner. Jake and Elyse had been late. Maybe that was why Dominic had invited me. Maybe it was all three of them working together and therefore all three were safe from being the proverbial *NEXT.*

It was Porter I really had to worry about. I had to keep him away from Abel; I had to keep him away from all of them. When this whole mess was over, my life would go back to normal. Porter was my *normal* and I was grateful I could hear him breathing through the thin wall separating me from the living room. I would have to keep a tight leash on him going forward.

— — — —

WHEN I WOKE UP, Porter was gone. So much for the tight leash. I opened the front door to make sure there weren't any more arms or messages. Mrs. Magnus's cat sat on the top step, spread eagle and licking itself. At least Porter hadn't killed it on his way out.

SEVENTEEN

DAYS LATER I STILL hadn't heard anything from Porter and I was in the car with Dominic bound for East Buford, Pennsylvania. He had discovered there was a behavioral school there and wanted to follow the lead.

"Did Abel ever say anything about this place?" I asked.

"No. He has no idea where she ended up. Once he signed those papers, he lost all his rights."

"Why would he do that though? Doesn't seem like him from what you've said."

"He doesn't like to talk about Marin, but he has mentioned a few times that he thinks she'll come back to him. He's not worried."

Gross. And so typical of my father's ego. It's so invasive and destabilizing for another person to believe they have such control over you. Even if it isn't true. Even if it is.

Hearing that should have been a catalyst for my own empowerment. Instead, I felt immaterial.

"Even if you're right," I said, "and James Calhoun brought Marin to this place, they aren't going to tell you. There have to be confidentiality rules out the wazoo at a place like this."

"How good are you at lying?" he asked.

"Average," I lied.

"We're going to pose as a couple with a messed-up kid. I've scheduled a tour already."

"Well, first maybe settle on a better diagnosis than *messed-up*."

He gave me one of those get-over-yourself looks before ignoring my input. "At some point I'll slip away and sneak into the records room."

"I'm going to ask you something and I want you to be completely honest with me."

"Okay," he said.

"Did you get this plan from *Ace Ventura: Pet Detective*?"

He hesitated for a second and then burst out laughing. "No, not on purpose, but you're right. It worked though."

"They're going to notice if one of us wanders off," I pointed out.

"I'll say I'm having stomach issues."

"This is giving *me* stomach issues," I muttered.

— — — — —

I'D SPENT FOUR MONTHS in upstate New York after my parents were arrested. James Calhoun had located a relative. More likely, Abel had told him where to look. He was an uncle, but distant. Generations of infidelity and children out of wedlock had left Abel's kin with loose connections.

The man was seventy-eight years old. Nimble enough to get himself to and from the local bar but not much else. He barely spoke to me or even acknowledged my presence much beyond bringing home highly processed snacks and tossing them in my direction.

James told me it would be short-term. Just enough time for the paperwork to go through. Once my uncle was given full custody, the rest was easy. The paperwork was sealed and I was in the custody of a relative in another state; the State of Massachusetts never gave me much thought after that. Oswald would eventually request the name change, sealing those records as well, and then Marin Haggerty would be nothing but a ghost. He just needed a little time.

I didn't know my place in the old man's home. I'd been treated my whole life as someone special, the center of the universe, and now I ranked somewhere between the armchair and the trash can.

Love, therapy, safety—all the things I probably needed—were none of the things I wanted and none of the things I got. Instead, I kept to myself, inside my head, surrounded by the teachings of my father, clinging to every memory, trying my best not to forget who I was.

There was comfort in being alone. I didn't miss the attention, the pressure to please my father, the punishments when I failed. No one expected anything from me. No one could hurt me. But it was lonely, and over time I started to accept I wasn't on some little break from my normal life; I was transitioning to something new.

James Calhoun returned unannounced on a Saturday afternoon. Everything was settled. I was Gwen Tanner now, and Gwen Tanner was newly enrolled in a boarding school somewhere in Pennsylvania. We left that day; nothing was exchanged with the uncle other than the five hundred dollars James had promised.

Over the next two days, the long drive, a night in a motel when we got there, it became clear to me that the boarding school was not going to be the plaid-skirts-and-legacy-admissions type. It was a *boarding* school in that students lived there full-time, but that was because these children were not welcome in their homes. It was a residential treatment facility more than it was a school, an educational institution with the emphasis on *institution*.

As far as the facility was concerned, my parents had died in a fire and I was having a hard time adjusting. I had no other close family and they shouldn't expect any visitors. James told me it was just a cover, a place to hide out until the dust settled, but there was a part of me that knew he thought I belonged there.

– – – – –

I FOLLOWED BEHIND DOMINIC, more timid than I would have expected. It had a different name now and the landscaping was better maintained. The bars on the windows were gone and there were new tan awnings—but the silhouette was the same. New windows couldn't stop old memories.

I remembered the day James brought me there—whispering in my ear to *stick to the plan* as he led me inside. I said goodbye to him in the reception area; he wasn't allowed to see me to my room, which was a real red flag. There were a lot of unsettling sounds on the other side of that door. I remembered hearing kids crying, yelling, TVs turned on way too loud to cover up other sounds. I didn't make a peep while an attendant led me inside.

I spent a whole month segregated in a sterile fish tank because of my fictional propensity for self-harm—an easy sell given the five carvings down my side. James said I had to pretend it was true so no one would wonder who had actually done it to me. I was technically under observation at first, but there wasn't much observing going on. Not much to see other than a little girl on a mattress on the floor.

I was eventually moved to a standard room where there was no lock on the door, and I could finally attend classes, which were a total joke. It was another month before I got a roommate. That little girl required a lot of attention and sometimes I think the staff forgot I was even there.

I didn't want to go inside. How had I ended up there again? My pace had slowed down and Dominic noticed.

"Are you okay?" he asked, stopping so that he could give me his undivided attention.

"Aren't you nervous? What happened to the guy who flipped out when Porter broke into the Haggerty house?"

"That was different," he said.

"Yeah, this is way worse."

"Not really," he argued.

I wasn't going to scare him out of this mission, and if I kept acting like this, it was going to start raising questions. "Just don't be stupid," I said.

"I'll try my best," he promised, content that my apprehension was directed toward his incompetence and not due to my paralyzing unwillingness to revisit this place.

The reception area was barely recognizable and it was immediately apparent that Dominic's plan wasn't going to work. There were several locked doors and a check-in desk behind a thin layer of glass. Behind the glass, behind the desk, behind a controlled-entrance door were the files—files that, for all we knew, didn't even go back the almost twenty years he needed.

I shot him a look full of judgment and disappointment, masking my true feeling of *Thank God.*

- - - - -

WE DROVE HOME IN mostly silence. I could tell he was embarrassed, and he should be. We'd suffered through a whole tour of that place with no hope of getting anywhere near the files. All it did was bring back more memories for me. It was eight years of my life that I had effectively blocked out. I had to use so much of my brain power to remember details from my life as Marin Haggerty that I think my mind was tired and needed a break when it came to those years.

After the first half hour in the car, the silence started to feel tense, more than it needed to be. I shifted around in my seat to try and reset the mood. "My neck," I said, massaging it. "I think I slept funny. Why is it always the neck? Why don't you ever wake up with anything else stiff?"

"Tell that to twelve-year-old me." He laughed; I had succeeded in resetting the mood. It was the perfect alley-oop for a dick joke, but I giggled like it hadn't crossed my mind. He needed to feel clever in order to stop pouting.

"Hey." He paused, ready to address his misstep. "I'm sorry for dragging you all the way out here for nothing."

"It's fine. Now I can say I've been to East Buford, Pennsylvania." I laughed. *Ha ha. What a strange little place that I totally have never been to before, ever, like, definitely never lived there.*

EIGHTEEN

G OING BACK TO THAT school had me totally on edge, reminding me of how sick and twisted the world was. My father was an outlier, not something to be extrapolated onto the population. The kids I'd met there, though, they'd felt like something much more pervasive—symptoms of our society, a microcosm.

I had shielded myself after I left that place, isolating socially, trying to forget I was ever there. I reentered the world as eighteen-year-old Gwen Tanner—a loner who worked three jobs to survive and tried to better herself—but I was also still a little bit Marin Haggerty, who, when given the opportunity, moved back to Boston, where she could casually walk by old crime scenes and remember her father. I was never the girl who lived at that facility; that was just the in-between.

AS SOON AS WE got back, Dominic ditched me for work and I headed to Jake's apartment. I hoped it was his little cult that was doing something with Porter; I'd rather someone be slicing up his stomach than cutting off his limbs.

"Hey, Gwen," Jake said, opening the door.

"Sorry to show up like this," I blurted out. I could tell he was surprised to see me.

"No problem. Come on in." He backed away to make room for me to enter. He was always so polite for a guy who worshipped murderers and cut up his friends for sport.

The place was different sans party. The curtains were pulled back, and even though it was dark outside, it still felt brighter than when they were closed. A couple of guys sat on the couches with their laptops; one was eating a burrito, the other sucked on a purple smoothie. They glanced up to wave at me, then went back to whatever they were doing on their computers.

"Is Porter here?" I asked, cutting to the chase, extending my neck, trying to peek into the bedrooms.

"No. Is he supposed to be?"

"I haven't heard from him in a few days."

"Are you worried?" he asked.

"I'm not sure."

"Come, sit." Jake led me onto one of the unoccupied couches. His face was thin. It was kind of like talking to an attractive Crypt-Keeper. Did I need to seriously consider this guy too? Was he sending me body parts? At least if it was Jake, I could get him out of the picture; Elyse was way too good for him.

"When's the last time you saw him?" I asked.

He thought for a second. "Sunday? At the party. He called a couple days ago, told me his parents kicked him out, and I said he could crash here, but when he didn't show up, I assumed he had figured something out."

"How did he seem?"

"Excited. Manic. He said he met someone, but he wouldn't tell me who. He kept saying it would blow my mind, but I didn't think too much of it. Hyperbole seems like Porter's thing." He smiled, but I didn't have time for levity.

"Do you think it was Abel Haggerty?" I asked.

"Abel Haggerty?" He recoiled. "Why would you think that?"

"He told me he wrote him a letter."

"Really? You should ask Dominic about that. He's obsessed with the guy."

"Yeah," I agreed. It was the obvious move, but I had decided not to mention it to Dominic. It wasn't like it hadn't crossed my mind fifty times during the long car rides, but there was something that always stopped me. Like a crossing of streams that felt dangerous. It would be naive not to consider Dominic as still very much in play, and I didn't want to risk that the information wouldn't sit well with him. The fragility of believing you are unique to my father was something only I could truly understand and I wasn't looking to shake that tree yet.

Jake considered it. "Even if he is communicating with Abel Haggerty, the guy's in prison. It's not like Porter could be staying with him. I think he's probably crashing with someone, maybe one of the guys." He turned to the others in the room. "Has anyone seen Porter in the last couple days?"

The guys shook their heads and Jake shrugged at me.

"Will you ask around?" I said. "Call me if you hear anything?"

"Of course."

"Thank you," I said. We exchanged numbers and I stood to leave.

"And hey . . ." he said, stopping me. "Seriously, come by anytime. Elyse really likes you. You're good for her."

Elyse really likes me. If Elyse was the one doing this, would he know? Would he be helping her? Did he mean *likes me* like a cat who brings their beloved owner dead rats? What was transpiring was not what I would have picked as the ideal display of affection. But what did I know about affection? Nothing about the kind that made a person feel warm and fuzzy. My father killed people and my mother didn't like hugs or quality time or me.

I walked out of the building, but that was as far as I got before I didn't know where to go next, unsure of even stepping to the right or the left. I was no closer to finding Porter. I had no idea who was doing this and no idea what else they had in store for me.

That was the message though. A succinct *WHO'S NEXT?* scribbled on my front door from whoever was out there killing the people I knew and throwing them in my face.

From the day I saw my name written on that note card, my real name, a change had begun. It was as if I'd started going backward, slowly at first, tiptoeing out of the safety and shelter of Gwen Tanner. Revisiting that school had taken it to another level, like a hand on my back, grabbing my shirt and pulling me. And now I was in it. I was that child again, standing on the street and wondering if every person who passed would be the next one to die.

It was not my father's actions but the anticipation that discolored my understanding of human life. I would detach, float through it, wait for him to whisper, "That one," which would ground me for a time, enough time for it to be done. Then I would float away again.

It was as if I were nine years old again, sitting on the basement floor, back vibrating against the washing machine as my father's bloody clothes went in circles. I would sit there, arms around my knees, staring forward, until the job was done. Then I would wait for who was next. It could be anyone, and there was nothing I could do about it.

There was no room for imagination in that life. No thought of what the future would be or even what I wanted for Christmas. It wasn't something that presented itself on the outside; I could play on the playground at recess, get a Happy Meal at McDonald's. It was instead something wrapped around my brain like an invasive plant, with moss clogging every synapse, vines restricting every thought pattern.

It had been a long time since I'd felt so out of control, but the feeling wasn't foreign. I was the institutionalized child of Abel Haggerty. Not every trigger is subtle; not every correlation is buried deep.

All I could think now, standing with my feet cemented to the sidewalk, fighting the urge to float away, was *Anyone but Porter.* I couldn't wait for who was next—not if it was him.

Porter had told Jake that he'd *met* someone. The implication was a face-to-face—maybe a phone call under Porter's patented exaggeration, but definitely more than an unrequited letter. Porter was serving himself up on a platter, and if it were me, that's how I would escalate things—take away someone who truly meant something to me.

I never gave much thought to how important Porter was to me until I was presented with the idea of him being taken away. I always thought it was my guarded isolation that was keeping me in control, but maybe it was the opposite. Having him—someone to talk to almost every day, someone who noticed me, someone whose dumb jokes let me exist in those moments—it was necessary.

If I wanted a say in the outcome, I had to be smarter, more like my father and less like his daughter.

I looked up and down the street. This person had to be following me, watching me. All I saw were cars. Lots of cars. It was a city. Unless my stalker drove the Batmobile, I wasn't going to notice. If it was someone I'd recognize, they wouldn't sit at a bus stop, peeking over a newspaper. The idea of a masked stranger crouching in the bushes was almost comforting. I'd happily choose that over the more likely option that it was someone I knew stalking me by talking right to my face.

That was it though. By targeting me, getting so into my business, they had actually given me the reins. This person was studying me, looking for a way to upset me. It was an opportunity.

I went back to work the next day and made a big deal about my weekend plans—something I'd never done before—and I definitely got some weird looks. "I can't wait for the weekend. I'm catching up with a close friend. I'm so excited. It's been way too long," I told everyone and anyone I interacted with; I needed my stalker to know. I texted Elyse. I texted Dominic. I texted Porter. One of them would say something to explain my absence to Jake and his friends. I texted Brian, who didn't respond. I even opened my old Facebook page and posted that I was **feeling excited about my weekend** 😎 🏃‍♂️.

I wanted to be in control; it was all that mattered. Childhood memories were something I lived with every day, but remembering what my childhood felt like, that headspace, that had to stop. If I wanted Porter to stay safe, I needed to suggest another target. I would decide who was next.

NINETEEN

CROSSED THE DRIVEWAY WITH my small duffel bag and knocked on the splintered door. A chair inside creaked, then I heard the clunk of a recliner folding shut. The door opened and Gustus stood before me. He had the type of body that could block out the sun. He didn't strike me as someone who had done the appropriate stretches in his youth to combat the inevitable breakdown of his super-long bones.

"Can I help you?" he asked, and I was relieved he didn't recognize me. He could have been acting, lying, covering up his mastermind psychotic murder plot against my loved ones, but the waistband of his Fruit of the Looms was sticking out from his jean shorts and I really had to let this suspect go.

"Is Reanne home?" I asked.

"And who are you?" He crossed his arms and leaned against the doorframe.

"A friend. Carol Griffin." Carol was a lady who'd worked with my mom at Kmart a million years ago. She'd had a bunch of kids to feed and was always eager to take shifts from Reanne when my mother was sick or destroying evidence or being cleansed by my father. When Abel was in one of his moods he would calmly tell my mother, "Better call Carol." Reanne would understand the reference.

"Hold on," Gustus said, and disappeared into the house.

I turned back toward the street. A neighbor was installing an air-conditioning unit in a downstairs window. Farther down I could hear a ball bouncing against the pavement. A car full of teenagers passed by. I didn't see any stalkers.

The door reopened and I whipped back around to face my mother.

She took the appropriate seconds to register it was me and not hardworking Carol. She knew how to proceed. She was intuitive and prison-smart. "Carol," she said. "It's great to see you."

"Sorry to drop in on you like this, but there's a burst pipe in my apartment and I didn't have anywhere else to go. I was hoping I could stay for a couple of days."

"Of course." Reanne smiled.

I lunged forward and threw my arms around my mother. It was a manufactured display of affection, trumpeted on the doorstep for my stalker, but it didn't make the physical contact any less real. I was enveloped by the deep stench of cigarettes in her hair and she hesitated a fraction of a second before wrapping her arms around my waist.

I loosened my grip and she separated from me, backing up to allow me inside the house. I stepped through the doorway knowing exactly what I was doing.

I stood on the edge of the living room, designed out of necessity rather than taste—mismatched furniture, stained carpet, a television six or seven versions behind the latest model. Gustus lowered himself back into a ragged recliner. If he was suspicious of who Carol was or how she knew Reanne, he wasn't going to say it.

"Baby," my mother addressed her husband, "why don't you go see your brother about the car so Carol and I can catch up?"

Gustus considered it, then leveraged himself against the armrests and back out of the chair. "How about a compromise? I'll go catch the end of the game at O'Brien's." He walked toward her, stopping to lean down and kiss her on the top of the head. It was kind of sweet. My mother's superpower was clearly getting awful men to love her unconditionally.

The door slammed shut behind Gustus and we were alone.

"Can I get you something to drink?" Reanne offered.

"I'm good, thanks."

"I'm surprised to see you," she said. "Is something the matter?"

"Yeah." I rested my bag on the tattered couch. "There's a burst pipe at my apartment." I repeated it with a bit of attitude toward her for not believing it the first time . . . even though it was a lie.

"Damn shame. Well, you can stay here as long as you'd like. And you don't have to worry about Gustus. He'll keep out of your business."

I took a seat, sinking into the couch. I was here, in the house, feigning a relationship with my mother. That was the plan; the rest was irrelevant. She sat down on the edge of Gustus's recliner, resting her hands in front of her and waiting for me to say something.

"You seem happy," I said.

She smiled in the affirmative. "I know it's not going to be all butterflies and rainbows, but it's good to be out."

"I'm sure."

"Tell me about you. I've missed everything." She scooted toward me.

"Someone cut off James Calhoun's arm," I blurted out, and she ceased trying to enter my space. "Probably killed him. Do you remember him?"

"I heard that," she said, shifting her body language back to what I was comfortable with.

"And the other guy, Oswald Shields. You knew him too."

"What's going on, Marin?"

She'd called me Marin again. Just like that. Out loud and so natural in conversation.

"I don't know," I said. "But be careful. Lock your doors and don't be stupid." I was actively trying to put her in the crosshairs of my stalker, but I guess I did feel guilty about it. Seeing her face, even though it looked like it had been soaked in a corrosive substance for the past eighteen years, I saw my childhood and I saw my family and I saw the last time I had belonged to anything. Maybe if I warned her, she would be ready and hit the asshole in the throat with a shovel or something. That was really the best-case scenario.

"Do you know who did it?" she asked, the casual delivery of her question reminding me that my family was different.

I shook my head. "I'm trying to figure it out."

"I'm sorry," she said.

I shrugged. "It is what it is."

"No, I mean I'm sorry that I'm your mother." Her head dropped and she broke down a bit. "I should never have had you."

I knew that, but I could have lived without hearing it. There was an uncomfortable silence as I saw her wheels turning, trying to make sense of her old life.

"I was in love with your father," she continued. "So in love, and I did horrible things. I bought into it. I believed he saw something the rest of us couldn't . . . and he wanted a child."

"That must have been a relief, then, once you got to sign away your rights to me." It was bratty of me to say, but c'mon.

"No, it wasn't like that. It was very hard. But I was going away for a long time and . . ."

"And he told you to do it."

She sighed. "Do you think you can ever forgive me?"

She was trying to be the better person I was sure she had told herself she would be once she got out. Living in the postprison honeymoon phase, she still believed she had changed; I didn't buy it. "Probably not," I said.

Her face contorted; she wasn't expecting me to be so blunt. It wasn't her fault. How could she have any idea who I had become over the past twenty years?

"Don't get emotional," I said. "We don't need each other. We never needed each other. You were Abel's wife and I was his child, not yours, not really. I know you think you're supposed to feel guilty about everything, but I know you don't feel that way and I'm telling you it's okay. Believing you're supposed to feel a certain way is exhausting. If Abel taught us anything good, it's that. Just exist as you are until it's over."

She stared at me like I was a freak of nature. I counted the creases across her forehead as she processed how the hell to follow that up.

"Reanne," I said. "Relax. Do you need a cigarette or something?"

"You look like him in the eyes," she said. Kind of a rude thing to say considering my father's wonky eye. "They move so fast and then they just stop when you get real into yourself. I'm not a great person and you can hate me, but you be careful. If you have to take after one of us, maybe I ain't so bad." She stood from the chair and grabbed a pack of cigarettes off the coffee table.

My newly righteous mother trudged into the kitchen to blow her smoke out the window. I picked up the remote and turned the game back on. My eyes stopped moving? That wasn't even a thing. Maybe it was the contacts.

— — — —

I STAYED WITH REANNE and Gustus for two solid nights. I did my best to not think of Reanne as my mother and it helped. We didn't have any more conversations like the first one. She didn't ask her husband to leave again. Gustus was actually funny. He was definitely lazy, but his social commentary was spot-on. So was his self-awareness. Every sick burn started with "I know I'm nobody worth sayin' this, but . . ." followed by something some person on TV shouldn't have said or worn or done. Fifty consecutive hours is a long time to spend with two people. I had established my place on the couch and we had worked out our group pizza-topping dynamic, but after breakfast on Sunday, Dominic called and Carol had to go.

It had taken Dominic a long time to contact me again after our trip and I was starting to get offended and self-conscious. I was less worried that something had happened to him and more worried that he had lost interest in me. Marin was the object of his obsession, but if he was innocent in all this, he didn't know I was Marin. To him I was just Gwen. Was Gwen a party pooper? Was managing all these secrets making me boring? Why couldn't he be interested in a different serial killer and then I could offer my own theories and give hilarious anecdotes instead of constantly negating him? But if it were any other serial killer, would I still be interested in Dominic? I was all right with this being a completely toxic relationship as long as the toxicity was reciprocal. I called him back as soon as I got into my car.

"Hey," he answered.

"Hi, yes, I missed a call from this number."

"Funny," he said. "You were the one who messaged me that you were going out of town."

"Yeah, but it's not like you couldn't have texted or something." I had to let this go.

"Sorry, I can be flaky when I get into something."

"So what had you so engrossed?" I knew it was me. Well, not me, Gwen, the clingy girl complaining he wouldn't return my texts, but me, Marin, the girl he thought was killing everyone.

"Can you blow off work tomorrow?" he asked.

"Are you serious? Attendance is not voluntary."

"Is that a no?"

"It's a *Why?*"

"I can't tell you yet because you'll never agree."

"But you think I'm going to agree to that?"

"Yes, because you're curious."

"Tell me."

"No." He chuckled. "Trust me."

"Give me a hint."

"It has to do with Abel Haggerty. That's all I'll say."

"I'm shocked," I scoffed, as if it weren't the exact piece of information I needed to hear in order to agree to this secret plan. "You know, I was saving up my days for a nice vacation." There was no truth to that. I had plenty of time saved and was never going on a vacation. The short notice was the bigger issue, but after making such a big deal about my weekend, I could say I had food poisoning.

"Last time, I promise," he said.

"Fine," I agreed, not at all appreciating the mystery of it. What if he was bringing me to Edgar Valley to introduce me to my own father? What if he thought that was some kind of honor? I would have to practice the appropriate fit I would throw in the parking lot if that was the case. Other than that, I guessed I had to wait until tomorrow and try not to lose my mind in the meantime.

— — — —

PAINTING POTS WAS ALWAYS slow when the weather was nice. Sunday was supposed to be Porter's shift, but since he had disappeared off the face of the planet, I was stuck with Jasmine, an actual high schooler. She was a great fit for the job—bubbly, patient with the norm# HAVEN'T KILLED IN YEARS

121

normkids, proactive with cleaning/restocking/setting up—but she was horrible with boredom. Why couldn't they have hired one of those teenagers who were glued to their phones?

Jasmine had huge, curly red hair that kept bopping into my periphery. She was buzzing around me. I tried taking my headphones out, thinking maybe she thought they were letting her presence go unnoticed, but then she started talking to me. She was sweet, but talking to her was doing the opposite of calming me down.

When stuck in conversations I didn't want to be a part of, my thoughts wandered from *what* they were saying to *how* they were saying it and *why* they were saying it. I couldn't help it. I listened for pauses, for emphasis, for word choice. I studied body language. It was a skill I was taught—a great tool, if only I could turn it off when inconvenient. I was at Painting Pots to numb my brain, not fixate on why Jasmine had first described her boyfriend as "chill" before shifting her weight and adding, "but, like, really passionate about everything." I couldn't have cared less about Jasmine's boyfriend, but when an insane man raises a child to expect coded messages, some of the wires get crossed.

I offered several times to watch the store if she wanted to leave early, but the damn girl was too responsible and insisted on staying until the end of her double shift. Finally, when the clock hit seven p.m., I made a peculiar cuckoo clock noise and she checked the time.

"Oh, wow. It's already seven." She hopped off the counter. "Are you gonna stay?"

"Yeah, just for a few."

I stayed another hour. I let my creation spin through my hands, chasing perfection, music blasting in my ears—finally the chance to zone out. It was late enough now. I could go home and go to bed, pretending that I would be able to fall asleep immediately, and then it would be tomorrow and all would be revealed. I flipped down the last light switch and Painting Pots went dark. I stepped outside and inserted the key into the lock.

"Gwen?" A voice that I knew well came from my right.

I turned to see Elyse step out of the shadows. The cojones on this girl never ceased to amaze me.

"What are you doing here?" I asked.

"Sorry, is this weird? I was walking to my car and saw you." She let out a nervous laugh. She was good, almost too good.

"No, of course not." I tucked my bottom lip in and bit down.

She glanced up at the Painting Pots sign. "I've never been to one of these places."

"Do you want to come in?"

"No, it's okay. I'm sure you want to get home."

"It's fine." I removed the key from the lock and pushed open the door. "I'll give you the grand tour."

I turned on the light in the back, just enough so that we could see but not enough for the place to look open, and she followed me inside.

"Do you work here?" she asked.

"No, but I have keys. I know the people who work here."

"Porter?"

I nodded, still very sensitive to his proximity to the world I was trying to separate him from.

I pointed at the shelves of gray unfinished pottery. "You pick a piece from there and then you paint it however you want and they fire it in the kiln in the back."

She walked toward the wall of pottery and perused the options. "That sounds straightforward."

I watched her meander around. I could barely recognize her as Cody Abbington's little sister, but there was something, the ridge between her eyes, that proved her identity. Did I have a marker like that, even after all the trouble I went through to alter my appearance?

"Do you want to paint something?" I asked.

She stopped and turned to me. "I can come back when it's open."

"It's fine. No one cares."

"Are you sure?"

"Yeah, pick whatever you want. I'll get some paints."

- - - - -

WE SAT TOGETHER AT one of the long wooden tables painting coffee mugs. I watched her trace the curve of the handle with yellow paint. She was so focused, so careful. Did she remember I was there?

She dipped the brush into the paint, *1-2-3.* "I never got to do anything like this when I was younger," she said.

"I'm sorry," I said, and I meant it because I understood it.

"You can ask me questions if you want," she offered. "Everyone always wants to."

"What kind of questions?"

"About my family. About Abel Haggerty and the murders."

"Kind of morbid," I said.

She shrugged and went back to her mug, using the blue paint to trace small circles. My eyes followed her strokes, putting me into a trance. She had three thin gold rings on her right hand—not ideal for killing. My father always wore his wedding ring on a thin chain around his neck, tucked under his shirt. I supposed it meant she didn't plan on killing me yet.

"I don't want it to define me," she admitted. "What happened to me. But it does. How do you deal so well with what happened to you?"

"What do you mean?" I braced myself. Was it time to go there?

"The fire, losing your parents," she clarified.

I exhaled. Yes, of course, my very tragic backstory. "Who says I deal with it well?" I watched her eyes come up and meet mine again. They blinked and it was a form of Morse code, communicating something, but I still wasn't equipped to translate her facial expressions. I wished that I could though.

The sound of the lock turning broke the tension.

We both twisted toward the front door, where Porter stood on the other side. He fumbled with the lock, dirty and disheveled. His sweaty shirt was covered with dark red stains that I knew from looking at him were not corn syrup.

TWENTY

JUMPED FROM MY SEAT and ran to Porter as he opened the front entrance to Painting Pots.

He froze in his tracks. "What are you doing here?!"

"What am *I* doing here?" I pushed him back out the door so that we wouldn't be overheard. "What the hell happened to you?"

He scratched at the back of his head, thinking about what to say.

"What?!" I yelled, demanding a response.

"Gwen, I did something . . . bad." He looked over my shoulder and noticed Elyse through the window. "What is she doing here?"

"Who cares? Tell me what's going on. Where have you been?"

He danced in place, incapable of stillness. "There's someone in my trunk."

"Some*one*, like a human being?"

"Yes, like a human being." He leaned in. "A fucking dead body." He shook his hands out like the words had landed on his fingertips.

"Oh my God. Why is there a dead body in your trunk? Did you kill someone?!"

"No, I didn't *kill* her." He groaned. "Please help me. Please don't call the cops." He scratched at his arms like he was tripping, and I hoped that he was just hallucinating something awful.

"What do you want *me* to do?" I asked.

"I need to put it in the kiln and you're here having a Girl Scout meeting." He peered back over my shoulder at Elyse with the audacity to be annoyed.

"You brought the body here?"

"I *told* you, it's in my trunk." He reached up and seized both of my arms. "You need to get rid of Elyse."

I rotated a hair to peek at her sitting there, watching. "Okay. Bring your car around to the back and I'll let you in once she's gone."

"Thank you," he said, spinning around and running to his car.

I went back inside and took slow, awkward steps toward Elyse. "I have to help Porter with something. Is it all right if we call it a night?"

She stood and met me halfway. "What happened? Do you need my help?" She reached up and touched my arm. I shivered from the sensation of her hand on my skin. Why was she touching me? She used her thumb to wipe at something. Porter had left a streak of blood on my arm.

I moved to scrub at it, getting her hand out of the way. "No, it's okay. He got in a car accident and is pretty shaken up. I'm going to help him get home."

"Whatever you say." She smirked in an insulting, accusatory way, but instead of pushing it, she brushed past me and out the front door—back into whatever shadow she had emerged from. I wanted to stare at the last place she was visible, transfixed, focused on the meaning of it all, but I couldn't stand around being a Jane Austen character when I had to help get rid of a dead body—reality, the enemy of romanticism.

— — — — —

I PROPPED OPEN THE back door as Porter reversed his ancient car toward me. I met him at the trunk, where he inserted the key, then stopped. "Are you going to be okay seeing this?" he asked.

"Just get it over with." What I meant was *Yes, please*. It had been so long since I had seen a dead body—a whole one anyway.

He popped the trunk and my throat closed.

She was loosely wrapped in a tarp and her frizzy auburn-and-gray hair was congealed with blood.

"It's Reanne Haggerty," Porter said. *No shit.*

"Who did this?" I choked out. "Why do you—"

"Just help me, okay?" He reached into the trunk and grabbed my mother by her armpits. "I'm going to puke," he said, gagging and burying his nose and mouth in his shoulder for a moment. "Grab her ankles," he ordered as he regained control of his stomach.

"Stop," I said, and he paused. "We're not bringing her inside."

Porter released the body, but glared at me for further explanation.

"We can't put her in the kiln. For a million reasons."

His stare was so blank. It wasn't because he was dumb. He wasn't dumb. It was because he was incapable of thinking logically anymore.

"Will she fit? Does it get hot enough? Is it going to smell? How long does it take? Will there be traces of her everywhere? Porter, you can't dispose of a body in the place where you work. You might as well try burying her in your backyard."

He sighed, bringing his hands to his face and rubbing them up and down. "What should I do, then?"

I took a step toward his trunk like an answer would present itself. I stood over her body. Her throat was slit—amateurish, too messy, a terrifying death, a millisecond of time when you think maybe the knife missed before you start catching your own blood in your hand.

I didn't like to admit it, but half of me had come from this woman. I'd never felt a connection, but I had grown inside her and she had fed me and dressed me and kept me alive before I was equipped do those things myself. Was I too hard on her? Was it just easier to hate her?

My plan had worked. Porter was with me, and instead, Reanne was dead. This was my doing. I had felt so smart concocting the plan. So why did I feel like complete shit now? Maybe it was because of Gustus. He was going to be heartbroken. He'd waited so long for her to get out of prison only for her to be taken away again. It had to be that. It wasn't possible these churning feelings were about losing her. I wasn't ready for that.

I knew for my cover I should be freaking out, but I didn't feel like it. The kid was too far gone; he didn't care if I was reacting appropriately. That was my fault too. I never thought it would come to this, but I knew he was susceptible. Not to anything specifically, but I knew he was young and lost and desperate for a place in the world. I had taken a kid like that, who I supposedly cared about, and thrown him right to the wolves.

"What happened to her?" I asked.

"I don't know," he insisted. "She was dead when I showed up— sitting on the couch, blood everywhere, throat slit. Her eyes were all open." He kept rubbing his hands forcefully over his face and through his hair, spreading bits of dried blood all over himself. "And my stuff . . . she had things that were mine."

"What do you mean?"

"Like some of my old hair was on the floor, covered in blood. There was a receipt on the table that I know was mine, covered in blood. My debit card was sticking out from between the cushions . . . *COVERED IN BLOOD.* Do you see what I'm saying? I was being set up."

"Why were you even there?"

"She asked me to go there. She said it was a friend's house and I could crash there. Once I saw the body, I didn't know what to do. I didn't do it, but it looked like I did."

"Who told you to go there?" I asked.

He turned toward me, bracing for my reaction. "It was her . . . It was Marin Haggerty."

TWENTY-ONE

WHAT DO YOU MEAN, Marin Haggerty?" I asked, trying to keep my voice steady and my hands from violently shaking Porter by the neckline of his shirt.

"I went to visit Abel, and when I left, there was a note on my car. It said to meet her at Old Navy."

"At Old Navy? Are you kidding me?"

"No, it said Old Navy, so I drove there and waited outside."

"And . . . ?!"

"What?" he protested, like I was being unreasonably impatient. "She walked up to me and we started talking."

"What did she look like?"

"I don't know. A regular person. Sort of pretty, blonde, a little awkward. She seemed nervous."

"And you've never seen her before?"

"No. I saw the picture from when she was a kid that Dominic had, but I'd never seen her in person."

"And you're sure it was her?"

"Who else would it be?"

I moved on, not wanting to overplay my hand. "What did she say?"

"She asked why I was visiting Abel . . . We just talked. It wasn't weird. She said it was hard for her to visit her father. I assumed she wanted me to help bring him messages. She was nice and she seemed scared. She didn't seem psycho or anything."

"Okay, but how did it go from that to this?" I pointed with gusto to my mother's body in the trunk.

"I thought it was cool, okay? Are you happy now? I thought I could bring her over and the guys would totally lose their shit. I wanted to impress them. I know. Don't say anything. I know it was stupid."

"And dangerous. You understand that, right?"

"Yessss." He elongated the word, frustrated with my completely justified frustration.

A motorcycle revved it's engine obnoxiously from a few streets over and it reminded me we weren't alone in the world.

"We have to get out of here. I'll take care of this. Take my car, the keys are inside. Go home. *Your parents' house.* I don't care what you have to say to them. You need to go home. I'll call you when I'm done."

Porter nodded.

"What about her house?" I asked. "Do we need to worry about that?"

"I used gloves. I found cleaning supplies under the sink. I cleaned it all up, I think." His face begged for me to agree that it was probably good enough.

"And she was alone? There was no one else there?"

He shook his head.

I guess Gustus picked a good day to get out of the recliner. I hoped wherever he was, he was with enough people to give him a good alibi.

"Okay," I said. "Wash up in the bathroom and then go. Do you understand?"

He nodded again.

"Go," I ordered. He turned around and went inside without a word. Porter—speechless. That's how I knew it was bad.

- - - - -

I DROVE TWO HOURS north to a pond in New Hampshire that I found on Google Maps by scrolling around the screen and not creating a record of searching for it. I wrote down the directions, then turned off my phone. I avoided any toll roads. I pulled over to pick up pieces of scrap metal I saw along the way—a discarded bumper, a piece of rebar, a rusty pipe-like thing, and a loose chain I saw hanging off a pasture gate.

I dragged the metal pieces and the body through the woods from the road to the edge of the pond. It took me three trips. I used the chain to attach the bumper to Reanne's neck. I shoved the rebar and the pipe under her shirt and then snaked them through her pant legs.

The water was murky, full of slimy overgrown plants. At least it seemed unlikely anyone would be looking to swim there. I dragged her in as far as I could manage, thankful she hadn't used her time in prison to bulk up. Then I made sure she sank to the bottom.

I didn't know if it was smart. I didn't know if her body would surface two hours later. I didn't know if it was a great fishing cove and some local was going to hook her eye socket the next morning. I only knew it was the best I could do given the circumstances. I'd spent a lot of my life thinking about killing and absolutely not enough time thinking about what I would do after the fact. I had to hope it was good enough, but I was confident the plan was a hell of a lot better than the kiln.

I texted Porter a few times once I was closer to home, but he didn't answer. I hoped that meant he was asleep. He needed it. I brought his car to a twenty-four-hour self-service car wash and did my best to clean it. Then I went home and did my best to clean myself.

The sun was starting to rise by the time I turned onto Porter's street. I pulled up in front of the house, but I didn't need to knock on the door to realize there was a problem. My car wasn't in the driveway. Porter hadn't gone home.

TWENTY-TWO

WAS AT ELYSE'S DOOR earlier than anyone could justify was reasonable. I brought the mug she'd painted, hoping she didn't notice I hadn't actually put it in the kiln. I buzzed her apartment from outside and she gave me the code through the intercom.

She met me at her door in a baggy ripped T-shirt and leggings. Her eyeliner was rubbed off but not washed enough for it to be completely gone. "Good morning," she said as she opened the door.

"I brought your mug." I shoved it in her face like it was a valid reason to have asked for her address at six in the morning.

"Thanks. Do you want to come in?"

"Is Jake here?" I asked, maneuvering past her.

"No," she said, a slight crease forming over her eyebrow, like it was weird that I had asked, leaving me wondering how serious they really were.

I looked around, postponing eye contact. There was something that seemed off about her place. At first I couldn't pinpoint it, but it was the emptiness. There was nothing on the walls, there were no picture frames, no candles, no books, no nothing. I figured she'd at least have some plants—she must get a good discount from her job—but there was only furniture and life things like dishes and lamps.

My curiosity overcame my apprehension and I had to confront her. "Why did you show up at Painting Pots last night?" I was so convinced she was involved, but Porter knew Elyse, and Porter had met *Marin*. If I really was wrong about Elyse, I needed more convincing. I wanted to be sure.

Her face scrunched, uneasy with my tone. "I told you. I was just in the area."

"Yeah, for what?"

"I like the sandwich place that's in that plaza."

That was a decent excuse; it was a good sandwich place. But she could totally be lying. It doesn't take a genius to pretend to like sandwiches. "They have a great teriyaki wrap," I said. "You should try it sometime."

"I'd love to." She smiled like what I said was an invitation.

I was attempting to interpret this conversation as an insidious metaphor, but I was failing.

She guided me to the couch. "How's Porter? Is everything okay?"

We sat together on the white couch that didn't have a single stain or throw pillow or evidence that we weren't the first two people to ever make contact with its surface. To answer her question, Porter was not okay. I stared at her, trying to compute where I should land between *Yeah, he's fine* and *Of course not and you know it*.

I had been awake all night. I was not making rational choices, and once our eye contact reached peak alignment, I couldn't help myself. "Elyse, are you fucking with me?"

She flinched at my boldness. "What do you mean?"

"If it's you, I get it, and I'm into it, so tell me and we can get dark and up the stakes and you can put a bomb in my car or something, but please tell me, because if it's not you—"

She reached up and touched my cheek. "I don't know what you're talking about." Her words were soft and her eyes stayed engaged. She was unbothered by the insanity I was spouting at her. Then she leaned in. Her lips touched mine.

It wasn't the answer I was hoping for, but it was happening and I let it. We had been playing a game after all, just not the one I'd thought we were playing. She pulled away, but I followed her and then we were still kissing. What was I doing? She was with Jake and I was up to something with Dominic, but that didn't seem too relevant in the moment. What did seem relevant was that my father had ruthlessly slaughtered her family.

I pulled away. I was hiding too much. She wanted to kiss Gwen, but she would never consent to kissing Marin. I leaned back and opened my eyes. "We can't do this." I looked at her before realizing that speaking wasn't enough. I stood up and backed away. "It's . . . not a great time . . . I have to be somewhere."

"Then why did you come here?" She forced a tight smile that didn't tell me anything about what she was really thinking.

I wanted to go back to the couch. Why not? What did I care that I was lying to her about everything? Deep down inside, I hoped she was lying right back. That was what made it exciting, right? That she could be just like me?

"Sorry," I choked. "I wanted you to have your mug." It wasn't the smoothest excuse.

My phone buzzed in my pocket and I reached for it, hoping and praying it was Porter, but it was Dominic.

Be there in 20.

It took me a second to register what that meant. So much had happened in the last twenty-four hours. Too much. Then I remembered. Dominic wanted to take me somewhere, somewhere he wouldn't tell me—a mystery that had to do with my father. If this wasn't going to be the confrontation and subsequent showdown with Elyse that I was hoping for, I guess I really did have somewhere to be after all. Even if I had completely forgotten about it. Even if I could be blindly walking into some kind of trap.

TWENTY-THREE

I RACED HOME FROM ELYSE'S to get there before Dominic showed up. I basically walked into my apartment, spun around, and walked back out the door at the sound of his text.

I climbed into his car and demanded an answer to where we were going. He made sure to put the vehicle in motion, and after a few tugs at his hair, he got into it. "I know the whole trip to Pennsylvania was a bust last time, but—"

"Are you serious?"

"Hear me out," he pleaded, offering up a greasy brown paper bag.

I yanked it out of his hand. I could eat the entire breakfast sandwich before the light at the end of my street turned green; it didn't mean I was agreeing to anything.

"I did some more research," he continued, hurrying to get it all out while my mouth was preoccupied. "The place has a different name than when Marin lived there."

"Allegedly," I chimed in, mouth full.

"Fine," he said, humoring me. "In the period of time that Marin would have hypothetically lived there, the place had a different name."

"And . . . ?" I swallowed.

"And it was owned by Care Vision, LLC. Not the same company that owns it anymore."

"Riveting," I mocked.

"Stick with me. Care Vision, LLC, ran into some major legal drama a while back. They were operating heavily in some gray areas between a school, a detention center, and a psychiatric facility, I don't know. Whatever they were calling themselves in whatever moment to manipulate funding and circumvent regulations."

"Okay . . ."

"They sold the facility to some big nationwide treatment center—that's not important. Care Vision, LLC, didn't disband. They got out of the kid business, but they still operate four halfway homes outside Philadelphia. And more than that, Care Vision, LLC, has an active lease on three storage units in East Buford, Pennsylvania."

"How do you know that—about the storage units?"

"I called the number on the website, pretending I was from the city tax office. I said I was calling to confirm they no longer owned or leased any property in East Buford and they quickly corrected me, afraid of more fines."

"Very savvy."

"So the files have to be in there, right? I mean, what else would they keep in there?"

"I don't know, furniture?"

"No one is going to pay rent to store some old furniture for ten years."

"You still have the same problem—controlled access." I couldn't let him know I was nervous, but I sure could let him know I was annoyed and hopefully thwart this before we reached the highway.

"You're driving me all the way out there again to be reminded of a thing called locks? There has to be a better way to go about this."

"I *did* have that same problem . . ." He paused, waiting for me to beg him for further explanation.

"Buuuut?" I obliged.

"I called the storage unit office. It's a mom-and-pop place, not one of those huge companies—just, like, a guy who's owned some units forever. I said I was performing a periodic security test and wanted to make sure the list of people with access to the units was up to date. The owner *faxed* me the list, can you believe it? He didn't know how to email it. I had to sign up for an online fax number."

"With your own name?"

"No, I used a fake email and that's all I needed. I mean, I'm sure some *Mr. Robot* cyber police could track my IP or something, but I'm not going to sweat it. We're not stealing the crown jewels."

"What are you going to do with the list?"

"I told the man we'd send someone over in the next week because we're thinking about going digital. He spouted off a ton of reasons not to go purely digital, mostly about the Chinese blowing up all our satellites, but he seemed very eager to keep Care Vision as happy customers. So I found the guy on the list who looks the most like me and John made me a fake ID."

"Who's John?"

"You know John. He lives with Jake."

"Oh, right," I said, having no idea who John was. All those guys looked the same to me. Not a lot of diversity, a lot of ripped black jeans and faux-faded graphic tees.

I was already in the car and his plan seemed a hell of a lot more solid than Operation *Ace Ventura*. I couldn't very well let him get to those files without me, so I said, "Fine."

"Thank you!" He beamed, adjusting in his seat, expressively getting into long-car-ride mode.

Spending five hours in the car and then five hours back with him, or anyone, was not particularly enticing, but I didn't really have another option. So many holes in the dam, but Dominic getting access to those files seemed to be the most problematic at the moment. I didn't know if there were files in those storage units, and even if there were, I didn't know if there would be one for me. I didn't want to think about what I would have to do if there was. Could I trust Dominic to keep my secret? Was it possible he already knew and this was all a ruse to torture me? Short of violence, all I could do at this point was wait and find out. So I sat quietly and thought about all the other problems I was ignoring in favor of this one.

I needed to be with Porter, wherever he was. He hadn't gone home like I'd told him to and he hadn't responded to any of my texts. I should have been looking for him, but short of reporting my car missing, I had no place to start.

And Elyse. What was I to even think about her anymore? She wasn't the person who'd met Porter at Old Navy. Was that enough to believe she wasn't involved? She could have hired someone—an aspiring actor. Or was it Dominic who'd hired someone? Dominic, sitting next to me, taking me on this trip, laughing on the inside about how dumb I must be. Taking cues from Abel or going rogue to impress Abel or going rogue to try to get the upper hand on Abel.

"Check it out," Dominic said, pausing my spiral by handing me the fake ID. "John did a great job."

Or John! Was it John? Whoever John was. I was getting worked up. I counted the buttons around the car radio, *1-2-3-4-5-6-7-8*.

"What are you doing?" Dominic asked.

"What?"

"You're staring at the radio. You can change it if you want."

"No, nothing. I zoned out. I'm tired."

"We can get a hotel tonight . . . so we don't have to drive all the way back."

"Yeah, maybe," I muttered, not really considering it.

"I just need a name," he said unprompted. "Whatever Marin is going by now. That would be game changing."

"Sure would," I said, knowing that if he had his way, we would be spending the next five hours talking about Marin Haggerty. I leaned my head against the window, closed my eyes, and welcomed the nap I desperately needed.

— — — —

IT WORKED. DOMINIC'S PLAN worked. I could have called ahead when we stopped for gas, warned the place they were getting scammed, but if there was something about my identity in there, better Dominic find it than the police. At least this way I had a chance to find it first.

The old man in the shoebox office handed over the keys without hesitation. He barely looked at the ID as he griped about the pitfalls of digital recordkeeping. All John's hard work for nothing.

Dominic hoisted open the door to the first unit, the rattling of the chains echoing across the cracked parking lot. There they were— stacks of aging bankers boxes. The door motion triggered a light inside, but the glow seemed almost imaginary, like an aha moment Indiana Jones might experience. Dominic ran his finger down the boxes in the first row, scanning the labels; they were arranged by birth year, too recent for me.

He moved to the second unit and lifted the door, the sound and the light less symbolic this time. Older boxes ran along the bottom.

He glanced over and raised his eyebrows, overjoyed with the possibility of getting something right.

I took a deep breath. Was this it? Was this dingy storage unit about to expose me? What was I even going to do about it? Knock Dominic over the head? Drag his body into the unit and lock it up? He's flaky. Who would even notice he was gone?

"Help me," he said as he started to pull boxes out and onto the pavement. "We need 1996."

A part of me was flattered that he knew such a specific personal detail, as if he had absorbed something I shared with him on a first date, not because he was obsessively trying to hunt me down.

Three layers in, there they were—the 1996 files. He pulled down the box labeled *A–H*, the one that *Haggerty* would be in.

"Grab one," he said. "Her name could be anything."

I skipped two boxes in favor of *S–Z*, the one where *Tanner* would be. Maybe, just maybe, while he was distracted, I could take the file out, slip it under my shirt.

We both started crawling our fingers through the files. I recognized some of the names. Eddie Slocum, we called him Eddie *Scrotum*—hilarious. Something bad had happened to him; something bad had happened to all of us. Some of the other kids were really mean to him—cruel, cutting insults. There was no room for sympathy when we were all just trying to survive.

Jillian Simmons—we'd shared a therapy group and she could scream like nobody's business. She had a really screwed-up ear. Her mother's boyfriend had cut her with a broken bottle. I think that was her.

I looked for my old roommate, Natalie Shea, but she must have been 1997, because I didn't see her file. She reminded me of this boy Declan, who was such a dick to her. He was a dick to everyone, really—the worst kind of insecure bully. I had such admiration for my father's cognitive restraint that impulsive dumbass boys had always tested my resolve.

My fingers reached the spot where Gwen Tanner's file should be, but there was nothing. It went from *Stanley* to *Thompson*. I kept going, but I reached the end of the box with no sign of *Tanner*. I should have been relieved, but now I was worried it was misfiled in one of Dominic's boxes.

Dominic's hands paused. "I don't see anything," he said, sighing. "No one that looks like her. You find anything?" He leaned back onto his heels.

I shook my head. He was so trusting. Even if my file had been there, would he have just taken my word for it? "Maybe she was never here," I tried. "Maybe James Calhoun was having an affair."

"Let's double-check each other." He shoved his box in my direction before reaching for mine. So much for trust.

— — — —

WE LOOKED THROUGH A trillion boxes . . . twice. He wanted it so badly that he convinced himself I could have been lying about my age and we had to go through years of boxes. When I moved into that place, I wasn't much removed from the school pictures Dominic had access to, and he knew that none of those little girls in the files were me. Despite his desperation, he finally accepted defeat. Only it didn't feel like the miracle I was hoping for; its absence was illogical. Instead, it was much more likely that someone had beaten us to it. Someone had purposefully removed my file.

TWENTY-FOUR

B EFORE WE GOT BACK to the car, I pretended to have to pee and raced back into the office. I needed to know who had been in that unit. I'd thought this trip might expose me; instead it could be what I needed to expose my stalker.

"Everything all right?" the man asked when I flung open the door and stomped in.

"Can you tell me who else has been in those units recently? Maybe in the last couple of years?"

"Those units? No one. I don't think anyone has been here since they first moved in. You all are the best customers I have."

"I know someone has been in there. Please, I don't care what happened." I reached into my pocket and pulled out my wallet, uncrumpling whatever bills I had. "Here's forty-seven bucks; it's all I have."

"I don't take bribes, miss."

"Please, just tell me and I'll go back to the office and talk up your Chinese satellite bullshit, convince everyone to give up on digital."

"It's not bullshit."

"Yes, I know. Sorry."

"But you'll tell 'em?"

"Yes."

He glared at me, wondering if I could be trusted.

"Okay, hypothetically . . ." He paused to acknowledge he was in no way admitting to this. "Hypothetically, we may have had a small break-in about a year ago. But nothing was taken. The office door was jimmied open, that's all. But I got new locks, double dead bolt," he was quick to point out.

"Do you have any surveillance cameras?"

"Well, we've got some fake ones. They say they're just as good of a deterrent."

"Clearly," I scoffed.

"Well, that's all I got for you."

"Thanks," I sneered, walking out.

"Don't forget the deal," he yelled after me. "One EMP from a basic rocket can wipe out the whole grid."

One rocket wiping out the whole grid actually sounded quite wonderful. Maybe all the doors at Edgar Valley would open, creating mass hysteria, then my father would escape, help me track down whoever was doing this to me, and choke the crap out of them.

— — — — —

I SLUMPED DOWN INTO the passenger seat as Dominic finished something on his phone.

"Good news," he said. "I got us a hotel room a couple hours from here. Kevin let me use some of his points. Two beds, don't worry."

I turned to him, unsure how I felt about that. The exhaustion was taking its toll on me and I wasn't looking forward to another five hours in the car, but it still seemed presumptuous of him. We had kind of discussed it on the ride there. I guess I didn't need to be bothered by it. There were too many other things to be bothered about. I nodded and grabbed my phone to fire off an email telling my boss that I was still throwing up, must not be food poisoning, must be a bug. I wouldn't be in to work the next day either.

- - - - -

ATTACHED TO THE HOLIDAY Inn was a heavily decorated Chili's knockoff restaurant called Tastes of the Pacific, which we found ourselves at soon after checking in. The hostess showed us to a pleather booth near the bathroom and we were greeted by our waitress, Heather, who appeared to be over us before we even spoke.

"What can I get you to drink?"

I scanned the drink menu, which was obscene and required a lot of reading to determine what all the themed drinks were actually comprised of.

"I'll take a Blue Bahama Breeze, please," I said.

"Candy rim?"

"What kind of candy?"

She looked at me like I had said something truly insane. "I don't know, honey, it's just sugar."

"Okay," I said. "Sure, sounds good. I wanted to make sure it wasn't, like, a Tootsie Roll or something."

"And you?" She turned to Dominic.

"Same thing," he said, possibly afraid to engage her further.

She strolled over to the bar and I went back to the menu, lifting the massive industrial plastic textbook in front of my face and shielding myself from Dominic.

"Hey," Dominic said, and I lowered my menu to see his blue eyes peeking over his own.

"Yeah."

"Can I ask you a serious question?"

I placed my menu back on the table, unsure where this was going, unsure if I should be nervous. "What?"

"Did you really think they might be putting Tootsie Rolls on the drinks?" He laughed out loud at my expense. "Like a bunch of Tootsie Rolls squished around the rim?" He mimicked affixing the chewy turd candies around a glass.

"I don't know," I said, laughing too.

"I would bet my life savings that no restaurant has ever done that. Ever."

"Well," I said, "the Bahamas also aren't in the Pacific, and yet, here we are." I held my menu up off the table as Heather came back with our two Bahama Breezes, neon blue with sugar crystals lining the rim.

Dominic laughed again. Heather did not.

—— —— —— ——

THE DRINKS WERE GOOD. Sugar for days. I had too many and I was going to feel like garbage the next day. Three hours in a car with a splitting headache for sure. Dominic led me back to our room. He hadn't had as many Blue Bahama Breezes as me, but he did have quite a few Jack and Cokes. The buzz from the first Breeze had given him the courage to ask Heather for what he actually wanted.

I flopped down onto one of the beds and he did the same on the other. We both stared at the ceiling and I started drunk thinking—amplified anxiety. My stalker was really getting the better of me. I was no closer to figuring out who he or she was. I had no clue what was going to happen next. I had kissed two of my suspects. For now, it was just par for the course.

The only round I could technically count as a win was getting Reanne killed instead of Porter, but once I saw Reanne's body, I ended up bummed, left second-guessing everything I ever felt toward her. Kind of hard to really consider that a win and not another victory for my adversary. Sure, Porter was still alive, but he was way more involved than I wanted. And missing. Maybe I was someone who could be messed with after all.

"You okay?" Dominic asked, rolling over to face me.

"I'm worried about Porter," I admitted. I had been tight-lipped on the drive out there, not wanting to say too much given Porter's situation.

"Why?"

I turned my head toward him, ready to shake the tree. "He went to visit Abel Haggerty."

"What?" Dominic swung up into a sitting position with more grace than I would have expected given the drinks.

"He visited Abel in prison and I think he got into his head."

"No way," he protested. "Abel doesn't let anyone else visit."

"Well, he did. Porter said Abel wanted to know about Elyse since you never talk about her."

"Yeah," he scoffed. "I don't think it's right to tell the guy who murdered her entire family about her. She's my friend. What if he did something to her because of something I said?"

"What's he going to do? He's in prison."

"I don't know, get some young impressionable guy to come visit, brainwash him, and get him to do his bidding."

"Like you?" I spat back.

"You think I'm doing his bidding?"

"Isn't that why you're really looking for Marin Haggerty? You're trying to find her for him?"

"I'm trying to find her because she's killing people!"

"And Abel told you about Oswald Shields," I pointed out. "He could have just said he didn't know the name. He told you Oswald and James hid her. Don't you think he did that so you would look into it?"

Dominic shook his head. "No, he told me she was a dead end. He told me to leave her out of my book or he would stop talking to me."

"And did that make you stop? Or did that make you more curious? Did that make you look even harder?"

Dominic squeezed his eyes shut and rubbed at his temples. I was making sense and he didn't want me to. He was too drunk to reason out another comeback and so was I. Not that I needed one. I was right.

My head started pounding, my brain sloshing around. I sat up, hoping for equilibrium, and scooted back against the headboard. I turned to Dominic, whose face was pleading for me to acknowledge that I didn't think he was being controlled, consciously or unconsciously, by Abel.

"Has anyone ever . . . approached you after visiting him?" I asked.

"What, like you did?"

"Yeah, but not me. Like, did anyone ever leave a note on your car while you were inside?"

"Someone left a note for Porter? What's going on?"

"It's nothing."

"Dammit, Gwen, why do I feel like you're more involved in this than I am? What do you know that you aren't telling me?" He flung his arms down on the bed, alcohol giving him his own sense of gravitas.

"Nothing," I said. "It just seems like everyone is so obsessed with this. It was twenty years ago."

"Yeah, and it's now. There are victims—James Calhoun, Oswald Shields."

And Reanne, I thought.

"It's not safe for Porter to be getting involved," he asserted.

"You sound jealous."

"I'm not jealous; I'm trying to figure out what the hell is going on."

"Don't act like you're so noble," I said. "You could have called the cops and told them what you know. You're only thinking about yourself and your great American novel."

"I'll call the cops right now. Is that what you want?"

"Sure," I said, calling his bluff.

He threw his head back, then rolled it around and returned to me. "And what if there's some hit out on Elyse?"

"Don't worry about Elyse," I said for no real reason other than I wanted him to stop talking about her. In reality, if she wasn't involved, I should be very worried about something happening to her. The idea that she could take care of herself was birthed from my own fantasy of who she was.

"What, are you her keeper now?" he asked.

"Shut up," I said. "You have no idea what you're talking about."

"*I* have no idea . . ." He nudged forward to the edge of his bed, as close as he could get to me without standing. "I have been communicating with Abel more than anyone has in years. What's going on now . . . it's not going to just blow over. There are bodies. Abel is letting Porter in. This is not some old ghost story from twenty years ago." He placed his hand down onto my comforter, inches from the tips of my fingers. I swallowed hard. His voice leveled out slightly above a whisper. "I think more people are going to die. Are you okay with that? Okay if Elyse dies?"

I crawled my hand forward to touch his. I was not okay with Elyse dying. Or Porter. Or Dominic. With my walls lowered from Blue Bahama Breezes, I realized maybe my mother had taught me something after all. I had complicated, angry, ugly feelings when it came to Reanne, but seeing her dead body, it was a different sensation than with all the others I had seen. She wasn't just a dispassionate representation of the meaning of life and death. She was my mother. Maybe more importantly, she was my father's wife, the only other person in the world who could understand what it was like to be us. It was my fault she was dead, and I wasn't used to dead bodies making me feel things. I didn't like it; I hated it.

I slipped my hand over Dominic's. It caused his body to inch an almost undetectable amount toward me. I pulled his hand closer and it brought him off his bed and onto the edge of mine.

We were both fired up, falsely empowered with how right we thought we were about everything, and it caused a carnal charge that my drunk brain couldn't ignore. I grasped his shirt and guided him to my face. He leaned in and kissed me. The whiskey was still strong on his tongue, but I didn't mind; my mouth tasted like I had eaten a warehouse full of Skittles.

I sat up off the headboard as we started to get more into it and my thoughts went completely numb. His hands reached for my shirt, lifting it up. I thought nothing of it as we parted lips so it could pass over my head and then we were back together.

I seized the opportunity to tug at his hair, see if I could enjoy it the way he did. *1-2-3.*

His fingers started under my arms and slid toward my waist. Then they stopped; his whole body stopped.

"Holy shit," he exhaled, with his mouth still full of my bottom lip. He flung me away, back against the headboard, and I scrambled to cover myself with my shirt.

He knew. Of course he knew. Why hadn't I considered that maybe he knew? It was never something I worried about. I'd always had an easy explanation for the Brians: a cool form of tribal design, an alternative to traditional tattoos that I had gotten during a year abroad that I'd never actually been on.

He reached over and took hold of my shirt, snatching it away. He zoomed in on the side of my rib cage. He was gentle as he ran two of his fingers over my scars, the small raised *X*'s from my father that ran down my side. Once he was convinced by what he was seeing, he returned his eyes to mine, refusing to blink. "Gwen . . . ?"

I said nothing. I just sat there, where I'd retreated against the headboard, waiting for him to make the accusation.

"These are the demon crosses," he informed me, like I didn't know what was on my own body—as if *demon crosses* was a term from a medical journal and not something dumb my father made up. "You . . . you're Marin?" he said.

I covered my face with my hands, rubbing them over my eyes, begging my brain to sober up. I lowered my hands back to my lap so I could see him.

He was looking at me differently now. At first it stung, but then it clicked. He hadn't known. Unless he was the greatest actor to ever live, he was genuinely shook. Dominic had had no idea I was her; he was not the one out to get me. I felt ten pounds lighter. It was relief.

He was not feeling that sort of way about it though. "Abel told me he marked Marin . . . you. He said it's what saved you."

I rolled my eyes.

"Did you kill those people?" he had the balls to ask as he inched away.

"No, you're kind of off base with your theory."

"Kind of?!" he shouted.

I reached for his hand—*Look, a nice touch*—but he jerked it away.

"You don't have to be an asshole," I said. "Do you want to know what's going on or not?"

"Yeah, I want to know what's going on." He got up from the bed and stomped over to a chair across the room, a ridiculous relocation.

I swung my feet off the bed and put my shirt back on. "It's not me, okay? I have nothing to do with any of this, but whoever does has it out for me. It started with messages and now she's getting into Porter's head, I think, to get to me."

"She?"

"A woman approached Porter and told him she was Marin Haggerty."

"What?" He tugged at his hair. "This is getting too crazy. I think we have to go to the police."

"Oh, c'mon, Dominic, what happened? I thought you were into this stuff—it gets you off. And now, all of a sudden, you can't handle it?"

"I wanted to write a book, not go to prison. Or die. Or wherever this is headed. You were supposed to be on my side and it turns out you're in on it."

"What is that supposed to mean?" I said. "I haven't done anything. I was just living my life, not bothering anyone."

"Don't act like you're some victim," he hissed. "You've been lying and manipulating me this whole time."

"You're the one getting your rocks off from people's real tragedies. I was a kid. Elyse was a kid. We're not here for your entertainment."

"I'm sorry." He sighed. "If I knew you were *you*, I wouldn't have involved you, not like this anyway."

"It's fine." I stood up and moved to the edge of his bed, closer to the asinine chair he had moved to. "I need you to trust me. I need to figure this out on my own—no cops. Not right now."

He left the chair and went to the other bed, ping-ponging around to avoid me. He lay down, probably too fast, because he grabbed for his head. "Who do you think it is?" The vitriol had left his words. His eyes were heavy and the alcohol was rapidly gaining ground on the adrenaline.

"I have no idea," I said.

The pauses were growing between the back-and-forth. I didn't know if it was the alcohol, the mental exhaustion, or what he could sense from my sincerity, but he was backing down.

"Are you all right?" I asked, not daring to try to move closer again.

"I don't know," he said as he rolled away from me. "I need to think."

"Okay." I stayed still for a few minutes to see if he would say anything else, but when he didn't, I turned off the lights and crawled into bed, the empty one.

He was just hurt and confused. He wasn't actually afraid of me. You tend not to defend yourself from a killer by going to sleep next to them. He could pout all night and I could try my best to sleep off the burgeoning hangover. I would wait for his sober reaction in the morning and then decide if this had ruined everything. Looking at him curled up in the bed next to mine, I didn't have the energy to pretend I would do something to stop him. I just wanted him to forgive me. I just wanted to be Gwen again.

TWENTY-FIVE

WHEN I WOKE UP the next morning, it was clear the night of sleep had done nothing to prevent a hangover. My mouth was dry, my stomach was an active volcano, and my head was being drilled into by an industrial force. They say drunk sleep isn't good sleep, but I didn't understand how I could be so dead to the world and not get any rest from it. That was what I'd been—dead to the world—because I hadn't even stirred when Dominic snuck out.

I checked my phone when I realized he wasn't there. He texted saying his keys were on the desk and he was taking the train back to Boston. I sat up in bed too quickly and thought I was going to hurl. The last thing I wanted to do was drive. Apparently the night of sleep hadn't eased his anger or fear or bruised ego or whatever he was feeling that required such a bold statement as sneaking out and taking a train. At least he wasn't running to the police. If he were, I'm sure he would have taken the car.

I lumbered into the bathroom and cupped water with my hands from the faucet into my mouth. It was hard to swallow anywhere near the amount it felt like my body needed. I started to gag and stopped, wiping the errant splashes from my face.

I made sure the car keys were on the desk as promised and then sat back down on the bed. I had lived in fear of this moment for so long, it seemed weird to not be running around the room in a screaming panic. I had been found out. Not only by my crazy stalker but by a person I had somehow, intentionally or not, let into my life. A person who was now thinking all sorts of horrible things about me—a person who right now could be running home and blowing the whole thing up.

I reached for my phone again. I knew he wouldn't pick up if I called, so I texted.

Me: Please don't tell anyone. Not yet.

Then I stared at the screen. Finally there were three dancing dots.

Dominic: Ok

That was it.

Me: I'm sorry

There was no response. The *Ok* would have to do for now—a sliver of time to figure out my next move.

- - - - -

THE NEXT MOVE WAS breakfast, or at least an attempt at breakfast. I had to get something into my stomach if I was ever going to survive the drive.

I headed back to Tastes of the Pacific and grabbed a seat at the bar like the lonely degenerate I was. I ordered one of the breakfast specials and took small, delicate bites until I was interrupted by my phone ringing in my pocket. I pulled it out and put it down on the bar.

It was Elyse.

I stared at it. To answer or not.

"You gonna get that?" a guy a few seats over asked.

I glared at him. Obviously that was a decision I hadn't arrived at.

"Well, reject it if you aren't gonna answer it."

I sighed and pushed the green button before lifting it to my ear.

"Hey," I said.

"Hi."

Then we were both silent. It was her place to speak given she was the one to call, but words didn't appear to be coming to her.

"Are you okay?" I asked.

"Yeah, sorry, I just wanted to make sure *we're* okay?"

We had kissed and I had run out of there on some mission that had ended up exposing me and throwing everything into complete turmoil, but she had been back home, living her normal life, worried about it.

"Yeah," I said. "It's totally fine. I'm not going to tell Jake or anything."

"Thanks," she said. "I doubt he would care."

I wasn't sure how to interpret that. He wouldn't care because they were on the outs or he wouldn't care because this was something Elyse did often? Kiss her girlfriends for fun with her boyfriend fully on board? It didn't matter to me if Jake cared that we kissed, but I was curious if Elyse did.

"Obviously, I won't say anything to Dominic," she said, misinterpreting my silence.

Yes, please, for the love of God, don't talk to Dominic about anything.

"Where are you?" she asked.

"Why?" I wondered how she knew I was *somewhere*.

"Just curious. The guys are having a party tonight if you want to come."

"It's Tuesday." I reacted like the grown adult I had accidentally become over the years.

"Yeah, but it's John's birthday."

"Okay, maybe."

Then there was silence again until she blurted out, "They found the other body."

"What?"

"Those arms. They found the second body, James Calhoun. I knew him, you know?"

I did know that, but I couldn't remember if Gwen knew that. Yes, right? Dominic told me all that stuff I already knew. I was hungover and this was getting harder. When you let people into your life, there are so many details. I knew that and I had ignored my own rules anyway.

"Yeah," I said, keeping it short.

"The police called to notify me personally, which was crap because they started asking me questions like I knew something about what happened."

"Shit," I offered as a condolence.

"And you know why?"

"Why?"

"The asshole carved *DEAR ABEL* into his chest."

The acid in my already-bubbling stomach churned. The days of hypothetical theories about connections between the arms were over now. The arms were connected to Abel Haggerty. It was only a matter of time before they discovered Reanne was missing, if they hadn't already. What was obvious to me was that it was going to become a lot harder to hide from everyone now that the world would be actively looking for Marin Haggerty.

TWENTY-SIX

GOT OFF THE PHONE with a vague promise that I would go to
Jake's that night, then explored whatever suburb I was in for
an hour, waiting for the breakfast and two Gatorades to do their
thing.

I ended up buying an outfit that spoke to me—black jeans with
carefully manufactured tears, not outright holes but the tantalizing
promise of them someday, and a dark gray sweater that had those
thumb holes at the ends of the sleeves. It wasn't like I could keep
pretending a pastel palette was going to help me hide anymore.

Was there enough information out there to really find me? My
stalker had killed everyone who knew my true identity and had stolen my file from the storage unit. The problem was, not *everyone* who
knew had been eliminated—not anymore. Dominic was on his way
home on a train, facing basically a death sentence if he opened his
big fat mouth to the wrong person.

It was time to suck it up and make the long drive back.

- - - - -

WHEN DOMINIC ANSWERED THE door, I dangled the keys out in front of me like they were a peace offering. He yanked them away and plodded back into the apartment building, leaving the exterior door open without explicitly inviting me in.

I followed him up the stairs and into his apartment, shutting the door behind me. "We need to talk."

"You think?" He had looked better. The train ride hadn't done him any favors.

"Let me try to explain and you can ask whatever you want," I said. "I really need you to understand you can't tell anyone, and I know that sounds selfish, and it is, but it's also because it will literally get you killed."

He huffed and puffed a bit as he rested against a stool at the breakfast counter.

"Listen, okay? Reanne is dead," I admitted, proof I was ready to be forthcoming.

"Seriously?"

"I don't know if the police know yet; I assume they do, but she's dead because of me."

"I thought this talk was you convincing me you weren't the killer?" He showed maybe, just maybe, a touch of a smirk behind his indignation and I sensed there was hope, even for the real me. I liked Dominic. He was no longer just a pawn but maybe a friend. I couldn't tolerate him hating me long-term.

"I didn't kill her," I clarified. "But I got her killed. Whoever is doing these things brought those arms to my apartment. I was the one who planted them to be found. Someone has been messing with me and I was really worried they would do something to Porter, so I went to see Reanne as a diversion."

"That's fucked-up," Dominic said, informing me of his opinion on the matter.

"I know."

"How do you know she's dead, then?"

"I just do. Please don't make me elaborate."

"Who do you think did it?" he asked.

"I don't know," I admitted. It was a simple answer that carried a lot more weight to me. I really had no idea. My father had raised me with an inflated ego that told me I was somehow better, that I was tougher, scarier, and smarter than other people, just like he was. The truth was I had no idea who was behind this, no idea what they wanted, and no idea how to stop them.

I covered my face. I needed Dominic to get over it so I could focus on everything else.

He inhaled, audibly, on purpose. I lowered my hands and he opened his arms. "Come here." A white flag.

I avoided eye contact, but went to him and let him wrap his arms around me. "I want you to let it go," I said into his chest. "Just for now. Let me figure this out. I promise, I'll tell you everything once it's safe." I pulled back so he could see me smile.

"Let me help you," he said.

"No, I can't worry about you too."

He sighed like he understood, and I hoped it was true. I knew I had a very small window to operate in before he would stick his nose in everything again, but any window was better than nothing.

I left him, closing the door with an unintentional borderline slam, and jogged down the stairs.

I flung open the exterior door, continuing my momentum directly into the cozy midsection of a woman—one of two official-looking people standing on the small porch, fishing for a way inside Dominic's building.

TWENTY-SEVEN

"E XCUSE ME," I SAID as I bounced back off the woman. From their ill-fitting bargain suits, I was pretty confident they were cops or IRS agents or bank managers, but cops were the most unfortunate option and therefore probably the reality.

"Hello, we're looking for Dominic Joyce," she explained.

I wanted to ask why or say he didn't live there or push them both down the five steps like maybe they would land in such a specific way as to snap both their necks. "Second floor."

The woman nodded while they both maneuvered past me and headed up the stairs. I knew I should get the hell out of there, but instead I found myself behind them, creeping back up to Dominic's apartment.

Dominic opened the door with gusto, thinking it was me knocking, back to be like, *Oh my God, I'm so sorry, I do need your help! You are the only person who can save me!* His body stuttered once he saw my two companions and then he furrowed his brow when he noticed me cowering behind them.

"Mr. Joyce?" the woman asked.

"Yes." Dominic's eyes darted between the three of us.

"I'm Detective Ellison." She held up her badge for him to see. "And this is my partner, Detective Hanson."

"How can I help you?" Dominic was fidgeting too much already.

"May we come in?" Ellison asked.

Dominic shot me a look as if I had sent out some sort of smoke signal that summoned these detectives to his door five minutes after I'd begged him not to tell anyone. I did the subtlest of shrugs to communicate that I had no idea what was going on.

I shadowed behind the two detectives into the apartment as if I belonged.

"And who are you?" Detective Hanson finally spoke.

"A friend." I hoped I could avoid giving my name.

"She can stay," Dominic said, tugging at his hair. "If that's okay."

Detective Ellison nodded and Hanson took his suspicious eyes off me.

"Do you want to sit?" Dominic asked them. "Or can I get you a drink? I'm sorry, what is customary here? I've never had cops in my home before."

"We have a few questions," Ellison said, almost smirking. Dominic's panicky consideration was adorable, if not insane. Ellison planted her feet and Hanson joined her—this is where the talking would take place.

"Right," said Dominic.

I tried to stay behind the detectives so that I could signal to him if he was blowing it, but Ellison noticed I was lurking behind her and rotated her upper body to stare at me until I acquiesced and sauntered over next to Dominic.

"Mr. Joyce, we're here in regard to Abel Haggerty. Prison logs show that you visit him quite frequently."

"Yeah, I'm writing a book about him."

"That's great. I look forward to reading it someday." She reached into her suit jacket and pulled out a small notebook, letting the silence build. She flipped it open as if she needed to check her notes. "Are you aware that Reanne Haggerty is missing—presumed dead?"

He was. I'd just told him. I was the reason he knew and was going to have to pretend he didn't.

"Huh?" he said, buying time to craft the appropriate reaction.

"She's missing, and we found quite a bit of blood at her home," Ellison said, watching him, then me.

Oh shit, I forgot I was there and had to react too. I crinkled my forehead and looked to Dominic for answers as if I was some dumb girlfriend in way over her head.

"She was murdered?" Dominic asked, stalling with another question. "Was it the same person who killed James Calhoun?"

Ellison glanced up from her unnecessary prop notebook. "We're looking into it."

"And what about the other man? Oswald Shields. Is it connected?" Dominic's voice regulated as he gained some control in the conversation. He was doing much better than I'd anticipated.

"We aren't at liberty to share those details," said Ellison.

"Sorry, I got too excited. You know, with the book and all. Anyway, how can I help you?"

"Have you had any interactions with Reanne Haggerty?"

"No. I was thinking of adding her house to the tour—I run the only Abel Haggerty–themed tour, by the way—but she lives in Saugus now and it's really out of the way. Plus I've found that when you give customers the hope that they might see someone and then they don't, they leave bad reviews."

"What about Abel?" Hanson asked, inserting himself into the conversation. "Has he said anything suspicious?"

Dominic thought for a second. "Well, he says a lot of suspicious things. He's a serial killer, after all, but he never said anything bad about Reanne, if that's what you mean. He's an old man with a lot of mental problems. If you think he's orchestrating some murder plot from his cell, I doubt it. He doesn't have much contact with the outside world, except me."

"And why are you so special to him?" Ellison asked.

"I have no idea, but I try to be grateful and not push it. He trusts me and wants his story heard."

Detective Ellison closed her notebook and shoved it back into her jacket. "We're going to need you to be available for further questioning. I hope you understand that your relationship with Abel Haggerty is not protected. If you know anything, you are obligated to share that with us."

"I understand."

The detectives turned and walked to the door. Dominic followed to let them out. Hanson left first, and as Detective Ellison crossed the threshold, she turned back toward me. "I'm sorry, what was your name?"

"Gwen," I said.

"Gwen . . ."

"Tanner," I whispered, hoping she couldn't hear but would accept that I had tried.

She nodded and left, reaching into her pocket, presumably for that stupid little notebook, as Dominic closed the door behind her. He didn't even look at me as he walked to the couch and flopped down.

"You were great," I said.

"Just go." He buried his head under a throw pillow. "If you don't want my help, at least try not to take me down with you." Muffled. Defeated. A little overdramatic.

"What's your problem?" I reached out and yanked the pillow from his face and threw it down on his chest. "You're one hundred percent to blame for the position you're in. Are you scared? You weren't scared before when you were trying to find Marin Haggerty, even though the Marin Haggerty in your mind wouldn't have hesitated to kill you. If anything, you should feel safe because Marin Haggerty actually likes you and has no interest in killing you. The real killer probably couldn't care less about you. That's a good thing."

That was a lie, but I had to say something to try to put him at ease, even if it was mean. If the real killer knew how fond I had become of Dominic, that would absolutely put him in the crosshairs. It's not like I was shy about spending time with him. He was probably on deck for a severed limb or exsanguination at some point.

"Great monologue," said Dominic, throwing the pillow at me. "If you don't want my help, then just get out of here."

"Boo-hoo," I said, mocking. "I need a few days to think and not worry about your arm being on my doorstep when I come home because you couldn't help yourself and revealed the wrong thing to the wrong person."

"I *get* it," he said.

"Good." I was not having his little tantrum. "And don't come to Jake's tonight." With that, I walked out of his apartment again, not knowing if I was helping him or hurting him by doing so.

– – – – –

JAKE'S PARTY WAS NOT where I wanted to be headed, but I wanted to see Elyse, and a desperate part of me still hoped Porter might be there.

I wore my new jeans and sweater and felt pretty good about it. *Hey, I might get you all killed, but don't I look kind of good in this?* I wondered how severe things would have to get for me to stop con-sidering what other people were thinking. Maybe that Chinese sat-ellite blackout thing.

The door opened and a guy stood there who I can best describe as: not Jake.

"Hey, Gwen!" He was happy to see me.

"Hey . . ."

"John."

It was John! Fake ID John! "Sorry, I know, I was spacing. Happy birthday!"

"Come in, come in." He ushered me inside to the sausage fest.

Thankfully no ritual mutilation games were taking place. Every-one was hanging out, drinking, smoking; there was music on. I got a few waves, but no real attention. I wished for Porter's arms to grab me from behind and assault me in some ridiculous yet welcome way, but I remained untouched.

I meandered toward the window to the fire escape, but when I lifted the curtain, the landing was deserted.

"Elyse isn't here." I heard over my shoulder.

I whipped around. "God, you scared me."

Jake thought it was funny.

"Where is she?" I asked, no need to pretend we both didn't know who I was looking for.

He shrugged. "I was hoping you knew. She's ignoring my calls and texts. I think she's mad at me."

"Why?"

"I don't know. She's been acting kind of odd."

I wasn't sure what *acting odd* meant to someone like him. Over his shoulder I watched a guy pour hot wax from a candle onto his friend's forehead.

"Well, she hasn't said anything to me." I wasn't particularly interested in talking about their relationship for multiple reasons. "Sorry," I offered, using it as an excuse to take a few steps back.

"You don't have to go. You can stay even though she isn't here. We all consider you one of the gang. Right, guys?" He yelled out the question as if anyone had heard what he wanted them to agree with. No one responded.

"Thanks," I said. "I'll grab a drink."

He seemed content with that, so I walked away. Once I was back in the kitchen, I went right for the door and headed out. *Where was Elyse?*

I heard the door open again behind me, but I tried to ignore it.

"Gwen!" Jake shouted down the stairs.

I turned, a little embarrassed to be caught running away.

"If you talk to her, tell her to call me? Tell her I'm sorry, okay? Please?"

I nodded with a reassuring smile. I wasn't sure what was going on between them, but I was probably a little to blame and definitely biased. Of course, none of that would matter very much if Elyse was already dead.

- - - - -

I KNOCKED ON ELYSE'S apartment door a half hour later and experienced an enormous sense of relief when she cracked it open. I could only see half her face, but I could tell she was upset; she needed to invest in some waterproof mascara.

"Why are you crying?" I asked as she allowed me inside. It must have been Jake and whatever fight they'd had. What an ass, hosting a party while she was at home crying. I hoped whatever was going on meant she was finally going to leave him and all of those supposed friends who were obsessed with her trauma.

She ignored my question at first, leaving me by the door.

"Elyse . . ." I said, stepping after her.

She turned to look at me and inhaled a ragged breath before speaking. "Marin Haggerty . . ." She paused. No verbs, no context, just the name.

I froze. Possibly I lurched forward first. She knew. Dominic must have told her. Or she already knew? But she was crying. Why would she be crying if this was the crescendo to her ultimate plan? What was she going to say next? How was I going to react?

Her lip quivered. "She's come out of hiding."

"Excuse me?" I said.

Elyse reached for her phone. She hit play on a video she already had queued up. The caption beneath it read, **I AM MARIN HAGGERTY.** Sitting in front of a blank wall, a blonde woman in a polka-dot blouse and white blazer read from a prepared statement. I knew those eyes. I knew that nose. I knew that jawline, and not from looking in the mirror. I had watched that face form during her prepubescent years. It was Natalie Shea—my old roommate, confidante, and accomplice.

TWENTY-EIGHT

NATALIE SHEA WAS THE first friend I ever made as Gwen Tanner. That was probably her biggest mistake . . . and mine. I had warned her not to mess with me, but she hadn't heeded my warning then, and she certainly wasn't heeding it now. What was being thrown right back in my face, though, was how I never should have messed with her either.

Seeing her on that screen, looking like me—well, looking like how she would assume thirteen-year-old me would end up looking— it made me rethink everything. She was only supposed to know me as Gwen, but she must have discovered my true identity somehow, and that had set her off. She killed those men from my past, chopped off their arms, left them on my doorstep, to what? Taunt me? Drive me crazy? I had to admit it was working. Not to play Monday-morning quarterback, but if I had to name one person I knew other than my father who was capable of it, it was Natalie.

Natalie was an absolute wild card. I'd really liked her, but we hadn't parted on the best of terms. I always assumed it was someone out to get Marin and never stopped to consider it could be someone who had it out for Gwen. What the hell was I supposed to do with that?

– – – – –

ELYSE STARED AT THE screen, clutching the phone in an unhealthy way. I gravitated closer to her as we watched together. Everything that had been taken from Elyse, it was my fault. All of it. It was my fault her family was dead and it was my fault it was all being thrown back in her face.

I wasn't practiced in processing these emotions. I wanted Elyse to die. I wanted her to drop dead at my feet to release me from this feeling. Only not really—not even close. I reached over and took her hand.

Natalie was a better actor than I would have guessed—tearing up over the loss of her mother, overwhelmed with having to revisit that dark time in her life, clueless about who would want to hurt all these people in the name of her father but begging them to stop. Elyse didn't know this was an act. She didn't know this was all for me.

When it was over, Elyse didn't flinch; she just gazed at the screen. "I'm going to kill her," she said, void of any rhetorical inflection.

"What?" I questioned, studying her profile, confirming I'd heard her correctly.

"Gwen . . ." She pressed her lips together as she put the phone down, considering what to say next. She rotated her whole body toward me, acknowledging my hand now, using her own to control the strength of our grip. "I want to tell you the truth. I don't know why, but I feel like I can trust you. Tell me I'm not wrong."

"You can trust me," I said, not sure of what was coming but sure she shouldn't trust me.

"I wasn't at the park when my family was killed," she admitted. "It's just the story I went along with when the police found me there."

My heartbeat became irregular. Bad things were coming.

"A couple days later, when James Calhoun came to see me," she continued, "I confessed that I'd been there. I told him it was Abel Haggerty who killed my family. Cody hadn't regained consciousness; that was a lie James told to explain how he knew to search the Haggerty house. They found so much evidence there that James said it was an unnecessary risk for me to come forward.

"Abel wasn't being shy about wanting Cody dead," she continued. "Once Abel's identity was released, tons of witnesses came forward, saying he had been at the hospital, on Cody's floor. Even with Abel in custody, they worried about what he could do, what connections he might have. James said if Abel knew I was the real witness, he would go after me. Better to let the truth die with Cody. James told me to keep saying I had been at the park the whole time. He really thought Abel would try to kill me if he knew."

She stopped for a breath and I lost mine. It hadn't been Cody who'd brought down my father; it had been Elyse.

"Because that wasn't the whole truth . . ." She paused so I could have the opportunity to stop her—a way out if it was already too much information to burden me, Gwen Tanner, with.

I abstained from casting a vote for my own salvation. She was going to keep going and I was going to hear it. I was detaching from her. I was detaching from myself. I knew what she was about to say.

"That day, I *was* playing outside. I was running around the neighborhood and I got hungry and headed back to the house. There was this loose board in the fence that I always ducked in and out through. I poked my head in and I saw my brother, Cody, in the backyard with Marin Haggerty."

I squeezed her hand too hard and she stopped talking. I let it go, but she yanked mine back like she needed to be connected in order to continue.

"Cody was trying to kiss Marin, but she kept pushing him away. Normal kid stuff, but it was exciting to me because I was young and kissing was a big deal." She almost smiled—how innocent she'd been back then; I couldn't relate.

"Cody started to get mad and was calling her names—nasty things," she continued. "But Marin wasn't having it. She kept staring at him—just looking at him. I don't know how to explain it, these evil eyes stuck on him. Then he spat at her and she lost it. She tackled him to the ground and grabbed a rock and started hitting him in the head. He gave up fighting, but she didn't stop."

Sometimes I tell myself I didn't realize I was killing him. How could a nine-year-old really understand the physics of it? But I knew. When his blood covered the rock, I knew. When he stopped moving, I knew.

"Marin Haggerty killed Cody," Elyse admitted, her greatest secret, *my* greatest secret.

She wanted me to react, but I could only count her eyelashes, *1-2-3-4.*

"I was so scared. I was only eight!" she exclaimed to fill the silence. "I crawled back under the fence and ran. I sprinted all the way to this river down the street like I could jump in and it would carry me away, but I got there and realized I didn't know what to do. I needed my parents, so I turned back. I got there in time to watch through the window as Abel Haggerty released Blake's neck and he slumped to the floor. I waited for him to leave and then I crept into the house. The blood was unreal. It was all over. I think he was trying to hide what happened, that Cody was killed by Marin first."

It was true. It was why Cody had managed to hold on for those excruciating five days; I had botched the job. I had disappointed my father and I remembered that being the worst part. I'd wanted to blame him somehow—I still did. It was his fault for not checking closer when he ran to their house to clean up my mess. He was the professional; I was merely the protégé. Cody must have still had a pulse, however weak. My father's faith in my abilities had clouded his reason. If my father had checked Cody's body, snapped his neck when he felt the pulse, then he would have been the killer, right? Not me.

"Why didn't you say something about Marin?" I finally spoke, wishing in that moment that Elyse had said something. How would my life have been different if I'd received the treatment I actually needed? How would hers?

"I did! I told James Calhoun everything and he said he would take care of it. Then I was shipped out to the Berkshires to live with my mom's aunt, who preferred to pretend I had fallen straight from God's hands into her yard rather than acknowledge what had happened to me. By the time I was old enough to understand how it had all played out, Marin was gone. There was no trace of her. It just felt easier to block it all out than let it take over my life. I trusted James Calhoun. Maybe I shouldn't have, but I did, and I thought he must have had a reason not to tell anyone."

I guess it explained why James had brought me to that school and why he'd never come back. He'd known exactly what I was, a monster like my father, but I was packaged in an "innocent" little girl's body and it must have left him conflicted. His hero complex had really screwed us. Elyse and I were more connected than I ever imagined.

"I tried to forgive her," she continued, glancing back at her phone, where we had watched Natalie. "Or at least forget her, but seeing her, I can't." She turned back to me. "I hate to say it, but when they found James Calhoun's body, I was relieved. It was justice—justice I didn't even realize I wanted. He shouldn't have let her get away with what she did. She shouldn't get away with it."

"Are you going to tell?" I asked.

Elyse shook her head. "She'll just deny it. After all these years, who would believe me?"

"I do," I said.

"It's not enough."

I knew what she was saying. I think if I were a normal person, I would have assumed it was all talk. I wouldn't have worried she would do anything to Natalie, but I knew what it felt like to live with that exact secret my whole life, and if I could do something about it, I would.

"If you do something to her, it will change you," I said. "What you're talking about is revenge, not justice. You think it will end these feelings, but it won't."

"You don't know that," she said, and she was right. Maybe revenge was just the ticket.

"Then let me help you," I said. Anything to ease her pain. Selfishly, anything to get her to keep me involved—anything to cling to in a situation I was clearly losing control of.

Elyse knew what had to be done and so did I. It didn't matter whether she was Marin Haggerty or Natalie Shea; the woman on the screen had to be put down. I had killed before and I could do it again if I had to—for Elyse and for me. One more time. It was the only way out. And a good one at that.

Natalie wasn't a kid anymore and neither was I. She was out in the world, severing arms. She had killed my mother. She was a ticking time bomb and I knew better than anyone that it would not be a good idea to let Natalie Shea explode.

PART
TWO

TWENTY-NINE

EIGHTEEN YEARS AGO

THE ATTENDANT ESCORTED TEN-YEAR-OLD Natalie Shea into her new room, hand on her back, applying force as needed. The girl clung to her bag, resisting him, her heels skidding across the tiles. Natalie was supposed to be in a room alone. She'd overheard that instruction plenty of times. *This one shouldn't share a room. Make sure you keep an eye on her. She's a lot stronger than she looks when she gets into one of her fits.* But Natalie wasn't going to be alone anymore.

Another child, about her size, sat under the glow of her bedside table lamp. Propped up on a stack of pillows, she was reading a chapter book as thick as the mattress she was sitting on.

"Gwen," the attendant said, addressing the girl, "this is Natalie. She's going to be your roommate."

Gwen lowered the book but remained silent.

The attendant gave Natalie a light shove, enough to get her weight off him.

"You girls play nice," he said as he closed the door and left the two children to sort things out among themselves.

Natalie shuffled toward her bed.

"How old are you?" Gwen asked with a raised eyebrow.

"Almost eleven," Natalie answered before placing her bag on the bed and crawling up to sit next to it. She was nervous. People made her nervous.

Gwen had still eyes that wouldn't move off her. When she finally spoke, it was penetrating. "Why are you here?" she asked—a question that felt like an accusation.

Natalie wasn't sure how to answer. "I get in a lot of trouble," she disclosed, fixating on her hands perched in her lap.

Gwen smirked. "Like what?"

Natalie shrugged. "I get angry and . . . I kind of black out."

Gwen considered that for a second. "Do you hurt people?"

"Sometimes."

"What kind of people?"

Natalie rubbed her fingertips together. She was ashamed. She wasn't a tough guy. She would give anything to not be like this.

Gwen gave up waiting for an answer. "Well, don't try anything with me."

"I won't," Natalie said, hoping it was true.

She unzipped her bag, but Gwen continued to pry. "What's the worst thing you've ever done?"

"None of your business." Natalie sulked, pulling her pajamas from the bag.

"Good answer!" Gwen smiled. "Don't tell anyone here anything. They'll use it against you."

Natalie yanked her scratchy sweater off over her head and threw on a softer sleep shirt. "Why are *you* here?" she asked.

"My parents died in a fire."

"Did you set the fire?" Natalie knew better than to assume anything but the worst.

"No." Gwen laughed.

Natalie went to take off her jeans and Gwen covered her eyes to extend a sense of privacy. "You're my first roommate."

"I'm not supposed to have a roommate," Natalie admitted, pulling her pajama pants up and sitting back on the bed.

Gwen uncovered her eyes at the sound of the springs. "Why not?"

"I don't know." Natalie glanced down at her hands. "Something's wrong with me."

"Who told you that?" Again, Gwen didn't wait for an answer. "My dad says most people have no idea what they're talking about. They think they're right about everything. He could tell when someone was full of crap right away. He was really good at it and I am too. And you seem pretty fine to me."

The sentiment was pleasing to Natalie, but she knew better than to hope Gwen's words were genuine, that this girl would see her differently.

"Why do you stare at your hands so much?" Gwen probed.

Natalie lifted her head, not realizing it was something she was doing or something to be noticed. Gwen's face was gentle. She didn't appear to be making fun of her. Natalie separated her hands. "Sorry."

"Doesn't bother me. Do you do it when you're nervous or what?"

Natalie wasn't sure what she was talking about. Then she found herself looking down again, rubbing her fingertips together, barely making contact, chasing the slightest friction between them.

"See?!" Gwen yelled. "You're doing it again."

Natalie picked her head up.

"No, don't stop," said Gwen. "Look at them again."

Natalie was skeptical.

"Just do it. Come on, please."

Natalie sighed and did as Gwen wanted.

"What do you feel doing that? Don't lie."

"I don't know," Natalie said to her hands. Then she was grazing her fingertips together again.

"And that?" Gwen asked. "That rubbing thing?"

"I don't know!" Natalie shouted, frustrated. What was the point of this? She separated her fingertips and lay down on the hard mattress, flipping away from Gwen and tucking her hands under her face. She stared at the wall. It was too much.

The bed springs across the room creaked. Gwen's feet made the subtlest scuff as they hit the floor. She had gotten out of her bed. *What was she doing? Where was she going? Please, please, leave me alone*, Natalie thought.

She rotated her head enough to see Gwen was standing next to her now, leaning over her bed. Natalie began to tense up. What was this girl going to do to her? What would Natalie do in return?

Gwen placed one of her pillows down next to Natalie's head. "It's okay," she whispered. "We can talk about it later."

Natalie's tension subsided.

"I thought it could be your thing," Gwen explained. "It helps me to have a thing. You can't freak out in here. They'll make you take drugs and turn you into a zombie. You'll drool and everything."

Natalie pulled the pillow under her head. She was fully aware of the lengths people would go to to keep her calm. There was nothing Gwen could do to stop them.

"Okay, good night, then." Gwen's footsteps pitter-pattered back to her own side, then there was a beat before the bed bounced under the weight of her jumping onto it.

The table lamp clicked off.

"Good night," Natalie whispered toward the wall, into the darkness.

Eventually her eyes adjusted to the dulled light from the hallway sneaking through the observation window in the door, the safety glass laced with thin crisscrossed wire—enough to remind her that even without a lock, she was still in a cage.

She could hear when Gwen fell asleep, her breathing becoming audible and rhythmic, a faint snore at the end of each inhale. Natalie was used to sleeping in solitary silence. One girl inhaling, snoring, exhaling over and over—it was too distracting for Natalie to relax.

She stared at the painted concrete wall, finding places the drips hadn't been caught before they'd dried. It was the first night Natalie didn't sleep because of Gwen, but it wasn't the last.

THIRTY

NATALIE

BEFORE THE ARMS

N ATALIE SAT IN HER car, watching Gwen through the window of
Painting Pots like she had so many times before.

When Natalie had first found her, Gwen had seemed to be doing
well. She'd been taking classes at a community college and would
meet up with people in the student center and spend long nights in
the library. She'd had a job at the campus store and waitressed at
night. It was all so normal.

Natalie had wanted to approach her. She could pretend to run
into her on the street. She could show Gwen how well she was doing
too. But every time she came close, Natalie's temperature would rise
and the tremors would start in her shoulders. What if Gwen would
bring up their last night together? What if that was all Gwen remembered of Natalie? What if Gwen didn't remember Natalie at all? That
would be even worse. It was better just to watch—wait for the right
time.

It had been almost eight years since she'd found Gwen, and Natalie had settled into this life. She had a job in a warehouse where

sustained manual labor and rampant turnover shielded her from any meaningful social interactions. She went through the motions when she had to, but nothing diluted her fascination with Gwen. She had no hobbies. She had no friends. She spent all her free time watching Gwen, waiting for the right time to approach her.

Natalie had been there to see Gwen briefly dye her hair red before dying it back to the fake brown color she'd stuck with since. She'd been there when Gwen dropped ten pounds she couldn't afford to lose and she'd been there when she gained twenty pounds back. She'd been there when Gwen started a new job downtown and moved into the apartment she was in now. Mostly she'd been there when nothing remarkable happened at all.

Gwen's job was a blessing and a curse for Natalie. When Gwen stepped through the rotating glass doors, she was gone. There was too much security and nowhere for Natalie to hide. But she needed that. She needed to be able to go to work herself. She would return later to be with Gwen for whatever the nights would have in store.

Natalie much preferred watching Gwen at Painting Pots. The storefront had big square windows that let her see almost everything. On slow days, when there was a clear view of Gwen sitting alone at the pottery wheel, Natalie wanted so desperately to walk in, but she never did.

There was a new guy working there. Well, by now it had been two years. Natalie didn't experience normal life markers that could help her process the passing of time in a relatable way.

The new guy was young, with bleach-blond hair that helped Natalie distinguish him from the other people Gwen interacted with. At first, Natalie didn't think much of him; Painting Pots had a rotating staff of unmotivated youths who Gwen couldn't care less about. As the weeks passed, Natalie noticed subtle differences. Gwen was smiling more. Their interactions were playful. Occasionally Gwen would bring him a coffee and he would hug her and lift her enough for her toes to leave the ground. It was a relationship Natalie couldn't quite understand, but he seemed to make Gwen happy and Natalie took note. She could make Gwen happy too. Once it was the right time.

— — — —

NATALIE STARTED HER CAR. It was a cold night and she needed to run the heat, crank it up for a few minutes, and then cut the engine, hoping it would last longer this time.

The final customers had left. The blond guy wiped down the tables while Gwen washed up at the sink. Natalie dug into a turkey sandwich she had packed. Gwen would be leaving soon.

The guy left first, as he usually did. He made a silly face at Gwen. She waved him off with a grin and he skipped out of the store and into the night to do whatever he did with the rest of his time.

Fifteen minutes later, Gwen exited the store and locked the front door behind her. Natalie repositioned herself in the driver's seat. This was the most stimulating part of the night; Gwen could be going anywhere. Once in a while, Gwen would go to the movies alone and Natalie would walk in a few minutes later and stay through the credits, and for those two hours, it was almost as if they were together.

Gwen grabbed dinner from the sandwich place two stores down and headed to her car, holding a brown paper bag and a medium fountain drink. She didn't always get a drink. It irritated Natalie that she couldn't find a reasonable correlation for why, but when Gwen opened her car door and maneuvered into the driver's seat with her hands full, a small white card fell from her pocket.

Natalie stirred. Once Gwen pulled out of the parking spot, Natalie got out of her car and went to the card. She picked it up and flipped it over. *Buy 5 sandwiches and get a free medium drink.* It had one stamp. Natalie shoved the card into her pocket and raced back to her car.

It was just a stupid promotion, one-fifth of the way toward a drink that couldn't cost more than a few dollars. She knew it meant nothing to Gwen and should mean nothing to her. She wasn't proud to fixate on objects solely because they were Gwen's. That had never been what this was about. But she wanted it. Just like she wanted the other things. She was not stealing; they were items destined for the trash.

Natalie caught up to Gwen's car, leaving two in between them for cover, and followed her home to her apartment. She parked in a spot far enough down the street to avoid raising suspicion but close enough to see Gwen's windows. The ones facing the street would remain dark until Gwen went to bed. Natalie reclined her seat and got comfortable.

It was nights like this that, while boring, made Natalie feel most at home. There were no distractions. She wasn't racing around town, trying to keep up with Gwen. She wasn't worried about being caught. She was alone and quiet and so was Gwen. It reminded her of the moments they'd shared as children, that small window of time at night when the girls finally heeded the attendants' warnings and stopped giggling—the minutes when they were together and silent before they were both asleep.

Natalie knew what she was doing wasn't normal, but *she* wasn't normal. What was the alternative for her? Her whole life she'd been told she wasn't right. She raged, she panicked, she attacked. If a little light stalking kept those things at bay, she wasn't going to feel guilty about it; it wasn't for other people to understand.

At ten fifteen the bedroom light came on, then the bathroom. Natalie watched Gwen's silhouette pass by the sheer curtains in the bedroom to the clouded glass of the bathroom and then back again. Five minutes later, the lights went out and Natalie started her car.

THIRTY-ONE

GWEN

NATALIE SHEA'S FACE WAS all over the place, or at least it felt that way to me as every internet algorithm had me pegged in no time. *Marin Haggerty* had returned—the blonde hair and light eyes that, to me but no one else, were blatantly unnatural.

I remembered the first time I met Natalie, more afraid of herself than anything the outside world could throw at her. What she hadn't known was that I knew the outside world was so much scarier than anything she could imagine. She'd hung on my every word. My father would have liked that. I liked that. I liked the control I thought I had over her and I let my guard down.

I'd really underestimated Natalie. Again. Part of me was impressed. How had she even found out the truth about me? I assumed that missing file meant someone had discovered that Marin Haggerty was Gwen Tanner. Was it possible instead that the missing file meant Natalie had discovered that Gwen Tanner was Marin Haggerty? The facility didn't know who I was, but there must have been some kind of contact information in there, or at least a record of who had dropped me off and signed me away—the hand that had held that pen was the same one attached to the arm that had arrived on my doorstep.

What was the use in hiding anymore? *Marin Haggerty* had been revealed. Why would anyone suspect I was someone other than the Gwen Tanner I said I was?

It was time to talk to my father.

- - - -

I SAT DOWN ON the stool they told me to sit down on. I put my hands on the short counter between myself and the glass, then I put them down in my lap, then back up. I sensed he was coming before I could see him. There was a catch in my throat that morphed into a shiver down my spine. Then I saw his beard.

My father landed on the other side of the glass and I kept my head low and let my hair fall to conceal my face. I watched him the best I could without untucking my chin. He reached for the phone and I did the same.

"Welcome," he said like a cult leader at a job fair. I was still Gwen Tanner.

I didn't know where to start.

He tried to kickstart the conversation he thought we were going to have. "You said in your letter that you know Elyse Abbington?" Of course I had mentioned her. I knew from Dominic and Porter that my father was as obsessed with Elyse as I was, and I needed Gwen Tanner on his visitor list.

I swallowed on par with the whale from *Pinocchio* before lifting my head. I wished what I felt was fear or anger, but it wasn't those at all. I exhaled for the first time in twenty years. My eyes locked on his, and in that moment, I would have followed him anywhere. I needed to feel that again. It was the reason I was there.

I thought my face would be enough, but I had done my job well. He didn't recognize me.

"Are you going to speak?" he asked. "No need to be nervous." He smiled and it was as rewarding to me as it had been when I was a child. His teeth had yellowed in prison, not that they were particularly white to begin with.

I didn't know what else to do so I rotated on the stool and lifted my shirt to show him the scars. He squinted at them and the phone fell a fraction from his ear. I dropped my shirt and turned back around.

"Mar—" he started before I grimaced, shaking my head, and he realized it was not something I wanted overheard. He combed his hand through his beard, grooming it to help him think. He stared at me as if trying to communicate telepathically. If it was ever going to work, it would have to be right then between him and me. That was our bond and that was his power, but I had no idea what he was thinking.

"I heard . . ." he mused, "my daughter has come out of hiding."

"I saw that," I said, finally ready to speak.

He nodded and it was clear we both understood what was going on. "Do you know her?" he asked.

"Yes, we met when I was a kid." I wasn't sure how to elaborate, nervous what details he would consider insignificant—the instinct to avoid disappointing him as poignant as ever. I waited for him to tell me what to say, think, know, feel.

"And now?" he said. "Did you know she was coming forward?"

I shook my head. Whatever was going on, if he was displeased, he needed to know it wasn't my doing.

He nodded again, a processing nod. "I think about my daughter every day," he said, an affection I wasn't prepared for. His head was still, but his eyes twitched, not following any pattern I could track.

I smiled. I couldn't help it.

His face relaxed into an idle stare.

I didn't know what to say next. It wasn't our relationship for me to lead the conversation. My job was to sit quietly, wide-eyed, and absorb every word of his gospel.

"I th-think . . ." I stuttered when he kept staring at me. "I think a guy named Porter visited you?"

"Yes, he did." He wasn't going to give me any more to go on. He was waiting to see what my angle was, how I knew Porter, why I cared to ask.

I psyched myself up, the mental equivalent of pounding my fists against my chest. "I don't want you to let him visit anymore."

"Is that so?" He tilted his head, curiosity showing in the arch of his eyebrows. His stare was squeezing my brain, the pressure building.

I didn't know what words wouldn't add fuel to the fire. My reason couldn't be for Porter's well-being and it couldn't be for mine. He wouldn't appreciate that my relationship with Porter was for my *well-being.* He would interpret it as a weakness. It would inspire him. There was only one reason he would respect.

"He's getting in my way," I said.

That jump-started his eyes again. He leaned in toward the glass, showing something very different in his face. "Explain," he said.

The intensity paralyzed me. I stayed quiet and he didn't approve.

"Now!" he demanded, shoulders flinching toward me.

I cowered at the tone of his voice and was grateful for the glass in between us. I broke the stare and shielded my face, burying it as far into my chest as my neck would allow.

"I'm sorry, my dove," he purred, causing me to glance back up at him. He lifted his hand to the glass.

I had no choice but to reach up and align my fingers with his.

"It's nothing I can't handle," I said. "But I don't need him here connected to you. It will complicate things for me."

"And you have a bigger problem." He finished my thoughts for me.

"Do you know about Reanne?" I asked, certain he did.

He nodded, short on words, but not in some calculated way. I could tell it bothered him, but whether he was sad or offended that someone had dared, I couldn't tell. "What do you know?" he asked.

"I think it was the same person who killed James Calhoun and Oswald Shields. I think your *daughter* might know."

He remained still, subtle twitches in his eyes showing he was processing what it all meant.

I had to speak before he could think much more on it. I lowered my head again, struggling to look at him when I spoke. "I have to do something, something I did once before."

He inhaled, and like the trained animal I was, I allowed it to suck my head back up. We locked eyes and I waited to see if he would infer what I meant.

"You haven't done it again?" he asked. Of course he knew what I meant. "Not since the first time?"

I shook my head.

He pulled his hand from the glass and ran it through his beard, watching to see if I was lying.

"You're surprised?" I asked.

"I am."

"Are you disappointed?"

"No," he said, teasing the possibility of humanity. "You're still young. I didn't understand my role until later in life either."

"It's not my *role*," I snapped, as much as I could while keeping my voice low. I was aware of how scarred I was by that idea—that I was supposed to be this, that nothing I could do mattered. It struck a nerve.

He stuck out his lower jaw and then rolled it back in—a familiar tic—and I knew better than to speak to him like that again.

I didn't want to dwell on the moment of my defiance. I needed to know one thing. The most important thing standing in the way of taking care of Natalie. "Are you involved in any of this? Something to drum up interest in your book, maybe?"

"No," he answered without fanfare, and I believed him.

What was happening, what Natalie was doing—my father had no control over it, no input, no proprietary insight. He didn't even know who she was. In that moment, extricating him from all this shifted something in the dynamic. It was immeasurable, inexplicable, and maybe temporary, but I think, in my mind, it minimized him.

He had to be involved; it was the only thing that had made sense. Everything in my life had revolved around him. Every decision I made, every thought I tried to hide from was because of him and what I thought it made me. But not this. This was mine. I had never really considered that was possible. That taken away from him, stripped of my identity and any influence he could have, I had caused this. I was the reason this was happening. I had created Natalie all by myself.

"I thought *Marin* might be involved," he said, unfurling a little grin. "That's what Dominic thinks."

I hadn't mentioned Dominic, but I had been stupid enough to make a dig about the book, and that's all my father needed to put it together. "He told you that?" I asked, remembering Dominic's inner struggle with whether or not to tell Abel his theory.

"He didn't have to."

Say what you want about my father—evil, crazy, narcissistic, heartless—but above all he was a gifted mentalist. He had an incredible talent at reading people and using it to manipulate them. If he had harnessed his powers into a job selling magic beans, we could have been rich. I'm confident that if it weren't for what I did, he never would have been caught.

"And what about Porter?" I asked. "What did he tell you?"

"He told me Elyse is doing well." A leading statement that I didn't want to fall for, but I bit the inside of my cheek at the mention of her name and he knew. "You care about her, I see."

"I know her. Why are you so obsessed with her? You used to only let Dominic visit, and now anyone who knows to mention her gets a free pass to Edgar Valley?"

"You say that as if it's a secret password. I'm not interested in performing a song and dance for fanatics. Until recently, those were the only letters I received. I have lost all connection to my family, *my daughter.* Elyse Abbington is my daughter's age, living with a connected past. I am confined in this prison and I admit that I've been tempted to entertain her as a proxy for my Marin."

"You would have killed her if she was there that day."

"Of course," he said, like whatever point I was trying to make was frivolous. "That's why I find such interest in her. *Marin* is the one I created on purpose; *she* is the one I created by accident."

That took me aback. Had he just summarized my infatuation with Elyse as well? The idea that our lives were both shaped so significantly by him, yet so different. Some kind of nature-versus-nurture experiment, but more like unyielding exposure to him versus one life-altering moment at his hands. And now what? He was waiting in his cell to see which one of us he had screwed up more? Desperate for any crumbs on Elyse, counting the days until I returned.

"If you miss your daughter so much," I said, "why did you arrange for her to disappear? Why would you do that if you didn't want to lose her?"

"I didn't want anyone getting to that." He tapped on the glass toward my face. It wasn't until he then pointed to his own temple that I knew what he meant: my mind. "*She* was as I wanted her to be."

I hated how he was looking at me, so proud. Was that the reason? Why he had worked with James Calhoun to make me disappear? Not because I was a witness he was worried about. Certainly not because he wanted me to have a chance at a normal life. It was something far more insidious. I was his investment. He'd put everything he had into me and had been waiting all these years for the return, literally and figuratively. And I was giving him exactly what he wanted. I had returned . . . and I was ready to kill.

No. I stopped myself. I closed my eyes. It wasn't like that. I was nothing like he was imagining me to be. If I was so impeccably trained, then how had Natalie gotten the better of me so easily? How had she taken down this infallible evil offspring? Again.

If I were anything like him, I would have killed her that last night we were together—claimed self-defense and brought my tally to two before I could even drive. The thought had never crossed my mind. He was wrong . . . I opened my eyes. "You don't know anything about *your daughter*."

"Perhaps," he said, beaming, lacking any doubt in his assessment. "Now, what was it you were talking about when you first sat down? You wanted to do something again? Something you had done as a child?"

I glared at him. I didn't *want* to do it. I didn't ask for any of this.

"Don't fight it," he whispered into the phone, holding my stare with the good eye, the wonky eye keeping steady just a hair off my face. "Listen to it." He put his hand back up to the glass for mine. "Listen to me."

The shift had been enough—enough for me to think, enough for me to trust my own read, enough to see his desperation. He was desperate for me to be like him. It was all he had. His life's work. It was all he wanted now and he was right; his want was a weakness. His weakness.

I didn't reach for his hand. Instead I jerked my body and hung up the phone—a poignant smack that released me from the moment.

"Stop!" he shouted, but to me, on the other side of the glass, it was as if he'd only mouthed it—what he wanted and what I wanted, structurally shielded from each other. It was the type of perfect metaphor that could give me hives.

I stood up and he slammed his fist against the glass. A guard appeared out of nowhere behind him, but Abel shot him a look, not struggling to find power even in the confines of prison. The officer backed off and I ran away before my father could turn around.

What I had sought from my father was a sort of reawakening, a belief that I had to go back to that place to be this person, but now I emerged with the clarity to see that I was his child, not his clone. He didn't define me and I didn't need his influence. I could do this my way—on my own.

I didn't *want* to kill Natalie. This was not a craving I had; no *beings* were telling me to do it; there was no impulse a tinfoil hat or a strong antipsychotic could subdue. I'd been raised with the tools to get it done, not born with the need to do it. The result would be the same, but to me, the distinction was cathartic. This was my choice; this was premeditated, and the only person telling me to do it was me.

And maybe Elyse. There had been dead bodies everywhere my

whole life, but she was *my* victim. I couldn't let her go over this ledge. I owed her this.

And I owed it to Natalie. She had killed three people. Maybe more. I hadn't seen or heard from her since I was thirteen, but I knew her. I knew she couldn't end up in prison for the rest of her life. Whatever she had done, whatever she had yet to do, I could not let her end up locked up again.

THIRTY-TWO

EIGHTEEN YEARS AGO

T HE GWEN AND NATALIE roommate experiment had proven thus
far to be a success. The first few nights, the staff had held their
breath, waiting for Gwen to start screaming and for them to have to
run in and tear Natalie off her, but the screams never came. It was
time to acclimate Natalie into other areas.

Gwen accompanied her to her first therapy group. "Remember,"
Gwen instructed her, "try not to say anything. It's easy. The little kids
will talk the whole time."

Natalie agreed, not looking to say anything anyway.

Gwen was right. There was one little girl in particular who
wouldn't stop talking. She didn't even have real feelings. She thought
hunger was an emotion. A boy named Declan, seated on the other
side of Natalie, told that girl to shut her fat ugly face and got in trouble. He was lanky and a couple years older than Natalie. She felt
uncomfortable around him and he picked up on it immediately, almost like he had a sixth sense.

"Look who they let out of the pen," he whispered.

Natalie tried to ignore him, but he reached over and flicked her arm.

"Declan!" the group leader yelled. "No side talking."

"Make her talk, then," he said, posturing.

"We don't make anyone talk until they're ready. You know that," she said.

He slid into an exaggerated reclined position in his chair. "Whatever."

The lady moved on, but Declan didn't. A minute later he sat back up. "Hey," he hissed toward Natalie. "You must have done something real bad if you won't say."

Natalie kept her eyes on her fingertips.

"Hellooo?" He leaned into her space. She could see his blackheads; she could feel his breath.

"Stop it!" Gwen scolded, reaching over and using her full palm to shove his head away from Natalie.

"What the hell?!" he squawked, jumping to his feet, ready to fight.

"Declan!" the lady shouted.

He moved to Gwen, towering over her, but she stayed in her chair.

"Don't fucking touch me ever again," he spat down at her.

She stared up at him, those still eyes.

"Declan!" the woman repeated. "Back in your seat!"

"Make her say she's sorry," he demanded.

"Gwen, apologize to Declan."

Declan glared down at the girl, waiting for a forced apology. Gwen cracked a devious smile then jolted toward him. It was enough to make him flinch.

Oozing with embarrassment, Declan took a step back around Natalie and kicked his chair, skidding it across the tile until it crashed down onto its side.

"Declan!" the woman screamed. "That's it, three strikes. Back to your room."

He recoiled, turning to her. "What? I didn't do anything."

"Out!" she insisted.

A bulky male attendant waiting by the door—idle meat, necessary in any group setting—uncrossed his arms and took two communicative steps toward the boy. Declan stomped off toward him.

Natalie looked to Gwen and smiled in thanks for the intervention. Gwen offered a thumbs-up, which made Natalie chuckle.

"Enough, girls," the woman muttered, exhausted with the session and probably her life. The attention only fueled the girls' snickers. It was infectious. Then more kids were laughing. It was all a chain reaction, but to Natalie, in that moment, it felt like acceptance.

— — — —

THREE WEEKS LATER AND Natalie had still not said a word during group. It drove Declan to corner her in art class, another of her newly earned rewards. Art was just a time during the day when kids sat in a room that had paper and markers. There was no teacher, only an attendant who sat in the front to make sure nothing went horribly wrong.

Declan slid into the empty seat next to her. "Nice picture, Natalie," he teased as he scooted his chair closer to hers.

She looked down at her drawing—a red dragon, peacefully asleep on a cloud. She wasn't much of an artist, but she liked drawing; she liked the idea of fantasy. Her hands gravitated toward each other, the one closest to him empty, the other holding an off-brand marker.

"Where's your pit bull?" he asked, referring to Gwen, as if the pet name would disguise his apprehension.

Natalie rubbed at the knuckle on her pointer finger, bent above the marker as it remained ready to return to coloring.

"Are you mute?" he asked. "Can you even talk?"

She continued to ignore him, staring down, maneuvering her full fist around the marker.

Declan reached over and grabbed her paper, shattering her focus.

"What are you doing?" she said.

"Ah." He revealed his teeth. "She does speak."

Natalie tried to take her paper back, but he yanked it away.

"Relax," he said. "You're going to like this." Declan picked up a black marker and took it to Natalie's picture. Just beyond the face of the sleeping dragon, he added an oversized cartoon penis. "Wakey-wakey," he pretended to say to the dragon before using the marker to shoot black lines from the tip of the penis into the dragon's face— over and over, until you could barely see any of the red drawing underneath.

Natalie tightened her grip on the marker she was holding. She knew this feeling so well. Her whole body tingled. She was angry, helpless, and starting to tune out. Then everything went quiet.

Natalie swung her arm around and jammed the marker into Declan's ear. Tears welled in her vacant, bloodshot eyes as she pounced, clawing at the boy's face. He tried to fight her off, but he was no match for her like this.

The attendant ran to pull Natalie away. His arm snaked around her neck, tearing her back with a choke hold until she was down on the ground. Another attendant ran into the room and the two grown men lifted Natalie to her feet. She was dragged into the hall, kicking and screaming, down to the infirmary, where she was restrained and drugged until she drooled, just as Gwen had warned.

— — — — —

THEY KEPT NATALIE IN isolation for two days after she stabbed Declan in the ear before bringing her back to her room to sleep off the remaining sedatives in her system. She barely remembered coming back when she woke up the next morning.

Gwen sat on the edge of her bed, staring as Natalie rubbed her eyes until they could stay open.

"Welcome back," said Gwen. "What happened?"

"Nothing." Natalie sighed.

Gwen raised her eyebrows. "I can't help if you don't tell me."

"I stabbed Declan with a marker."

"That's it?" Gwen said. "I saw his face."

If she knew, then why did she ask? Natalie didn't want to talk about it, but Gwen didn't care.

"Why'd you do it?" Gwen asked.

Natalie shrugged. "He was bothering me."

"You can't go berserk whenever someone makes you mad," said Gwen. "Everyone here is going to make you mad. You have to stop. No more freak-outs. Do you want to be a zombie all the time? Do you want to be alone again?"

"It's not like I can help it," Natalie insisted.

"You need a thing."

"I tried that, looking at my hands like you said. It didn't work."

"Well, then, you have to try something else. You know what I do? I count. I count everything. You should try it. When you get mad, check out—not like you normally do, but find something and count it."

"That's not going to work," said Natalie. "I can't even think when I get like that. You don't understand."

Gwen lay back on her bed, fingers interlaced behind her head.

"What are you doing?" Natalie asked.

"Shh, I'm thinking."

Natalie inhaled and followed it up with an exaggerated exhale.

Gwen had pelted her with questions before she was even fully awake and now she wanted quiet time?

Gwen stared at the ceiling. "Tell me what happens. Like, you're totally normal and then you're stabbing someone . . . What happens in between?"

Natalie said nothing at first, only dropped her head.

Gwen looked over, awaiting an answer. "Don't be embarrassed or anything. I don't even care that you attack people. You just have to be smarter about it. I don't want them to take you away all the time."

Gwen wanted Natalie around. It wasn't something her birth mother or any of the foster homes she'd ever been in wanted, but Gwen did. Natalie's fingertips drifted together and she rubbed them as she contemplated the question.

"I guess, I don't know . . . I go really numb?"

"Don't ask me." Gwen laughed.

"Sorry." Natalie smiled before resetting. "I don't want to hurt anyone. I really don't."

"I know."

"But the harder I try . . . the madder I get and then I lose it. Sometimes I don't even realize what I'm doing until I snap out of it."

"Hmm . . ." Gwen went quiet again and Natalie wasn't sure if she was supposed to say more. Then Gwen popped up, back to sitting on the edge of the bed. "I have an idea."

Natalie's eyes widened and her fingertips separated. She was open to anything.

"What if instead of trying not to freak out, you react immediately?" Gwen smacked her hands together for effect.

"What do you mean?"

"Okay, so Declan was bothering you, right?" Gwen scooted farther off the edge of her bed, jittery, excited. "He was being a jerk before you attacked him. What was the very first thing he did?"

Natalie tried to remember. He had ruined her picture, but if she was being honest, she had started to tingle the moment he sat down. "He wanted me to talk. He didn't like me ignoring him."

"Okay, what if the second he said something to you, you reacted? Like, you had to know he was there to bother you. Declan doesn't do anything but bother people. So the second he even looked at you, what if you had called him an asshole? Screamed it out. Or kicked him in the shin? I'm not talking about going lights-out and trying to kill him; I'm talking about a little kick on purpose."

Well, that was an idea that no one had ever presented to Natalie before. No social worker, therapist, or teacher had ever encouraged reacting. It had always been about new techniques to *prevent* a reaction, as if Natalie had never before considered deep breathing or walking away.

"Won't I still get in trouble?" she asked.

"Yeah, but, like, going to your room early or missing some dumb activity. They're not going to restrain you in the infirmary because you called someone a name or threw something. I bet right now there are three or four kids getting in trouble for those exact things."

"Yeah . . ." agreed Natalie.

"The second you feel uncomfortable, if I'm not with you, do something about it," said Gwen. "Don't fight it. It's not about pretending you don't have these feelings. It's about controlling them."

"Okay," said Natalie. "I'll give it a try."

THIRTY-THREE

NATALIE

N ATALIE LIVED IN A tiny apartment in Malden, close enough to
Gwen, but not too close. The main house had belonged to an
elderly woman named Denise who never went outside. Her sons had
converted the space above the detached garage into a studio apartment and rented it to Natalie to help cover costs. Natalie had only
seen Denise a handful of times over the years. The last time had been
when the paramedics wheeled her out on the stretcher—her body
had finally given up on a mind that had packed it in long ago.

A week later, Denise's sons had showed up with a truck and a
dumpster and emptied the place in a weekend. They'd furnished the
main house with cheap furniture and tacky decor and listed it on
Airbnb. It wasn't much of a vacation destination, but there was a
wedding venue fifteen minutes away and they hoped it would drum
up some demand, at least through the winter, when there wasn't as
much competition from the coast or the city.

Natalie pulled into her assigned parking spot behind the garage.
She entered through the side door and flipped the light switch. It

took her a moment to adjust to the latest tenant's car, a white Suburban. After years of Denise's rusty Windstar practically rotting into the concrete floor, the rotating cars still caught her off guard.

Natalie hiked the stairs to her apartment. She unlocked the door, slid her hand inside to turn on a lamp, and then killed the lights to the garage. She crossed the room to her nightstand and lifted a faded shoebox from the open shelf below the drawer. She placed it on the bed and sat down.

She lifted the top of the box to reveal her collection. Priceless items with no monetary value. Several receipts, a hair tie, a small jewelry tray from when Gwen used to actually finish her pottery. It was chipped and Gwen had tossed it in the trash can outside the sandwich shop after she'd noticed. Natalie pulled the sandwich card from her pocket, placed it inside the box, and closed the lid. She went to put it back on the shelf, but something caught her eye.

The shelf was dusty. She didn't take the box out very often. She wasn't a freak. She didn't get the items and stare at them all day and night; she just liked to keep them. So the dust wasn't a surprise. The surprise was that the area free of dust was not a single rectangle in the shape of the box; it was as if two boxes slightly overlapped, the corners less dusty than the overlapping area. The box had moved.

Could the box have shifted on its own? Natalie heaved back on her bed, seeing if the motion would move the nightstand. The box didn't move. She reached over and opened and closed the drawer above the shelf. She even tried pounding her fist on the top of the table, but the box didn't budge. She sat back on the bed. Her fingertips gravitated to each other and she rubbed them together.

Had the box really moved? Even if it did, had she kicked the nightstand some night she couldn't remember? Had she rolled over in her sleep? Was she taking the box out without realizing it?

This was supposed to be her safe space, but she couldn't escape the idea that someone had moved that box.

Almost as if on cue, the garage door below her rumbled and squealed as it opened.

Natalie rose from her bed and went to the window. The curtains were parted enough for her to see the main house and driveway. The front door was open and she stared, waiting for a monster or an axe murderer—something to match her bubbling paranoia.

A stocky man emerged, pulling two suitcases behind him. He struggled to yank both suitcases down the stairs. Natalie watched him walk across the driveway until she couldn't see him anymore. Then she could hear him below her, opening and closing the trunk of his SUV.

Natalie held her breath. A tiny part of her worried he was about to come up the stairs. This man who had maybe been in her apartment, moving her box. She tried to shake it off. It was in her head. She was struggling with the Airbnb and all the strangers it put in her own backyard. She tried to ignore them, but some were loud—sometimes they would fight, sometimes the opposite. It was so easy to watch from her window.

"Tom!" a woman yelled.

Natalie looked back at the house. The woman stepped outside with two full grocery bags. The man appeared again from the garage and grabbed them. Ten minutes later, the house was locked and their SUV pulled out of the driveway.

The house was quiet for several days, but the next weekend, another couple showed up. On the second night, Natalie watched the woman, intoxicated after presumably attending a wedding, still in a beautiful dress, show the man something on her phone and then slap him across the face. He ripped the phone out of her hand, shoved her to the floor, and then dropped it in the toilet. It was tense and Natalie worried things would escalate. She hated violence. It reminded her what she was capable of.

Eventually the couple went to sleep, the woman in the bed, the man somewhere else. Natalie went to her fridge and took out a cucumber. She crept down the stairs into the garage and checked to see if their car was unlocked. It was, and she slipped the cucumber under the passenger seat. It would go unnoticed until it started to rot. The smell would intensify, torturing them until they found it.

Natalie crawled back into bed and reached for her journal. The idea had just come to her. It was harmless—for them anyway. For her, it was dangerous. She promised herself she wouldn't do anything like that again.

After she wrote a few paragraphs about the couple and the cucumber, she turned the page to write about Gwen. There wasn't much to note that day, but that was okay—that was safe. She needed to stop watching the people in that house. She needed to focus on Gwen. Natalie could feel it. She'd been saying it for years, but this time she meant it; she was sure of it. She was almost ready to approach her.

THIRTY-FOUR

- - - - - - - - - - - -

SEVENTEEN YEARS AGO

N ATALIE HAD NEVER FELT so good about getting in trouble before. She missed a lot of afternoon recess and almost always lost
her TV time, but it never went much beyond that. Maybe she reacted
too quickly, maybe unnecessarily at times, but it was working and
she wasn't going to take any risks.

Natalie stuck to Gwen like glue. Sometimes she worried that she
was annoying Gwen, being too much of a burden, but it had been
more than a year since they'd become roommates and Natalie was
starting to think the dependence might be mutual.

Gwen never hung out with anyone else; it wasn't like she was
dragging Natalie along out of some sense of obligation. Gwen had a
special way about her. Natalie never felt like a charity case. She never
sensed any pity. Gwen was confident. There wasn't anything wrong
with Natalie, but she had never been taught how to deal with the
world. Everything Gwen said was the opposite of anything anyone
had ever told her before, and Natalie had completely bought in.

This place wasn't so bad. Compared to some of the other kids,

Natalie was almost normal. She didn't feel like she was walking around with a big sign that said *freak* over her head. They were all freaks; it was implied. The "schooling" was way easier than a traditional classroom and she enjoyed not having to think she was stupid every day.

Gwen and Natalie talked most nights until an attendant would pound on the glass and tell them to be quiet or they would be separated.

"Do you think you'll get married?" Gwen had asked her one night out of the blue as they lay in their beds.

"I don't know," answered Natalie, her usual answer to Gwen's questions before Gwen could pry more out of her.

"Why not?"

"I don't know."

"You always say you don't know," complained Gwen. "Obviously, you don't *know*, but what do you think? Like, best guess?"

Natalie thought for a second. "Probably not."

"Why?"

Natalie considered the why but didn't want to say it. She didn't think anyone would want to marry her. She was not someone people liked to keep around. Well, other than Gwen.

"You better not be thinking anything sad," said Gwen, knowing without knowing.

"I'm not," Natalie insisted.

"You have to start thinking about these things," Gwen said. "We're not going to be in this place forever."

"You always say that."

"Well, it's true! Do you see any forty-year-olds locked up around here?"

"No." Natalie giggled.

"I don't think I'll ever get married," Gwen mused.

"Why not?"

Gwen thought about it. "It just seems weird. What if you don't want them to know something about you? What if they're mean or stupid or get really ugly? Do you think you could really trust them?"

Natalie shrugged. "You could get a divorce."

"I guess." Gwen pulled her legs out from under the covers and flopped them back on top of the bed. "Unless they're abusive. Then what do you do? Kill them? Now you have to be a murderer because you married some guy who used to seem perfect."

"I don't think you would have to kill him," said Natalie. "Couldn't you just run away?"

Gwen laughed out loud at the suggestion. Natalie wasn't sure why but was embarrassed that it was such a laughable idea.

"You make it sound so easy," said Gwen. "It's not easy to go into hiding. Where are you going to go? With what money? How are you going to change your looks enough so some man you slept with every night won't recognize you? And even if he's just a lazy piece of crap who won't come looking, you're still going to worry he will. You want to live your whole life looking over your shoulder? Or don't you just want to be single?"

"Single, I guess," said Natalie.

"Don't say that just because that's what I'm saying. Maybe you will be a perfect wife someday."

Natalie shrugged. She wanted to please Gwen with her answers, but sometimes she felt like there was no answer that would please her.

"What about your job?" asked Gwen. "What kind of job do you want to have?"

"I don't know," said Natalie, before wincing. "Sorry, umm . . . I really don't know."

Gwen considered it. "Okay, but you're supposed to think about it; don't you think about it? In a perfect world, don't you think about being a movie star or a veterinarian or something?"

"No."

Gwen looked at her funny. "Interesting."

"What does *that* mean?" asked Natalie.

"I mean it's interesting. Don't get mad about it; it's not a bad thing. I like the way you think about things. Or don't think about them." Gwen chuckled.

"Are you making fun of me?"

"Oh my God." Gwen threw her head back. "No!" She tossed her pillow playfully across the room at Natalie. "Trust me, you will know if I don't like you."

"Okay," said Natalie, sliding off her bed to dutifully return Gwen's pillow.

Gwen grabbed it and shoved it back under her head while Natalie returned to her own bed.

"I think you should try writing in a journal," suggested Gwen. "Maybe if you write things down, it will help you think. It will give you more ideas."

"About what?"

"Anything. Your life. Maybe you won't say *I don't know* to every question I ask. Plus, we've figured out it's much better for you not to keep things bottled up, don't you think?"

"Yeah."

"Just try it. It couldn't hurt. Remember, we aren't going to be in this place forever!" Gwen barely got the sentence out before she burst out laughing. Then both girls giggled until there was a familiar tap against their door.

"All right, girls, that's enough . . . lights out."

"Ugh." Gwen rolled her eyes and flipped off her bedside table lamp. "Good night," she whispered.

"Good night," Natalie whispered back.

Gwen was asleep within minutes. Natalie was used to Gwen's snoring now and even found it comforting. This last-resort lock-and-key children's institution had turned out to be the place where Natalie could finally feel at home. And, dare she say, optimistic?

THIRTY-FIVE

GWEN

ALL I THOUGHT ABOUT was killing Natalie. What it would feel like. What it would mean. How I could continue justifying that it was nothing like what my father did when he took a life. How I could go back to work and to Painting Pots and on dates with Brian knowing I had killed again, telling myself it was different this time.

I was glad I had finally visited my father, confronting what I had long been afraid would happen if I did so. It felt good to defy him, to deprive him of what he wanted, but my mental state was like that of a zoo animal set loose into the wild—appreciative of my newfound freedom but ill prepared to survive on my own. It didn't help that I was focusing so much of my attention on Natalie and what I was going to have to do to her. The mental gymnastics required to feel free from my father while planning a murder were causing my brain to overheat.

I craved being near Elyse. She was a release valve for the pressure in my head. I had earned her trust somehow—I was the worst possible person in the world for her to trust, but she did. She didn't know I was Marin Haggerty, but she'd figured out that Gwen Tanner was dark and fucked-up too. My parents dying in that fire must have really affected me, because I was not appalled by her plans or the callousness with which she discussed them. I encouraged her to talk about killing Natalie, letting her say all the things out loud so that I didn't need to think them alone.

I sat in Elyse's aesthetically dull kitchen. I watched her run a sponge around the edges of the sink, pausing in spots to scrub hardened grossness away.

"I was thinking about motive," she mused. "If I take a bunch of things like jewelry and her wallet, the cops will think it was a robbery gone bad."

"Marin is too much in the public eye right now," I cautioned. "It's going to be suspicious no matter what you do."

"They're going to assume it's whoever did the other killings."

"But how are you going to actually do it? The act?"

"Stab her?" Elyse kept scrubbing at the counter that was already spotless five minutes ago. "What do you think?"

"I think stabbing is really personal," I said. "You'll have to be so close to her and she's going to look you in the eyes. She'll beg you not to do it. If you panic and don't finish it, you're done. You'll go to jail and she'll be a hero."

Elyse pulled the sponge away from the counter to look at me. Her face was unaltered by my attempt to set the chilling scene. "I can stab her from behind," she suggested. "I would surprise her."

I had to remember who I was dealing with. She had seen her whole family dead, splayed out, covered in blood. The thought of her nemesis in that condition was not going to spook her. My only chance was logic. "You have to hit an organ or cut a vein. There are lots of places you can survive a stab wound."

She was scrubbing again. "What do you think? I should shoot her? I don't know how to get an untraceable gun."

"Guns are too loud."

"What, then?" She pressed for my advice, frustrated. "It has to be something quick."

"I don't know," I said. "It's not like there's an easy answer. Getting away with murder is supposed to be difficult."

"Are you trying to talk me out of this?" She turned back from the sink. "I get it if you don't want to be a part of this. I know it's a lot." She tried to inhale, but her breath caught in her throat and she flipped up her palms, gesturing defeat. "I know it's really crazy and you don't owe me anything."

"I said I would help you and this is me helping you. You can't half-ass it. Every detail needs to be worked out and you have to know one hundred percent that you want to kill her. I mean, she *was* just a kid."

"*I* was just a kid!" Elyse threw the sponge into the sink for good. "You don't do that and then puberty turns you into a well-adjusted person, while I'm stuck sitting in this apartment watching her crush my brother's skull over and over again."

"It won't make you feel better," I insisted. "Any relief you'll get from her being dead will be marred by the act *you* committed. You'll watch her life fade away at your hand. There will be blood spilling out. She'll cry and beg you for help and you can't help her. Then she will just be a body and her eyes will be glued open and staring at you." I leaned over the table, trapping her eyes symbolically with mine. "That's what you'll see every day for the rest of your life. If someone cuts you off in the street and you think a bad thought about them, you will see them dead, because your mind will know what you are capable of. It will not end. It will be who you are now."

"Good," she said as she stood back up and walked away.

Her cold indifference sent a charge through my body—an attraction clouded by guilt. Elyse was innocent and the point was to keep her that way. She wasn't like us. I didn't know what had happened to Natalie or why she was doing this, but regardless of any aliases or wigs, this was our mess alone—mine and Natalie's.

THIRTY-SIX

NATALIE

I T WAS ANOTHER EFFORTLESS night watching Gwen. Painting Pots, then back to her apartment. Natalie wished Gwen would do something different. Go on a date, find a new hobby, change jobs. The ease with which Natalie could watch her at Painting Pots was, for the first time, starting to feel monotonous. When she didn't have to think about Gwen, it was harder for Natalie to ignore the people in the house.

After a couple of hours, Gwen finally went to bed and Natalie headed home.

There was a car in the garage. Natalie climbed the stairs into her apartment, but once inside, she didn't go to the window. She didn't want to think about the car or the fact that it meant someone was in the house. Instead, she went into the bathroom to wash her face, turning the knob on the sink and letting the water run. It took a minute for the shoddy garage pipes to heat the water, and while she waited, she picked at the dry skin around her nostrils. As she passed her hand under the stream, testing the temperature, feeling it cross the threshold into lukewarm, there was a knock at the door.

Natalie hit the faucet to cut off the water. Then it was silent. She waited. Maybe it wasn't a knock; maybe the wind had tipped something over in the garage. Then she heard it again. It was definitely someone knocking on her door.

She left the bathroom with nothing but her clenched fists and opened the door to a man in a pristine white baseball hat, fitted joggers, and a quarter-zip. His hands were tucked in his pockets and if he was dangerous, it wasn't presenting as an immediate threat.

"Hi," he blurted out with a sheepish smile.

"Hi," said Natalie.

"I'm sorry, I know it's late, but you're a hard person to run into. You must be a busy lady." He waited a beat as if he had asked a question but then regrouped. "I'm sorry, I'm Wesley. I moved into the house last week." He held out his hand.

"Natalie," she said, meeting his hand. She wasn't sure what to say. She didn't really talk to anyone, let alone in the middle of the night in her apartment—her safe space.

"I'm sorry," he apologized again, the third time in twenty seconds. "I suppose it's kind of rude for me to show up so late. I swear, my intentions are noble. I just wanted to introduce myself since I rented the place through the summer. If you need anything, don't hesitate to knock on the door."

"Thanks," Natalie managed.

"Okay, great. Well, I'll leave you alone. It was nice to meet you, Natalie. Hopefully I'll see you around once in a while."

Natalie assembled a small smile and Wesley backed away from the door, not turning until he reached the stairs, where he spun around and jogged down them. Natalie closed the door and inhaled.

A nice neighbor doing a nice thing and she'd handled it like a normal person.

She didn't bother going back to her bathroom routine and instead climbed directly into bed. She stretched the blankets up over her shoulders and closed her eyes.

As her body relaxed, so did her mind—not in a way that brought peace, but in a way that brought clarity. There was someone in the house and not just for the weekend. A man she didn't know anything about. A man who came to her door uninvited in the dark. Natalie sat up in bed. She couldn't see anything through the curtains.

It wasn't a conscious decision, but she found herself at the window, pulling the curtain back—barely enough to peer through. Wesley was in his bedroom now; she had a direct view across the driveway, not obstructed by any curtains or shades. He paced around the room, typing on his phone with purpose, still fully dressed, looking exactly like he had at her doorstep.

Finally he flung the phone down on the bed and reached for the waistband on his pants. Natalie averted her eyes. She wasn't like that. She waited before looking back, but when she did . . .

Wesley was at the window.

Can he see me? Is he looking at me?

IT HAD BEEN ALMOST a week since Wesley had come to her door, and Natalie sat in her car outside Painting Pots. It had been a long day at work and she hadn't been sleeping well. There was a fog in her brain that could almost let her relax, but when Gwen walked out in a striped blouse with her hair down, Natalie knew she wasn't headed home, and it was like a shot of adrenaline.

Natalie sat up in her seat. She grabbed for the keys in the ignition, but when Gwen walked right past her own car, Natalie froze.

Gwen was headed toward the train station. She must be going into the city. It had to be a date. Why else would she be going into the city looking so nice?

Natalie hopped out of her car and hustled to the trunk. She rummaged around searching for something warm she could put on over her baggy long-sleeve T-shirt. She ripped open a thin trash bag full of old clothes she had been meaning to drop off at Goodwill. She knew there was a black fleece in there. The inside lining had completely worn through, but at least it was something. She wasn't sure if Goodwill would even accept it, but she didn't have the heart to throw it away. That's why the bag had remained in the trunk; every time she debated pulling up to the donation center, she worried they would tell her everything she had was trash, so ugly and worn that not even a person in need would want it.

She found the thing and zipped it all the way up. It was better than nothing. She slammed the trunk and ran out of the parking lot, slowing to a normal pace once Gwen was in sight.

The train was always tricky for Natalie. She couldn't very well ride in the same car as Gwen—public transportation inspired stares, the dense crowd failing to provide cover, instead giving people the confidence that their gaze could go unnoticed.

Natalie boarded the car in front of Gwen's, staying at the door, standing and ready to disembark in an instant. There were really only a few stops she had to worry about if Gwen was headed downtown and not looking to switch trains. When the train stopped at State Street, Natalie caught a glimpse of Gwen's brown hair on the platform and lunged off the train, pushing through the people who had already started boarding.

Natalie ascended the stairs out of the stifling underground station and into the fresh, cold air. She tucked her hands into the coat pockets, feeling the scratchy remnants of the liner. Gwen's jacket looked much warmer, and when she paused to zip it, Natalie shielded her face, pretending to check her phone. Then Gwen was on the move again.

Natalie stayed close, but not too close, a distance she practically had down to a science at this point. Gwen cut through a few side streets and crossed a main intersection on her way toward Faneuil Hall. Natalie's teeth were chattering; where was spring?

Ultimately, Gwen dipped into a bar off Congress Street and Natalie slowed in front of the window. It was crowded inside, full of the after-work crowd. Tall bar tables lined the windows; Natalie couldn't get away with standing there all night, noticeably gawking, not that she could tolerate the cold much longer anyway. She didn't have much of a choice; if she wanted to watch, she had to go inside.

Natalie took a deep breath and pulled open the door, a cacophony of conversation pouring into the street. The door closed behind her, sealing her inside with the people and their gossip or their flirting or their complaining—whatever was making all that noise.

She scanned the room for Gwen and found her sitting at one of the tall tables near the bar. Across from her was her date. He didn't look too threatening. He seemed to be around their age, too young and single to own a house. No house meant no basement. No basement meant no dungeon. There wasn't much else for Natalie to surmise from first appearances. She found a seat on the opposite side of the bar, facing them but slightly obstructed by four guys huddled around two stools.

"What can I get you?" the bartender asked, sliding a cocktail napkin in front of her.

She ordered a club soda and settled in for what would probably be two or three drinks on Gwen's end.

- - - - -

HE TALKED A LOT. Way more than Gwen. Probably an 80-20 split. And he kept touching her hand. *Stop touching her hand,* Natalie thought. *She doesn't like to be touched like that; she pulls it away every time.* Gwen excused herself to go to the bathroom, probably to wash her hands, maybe just to pee.

The date sat alone now. Their drinks were empty, waiting on the waitress. He pulled his phone from his pocket, checked something, then slipped it back in.

"Excuse me," a voice came, penetrating Natalie's bubble.

She turned to see a man standing there.

"Yeah?" she said, trying to keep her eye on Gwen's date.

"Is this seat taken?" He pointed next to her.

"No," she said, watching the waitress arrive at Gwen's table with another round of drinks. No sign of Gwen.

"Are you here alone?" He kept talking as he sat, but she ignored him.

"Hey!" he barked, startling her.

Natalie's whole body tensed as she whipped her head around to the man, unsure what was happening or what she would have to do.

"Sorry," he said. "I thought you couldn't hear me."

Natalie gave the slightest smile to forgive and hopefully dismiss the man before looking back to Gwen's table. The date was pulling his hand away from Gwen's drink.

Why was he touching her drink? Natalie wondered. *Maybe the waitress mixed them up? Maybe she put it down too close to him? Maybe he slipped something in there when Natalie wasn't looking?*

Gwen reappeared, smiling politely as she climbed back onto her stool. She put her hand around her glass and brought the tiny straw to her lips. Natalie held her breath. Gwen didn't drop dead, not yet at least, and Natalie exhaled.

They finished their drinks. He was still reaching for Gwen's hand. Maybe it was a nervous tic; he was doing it so frequently. Gwen pulled her hand back and rubbed her forehead. She didn't look good. She was flushed, taking deep breaths, leaning her elbow on the table. Her posture was flimsy and weak.

Gwen slid off the stool. She was going to the bathroom again. She'd just been to the bathroom. Something was happening to her. Her drink.

The guy adjusted in his seat. He glanced around the bar. *What are you looking for?* Natalie wondered.

He got off his stool and stood next to the table; his eyes were shifting all over the place.

Natalie crawled her fingers over to an abandoned plate at the seat next to her, the fatty edges of a steak waiting to be bused away. She grabbed the knife and slipped it under the bar.

The date started walking. He was headed toward the bathroom. He was looking for Gwen. He was going after her.

Natalie jumped off her stool. She was on the move. She gripped the knife.

He turned the corner into the hallway where the bathrooms were and Natalie lost sight of him. She shoved a couple of people out of the way, picking up her pace. She rounded the corner, crashing directly into the date.

"What the hell?!" he exclaimed. He was standing at the waitress stand, next to the kitchen, talking to their waitress, getting the check.

"Sorry," Natalie muttered, confronted with the reality of the situation. She turned and ran out, dropping the knife on a random table.

She burst into the street. *What was I thinking? What was I doing?*

Natalie waited in an ATM vestibule across the street until Gwen and the man left the restaurant. When they parted ways at the entrance to the train station with a peck on the cheek, it cemented Natalie's overreaction. Her fantasy of being some kind of savior had almost ruined everything. She had nearly stabbed the man with a steak knife. She had to be better.

The train ride back to her car was agonizing. If Natalie couldn't control herself, she'd need to adjust, but she didn't want to. She didn't want to have to wait in her car all the time because she couldn't trust herself anywhere else. Her own actions were betraying her, like they always did.

Natalie drove down Gwen's street. Her car was in the driveway and there was a light on in the bathroom window. Gwen was inside. She was safe; there was no use in Natalie staying until Gwen went to bed. Natalie hadn't been sleeping well. It was affecting her temperament. Maybe that's all it was.

She didn't want to admit to herself the real reason she wasn't sleeping well.

She was watching the man in the house. She was lying awake, wondering if he was watching her too.

THIRTY-SEVEN

SIXTEEN YEARS AGO

NATALIE HAD BEEN ON her best behavior all day and hadn't lost any of her TV time. Natalie and Gwen sat together in a jumbo beanbag chair, watching a family sitcom that one of the attendants had turned on, but Natalie's bladder was bursting with watered-down juice. She held out for a commercial break and once the show cut away, Natalie rolled out of the chair.

"Have to pee. Be right back."

"Okay," said Gwen as Natalie sprinted into the hallway.

There were two single bathrooms off the recreation room and Natalie shoved into the first door. It was locked and a high-pitched voice screamed, "I'm in here!" so she bounced off the door and into the next bathroom. As soon as she felt the door give, she knew it was unlocked and started to undo the button on her pants. She had to be quick to finish before the show came back. She lowered the zipper as she stepped through the doorway onto the tile floor.

She was not alone.

Declan was standing over the toilet.

"Sorry!" Natalie exclaimed, yanking her zipper back up and turning to leave.

"Hey, hey, hey!" Declan said, grabbing her attention back before her brain could catch up.

As Natalie turned back around, Declan rotated from the toilet and started peeing, his stream of piss landing on Natalie's socks.

"Stop it!" she yelled, but as she stepped back, he stepped forward.

She turned away, but then she could feel it spraying the backs of her calves as she reached for the door.

"Just marking my territory," he mocked.

Natalie swung around and kicked Declan right between the legs. He groaned as he bent over, but Natalie whipped the door open and ran from the bathroom. She hadn't hesitated. It was the perfect reaction.

- - - - -

"YOU SMELL LIKE PEE," Gwen announced as soon as Natalie plopped back onto the beanbag chair.

"Sorry, I tried to clean it."

Gwen cringed before her face softened. "Are you okay? Did you have an accident or something?"

"What? No!" Natalie insisted. "It was Declan. He peed on me."

"What do you mean he peed on you?"

Natalie huffed. "I mean what I said. I went into the bathroom and he was in there and he turned and peed on my feet."

"That's disgusting," Gwen said.

Natalie rolled off the chair and stood up, towering over Gwen now. "I know, okay? I know it's disgusting."

"Calm down," said Gwen. "I mean *he's* disgusting. It's not your fault. I didn't mean *you* were disgusting."

Natalie relaxed her shoulders. "Well, I kicked him and left before it got any worse."

Gwen smiled. "That's great. That's really great."

Natalie couldn't help but smile.

"Now, sit back down," Gwen instructed, and Natalie did as she was told.

They were both quiet for a few minutes, Natalie relieved to have moved on.

"You did really great," Gwen repeated out of nowhere, past the point it made any sense to still be talking about. "But that doesn't mean he should get away with it."

THIRTY-EIGHT

- - - - - - - - - - - - - - -

NATALIE

NATALIE PULLED INTO HER driveway a little after eleven, setting off the light over the garage. She parked in her usual spot and walked around toward the door.

"Hey there," came a voice across the driveway.

She jumped as she turned to see Wesley sitting on the steps of the main house, sipping on a bottle of beer that he held around the neck like chopsticks.

"Sorry, I didn't mean to scare you," he said.

"It's okay." She brushed him off, continuing toward the door.

"How was your day?" he asked before she could put her hand around the knob and escape the interaction.

"Good, thank you."

"You're very welcome," he said, teasing her for her performative manners. "Care to join me?"

"In what?" Natalie asked rationally instead of participating in social norms.

"I don't know, sitting?"

"It's cold out here," she said.

"You have a coat though, and look, I'm only wearing a button-down."

Natalie gravitated across the driveway toward him, knowing she shouldn't but doing it all the same. The closer she got, the stronger the scent of alcohol became.

"Can I get you a drink?" he asked, with long, extended blinks as he waited for her answer.

"No, thank you," she said, taking a seat next to him on the front steps.

"I shouldn't be talking to you like this," he said, chuckling.

"Why?"

"I've had too much to drink." He grinned at her with an unspoken *obviously*. "I don't want to say anything I shouldn't."

Natalie's fingertips grazed together as she rested her hands in her lap. She didn't know what she was supposed to say.

"Where do you go all the time, Ms. Natalie?" He turned his face toward her.

"Work mostly."

"You must work a lot." His stare was absent. It wasn't a question, but it was like he was waiting for an answer.

"Do you have a job?" she asked.

Wesley nodded. "I'm a journalist."

"Is that why you're here?"

"Yeah, I'm working on a story in the city, so I grabbed this place for a few months. The drive back and forth to Jersey was killing me."

"What's the story?"

He grinned. "Nice try."

Natalie looked down at her hands. She didn't really care. She was just trying to be polite.

"It's not that exciting," he offered. "Well, I'm hoping it will be, but corporate fraud . . . nobody cares if you can't humanize the victims. Ahh . . ." He grinned. "I've said too much!"

It was playful and they both laughed before falling into silence. Wesley took another sip of his drink before rotating his head toward her. His neck muscles seemed weakened and his head flopped over enough to make his stare verge on puppy-dog.

"I have to go," said Natalie, standing and walking away without giving him the opportunity to protest.

"Good night!" he yelled after her.

Once she was inside her apartment, she looked back at him through the window. He rose to his feet slowly and wobbled up the steps, so unsteady, barely making it inside. She liked him this way.

As she changed into her pajamas, Natalie couldn't stop thinking about Wesley. He was drunk and a little too friendly. It had unnerved her, but now she wondered if she could have stayed a little longer. She headed back to the window.

Wesley was still downstairs. She watched him stumble around in the kitchen, then into the bathroom out of sight, then back again. He hadn't rebuttoned his pants and he lumbered forward, trying to kick them off.

Then he tripped, caught on his own pants. He fell to the ground, but not before his head bounced off the kitchen island. His body didn't move. All Natalie could see now were his lower legs, one on top of the other, pants around his ankles.

Every bone in her body was telling her to go to bed. Wesley was messy—a distraction she couldn't afford. She'd worked so hard to be with Gwen and didn't want to do anything to jeopardize that. But what if Wesley was lying there, bleeding out, and would die without intervention?

— — — — —

NATALIE WAS STANDING ON his porch before she could talk herself out of it. She pushed the door open like in a horror film where the door swings open but the person just stands there in the doorway. She waited and listened for any sound that would change her mind. A soothing hum came from the ceiling fan in the living room.

She entered the foyer and pulled the door closed behind her. Her footsteps were silent and it was only in that moment she realized she hadn't even put shoes on. Her thin white socks were filthy from the driveway.

Natalie moved closer to the kitchen island. Wesley's hands and forearms matched his legs—the right one draped over the left—two useless limbs that had done nothing to break his fall. She stepped farther into the kitchen and around the island until her view was no longer obstructed. There was no blood, and within three stressful seconds, she could tell he was breathing.

She knew she should leave. She did what she had come for. Her conscience could be clean, but instead, she dropped down to one knee beside him. She reached out toward his shoulder and paused, her hand not quite making contact, not yet.

It felt strange to be so close. She could see his stubble. She leaned forward and let her fingers meet his cheek.

A moan broke the silence as if she had set off an alarm on his body. Natalie jumped back and fell onto her ass. Wesley began to stir and she crab-walked away from him and around the corner of the kitchen island as he rolled onto his back. She leaned against the island, pulling her knees up to her throat and hoping he hadn't seen or heard her. She buried her face in her knees and let her nerves take her elsewhere.

She thought of all the times she had almost been caught by

Gwen. Years ago, when Natalie was too eager and unaware she was even someone to be perceived—when she worried she had parked too close or walked by the window too many times. When she would sprint home and hide in her bed and pray she would never see the look of disappointment and disgust that she'd seen the last time Gwen had looked at her.

Natalie snapped back to reality, face pushed so hard into her knees that, as she lifted her head, it took time for her cheeks to regain feeling. The only sound was the ceiling fan, and the rhythmic rotation of the blades returned her to the moment. She leaned to the side, enough to peer around the island. Wesley was gone.

She rose to her feet with extreme caution, but once she was upright and could confirm she was alone, Natalie hustled for the door. She slithered out and ran across the driveway. Once safely back in her apartment, she chucked her dirty socks into the laundry basket and ran to the window. In the light of the moon, she saw Wesley had found his way into bed.

Natalie crawled under the covers, her heart beating rapidly. She rubbed her fingertips together, remembering the texture of Wesley's face. She didn't think about Gwen again that night, only about what would have happened if Wesley had caught her.

─ ─ ─ ─ ─

DAYS HAD PASSED SINCE Natalie had last talked to Wesley on the front step, since she'd gone into his house, since she'd touched his face. As soon as Gwen went inside her apartment for the night, Natalie raced home.

When she opened the door to the garage, it was empty; Wesley's car wasn't there. Natalie was furious. She had left Gwen early for nothing. It couldn't be for nothing.

Natalie went back to her car, where she sat for hours, parked behind the garage, waiting for his headlights to blast through her windshield, and when they did, she climbed out as though she had just arrived.

The one-sided clandestine meeting in the driveway didn't go as Natalie had hoped. She wasn't sure what she'd hoped would happen, but it wasn't that. Wesley brushed her off. He barely stopped to acknowledge her, only enough to tell her that he wasn't feeling well. He gave her a smile and then coughed a few times, but the coughs seemed even more forced than the smile.

Did he know she had gone into the house? Was he mad at her? Was he afraid of her?

Natalie hated this feeling. Wesley had come to *her* door. He had called *her* over to the steps that night. He couldn't all of a sudden hate her. It wasn't fair. Maybe he really was just sick. Maybe that's all this was. She had to know.

She decided to bring him soup. That seemed like the neighborly thing to do. Then he couldn't ignore her.

– – – – –

NATALIE WAS AT THE grocery store first thing the next morning. Two cans of low sodium chicken broth rolled around in the shopping basket as she reached for a produce bag. She rubbed the end between her fingers, waiting for the right piece to catch and separate. Over and over, but the thing stayed sealed tight.

She could sense a man behind her, waiting for his turn to grab a bag, but keeping his distance so as not to embarrass her. It didn't work. She felt the pressure and started moving her fingers faster, not getting any closer. She couldn't take it anymore and crumpled the useless bag into a ball and chucked it down among the cucumbers. She threw the celery into the basket before grabbing a package of carrots, and as she breezed past the display of onions, she snatched one off the top. That would have to do.

The basket had some weight to it now and Natalie hooked her elbow through the handle for more leverage as she made her way to the cash register. She was content with her ingredients until a thought came to her, a sick thought she tried to brush off, but it came back. She could just buy it. It didn't mean she would use it. She would just buy it.

The self-checkout line was empty and she went straight to the register. With the basket still hooked around her arm, she scanned her items. A three-pound whole chicken, two cans of broth, celery, carrots, an onion, and a Mouse Killer Disposable Bait Station.

THIRTY-NINE

SIXTEEN YEARS AGO

B IRTHDAYS WERE WHAT YOU made of them at the facility; no one in charge was going to do anything for you. About half the kids had families who would visit and that was something. If the woman in the kitchen liked you, she might slip you an extra dessert. But Natalie didn't have any family and the woman in the kitchen still held a grudge from the time Natalie had thrown her milk against the wall when given meat sauce that the lady wouldn't let her swap for marinara.

"Happy birthday!" Gwen yelled, whipping Natalie's blankets off her.

Natalie's eyes shot open as she struggled to get her bearings.

"Finally, you're thirteen," said Gwen. "You're a teenager! And it means absolutely nothing," she teased.

"Thanks," Natalie said as she sat up in her bed.

"What do you want to do today?" Gwen asked.

"What do you mean?"

"It's your birthday."

"It doesn't matter," argued Natalie.

"Oh, Natalie." Gwen sighed. "You've got to learn to make the most of things. We can't go to Disney World, but we can play checkers or something."

"Okay, we can play checkers," she agreed, to the frustration of Gwen.

"That was an example!" chastised Gwen. "You hate checkers."

"I don't hate checkers," Natalie protested.

Gwen rolled her eyes. "That's what you want to do today? On your special day? You want to play a dumb game that we never play that's missing half the pieces?"

"Then why did you say it? You suggested it and now you're acting like I'm so stupid for agreeing."

Gwen sighed. "Okay, reset. Forget checkers. Pretend I never said anything about it. I want you to think of something that you want to do today that will feel special, that's all. No pressure. If you think of something, tell me and we'll do it, okay?"

Natalie nodded.

"And if you don't think of anything, that's fine too. Okay?"

Natalie nodded again, this time with a smile.

Natalie wanted to think of something to tell Gwen. She wanted to feel special, but more importantly, she wanted to please Gwen. She almost suggested a few things, but she didn't want to upset Gwen like the checkers had. As long as she was with Gwen, she was happy. There wasn't anything to do within those walls that would bring Natalie any more joy than that.

Natalie brought her dinner tray to the table and sat in the same seat she always did. Not only was she not afforded an extra dessert, the one she got was blueberry crumble, her least favorite. The blueberries probably weren't even real. They were sour and mushy and the crumble was more like a paste.

"Happy birthday, Natalie," came a voice from behind her.

Natalie looked over her shoulder to see Declan. "Thank you," she said, hesitant to outright ignore him.

He slid into the seat next to her and placed his tray beside hers. He never sat with them. This was going to be a thing.

"Gwen's sitting there," she tried.

"I wanted to offer you my dessert. You know, for your birthday." He grinned as if he weren't trying to convince her he was being kind.

"No, thank you."

"Really, I insist." Declan scooped a spoonful of the blueberry slop and dropped it directly on top of her rectangular pizza.

Natalie closed her eyes. He wanted her to react. He knew what would happen to her if she did. She didn't want to be sent to her room for the night. She hadn't thought of anything special yet.

Another spoonful hit her tray, and when she opened her eyes, it covered her french fries. Declan grabbed one, only a dot of blueberry on it, and shoved it into his mouth. "Not bad," he said.

Natalie looked for Gwen, but she was still in the food line. She would be a few minutes and Declan wasn't going anywhere. He started humming; it was the tune to "Happy Birthday." It started soft, but each time he repeated the verse, it would get louder, more aggressive, his head moving closer to her ear. She started to tingle. Not now. She couldn't do this now.

She reached over and shoved his tray away. It slid along the table until it went crashing to the floor.

An attendant was at their table before the tray had finished reverberating against the tile. "What happened?"

Declan pointed at Natalie. "She pushed my tray. I wasn't even doing anything. She always does this stuff to me."

"Go get another dinner," the attendant instructed. "And sit somewhere else."

Declan slid off the stool and shielded his face enough to wink at

Natalie without the attendant noticing. Then he was gone and only the effects of him lingered.

"I'm sorry," said Natalie. "I didn't mean for it to fall."

"Then you shouldn't have touched it. Now, finish up and then head back to your room."

"Please," she begged. "It's my birthday."

"Happy birthday," he said. "You have ten minutes." He made a point of motioning to the wall clock as he walked away.

Natalie stared down at her blue dinner, breathing and waiting for her emotions to regulate, waiting for Gwen.

"Ew," said Gwen as she sat down and noticed the tray. "Did Declan do that?"

Natalie nodded, hoping Gwen would be mad, but instead she smirked.

"He's such an idiot." Gwen slid Natalie's tray away and put her own down in between them. "Here," she said, handing her the plastic knife, "cut mine in half. We'll share. I'm not that hungry anyway. Plus . . ." Gwen reached into her pocket and pulled out something wrapped in a napkin.

Natalie put down the knife and grabbed the napkin, unfolding a brownie, her favorite.

"How did you get this?"

Gwen shrugged. "Nancy owed me a favor."

"Thank you," said Natalie.

They ate in silence for a moment, Natalie staring down at her food, Gwen with her eyes up, always aware of her surroundings.

"Did you think of anything yet?" Gwen asked. "Anything special for your birthday?"

"No," said Natalie. "But I have to go to my room once I'm done, because I threw the tray. This brownie is special though."

"Eh," said Gwen. "I have a better idea."

Natalie perked up. "What?"

"Look," Gwen whispered as she nodded toward a small plastic container in the corner of the room—a poison bait station for the mice that ran willy-nilly through the place.

"So what?" asked Natalie.

"Go get it. I'll distract the guy."

Gwen headed over to talk to the attendant and Natalie slipped out of her seat. She made sure no one was looking, especially Declan, and then she swiped the container. It was gross, dusty, with cobwebs trailing from the wall, but Gwen wanted it, so she happily shoved it into her pocket.

FORTY

- - - - - - - -

NATALIE

NATALIE PULLED OUT A pot from the drawer next to the oven and turned a burner to medium. She dropped in the chicken and broth to cook while she chopped up the vegetables. Then she dumped them in too. She left the box of rodent poison in the paper bag on the floor, like there was nothing nefarious behind it, like she had purchased it for the sole purpose of eliminating mice.

She checked the clock. It was half past nine. Gwen would get to Painting Pots at eleven, when it opened. She never went early on the weekends since she didn't have to leave for work.

The soup smelled pretty good. Natalie skimmed the top with a spoon and brought it to her lips. She blew on the liquid, sending a ripple through it until it was a safe temperature. It was salty and flavorful, all thanks to the prepackaged broth and not any real culinary skill or effort.

She moved the pot to the back burner to cool and reached into the drawer that housed her collection of glassware, neatly sorted and stacked. She pulled out a small round container and its complementing top. As she closed the drawer, the brown grocery bag stared directly at her, unobstructed. She placed the container on the counter and reached into the bag.

Natalie held the box in her hand. Wesley was a grown man. It probably wouldn't even do anything.

She put the box down, only for as long as it took to pour the soup into the container, and then it was in her hands again. She peeled open the box and slid out the contents. The bait wasn't in powder form, not like she remembered; it was a green cube. She freed it from the plastic packaging and stared at it on the counter. It was a sign— a sign not to do it. A sign she didn't listen to.

From her junk drawer, Natalie pulled out an all-in-one multitool. She gripped the handle and slammed the hammer end down onto the green cube. Chunks broke off from the edge. Then she smashed the smaller pieces until they turned to powder. She held the soup container below the counter and scraped the powder over the edge, watching it disappear into the broth.

She cleaned up the unused poison, and as she washed her hands in the kitchen sink, she caught a glimpse of the microwave clock. It was 10:45 a.m. She was never going to make it to Painting Pots by eleven. How had she lost track of time? It was so unlike her.

She left the container of soup in front of Wesley's door with a note that said, *Hope this helps you feel better—Natalie.*

She would need to catch every green light to make it to Painting Pots on time to see Gwen arrive, but she wouldn't have any trouble speeding with the adrenaline coursing through her veins.

- - - - -

GWEN WAS ALREADY INSIDE. Natalie had missed her arriving, missed her walking through the parking lot, missed her finishing her coffee. Natalie slammed her hands against the steering wheel.

She had wasted her morning on Wesley. Why had she done that? She watched through a sea of children as Gwen sat at the pottery wheel. She looked sad, like she knew Natalie had let her down. Natalie could feel her chest tighten. She clenched her hands against the steering wheel and stared through the big square windows into the ceramics store. She tried counting the raw pottery on the shelf, *1-2-3-4-5-6-7-8-9-10*. It didn't work. Counting didn't work for Natalie; that was Gwen's thing.

Sounds began to dull. It always started this way, a warning. She took a deep breath, then another. If she didn't stop it, what would she do? She focused on Gwen, watching the clay rotate in her hands. Natalie had to claw it back or who knew what would happen. She needed to leave—get away from Gwen in case she couldn't stop. If she had a fit there, she might go inside. She might approach Gwen like this; it would ruin everything.

Natalie started the car, putting it in reverse, and hitting the gas. The car jerked back.

Thud.

It was a thud so poignant it penetrated the sounds she was muting.

Natalie slammed on the brakes. She looked up at the rearview mirror.

The guy with the bleach-blond clump of hair stood behind her car. He punched her trunk one more time for effect. *Thud.* "Watch it!" he yelled.

Natalie sank into her seat. He wasn't supposed to see her—ever. She wanted to take off, but he would remember that and then he would remember her car. He would notice her in the parking lot. She faced forward, but lifted her hand. "Sorry!" she yelled back.

He tapped the trunk. *Tap-tap.* Apology accepted and he scampered off across the parking lot.

Natalie regained her composure. Almost killing Gwen's only friend had been the distraction she needed to snap out of it. She watched him swing open the door to Painting Pots, all the way, the door catching itself right before it would have smacked into the window. He skipped toward the back of the store, and when Gwen looked up from her work, he bowed. A smile appeared on Gwen's face as she grabbed a small wad of clay and chucked it at him. He dodged out of the way and they both laughed.

Natalie smiled too. It had passed. She could stay a little bit longer.

— — — — —

GWEN WENT TO THE movie theater that night. Natalie couldn't believe it. She was so happy she had been able to stay, to calm herself down after she'd almost lost it. She walked through the big glass doors to the multiplex with practiced timing to watch Gwen collect her ticket from the self-serve kiosk. Gwen headed toward the usher and Natalie lurked with just the right distance to hear the teenager tell her, "Theater two on your left."

Natalie purchased her own ticket while Gwen bought a medium popcorn and small cherry Icee. Once Gwen headed into the theater, Natalie stepped up and ordered her own medium popcorn and small blue raspberry Icee. She didn't like the cherry; it was too sour.

She waited in the wings until the house lights lowered and the first preview began. With her potential visibility at its lowest point, Natalie hustled up the steps all the way to the top of the theater. She scanned the audience for the back of Gwen's head. She was easy to spot; she was the only person there alone. Well, other than Natalie, of course. Natalie trotted back down five rows to land three rows behind and two seats to the left of Gwen. Perfect.

— — — — —

NATALIE DIDN'T GET HOME until after eleven. She climbed out of the car, sucking at the melted blue sugar water in the bottom of her Icee, slurping into the quiet night, but as she reached the door to the garage, another noise dwarfed her slurps.

Intense, pained heaves echoed from the main house. Moans mixed with cries, then heavy wetness pouring into porcelain. There was a velocity to it that didn't sound human. Projectile vomiting. Wesley puking out the poison. Natalie had forgotten. She was simultaneously reminded of what she had done and notified that it had worked.

Natalie flung open the garage door and ran up the stairs into her apartment. She left the lights off and tiptoed toward the window. His bedroom window was open, fresh air necessary given the current state of Wesley and his bathroom. All Natalie could see were his feet through the doorway to the en suite. They were bare, their tops pressed against the tile floor, supporting a man stuck on his knees with his face in a toilet.

Natalie crept forward and opened her own window a few inches, enough to hear Wesley heaving again. Heaving, coughing, spitting, then eventually another round of liquid, expelled from somewhere deep inside. Natalie slinked back a few steps until she could sit on the edge of her bed. It wasn't much to see, more of an audio performance to take in.

Not long after, the noises ended. Natalie watched Wesley fall back on his heels, then flop over to sit against the wall, using a hand towel hanging from above to cradle his head. He looked too weak to move much farther and too nervous to put any real distance between himself and the toilet.

Natalie tried one last time to suck up any remaining drops of her Icee but came up empty. She sat alone in the dark in her silent apartment, staring at Wesley, whose head fell into his hands—the visceral surrender only a violent stomach issue can inspire. Natalie's whole body tingled.

FORTY-ONE

- - - - - - - - - -

SIXTEEN YEARS AGO

W E CAN'T DO ANYTHING tonight," insisted Gwen, sitting on her bed across the room from Natalie. "It's not smart. Everyone knows you threw his tray at dinner and got sent to your room. You'll be suspect number one."

"Everyone hates Declan," argued Natalie. "They won't know I have anything to do with it."

"Everyone hates Declan, but not everyone goes super crazy on him all the time."

Natalie hung her head.

"Sorry," said Gwen. "I didn't mean it like that. I just mean that as long as you are the one getting in trouble for doing stuff to him, we can't poison him."

"He's the one who does stuff to me!"

"Natalie . . ." Gwen exaggerated an exhale to elicit one out of Natalie. "I know Declan is the problem. Not you. That's why we're going to poison him. But you have to understand that it doesn't matter what I think."

Natalie crossed her arms, pouting, petulant. While Gwen came off well beyond her years, Natalie had a propensity for the opposite. "You said I could pick something special for my birthday."

"And you didn't think of anything," Gwen was quick to point out. "This was my idea and I don't want to be mean, but we're going to do it my way."

"Tomorrow?" Natalie asked, eyes wide.

Gwen smiled. "Maybe."

- - - - -

NATALIE HAD BEEN THIRTEEN for almost two months and Gwen still hadn't poisoned Declan. Natalie needed it to happen; she needed *something* to happen. She was doing her best to show no reaction at all to Declan, to make herself an unlikely suspect, but it only made him target her more. He wanted a reaction and it was only a matter of time before she snapped. Gwen knew she wasn't supposed to hold things in. *Why wouldn't Gwen just do it already?*

Earlier that day, Declan had spit directly on the back of Natalie's head. A loogie—snot she'd had to rake from her hair with her fingers. His only punishment: going to his room fifteen minutes early.

Natalie had begged Gwen to do something, but she'd said no. Again. Because he had spit on Natalie and the staff knew. *So now Gwen's excuse was because of what Declan did? Even when I didn't react at all? How was that fair?*

All Gwen said was that they couldn't do anything reactionary. That it would be too obvious. She said the same thing she always did—*We have to be smart about it*—the same sentence that made Natalie feel so stupid. Gwen wouldn't keep saying it if she thought Natalie was smart.

But Declan wasn't tormenting Gwen. He was tormenting Natalie. Maybe it was *smart* for Gwen to wait, but every day it was getting harder for Natalie not to react. One of these days, she was going to lose it. Then what?

So that night, while Gwen slept, Natalie slid out of her bed. She grabbed some clothes from the closet and bunched them up under the blanket. Convinced it was passable for her body, she went to Gwen's nightstand and opened the drawer. The poison was sitting there, collected and stored by Gwen in a plastic animal crackers package. Natalie grabbed it and slipped it into her pocket. She waited to see if Gwen would wake up, but her little snores went on uninterrupted.

Natalie crept to the door and opened it a crack. She was not sneaky like Gwen. She was so nervous she would be caught. She could say she was going to the bathroom, but that would only work on their side of the floor. Once she crossed the stairwell, she would be out of excuses.

The hallway was silent and she closed the door carefully behind her. Her socks kept her footsteps faint and she hadn't seen or heard anyone by the time she reached the bathroom—her last chance to turn around. She touched her leg—confirmation that the poison was still in her pocket. Then she was walking again.

Declan's room was at the far end of the boys' side. There was a small desk for an attendant between the two sections, but it was unoccupied. Gwen had told her that once the kids were asleep, the overnight crew played poker all night in the staff lounge. She didn't know how Gwen knew that, but Gwen knew a lot of things.

Once Natalie was past the desk, she picked up her pace and was at Declan's door in seconds. She lifted onto her tiptoes to peek through the window, laced with wire just like theirs. Declan and his roommate were both asleep. Declan was on his back, one leg out of the covers, one leg under. His roommate was buried under his blankets, looking remarkably like the clothes Natalie had left in her own bed.

She turned the handle and waited for a reaction. Nothing. She pushed the door open and there was a creak. She paused, but neither boy moved.

What am I doing? What is Gwen going to think? I shouldn't risk it. This is stupid. I should go back and wait for Gwen to tell me the right time.

A noise down the hall made the decision for Natalie. Someone was coming up the stairs. Natalie slipped into the room and shut the door behind her.

She leaned against the wall next to the door, holding her breath until she couldn't anymore. Footsteps approached and she jammed her eyes closed. She couldn't lose it. She had to control herself. She pictured Gwen in her bed—asleep and unaware of how badly Natalie was ruining everything in that moment. Natalie imagined herself back in the room, safe with Gwen. The numbness subsided, but the footsteps were closer.

Suddenly a light was shining in the window—a flashlight. First it illuminated the roommate, then Declan. Then the light was gone. That's all it was, an attendant on rounds, doing the bare minimum.

Natalie waited until she could no longer hear footsteps, waited until she was sure it was safe to open the door. She was about to make a run for it when she noticed Declan's water bottle on the ground, exactly what she'd been hoping would be there when she'd first climbed out of her own bed. He'd been scolded earlier that night for putting too much fruit punch powder in there, so the flavor must be strong. It was why it had to be tonight.

Natalie lowered herself to the ground and crawled toward Declan's bed. She grabbed the bottle and unscrewed the top, bringing it to her nose. The chemical smell of "fruit" was so potent. From her pocket, she pulled out the plastic package of mouse poison and dumped it in, watching it dissolve without a trace into the bright red liquid.

FORTY-TWO

- - - - - - - - - -

NATALIE

NATALIE TOSSED AND TURNED all night. *Would Wesley know it was the soup that made him so sick? Would he suspect there was anything to it beyond a little food poisoning? What would he do about it if he did?*

By seven a.m. Natalie was out of bed and at the window. Wesley was a lump in his bed. She microwaved a cup of instant coffee and dragged a kitchen chair over to the window. After all the vomiting the night before, he needed his sleep. She brought the mug to her lips and inhaled the scent before taking a sip.

An hour later, Natalie got up and put a slice of bread in the toaster. There was a noise from outside and she sprinted back to the window, but he hadn't moved. It must have been a squirrel.

By nine a.m. she had eaten two pieces of toast, chugged three glasses of water, and dragged a comfier chair to the window. Still no movement. She was getting nervous. He should have at least rolled over.

By ten a.m. Natalie was getting really nervous. Wesley still hadn't moved and she needed to be at Painting Pots by eleven to see Gwen arrive. The thought did cross her mind: *What if Wesley isn't sleeping? What if it was too much poison?* Natalie hurled the comfy chair across the room and it landed in the vicinity of where it belonged. She went to the window and slammed it shut. It was loud, but not sharp enough to startle someone awake. She pushed it open again and coughed as loud as she could a few times, but nothing.

She looked at the clock. There was no way she was going to be late again today. Not after yesterday, when she'd hit the blond guy with her car. She needed to wake Wesley up and she needed to do it now.

Natalie yanked open the fridge and scanned for something that would work. She slid the coffee creamer out of the way and grabbed for the jar of pickles. Without even closing the fridge, she stomped back to the window and lifted the jar above her head. She hurled the jar to the floor. The glass shattered, the juice sprayed everywhere, the pickles rolled past her feet. The smell was strong. She should have dumped it out first, but she didn't care much about the cleanup when she looked across the driveway and saw the blankets move.

Wesley rolled over and reached for his phone on the nightstand. He was alive.

Natalie exhaled before dragging the trash can and a roll of paper towels over to her mess. 10:20. She had plenty of time to get to Painting Pots. She could do this, balance both Gwen and Wesley. She would make a choice if she had to, but for now she could keep them both.

- - - - -

NATALIE WAS IN THE Painting Pots parking lot by 10:45. While she waited for Gwen she ran her finger back and forth across her palm where the pickle jar had sliced her.

Ten minutes later and someone was unlocking the front door to Painting Pots. It was the girl with the big, curly red hair, not the boy with the bleach-blond hair. Natalie sat up in her seat. On Sundays the boy opened. That was why Gwen would go there when it opened.

Natalie scanned the parking lot, nerves heightening. *Where is Gwen?* This was not the routine.

She waited another hour. Stupid moms and stupid kids filing in, but no sign of Gwen.

At twelve on the dot, Natalie peeled out of the parking lot. She drove to all the likely spots. Gwen wasn't at home, not at the grocery store or the movies. She wasn't at Target or the taco place next to the hair salon. She drove to Gwen's apartment four times. No sign of her or her car. Something was wrong.

Natalie pulled at her face. She pounded her fists on the steering wheel. Hours. Gwen had been missing for hours. She didn't know what to do. It was almost three o'clock. If the boy and the girl had switched shifts at Painting Pots, he would be showing up soon. Maybe that's all it was. Maybe *he* had changed the routine, not Gwen.

Natalie raced back to Painting Pots, driving up and down the rows of the parking lot looking for Gwen's car or the blond guy's. No sign of either, so she parked and waited. She picked at the scab on her hand, undoing any healing, and let the blood leak out before licking her finger and rubbing it away. When it scabbed again, she repeated the exercise.

At seven o'clock the redhead locked the front door and left. Natalie gripped the steering wheel, the skin under her fingernails dyed red from wiping the blood for hours. *Where is Gwen?*

Out of ideas, Natalie parked on Gwen's street, knowing she wasn't inside, and waited. A little after eleven, a car Natalie didn't recognize turned onto the street and came to a stop in front of Gwen's apartment.

There she was.

Gwen climbed out of the passenger seat. Her hair was a little messy. She held her cardigan in her arms. *Where had she been? Who was this guy?*

Gwen mounted the front steps and disappeared inside. Natalie wanted to stay, to finally relax knowing Gwen was there and safe. But the car was pulling away. How would Natalie get any answers if she didn't follow him?

An hour later and Natalie had been to a twenty-four-hour car wash and two bars. There was no special place in Gwen's heart for this new man; he was an Uber driver.

Natalie went home. She was exhausted and confused. Something was going on with Gwen and she wasn't sure how she was going to figure it out. But she had to.

There was no car in the garage. Wesley was gone too. Natalie couldn't worry about where he was. She had to stop thinking about him. Look what had happened when she got distracted. She had lost Gwen.

- - - - -

THREE DAYS LATER AND Natalie had still not seen any sign of Wesley. It was possible he came back to the house while Natalie was at work or with Gwen, but three nights straight, he hadn't slept in his bed.

What if he had gone home? What if he'd finished his story and moved out without saying goodbye? The thought bothered Natalie. She had never needed anyone except Gwen, so why was she feeling this way about him? His casual nature, his proximity, the lack of any true details to interfere with whatever she wanted to believe about him.

Or do to him. Natalie had manufactured his significance and was now struggling to unwind it all back to reality.

On the fourth night, Natalie did something she had promised she would stop doing. She left Gwen's place early. Gwen was still awake, presumably on the couch, but Natalie was dying to know if Wesley had returned.

It started raining as she drove back to her apartment—cold, relentless rain that wouldn't last long, only long enough to make Natalie's drive home unbearable. It began to weaken as Natalie pulled into her driveway, but the pavement was flooded and she took the turn too fast. The bald tires on her car hydroplaned enough for her to bump into the garbage bins before coming to a complete stop. There was no damage, only an instant of panic when the tires couldn't catch.

There were no lights on in the house, no signs of Wesley. Only, as she stepped inside the garage, there was his car.

Natalie sprinted up the stairs and into her apartment, racing to the window. She couldn't see anything. The house was pitch black. She would have to take enough comfort in his car parked below.

She ripped off her shirt and had barely changed into dry clothes when there was a knock at the door.

Wesley stood on the small landing. *Was he just sitting in the dark waiting? Waiting for me?*

"Hey," he said. "I saw you hit the garbage cans. I wanted to make sure you're okay."

"I'm fine."

"Are you sure?" He raised his eyebrows, skeptical and not afraid of letting her know that.

Natalie's face contorted. *Why did he say it like that?*

He sighed, teeming with pity. "I don't think you've been okay for a very long time."

"Why would you say that?" she asked, suddenly defensive.

His eyes wandered over her shoulder. "Can I come in?"

"No," Natalie spat back.

He held up his hands. "Sorry, I didn't mean to offend you."

"It's fine." She didn't need someone who felt sorry for her. Or worse, someone paying enough attention to feel sorry for her.

"You know," said Wesley, "I got quite sick from that soup you made me."

"Really?" Natalie said, worried about her acting skills.

"Yeah, in case you saved any for yourself. You probably want to trash it." Wesley looked away, taking a moment in his own head before letting out an odd little laugh. "I really think you should let me in."

The hairs on Natalie's neck raised. She had developed a good sense over the years of when someone was intending to bother her.

"It's not what you think," he said. "Whatever it is you're thinking. I just want to talk. I haven't been completely honest with you." He paused for a reaction he wasn't going to get yet. "The story I'm working on . . . it's not about corporate fraud. I'm sorry I lied to you. But you'll understand if you just let me—"

"What are you talking about?" she asked, genuinely unable to keep up with what he was trying to say.

"I need to talk to you about Gwen Tanner."

Every fiber of Natalie's being told her to shove him down the stairs for uttering Gwen's name. Instead, she took two steps back and allowed him inside.

FORTY-THREE

SIXTEEN YEARS AGO

NATALIE BURST BACK INTO her room, forgetting for a moment to be quiet. It didn't matter; Gwen was already awake.

"Where were you?" asked Gwen, sitting up in her bed.

"I'm sorry," said Natalie, afraid to tell her, afraid Gwen would be upset with her.

"What is it?" Gwen asked. "Are you okay?"

"I'm sorry," Natalie repeated, shaking her head, working herself up.

"Natalie! It's okay," Gwen insisted. "Come here."

Natalie did as instructed and plodded over to Gwen's bed. Gwen moved to the wall to allow Natalie to crawl in.

"What happened?" Gwen asked once both girls were repositioned next to each other comfortably.

"I did it," said Natalie, still hesitant to spell it out.

"Did what?"

"I put the poison in his water bottle. I know you said to be patient, but I don't know, I just thought about it and I couldn't sleep and—"

"Oh," said Gwen, cutting her off without anything to say.

"Are you mad?" asked Natalie.

Gwen thought for a second. "No, I'm not mad."

"You seem mad."

"Well, I'm not," insisted Gwen, but her harsh tone wasn't helping.

Natalie climbed out of her bed, hoping Gwen would tell her to stay, but when she didn't, Natalie sulked back to her side of the room. "I'm sorry," she repeated.

"Sorry doesn't really help anything," said Gwen.

"What do you want me to say, then?"

"I don't want you to say anything. You should have listened to me."

Natalie collapsed onto her bed, crossing her arms. "What do you think is going to happen to him?" she asked.

Gwen shrugged. "I don't know. Hopefully it doesn't kill him."

"What?!" Natalie's face whipped toward Gwen, her mouth agape.

"It was a bunch of poison, Natalie. I don't know what it will do."

"It was your idea!" Natalie shouted.

"Yeah, and it was my idea to wait and be smart about it. Not go dump all of the poison in his water bottle. It was supposed to be a little at a time." Gwen sighed. "What if you were caught?"

"I wasn't!"

"Not yet."

"Well, your idea was stupid," said Natalie. "You know I can't control myself. You wanted me to ignore Declan and I did for like two months. Do you know how hard that was? What if I had lost it? Every day I prayed he would leave me alone and that I wouldn't do anything stupid to him and then you would say it was time. But every day you said, *Not yet*. I don't think you were ever going to do it. I think you were just pretending you were going to help me!"

"Pretending? Natalie, all I've ever done is try to help you!"

"Well, you aren't helping me. You think you have all the answers, but I don't need your help anymore. I did it myself."

"Yeah, and we'll see how great that turns out." Gwen rolled over. She was done with the conversation. She wouldn't be coddling Natalie tonight.

‒ ‒ ‒ ‒

NATALIE LAY IN HER bed, unable to sleep. She shouldn't have said those things to Gwen. She hadn't meant it. She knew Gwen wanted to help her. She shouldn't have used the poison, not without Gwen. Hopefully Declan didn't drink it. Hopefully, if he did, he would be fine.

What would Gwen think if I really hurt him? Gwen said it could kill him. What would Gwen think if I killed him? Would she be afraid of me . . . It was too much.

Natalie felt her teeth clench and her cheeks warm. She rubbed her hands together to fight the tremors, but they came. Then she was standing in the middle of the room holding her pillow—silence—blinks of sanity amid unconscious rage. She had been holding in so much.

Then she was at Gwen's bedside. Gwen looked as peaceful as that sleeping dragon Natalie had drawn, before Declan ruined it. Before Declan ruined everything. Natalie lowered the pillow over Gwen's face.

Suddenly Natalie was on the floor, gasping for air.

She peered up at Gwen, who glared down at her. "You can't do that," Gwen said, almost too calm. "I told you the day I met you not to mess with me. What is wrong with you?"

Natalie coughed. "I can't breathe," she strained.

"You got the wind knocked out of you," said Gwen. "You'll be fine. Now go to bed and don't come back over here or you really won't be able to breathe." Gwen didn't turn away, but she made a scene of averting her eyes. Natalie knew it was because she was afraid to roll over; Gwen was afraid of her.

Natalie crawled back to her own bed as she started to find more oxygen. She hadn't meant to go over there; she definitely hadn't meant to hurt her. Natalie loved Gwen. Natalie didn't sleep at all that night. She didn't think Gwen did either. She craved the sound of her little snores, but instead it was silence.

Natalie counted the blocks of the concrete wall over and over again, afraid of what she would do if she stopped.

- - - - -

IN THE MORNING GWEN was quiet. Natalie was afraid to apologize again. She knew how much Gwen hated that she was always saying she was sorry, so both girls headed to breakfast without acknowledging what had transpired in the night.

When Natalie saw Declan sitting across the room, she was reminded of what she had done before everything went so wrong with Gwen. She didn't see his water bottle. He seemed fine.

Natalie looked to Gwen for guidance, but she was walking away, not noticing that Natalie wasn't following—maybe she didn't care. Natalie was paralyzed. Should she warn Declan? Should she run after Gwen and beg for forgiveness?

A loud screech pierced the room. Declan had pushed his chair back, scraping it against the floor as he stood. It was almost slow motion, but when he keeled over and projectile vomited all over the floor, Natalie ran to him and helped him stay on his feet. The vomit was so red, shooting out of him onto her shoes.

Once he found a moment of relief and noticed it was Natalie holding him, he pushed her away, and something inside her broke.

Other kids were yelling for help, some gagging, threatening to throw up themselves, but Natalie couldn't hear them. Her eyes clouded. She lunged at Declan. She pushed him down. He tried to squirm away but he was pale and weak from the poison. An older boy grabbed Natalie, but she bit him, and he hurled her away.

"What did you do to me?!" Declan screamed at her before more vomit exploded out of him.

The nearest attendant, a slight woman who'd been there less than a month, darted toward them.

Natalie grabbed the closest folding chair and swung it at Declan, whacking him from behind and sending him to the floor in a pool of his own barf. Then she was on top of him again, taking his hair in her clenched fist and slamming his head down onto the tile, blood from his nose starting to mix with the red bile splashing around them.

"Stop!" the attendant yelled. "Get off him!"

Natalie reached for the chair again and whipped it at her, capping her in the knees. The woman screamed, frightened and physically weaker than the hefty male staff members Natalie was used to. The helpless sound of the woman's scream pierced the girl's dark fog, freezing her rage. Natalie steadied on her feet only a second before collapsing. She had messed up again. Only this time, she didn't think Gwen would care.

FORTY-FOUR

NATALIE

WESLEY HAD UTTERED THE two most important worlds in the whole world to her—*Gwen Tanner*—and now he needed to say a lot more.

He helped himself to one of Natalie's chairs. "Where should I start?"

Natalie lowered her defenses enough to take a seat across from him.

"I want to be delicate about this," he said. "How well do you know Gwen?"

"What do you mean?" asked Natalie, debating how oblivious she could play this. He knew something. He knew enough to come to her doorstep and say Gwen's name.

"Do you know who she really is?" he asked.

Natalie wasn't sure how to answer that.

"Her real name," he clarified. "Gwen Tanner is not who she says she is, but my question is, do you already know that?"

"What?" Natalie asked. "Her name?"

Natalie didn't know what he was trying to say, or if whatever he was trying to say even mattered to her. She watched Gwen every day. As children, for years, they'd slept in the same room. How could this random guy have anything to say that would alter her perception of Gwen?

"Her real name is Marin Haggerty," he said, waiting for any reaction, but the name meant nothing to Natalie. *"Abel Haggerty* is her father." His eyes slivered, seemingly unsure of how his words would land but certain they would have an impact.

Natalie remained expressionless. "The one who died in a fire?"

A sly smile grew in the corner of Wesley's mouth. "No, Natalie, no one died in a fire. There was no fire."

Natalie's fingertips converged. She stared down at them, getting Wesley out of her sight while she processed. There had been no fire. Gwen's parents hadn't died in a fire. Why would she lie about that? Why would Gwen lie to *her* about that? Natalie didn't want to talk to Wesley anymore; she wanted to talk to Gwen, but that was a fantasy.

She looked back up at him, but she didn't need to ask. Wesley was brimming with world-shattering information to unload on her.

"Her real father, Abel Haggerty, is an awful man. He was a serial killer and is in prison for life. That's why she changed her name. That's why I'm here. It's what this is all about."

Natalie struggled to keep up with what he was saying. She was struggling to hear someone else talk about Gwen at all. She wanted to tell him to shut up, to tell him he was wrong, but in reality, Natalie had no idea what the truth was. Was it possible she had no idea who Gwen really was—not anymore and maybe not ever?

She was supposed to be shocked about Gwen's father being a

murderer; Natalie knew that was alarming, but she could only fixate on what this all meant for her and Gwen.

Natalie's eyes were burning. She knew they were turning red, if not so already. She glared at Wesley and he started to squirm.

He sat back against the chair and held up his palms as if he could push her budding reaction back inside her. "I'm just here for the story," he insisted.

"What *story*?" Natalie asked.

"Marin's mother, Reanne, was just paroled. She was in prison for helping Abel. I grew up in the area. I was familiar with what happened, and when I saw she was getting out, I thought it would be a good story. You know . . . Is she remorseful? Would she be more forthcoming about her experience? What had she left in her wake? That sort of thing. It was ripe for a headline, *Mommy Dearest Returns* or something titillating like that. But it only took me a minute to realize the daughter, *Marin* Haggerty, didn't exist anymore. She had disappeared."

Natalie was starting to go numb. Gwen was in hiding and Wesley had gone and dug up her secrets. He was going to write about them and expose her.

"It wasn't easy to find her," he continued. "But once I had her new name, Gwen Tanner, I started following her. Not in an inappropriate way. I wanted to figure out the best way to approach her, but that's when I noticed she already had someone following her."

Natalie had never worried anyone would notice her other than Gwen. No one existed other than her and Gwen.

"So I had to know," said Wesley. "Who you were. Why you were following her. I was worried someone else was working on *my* story. But you never approached her."

Natalie's temperature was rising and Wesley's face was starting to blur around the edges. She couldn't let this man ruin everything. Natalie's fingers curled up into fists.

"You spend so much time watching her." He leaned forward into her space. "Why are *you* following Marin Haggerty?"

Marin Haggerty. Natalie didn't know *Marin Haggerty. Marin Haggerty* didn't exist.

FORTY-FIVE

- - - - - - - - - - -

SIXTEEN YEARS AGO

WEN SAT ALONE IN her room, trying to read but too distracted to absorb more than a few words at a time. They had sent all the students back to their rooms, afraid that whatever Declan had might be contagious. Stomach bugs weren't uncommon around there, and always unfortunate.

It had been at least a couple of hours and still no sign of Natalie. Gwen expected as much. She didn't think she would see Natalie again for a few days. They'd have her isolated and on some kind of pills for at least that long after what she'd done to Declan and that poor lady at breakfast. This time, though, Gwen was grateful they had her locked up; the night before, Natalie had tried to kill her while she slept.

Gwen had missed something. She'd known Natalie was capable of violence, obviously, but not against her. After all she had done to help her, Natalie was supposed to be dependent, obedient even.

How many times had her father warned her about this very thing? The second you assume anything about another person, you lose the upper hand. Natalie could have done anything, any night, while Gwen slept peacefully a few feet away. Gwen had never even considered it. She'd always seen herself as the monster and Natalie as someone she could control.

Gwen was disappointed she had been so overconfident, embarrassed she had been so vulnerable. If only her father could see her now. Weak and exposed.

He had told her she was special, but maybe Gwen didn't have what it really took to be like him—someone immune to tricks and charm, someone who couldn't be manipulated. Gwen was the opposite of all of those things. Her father had controlled everything she had ever done. Was Natalie really the one who shouldn't be messed with?

Gwen was agitated. She needed to fix this. Her strategy with Natalie had been all wrong and it had almost gotten her killed. She had underestimated Natalie. She had missed the potential—the possibility of having a true companion instead of a disciple.

Gwen assumed she was destined to be alone in the world, that no one could ever accept the real her—where she was from, what she had done. But maybe there *was* someone who could. Maybe Gwen had sensed it all along, in the hours they spent together, sometimes giggling about nonsense, sometimes hoarding poison. A girl so eager to hurt the boy who bullied her that she couldn't help herself. If there was anyone in the world Gwen could trust with the truth of what she had done to Cody, it was Natalie. She would understand.

Things would be different when Natalie came back . . . if she ever did.

FORTY-SIX

- - - - - - - - - - -

GWEN

NATALIE'S FACE WAS EVERYWHERE. Every mention of the murders of James and Oswald was accompanied by a still of her from that video. I couldn't believe it. I wanted to hate Natalie, but I didn't. She was a girl I had known when I was thirteen. It had been easy for me to erase her significance since then, dwarfed by my sick brain's devotion to my father. But the more I looked at Natalie and the more I remembered, the more it seemed it might be that the reunion we were denied all those years ago was simply inevitable.

She had been my friend and this was what people who were friends with me turned into. Look at her now. Look at Porter and Dominic and even Elyse. I had always been the problem. It wasn't fair to keep blaming everything on my father. I could ruin lives all on my own.

Now Natalie wanted some kind of revenge. She had killed everyone from my past who knew me as Marin Haggerty. For what? What was her goal and how far was she willing to take it before she came for me?

I gripped the bag holding my chicken wrap and used it to push open the front door to my apartment building. Mrs. Magnus's cat was sprawled across the bottom step with his butthole exposed as usual and didn't even flinch as I stepped over him.

I heard a board creak above me and I stopped, straddling the feral feline exhibitionist. I'd thought this part of the game was over. We'd escalated far beyond arms and bloody messages. It was almost too on the nose for it to be her.

I crept up the stairs, ready to defend myself with my keys and a sandwich. I rounded the corner and landed in a sort of half crouch, ready to kick or stab or smother with a wheat wrap.

"Dammit!" I exclaimed when I saw Porter slumped against my door. "You could have called, you asshole."

He had dark circles under his eyes and pale flesh. His hair was growing back into an unsightly fuzz. I went to him and pulled him to his feet. The putrid smell of his neglected hygiene slapped me in the face. I unlocked the door and shoved him inside.

My phone buzzed in my pocket and I slipped it out as I closed the door behind me. It was Elyse. I rejected it. I had to deal with Porter first—one torpedoed friendship at a time.

"Where have you been?" I asked.

"Nowhere," he said.

"What does that mean?"

He flopped down on the couch. "It means it doesn't matter."

"No, get up. You're disgusting." I grabbed his arm and hoisted him back to his feet. I dragged him to the bathroom and shoved him against the wall while I cranked on the shower. Then I yanked him off the wall and pushed him over the edge of the bath. His knees buckled and he dropped into the tub.

"Stop!" he screamed.

"This is over," I said, pushing him down. "I don't have time for this." I held him by his shirt and let the freezing water fill his nose and mouth. He shook his head and coughed and spit and I pulled him back from the stream. When he started breathing regularly, I shoved him back under.

－ － － －

A HALF HOUR LATER, Porter sat on my couch with a blanket around him, shivering like he'd barely survived the *Titanic*.

"Where have you been?" I asked again.

"Around."

"Yeah, you look like you've been around; you look like you were living in the sewer."

"I don't know if you remember, but I was in that house, I moved that body, and now the cops are everywhere. What if I left fingerprints? What if I didn't find everything she planted?"

"Okay, well, I also moved the body and I'm functioning." I had to stop being salty and act more like an innocent person. "Do you think I wanted to take care of that body? I was freaking out. I *am* freaking out. You brought this upon yourself and you dragged me into it." Saying that was hard to stomach given the irony.

My phone vibrated on the coffee table and I scooped it up. It was Elyse. Again.

Porter continued to whine, making it impossible for me to answer. "I'm going to go to prison if they catch me. I need to get out of here. Leave the country. Get plastic surgery. Change my name."

I rejected Elyse's call. I would call her back in two minutes, once I talked Porter off the ledge.

"At this point, I think you need to be more worried about being murdered. You're the one on Marin Haggerty's radar."

"That's not helping!"

"Do you have somewhere you can go?" I asked. "I mean a reasonable place like an aunt in Nebraska or something?"

"Do I look like someone with an aunt in Nebraska?"

I shook my head at his taking offense to that.

"What if I go to the cops?" he asked. "Tell them everything. I think I know where she's hiding out. There must be evidence there. They can protect me, right? Give me immunity?"

"You know where she is?"

"I think so. She paid for this room for me in a motel for a couple nights. You know, before I knew she was a psycho. I'm pretty sure she was staying there too."

I landed on the couch beside him and paused my barrage of questions. It was exactly what I needed to know—where to find Natalie. Only now I'd have to do something I didn't actually want to do. Something I had never wanted to do—hurt her.

FORTY-SEVEN

- - - - - - - - - - - - - -

GWEN

I SENT PORTER INTO THE city with the five hundred dollars' cash I kept in my apartment for emergencies and told him to get noticed. I told him to put a hotel room on his credit card for the night and I would reimburse him. I needed him to have an alibi and I couldn't have him coming back to my apartment if I was about to do anything in the realm of what I was telling myself I was about to do.

He sent me to look for Natalie at a cheap, grungy motel in Revere Beach. It was two blocks from the actual beach, enough distance to obstruct any view of the ocean but close enough to give it a vaguely nautical name. It was the end of the offseason and there were only a few cars in the parking lot.

Most of the motel was dark. There was a light on in the first-floor room that was two doors to the left of the vending machine—the one Porter thought she was staying in.

It was forty-five minutes before I saw her silhouette pass by the window. I couldn't know it was her for sure, but it wasn't a three-hundred-pound man, so it was enough to make me sit up in my seat.

Stalking was not nearly as exciting as they made it seem on TV. I should have kicked the door down the moment I got there; sitting quietly in the dark had really deflated my sails.

There was no sense of urgency. She wasn't going anywhere and I didn't know what I was going to say or how I was going to say it. It was Natalie. I needed her to listen to me. I needed her to stop. But nothing I had ever tried before had worked.

- - - - -

TWO HOURS LATER AND nothing had changed. She hadn't left the motel room and I hadn't left the car. Maybe she was done with the whole thing. Maybe she was going to slink off into the sunset and I wouldn't have to hurt her. I'd never wanted to hurt her.

I yawned. Then I thought about leaving. Tomorrow night might be better for escalation and murder. I'd have a late-afternoon espresso and skip the stalking part. But before I could wimp out under the guise of strategy, her silhouette appeared in front of the curtains again—at least I assumed it was her. The figure stayed there for a moment, staring out onto the street. It was as if she were looking at me, but I couldn't tell if the curtains obstructed her view the way they did mine.

Then I saw the curtains separate, enough for her to get a good look outside and for me to get a decent enough look at her face. It was definitely her. She released the curtain and slipped away.

I popped open the glove compartment and pulled out the largest, pointiest knife I'd been able to find at the thrift store, originally for self-defense and not necessarily to ambush my old friend with. I didn't want to use the knife and I still hoped there was a chance I wouldn't have to.

I gripped the handle in my sweaty hand and waited. Minutes passed and I started to second-guess the whole staring-at-each-other-across-the-parking-lot moment. Had she even noticed me or my car? Stalking was hard. I understood why my father preferred impulsivity when it came to killing.

I almost put the knife back in the glove compartment, but then the motel door opened and Natalie stepped out onto the paved landing.

Then there was no doubt she was looking directly at me.

FORTY-EIGHT

GWEN

THE IRONY OF IT all was that none of this would have happened if I had stayed Marin Haggerty. I never would have met Natalie, and maybe more important, she never would have met me.

She stood outside her motel room, staring at me but not moving. I took a deep breath and ran my tongue along my bottom teeth. I closed my eyes and let myself go back to Cody. I didn't remember much from before I attacked him, but I remembered everything about it once I'd started. The first hit had satiated my need. I'd been feeling helpless and then I suddenly wasn't. But I didn't stop. The second hit against his skull elevated me to powerful. The third hit was to convince myself I was in control. Each hit after that proved the opposite; I had lost control. I was staring down at Cody's still body, tugging at his shirt, slapping his face, unable to garner a reaction. There was no power there, no control; it was true helplessness. It was nothing like my father had promised me it would be.

I slipped the knife into the large front pocket of my hooded sweatshirt—a wardrobe choice I had made specifically for that reason. It's difficult to conceal a long, sharp knife with no sheath, but I was going to have more than a rock at my disposal this time.

I stepped out of the car and closed the door. I was standing, but that's about all that changed. She didn't move. After everything that had happened, she was still waiting for me to tell her what to do, timid all of a sudden, like she hadn't already taken matters into her own hands.

I started to walk in her direction, fast at first but then slowing down so she understood she should come and meet me in the parking lot. I wasn't looking to be trapped inside an enclosed space with her.

Her face was blank. It was a face I'd seen many times before. I had always been so intrigued by the way Natalie's brain worked. It was as if it had an energy-saver mode. When she wasn't thinking about something specific, it was just . . . off. Only, how could she not be thinking about something in this moment? Seemed like a pretty big deal to me.

I came to a stop, making sure I was more than arm's reach away. She stopped when I did.

"Hi, Natalie," I said for lack of anything wittier.

"Hi," she said.

The interaction was anything but verbose so far, but it came with the weight of the world. I had seen her in that video, but this was different. Her dyed-blonde hair was frizzy, she wore no makeup, her shirt was oversized and worn. She looked at me almost doe-eyed, but I knew there was nothing innocent behind her gaze.

"How are you?" she asked, and I smiled, nervous but also because it was kind of a funny question given the situation.

"Um," I stalled, "not doing really well. I think you know that."

She nodded, processing, and I was struggling to understand why she had gone to so much trouble for this awkward conversation to be the point of it all.

"Why are you doing this?" I asked, and her face contorted. Her brain was booting up.

"What do you mean?" she asked.

"You found out my real name, who my father is, okay . . . but I don't understand. Why do all this? Just because I lied to you when we were kids?"

"What do you mean?" she repeated, and I was getting frustrated. I had forgotten how difficult it could be to communicate with Natalie. As interesting as her mental processing could be, sometimes I just wanted to slap her across the face to wake her up.

"Natalie!" I regretted raising my voice immediately. "You killed those people for what? I don't understand. All I want to know is why. I know the last time we were together wasn't great, but we were friends. Don't you think we were friends?"

"Of course!" Natalie smiled as if I'd only said the last part.

"Then why?" I asked. "Why did you have to kill them?"

Her smile melted and a scowl grew. "I didn't kill anyone . . . ?"

I exhaled, exasperated, becoming jerkier in my body language than I would have liked. "James Calhoun? Oswald Shields? My mother?!"

"*I* didn't kill them." Natalie crossed her arms. "I would *never* hurt you."

"Natalie!" I rolled my eyes and took a breath. I had assumed she wasn't all there, but I hadn't anticipated having to work so hard for answers. "We aren't at some high school reunion. You're going around pretending to be me."

"We're trying to help you!" Natalie snapped.

Who was *we*? The implication was that Natalie had an accomplice, only that seemed impossible. Working with others had never been her strong suit. I could hear her words, but I could also see what was happening in her head. Her eyes were glazing over. Her fists were clenched. She wasn't mad; she was desperate for me to understand.

"I would *never* hurt you," she repeated, her cheeks flushed. "You were the only good thing I ever had in my whole life. I didn't mean to do anything to you. That night with the pillow was a mistake. If they had let me come back, I never would have done that again. I promise. It was just Declan and I was scared and—"

"Natalie . . ." I stopped her, starting to realize that she might not have an *accomplice* after all. She was telling the truth or . . . what she thought was the truth. Whatever was going on, Natalie was just a pawn.

I softened my face to try to calm her down. Her head dropped. "Breathe. Look at me. You need to reset. You don't want to lose it. We're just talking. I'm not upset."

"I knew you were in trouble! I knew about those arms and the men who were killed! That's why I did *everything*!" She wasn't hearing me, and when she looked back up, I saw her face—that dangerous look she'd get when whatever she was doing to stay in control wasn't working. I slid my hand into the front pocket of my sweatshirt.

"What are you doing?" she asked. "What's in your pocket?"

"It's nothing," I said, ripping my hand back out like I'd been caught in the cookie jar. "Natalie, who is *we*? You said *we're* trying to help you."

She tilted her head at me for being so obtuse. "Wesley."

"Who?"

"You know," she said, "the reporter you've been talking to."

I took a step back and looked away. I needed to process that for a hot second. Who was Wesley? And why did Natalie think I would know who the hell she was talking about?

"Why would a reporter come to *you*?" I asked. "How did he even find you? I haven't seen you since we were teenagers."

Natalie grimaced. I didn't know those were minefield questions, but it was clear I had stepped into something there.

"It's okay," I said, trying to keep her stable enough to get more out of her. I wasn't sure how to explain that I had no idea who she was talking about in a way that didn't discharge the fireworks. "And he's trying to help me?"

"Yes," she said. "We're trying to find the killer."

I nodded, knowing I needed to allow for a quiet pause before my next words. Being reactionary wasn't going to help keep a lid on her. "And you trust him?" I asked. I couldn't tell her what to think. That wouldn't work on her.

She looked at me funny. She was wondering why I would even ask that. I had to plant the seed of doubt before I tore up the lawn.

"I have to tell you . . ." I paused again. "I've never met anyone named Wesley. And I haven't talked to any reporters."

I watched her fingertips come together as I had so many times before. "He said he talked to you." She studied my face. "Why would he lie about that?"

She was begging for an answer that made sense, but I knew the answer that made sense was going to upset her. "I'm just . . ." I hesitated to get it out. "Is it possible . . . maybe . . . that he's . . . involved in some way with those murders?"

Trying to ask in a nonthreatening, borderline-cutesy way didn't help. Her eyes narrowed as they reddened. Then she hung her head, rubbing her fingertips back and forth, and I knew her brain was in overdrive now. If only there were a button to put it back in sleep mode.

"Natalie . . ." I tried, flirting with the possibility of approaching her.

She glanced up and whispered, "I think I messed up again."

I stepped toward her, but she lunged forward and shoved me in the chest. I stumbled over the parking barrier behind me and fell to the ground.

Then she was gone, sprinting away, out of sight before I could get back to my feet.

I knew that shove. I'd taught her that shove. It was her way of staying in control. She didn't want to lose it; she didn't want to hurt me either. Natalie wasn't the mastermind behind all this, but whoever Wesley was might be. Some random guy I'd never even heard of. Great.

FORTY-NINE

GWEN

I DROVE AROUND THE STREETS surrounding the motel for what felt like two hours when in reality it was about fifteen minutes. It wasn't that I didn't have the motivation to find Natalie; it was that it was dark and she was clearly hiding or already gone. I wasn't going to suddenly spot her on a park bench and tackle her.

Instead, I pulled back into the motel parking lot. The door to her room was still ajar and the prospect of finding something in there that could help me locate her seemed more reasonable than sniffing around the neighborhood like a hunting dog.

The room was tidy but lived-in and I wondered how long she'd been staying there. A notebook rested on top of the nightstand, which was the obvious place to start. I flipped it open and knew right away that it was her journal. She used to keep a journal when we were together. It was my idea.

From the first page, it became clear Natalie had been stalking me, and I mean really stalking me. My foray in sitting outside her hotel room for a couple of hours was not even in the same strato-sphere. I was pretty sure she had been watching me every day. I felt bad. What a horribly boring person I must have been to stalk.

I riffled forward in time in the journal, flipping to the last pages. I wanted to read all of it. I wanted to read about everything she had done and I wanted to read everything she thought about me while doing so. I wanted to sit for hours and hope to find answers. There were a lot of answers I wanted, but really only two I needed. Who was Wesley? And where was Natalie?

When I read an entry where she complained about the water tem-perature in the garage pipes making it hard for her to shower at home, I knew no matter how badly I wanted to keep reading about myself, I needed to find where *home* was.

I went to the small desk that was also food storage and yanked open the top drawer. There were several pieces of opened mail inside. I guess people from your fucked-up childhood who suddenly re-emerge amid several murders still have bills to pay. I guess they also don't necessarily go paperless.

Good old-fashioned mail was the best clue to where Natalie had gone. There was an address right on the front. Obviously. That's how mail works.

— — — —

IT WAS A DECENT house. Much bigger than any place I'd ever lived in, and I wondered how she could afford it until I spotted the two mailboxes and remembered the garage pipes.

There were no cars in the garage and I made my way to the stair-case, headed straight for an enclosed space, something I'd been so adamant about avoiding a couple of hours earlier. At least I still had a kitchen knife in my pocket.

When I reached the door, I knocked. I was, in theory, trying to catch her, but I didn't want to scare her and I didn't really know what else to do.

I waited and I listened. Then I heard something.

It was a wet slap coming from inside, like maybe there was a seal in there clapping for a sardine. I wanted it very much to be that. A cute little seal rescued from captivity—or not even rescued; I'd have been content with stumbling upon an underground exotic animal crime syndicate.

I reached for the knob and opened the door. The fact that it was unlocked was not a great sign. I had spooked Natalie by showing up at the motel. If she were hiding inside, she would have locked the door.

It was a studio space. One room with a bed and a couple of chairs. That's about as much as I could take in before I saw her.

She was collapsed on the floor, curled up on her side, her hand tapping against the vinyl, smacking her own blood, which was pooling around her. Her last movements, trying desperately to get someone's attention.

I dropped to her, not thinking clearly, and rolled her onto her back. There was so much blood, I couldn't tell where it was coming from. I put my hand down on a few likely spots, trying to make it stop, but I only had two hands.

She let out a weak cough, choking on the blood that I had caused to pool in her mouth by rolling her over. I turned her back onto her side and the blood drained out of her throat and down the corner of her mouth.

I leaned closer to the ground, trying to look her in the eyes, eventually giving in and lying down on the floor next to her. I knew that even if I had walked into her apartment and she was dancing naked in front of a shrine to me, I still wouldn't have been able to hurt her.

She tried to speak, but her mouth was full of blood.

Fading away, realizing speaking wasn't an option, Natalie crawled her hand to her head. She pawed at her hair, now thick with blood, pushing it away from her face so she could see me. She grabbed at it, desperate for it to stay back.

"Oh, Natalie." I sighed, reaching out to help her. Her hand fell and I continued to push the hair off her face. "What happened to you?" I pleaded.

Natalie didn't try to speak anymore. All movement had stopped. She was looking at me, but her eyes were stuck now. I should have looked for her. I could have found her. I could have been in her life and had her in mine. The sight of her had completely rocked me to the core. She wasn't the bad guy I wanted her to be.

I pulled my hand back. I wasn't comforting her anymore; I was petting a dead body.

I climbed off the floor and washed my arms and hands in the sink, then wiped off anything I thought I'd touched.

"I'm sorry," I said to her corpse, and then I left her there.

I wanted to know what had happened to her in all the years since I'd last seen her, but what had happened to her in the last twenty minutes was more pressing.

Up until that night, there had been only one other person who I knew was out to kill her. After seeing Natalie brutally slain like that, did I really think Elyse was capable of it? It was so eerily similar to how her family had looked after my father killed them that it *was* believable.

She had called multiple times while I'd been dealing with Porter. What if she'd been doing what I had begged her to do—call me before she did anything to *Marin*? What if Elyse had followed me to that motel and when Natalie had run, she'd followed her?

Still, I was more concerned about Wesley. Whoever the hell Wesley was. This reporter who was so involved in my life story but had never introduced himself? He was either the world's worst reporter or really fucking suspicious.

FIFTY

- - - - - -

GWEN

I JUMPED INTO MY CAR and drove away, careful not to speed and draw any attention. When I was forced to stop at a red light, I ripped off the hooded sweatshirt, knife and all, before contorting my body over the center console to rummage around the back seat for anything I could change into. I found a light jacket and wrestled in my seat to get it on and zipped over my shirt, succeeding as the light turned green.

I drove with one eye on the road, one eye inspecting myself in the rearview, licking my thumb and trying to rub off the speckles of blood that I had missed. Content that I had put enough distance between myself and Natalie's body, I pulled into an empty parking lot to read the rest of the journal.

It was a slow start. The first third was missing a good hook. I hadn't been a very interesting person to stalk, not back then at least. I couldn't tell how long she'd been watching me, but this notebook wasn't the first volume. It got interesting once she started worrying about the Airbnb guests. Then even more so when she started doing things to them.

I couldn't believe she'd almost attacked Brian because she thought he had roofied me. *It was just period cramps, Natalie.*

I got the sense she'd been as bored with my life as I was and had been desperate for something more to happen, something to justify her dedicating her whole life to stalking me. If she had known this was how it would end for her, she would have been grateful I'd spent most nights getting takeout and sitting in my apartment.

My heart started beating faster when Wesley made his first appearance. So did hers.

A man came to my door. His name is Wesley and he's staying in the house. He's going to be there all summer. That's a long time. I don't think I want him to be there for so long. Why is he here? Why is he alone? Is he going to come to my door again? I don't like that.

At first I couldn't help being worried for Wesley, like he was nothing but a character in a book. Natalie had fixated on him almost immediately and I suspected he would get worse than a rotting cucumber. My instincts were spot-on.

I didn't think I put very much in the soup, but maybe I put in too much. I think it was less than I put in Declan's water bottle. They both threw up so much. I'll see how Wesley is in the morning.

The same way she had poisoned Declan—it was chilling. I'd seen a lot of people brutally murdered in my day, but this was different;

this was a strange mix of disturbing and just plain sad. Everything that we had experienced together as children still occupied her whole life. To me, it was my distant past. She didn't have the same luxury.

My sympathies for Wesley dissipated once he blew up my whole spot.

Gwen is not Gwen. That's what he said. Her father is a serial killer. Wesley told me all about him, but it was hard for me to pay attention. He was saying so many things, so many names I don't know, and everything was so long ago, and I just couldn't follow it all. Maybe it's because I don't care. I could tell he really thought I should, so I tried. But it had nothing to do with Gwen. I don't understand what I'm supposed to think.

I appreciated the sentiment that what my father did had nothing to do with me. If only that had been the truth. I had experienced such liberation at the idea that this had all been Natalie and nothing to do with my father. That was gone now—right out the window— as I read on and watched her be unwittingly sucked into a situation she had nothing to do with.

Wesley says I can't watch her anymore. He didn't say that exactly, but I know that's what he meant. I told him I would stop, but I don't know if I'm lying. I want to stop. I don't want her to see me. Not like that. The cops found an arm and Wesley thinks it has something to do with Gwen's father. He thinks someone is trying to find her. He's going to talk to her. He wants to warn her. I know once he tells her, she's going to pay more attention to everything. To who is parked on her street. To who is in the parking lot at

Painting Pots. To who is in the rearview mirror. Everything. There is nowhere for me to be. So I have to stop. At least for a little while.

That had been a lie. He'd needed Natalie out of his hair and after the way things had played out, I wished he had just killed her then and there.

There was an obvious change in Natalie's writing after that point. Stuck at home without her routine, all she did was worry about me. Her entries became repetitive. She was putting more pressure down on the pen.

She waited in her apartment, day after day, night after night, for Wesley to show up and update her, to tell her I was okay, to recount the fictitious interactions we had on occasion—not too much to overplay his hand but enough to satiate Natalie's cravings. Then, when there was another arm, and then bodies, she couldn't take it anymore. She begged Wesley to let her do more; they needed to do more.

Wesley brought over pictures for me to look at. It was the blond guy from Painting Pots. His name is Porter. Wesley has been following him. Porter looks so different. His hair is gone. His clothes are different. He's with all these other strange guys. They all wear so much black and hang out in this dark apartment. Wesley showed me pictures he got from the building across the street. You could see inside. Posters of mug shots. Wesley told me they were of other serial killers. Wesley is worried that maybe we were wrong about everything. Maybe the killer isn't looking for her. Maybe the killer is someone she knows. Wesley hasn't told Gwen about Porter yet. He told me first. It's how I can help Gwen. Wesley has an idea.

Of course Wesley had an idea. Showing her pictures of Porter with Jake and his friends would be shocking; it would be suspicious. Maybe it would have been to me too if I hadn't been the one to introduce him to them, to watch him become one of them.

Then Wesley dropped a bomb.

Porter is going to visit Abel Haggerty in prison. Wesley bribed a guard to tell him who was going to see Abel, and Porter is on the list. This isn't right. Porter could be dangerous. I should have just run him over the day I hit him with my car. Wesley needs to tell Gwen. I will if he doesn't. Somehow. I'll figure out some way to tell her. But Wesley wants to try something first.

He'd had a plan. Natalie would leave her apartment and move into a motel. She would dye her hair. He would get her new clothes and colored contacts. She wasn't going to be Natalie Shea anymore. She was going to be me.

That was when "Marin Haggerty" had approached Porter—the fateful Old Navy rendezvous.

I told Wesley I don't think Porter has anything to do with this. He was very nice. He really believed I was her. I pulled it off. I like that I could be her. That someone could believe I was her. If Porter had anything to do with this, he would have known I was just an impostor. I didn't like how he asked so many questions, but I just thought of Gwen. I thought of how she would talk, what she would say or not say. It was easier to talk to him as her. Easier than it ever is for the real me. He wanted to get coffee, but I said no. He invited me to a party, but I said no. I think he really liked me. I think we could be friends too. Once Gwen and I are friends again.

Of course Porter was not this sinister figure Wesley had planted in Natalie's mind, but I think he knew that. What Natalie thought was a fruitless endeavor had accomplished exactly what it was meant to do—leave Porter thinking he had met Marin Haggerty. He wouldn't be able to keep that to himself and it would set off the next chain of events. While finding answers was nice, I was irritated at how flawlessly Wesley's little plans had worked.

Until they hadn't.

If Porter tells anyone that he met her, he will be in real danger. If we were right the first time and someone is doing all of this to find her, they will kill Porter to know what he knows. The killer doesn't know it was just me pretending to be her. I shouldn't have done what I did. This is my fault. Wesley keeps telling me Porter will be okay, but I know he's just saying that to make me feel better. He says he's going to figure something out, but if he won't do anything to keep Porter safe, then I will.

Oh, Natalie, I should have known you were in there somewhere. When you think you have Natalie figured out, when you think she's a puppet at your disposal, Natalie is going to Natalie.

He underestimated the urge she would have to fix what she had done by putting Porter in danger, the responsibility she would feel. She got Porter a room on the other side of the motel she was in. He needed a place to stay and she needed to keep an eye on him. She didn't tell Wesley.

Wesley has a place Porter can stay. Some friend who lives in Saugus is out of town for a while. He gave me the address so I could give it to Porter. I didn't tell him Porter was here. He's upstairs, on the far end. I paid for two nights, but I can't afford to keep him here with me forever. This is a good option. I'm glad Wesley meant it when he said he would help Porter.

If only Natalie had known where she had really sent Porter . . . what he would find when he got there. I was glad she would never know, but I hated that it had renewed her faith in Wesley. Even if it was short-lived.

Gwen's mother is dead. The killer is getting closer to her. I can't sit all day in the motel hiding. I want to do more. I begged Wesley to do more, but he says we need to be patient. He told me we had to be smart about it and I hated that. I can have good ideas too. I know her better than anyone. And you know what? I do have an idea.

I miss having Porter at the motel. It was nice having someone to watch again. But it's not safe for him to be here, because if the killer knows Porter met her, then . . . But what if the killer didn't need Porter to know who she was? What if the killer could find the same woman that Porter did? Then Porter would be safe. Then the killer wouldn't be looking for Gwen anymore. Maybe Gwen will see me, but when this is all over, I will explain everything. I will tell her what I did to keep her safe.

She'd wanted to be the hero—my hero. Natalie had released that video. The one I'd watched, holding Elyse's hand, about to learn that Elyse knew the truth of what I'd done to her family. Natalie had disobeyed Wesley, but if he had known how much her actions had actually hurt me, he would have been thankful.

Wesley is not happy. He says I'm in danger now. He says the police will be looking for me and so will the killer. That if I'm dead, I can't do anything to help Gwen. I think he's right. I was frustrated and impatient. I acted out and now I might have ruined everything.

Why do I always do this?

The journal entries slowed as I read the final few pages. She had spent her last days sitting alone in that motel room, eating Easy Mac and watching *Criminal Minds* reruns, worried someone who had seen her as Marin Haggerty would come for her.

Finally someone had. But it was only me.

Natalie wasn't the psycho killer I'd thought she was. Instead, she was the person who'd cared the most about me, even if she had a funny way of showing it. And, of course, now she was dead too.

I talked a big game about being a loner, but she was yet another person killed just for being in my life. She was by far the most devastating one yet, but it was hard to wallow in the sorrow of it when all I could think was *How was this going to end?*

PART
THREE

FIFTY-ONE

N SOME WAYS, I was back to square one. It wasn't Natalie. I had no idea who Wesley was. It's not like her journal had included a scan of his passport. She never even described any physical attributes I could use.

I threw the journal down on the passenger seat.

I grabbed my phone and searched some combinations of **Wesley Reporter**, **Wesley Editor**, et cetera, but I knew it was about as likely he was a proctologist as actually some kind of journalist.

I tried **Wesley alias** and **Wesley criminal record**, but nothing. I looked at a lot of local Wesleys on social media but didn't find anything constructive.

I knew my best shot was probably the house. Can you rent anonymously? Or under an alias? Maybe not technically, but it wasn't like this guy hadn't gone to great lengths on everything else.

I should have been going full Nancy Drew, but I'd just lain in the blood of my only childhood friend and pulled an all-nighter and the sun was barely up. I couldn't have one of those montages where I combed through microfiche at the library or pulled liquor store security camera footage. Nothing was open yet and I didn't want to be alone.

I started my car.

— — — —

I PUNCHED THE ENTRANCE code into the panel—the code she hadn't hesitated to give me. I pushed the square elevator button, *1-2-3-4-5*, imploring it to turn green. It was too slow. I gave up, flinging open the door to the stairwell and running up to the third floor.

I banged on her door until it opened.

"Hi." Elyse stood before me in tiny flannel shorts and a crewneck sweatshirt that hung off her shoulder.

I lunged past her into the apartment. "She's dead," I blurted out, no compassion for clearly having woken her up.

Elyse approached me, extending her arms, not to touch me but more like to wrangle in my chaotic energy. When I stopped moving she glanced below my neck, the triangle of my blood-splattered shirt showing above the jacket zipper. She reached slowly toward the zipper and I let her yank it down.

My shirt was undeniably bloody and she inhaled before speaking. "What hap—"

"I found her," I said, "but she was dead."

"Who?"

"Nat— Marin Haggerty is dead!" I shouted. "Did you have something to do with this?"

Elyse's eyes grew and then she took a step back. "What? What happened? I didn't have anything to do with it." She was disgusted by the accusation, as if she hadn't been saying it for weeks.

I explained what had happened as best I could. It made sense to her that someone had killed Natalie, given Elyse thought she was

Marin and someone was out doing kills for Abel's attention. There was so much I wanted to say, but I didn't want to push my luck with Elyse. I wasn't confident that I was coherent enough to juggle all the secrets and lies, and if I let the wrong details slip, it could ruin everything. Or at least the little bit I had left that wasn't already ruined.

She brought the conversation to an end when she looked me square in the face and said, "I'm sorry I involved you, but I'm glad Marin Haggerty is dead."

She gave me, Gwen, a fresh towel and a set of clothes to change into. I took a shower while she made me a breakfast cocktail that would help me relax. She took excellent care of Gwen, relieved Marin was dead.

Elyse's all-white bedding was so clean and sterile it reminded me of my bed at the facility, only hers was much more comfortable—significantly higher thread count, pillow top, an actual box spring. Crawling under the covers, fresh from the shower, swimming in an oversized sweatshirt of hers, it was almost like I could relax for a minute.

She climbed onto the other side of the bed, staying on top of the blankets, allowing me the privacy of being alone underneath. There were a million things we should talk about, but I wanted to enjoy this break as long as I could. I wanted to pretend I was Gwen Tanner.

"Why did you call me so many times last night?" I asked.

"Oh." She sighed. "Jake and I were fighting."

"Why?" I rolled onto my side, tucking part of the blanket under my cheek.

"We've just been fighting a lot. All the time, really. We both pick stupid arguments over nothing. We have very different ideas of the future and he struggles with how the past affects me." Her voice cut out, her breath shaky. I was reminded again what I had taken from her—how horrible her past was.

"Tell me about your family," I said.

"It's okay," she said, trying to hide that she was upset.

"Really," I insisted. "I'd rather listen than talk right now."

"What do you want to know?"

"Whatever you want to tell me."

She thought about it. "I don't remember that much. I was so young. I guess I should be grateful for that."

I didn't respond. She was grasping for a way out of the conversation, but I wanted to hear more. I wanted to know what kind of family I had destroyed.

"My parents weren't really the lovey-dovey type. I think they were tired. The three of us were a lot, me and my brothers." She picked at her fingernails. "I miss Blake the most," she continued. "He was the nicest to me. He was nerdy; puberty was hitting him hard. He didn't have a lot of friends, so he was one of the only people who enjoyed my company."

"What about your other brother?" I asked. I wanted to know what she thought of that little shit. Maybe there was room for forgiveness if she didn't like him either.

"Cody was tougher. We were too close in age. He was big for ten, kind of a bully. Blake and I naturally got along better. But Cody could be sweet sometimes. If no one was looking."

"I'm sorry," I said. I was sorry her family was brutally murdered, and I was sorry I was the reason why.

— — — — —

AT SOME POINT AFTER that, I fell asleep. I don't know how. I must have been so exhausted. I must have felt safe enough to close my eyes. Elyse might have put something more in that drink, but I wasn't complaining.

When I woke up, I was disoriented and it took me a minute to remember where I was. I was in Elyse's bed and I was alone. It was much brighter outside than when I'd arrived. There was no sign of her. I reached over to the nightstand where my phone was and saw a text from her saying she had to go to work but didn't want to wake me.

No one else had texted. I shot off a round of messages that seemed routine by now.

A few to Porter.

Me: Where are you?
Me: Please text me back ASAP.
Me: Or call. 🙏

And then Dominic. I'd asked him to lay low, but given what had transpired since, this was too low.

Me: I really need to talk to you.
Me: I'm worried.
Me: Please 🙏😔😈

I slipped out of bed and went in search of something I could wear home. I found yoga pants and kept the sweatshirt that I didn't think she would mind me borrowing. In her closet, I found a pair of flip-flops. They were too small and my heels hung off the back, but at least they weren't covered in blood.

I grabbed the trash bag of bloody clothes and left.

— — — — —

I ADDED THE HOODED sweatshirt and knife to the trash bag and flung it into a fly-ridden restaurant dumpster, hoping there was no reason for anyone to go looking there. I stopped to buy cleaning products with cash, two towns away from the secluded spot I found where I could park and scrub my car clean. When I ran out of evidence to conceal, I headed home. It didn't feel right going back to my apartment, but I had nowhere else to go. It was Gwen Tanner's apartment and I wasn't feeling very Gwen Tanner at the moment.

Mrs. Magnus's cat sat sprawled across the landing outside my door, but when he saw me, he jumped to his feet and scurried back downstairs like even he found me unrecognizable.

I sat on my couch. I didn't know what to do next. I should want to do something. Something to find Wesley—whoever he really was. That had to be an alias. It was all so personal. It had to be someone connected to me or my father. Someone I had met. I'd gained nothing from finding Natalie or from her death. I was right back in the same place and all I wanted to do was lie down.

Where was the spiraling panic from having no control—the thing that had driven me to do so many stupid things? Instead, it felt like nothing I could do would matter. This was new. Was this worse?

I wasn't a detective. I just thought I was smart because of a bunch of ardent slogans my psycho father had brainwashed me with. I was happy to have been on the journey, realizing I could be something other than my father's daughter, but I did miss thinking it gave me some kind of advantage over other people.

I still had the house lead, but it seemed like a lot of work to find out that he had rented it using the same dumb fake name. He would have needed ID though.

I sat up.

Despite being almost thirty, I knew someone who made fake IDs. The birthday boy—John.

FIFTY-TWO

WENT TO THE GUYS' apartment, but I found no John. There were only two guys there and I couldn't have told you their names for any amount of money. One of them gave me John's number, but he wasn't answering. That seemed bad. If John had made someone a Wesley ID and that person knew I had talked to Natalie, poor John might have become too much of a loose end. At least he wouldn't have been murdered because of his relationship to me. Just more of an old-fashioned cleanup job. RIP, John. Maybe.

If I couldn't find the person who made fake IDs, I wanted to find the person who'd told me about John's talent in the first place. The problem was, he wasn't answering any of my texts. He hadn't been for days. I started to hope it was because he was Wesley and not because he was another loose end that had to be dealt with.

I didn't think I could handle him being dead.

- - - - -

DOMINIC'S APARTMENT DIDN'T HAVE a fancy buzzer like Elyse's or an annoying carpet that prevented the front door from closing like mine. It relied on the old-fashioned system of texting the person you were there to see and waiting for them to come down. That wasn't going to work for me since Dominic wouldn't answer any of my texts.

With the lack of a better plan, I knocked on the front door. I waited for reactionary sounds, a floorboard creaking or a chair skidding, but there was nothing. I took a step back from the door to look up at the second-floor windows. The two I could see were both open, letting the breeze pass through the screens. If Dominic was actually inside, he was being still and silent, and that wasn't a good sign.

Was I really going to climb on the trash can and break in again? I jogged back down the porch steps and drifted toward the narrow path along the side of the house.

"Can I help you?" A voice met my back and I combo jumped and spun around.

"Hey. Hi. Hey," I said as the best defense of my actions.

I realized who it was right away. "Kevin, right?"

"Yeah," he said, still confused by who I was and what I was doing.

"Sorry," I said, moving closer and getting some distance from my suspicious positioning in the path. "I'm Gwen, Dominic's friend."

His posture relaxed immediately. "Oh, sorry. I didn't know." Kevin looked nothing like Dominic or Jake or even Megan for that matter. He was fit and clean-cut, with well-fitting khaki pants and a tucked-in shirt. He was more like a Brian, and in a different context, I would have been open to grabbing a meaningless two to three drinks with him.

"Is he home?" I asked.

"I don't think so." He glanced up toward the open windows. "I got back a couple nights ago and haven't seen him."

"Is that normal?"

He shrugged. "Sure. I mean, he goes to visit Barbara sometimes."

"Can you try calling him?" I asked.

"Why?"

"I forgot my phone and I'm trying to get ahold of him." I prayed I wasn't about to have one of those sitcom moments where my phone beeps in my pocket the moment I lie about not having it with me.

Kevin took his phone out and tapped the screen a few times before holding it up to his ear.

While it rang, he stared at me. Too closely for my liking.

He took the phone from his ear. "Didn't answer."

I rubbed my hand across my forehead. Dominic of all people should know that I would be assuming the worst if he wasn't responding to anyone.

"I wouldn't worry about it," said Kevin. "If he's at Barbara's, he probably doesn't have service."

"Can I give you my number?" I asked. "And if he calls you back, will you text me?" I pulled my phone from my pocket.

"I thought you didn't have your phone."

Shit. I was literally a disaster; I didn't even need my phone to give him *my* number. To think I was anything like my father was becoming comical. I didn't know what to say; instead I made a face that was equal parts *I'm embarrassed* and *This is awkward*.

"I don't want to get in the middle of anything," he said.

"No, no," I insisted. "I'm just crazy." Self-deprecation for the win. "When someone doesn't respond to me, I always think the worst— death, destruction, you know? I'm working on it, but it would help if I had confirmation he was alive."

He shook his head but handed me his phone and I entered my contact information. I gave it back and he did his best to comfort me. "Seriously, don't worry about him. He's probably with Barbara and he's a space cadet anyway. Really bad about checking his phone."

"Thanks," I said as he stepped past me toward the porch.

"See you later, Gwen," he said, looking back with a smile before unlocking the front door and leaving me on the curb.

Kevin could be right. Dominic could be with his mother. She lived in the sticks in New Hampshire and it was nice to think he was there taking care of her with no cell service. He wasn't ignoring me because he was dead; he was busy being a doting, selfless son. While Dominic being with Barbara was an optimal explanation, it was a complete guess from Kevin, who was probably just trying to get Dominic's crazy girlfriend off his property.

Could I accept that Dominic was visiting his mother? Swallow that excuse to make myself feel better? No. I kept thinking about him being dead. He wasn't returning any calls because whoever was behind this had chopped him into bits. Or, worse, had buried him alive, and instead of searching for him, I was like, *Oh cool, he's with his mom.*

Whoever was behind this was definitely winning. I was losing it. I had to get out of the city. Time for a little road trip. New Hampshire's lovely in the spring.

FIFTY-THREE

BARBARA COOK LIVED IN Franconia, New Hampshire. A quick search on a website called VerifiedData.com gave me her address with minimal effort. It was so easy I ended up googling Gwen Tanner and Marin Haggerty. Gwen Tanner showed my current address and the one I'd had before that one, and I regretted every credit card I'd ever opened. The Marin Haggerty search came up empty at least.

It took around two hours to drive there. It was a pleasant little town, with a ski resort closed for the season and some other nature-y stuff—thankfully nowhere near the pond my mother's body was hopefully still submerged in.

The house was small and it didn't look like more than a couple of people could live there comfortably. There was no sign of Dominic's car or the tour van. The only vehicle in the driveway was a silver Honda Civic that I didn't recognize.

I followed a stone path from the driveway to the front door, taking smaller-than-usual steps to stay on the stones. I reached the door, but it opened before I could knock. A middle-aged woman in nurse scrubs greeted me.

"Thank you for coming," she said, dipping back into the house and allowing me to follow.

She scrambled around for her purse and coat and it was obvious she thought I was someone else. "She's easy—already asleep and probably won't wake up. If she does, you can usually take her to the bathroom and then she'll go back to sleep. She can be a little disoriented, so if she's upset, you can turn on the Game Show Network."

"Okay," I said, knowing I should explain that I was not there to relieve this caretaker—that I was actually a complete stranger with zero medical training—but how would that help anyone? This lady clearly had somewhere to be. Whoever she thought I was would show up soon. No harm, no foul.

The home nurse, or whatever she was, left me there having asked only one question: "Do you have any questions?" When I shook my head, she was satisfied and that was that.

I stood alone in the living room. The furniture was dated and sparse. There was a worn couch with a quilted blanket placed over it and a recliner that seemed wider than the doorway. The small table next to the chair was crowded with cups, pills, tissues—things that informed me it was mostly where the sick lady sat.

I meandered toward the kitchen, peeking my head in, feeling that if I stayed in the living room, I wasn't quite trespassing yet. The kitchen was tiny like everything else, one counter with a row of wooden cabinets that had a shoddy coat of white paint over them and one rectangular table against the wall, with room for four chairs if anyone ever pulled it back, but it seemed content now with only two seats.

I moved away from the kitchen toward the hallway. The carpet was the same, running uninterrupted from the living room. There were three doors all in a row, *1-2-3*, all closed. I put my ear to the first one and could hear her breathing. They were weak, raspy breaths, the kind I thought might stop at any moment and she would be dead, but she kept breathing and I moved to the second door. There was no part of me that wasn't going to open that door, but I inhaled, pretending I had seriously debated it, then turned the knob on the exhale.

It was a bathroom, super anticlimactic. Toilet, shower, sink, lots of grab bars to help someone in her condition function. I closed the door and moved on.

I wasn't looking for anything in particular, but I had driven all this way and had a history of breaking in and snooping around Dominic's life. It was our thing. I remembered how that freak had known I was there in his closet and had played the whole thing out just to mess with me. What an interesting guy. Definitely a weirdo, but in an appealing way. I tried to stay breezy about it, but I knew I would be devastated if he was dead.

The third room was finally something I could enjoy. It was a second bedroom, with a twin bed in the corner, but more accurately, it was a storage closet. Hard to tell if it was last month or ten years ago, but his mom had definitely been moved there hastily. There were boxes stacked to the ceiling with minimal labeling. A few had *kitchen* or *bathroom* scribbled on them with a Sharpie, but most were nondescript.

I pulled one of the boxes without any labeling down onto the twin bed. It was full of toys, old toys that maybe could be worth something. It made me all sorts of nostalgic, not from memories of playing with those toys but from memories of seeing the commercials for them on the box TV in the recreation room at the facility. I used to tell Natalie how much each thing cost as if I had any idea. I would confidently report to her, "That game costs $12.99. It's not worth it.

Those pieces are going to break the first time you play." She'd believed every word I'd said and it made her a little less sad about the fact that we were never going to have any of those toys.

Stop. Don't think about her, I scolded myself. This was new. It was unusual for the memories of Natalie that bubbled up to be pleasant—to elicit a warm feeling. The norm was for every memory of our time together to be framed by how it had ended. As it turns out, that night in our room as teenagers wasn't how it had ended after all. Instead, I'd held her in a pool of her own blood after my stalker had slit her throat. I guess now that she was gone, dead because of knowing me, I could remember her differently. I was becoming such a sap. It was hard to recognize myself.

I took an old Nintendo DS out of the box. The edges were scuffed and some of the color had worn off the buttons. I tried to turn it on, but who knows how long the thing had been in storage, and it might as well have been a rock.

That box was fun, but I moved on. There were *a lot* of towels, dishrags, washcloths. Some of them were crunchy. Why on earth had these survived the move? There had clearly been some depression-era thinking in the packing process. The stuff was too old to even be Barbara's, more like her parents'. Hoarding passed down from generation to generation. When Barbara died, would Dominic move all this shit into his apartment?

There were lots of souvenirs, like those tiny spoons, a million magnets, postcards from friends with the most generic greetings-from-wherever messages. Barbara had lived a nice life, which made it even sadder to think of her in the room two doors away, her days filled with the Game Show Network and deciding whether to stay in bed or sit in that chair. She couldn't be that old, but the illness had robbed her of years, leaving her with the existence of a lonely elderly woman.

I stumbled upon a box of Dominic's old art projects. They were cute, of course, but I didn't think he was very creative. Lots of dogs. Everything was a dog or a blob where the teacher had labeled it *"Dog"—Dominic, Age 5.*

Finally I came across some pictures. There was a smaller box inside one of the bigger boxes stuffed with those paper envelopes that pictures used to come in when you had to get them developed. I flipped through a bunch—people I didn't know, fluorescent fashion, feathered hair, the occasional kid I thought must be little Dominic, a man who was maybe his father, then more men who were pretending to be his father. Barbara had been a total babe.

There were a bunch of loose pictures at the bottom, not part of any particular roll. I grabbed a stack of them. More of the same, too many pictures of buildings and landmarks from trips, multiples of the same group posing with slightly different looks since the luxury of deleting until you got the perfect picture hadn't existed back then.

I was ready to move on to another box but reached for one more little stack. There were pieces of faded tape in some of the corners, and the chunk of photos stuck together as I tried to separate them. They had clearly been in an album at some point, removed and relegated to this box within a box.

The clumped pictures all featured a lady I didn't know, which wasn't much different from my entire experience thus far, but I didn't recognize her from any of the other pictures. She wasn't a stone-cold stunner like Barbara, but she had a perfect smile and I could see why someone would keep a nice little collection of her photos. Maybe she had been Barbara's secret lover. This box of pictures—all the boxes, really—had turned out to be a disappointment, pretty boring, and the thought of Barbara and this woman having a secret love affair brought me back to life.

I just needed one picture to confirm my suspicions. A picture of them together. My hands moved faster, sliding each picture from the stack onto the bed to reveal the next one. It took seven pictures, *1-2-3-4-5-6-7*, before the mystery woman wasn't alone. She sat in a folding chair in some backyard. Her symmetrical smile, a crop top, and a pair of jean shorts. Behind her, picking at the food table, was Oswald Shields, sideburns and all.

I TOOK THE STICKY picture and ran out into the hallway. I burst into Barbara's bedroom like I had every right to be there. She didn't wake up on my arrival. She slept propped up on a row of pillows, a thin tube running under her nose providing oxygen.

I went to her bedside and reached for her shoulder.

"Excuse me," I said, probably not whispering as much as I liked to think I was.

I shook her shoulder a bit and she stirred. I pulled my hand back and she went still again.

"Excuse me!" I basically yelled in her face.

Her eyes shot open and she saw me. She scurried back in her bed, trying to sit up, but too weak to move fast. She started struggling to breathe and I was reminded way too late that what I was doing was terrifying. I'd been so freaked-out by the picture of Oswald Shields in my hand that I had screamed awake a very sick stranger in her own bedroom.

"It's okay. It's okay," I insisted, backing away from her, lowering my voice. I reached for a lamp behind me and turned it on so she could really see me, see that I was a nonthreatening young lady.

"Where's Marissa?" she wheezed.

"She had to go. Everything's okay." I crept back toward her, making sure each step was approved. "I need you to tell me something." I raised the picture in front of me.

"Who are you?" she asked.

I didn't have time for that. I needed to know how Dominic knew Oswald Shields. I suddenly had much greater concerns than him being dead. What did it mean? It was such a random connection. Was it enough to prove it had been Dominic all along? Pretending that his interest in Abel was innocent and born out of career ambitions? His reaction to discovering my identity had all been a ruse? I had let him seep right into my life, exactly what he'd wanted. He'd wanted to convince me he wasn't involved, make me worry about him, and then, when I discovered it was him, it would break me.

"How do you know this man?" I asked, bringing the picture closer to her.

She wanted more answers from me, but I was still being kind of scary and she acquiesced, focusing on the picture. "I don't know," she said. "I don't know who that is."

I flipped the picture back to look again. Maybe I had hallucinated Oswald Shields out of boredom and concern over Dominic, but he was definitely there.

"Why do you have this picture, then?" I shoved it back at her.

"I don't know," she repeated.

"Who's the woman?"

"That's Eva, my ex-husband Mitchell's first wife." Barbara started coughing and sucked for breath until it passed.

I looked at the picture again as if Eva would mean something to me.

"Why would you have this? Why would you have a picture of your ex-husband's ex-wife?" I pressed, not understanding and knowing there was a zero percent chance it was a coincidence.

She grabbed a tissue to wipe away the tears that generated during her coughing fit. "It must have been the kid's. When Mitchell and I split, he left tons of stuff in my house." She started coughing again; stringing so many words together was tough.

"What kid?" The question was guttural. I had been so desperate for answers, but now I only felt queasy.

"Evie's son. Mitchell had adopted him before she died. He was a few years older than mine, but he wasn't smart like Dominic. He was a bizarre kid. Seems okay now though. The boys are still close."

"What was his name?" I asked even though I had a good guess.

She coughed again. "Jacob," she choked out before more coughing prevented her from saying anything else.

FIFTY-FOUR

TOOK THE PICTURE OF Oswald Shields with me. I shoved it in my pocket and left Barbara. Hopefully Marissa's actual replacement would be there soon. I had turned the Game Show Network on for her and apologized. Maybe in the morning she would think it had been a fever dream. There were a bunch of pill bottles next to her bed that could explain that sort of thing.

It was hard to concentrate with all the freaking out. I used to be so calm and calculated about everything. I guess it was because I didn't really have much to deal with. I had crafted a life with precision to explicitly avoid this sort of emotional investment and subsequent breakdown.

Jake's mom had known Oswald Shields. Okay. So what? Did that mean she'd known Abel? Abel had barely known Oswald. Dominic said it was James Calhoun who'd known Oswald. Was Dominic a reliable source? At the mention of Jake's name, I had acquitted Dominic, but Dominic was only one more degree of separation from Oswald Shields than Jake.

Dominic didn't seem the type—a little goofy, always nervously tugging at his stupid hair, rocked to the core when he saw my scars—but it could have been an act. I was an act. Why couldn't he be? That hair. The incessant touching. I reached to my own head and gave my hair a tug. Didn't do anything to calm me down. Then I thought of someone else. Natalie. Seconds from death. Using her last ounce of energy to reach for her hair when I asked her what happened. Was she trying to tell me something about her killer? Like maybe he kept pulling on his hair?

What if Oswald had told them about me? Bragging about his one claim to fame like a good old drunk. It would have appealed to Jake and Dominic, two floundering young men on the fringe, looking for a purpose. Their proprietary relationship to Oswald turning them into Abel Haggerty sycophants, obsessed with anything and everything he had touched. All I knew was that I was pretty sure I had narrowed down the search for Wesley to two.

But I wasn't the only one Abel had left behind for them to salivate over.

I had to get back to Elyse.

- - - - -

I POUNDED ON ELYSE'S door. My almost-three-hour drive back from New Hampshire had me imagining all sorts of twisted scenarios. If Barbara had called Dominic after I left, if he had answered and she had told him about me and about the picture, Elyse could be dead, waiting for me on the floor of her apartment just like Natalie.

I couldn't breathe until the door opened, but even that was short-lived.

Jake stood on the other side. "Hey?" He held his position like he wasn't so eager to let me in.

Of course he would be there now. Not any of the other times I had shown up there unannounced, but now, the worst possible time for him to be there. It was hard to deny that it was probably another really bad sign.

"Where is she?" I asked.

"At work, should be home soon. Do you want to come in and wait?" He backed up to allow me the space to enter and I slid past him.

I wanted to believe he was telling the truth, but I wouldn't be content until I saw her alive. I moved farther inside without taking my eyes off him. He closed the door and followed.

"Have you heard from Dominic?" he asked. "Kevin said you were looking for him."

I shook my head. I wasn't sure of the best approach. I had raced there to make sure Elyse was alive, ready to tell her what I'd found— then we could make a plan together. I was not prepared to confront Jake. Not now, not alone. "When did you say she'll be home?"

"I don't know." He shrugged. "Is everything all right? You seem kind of anxious."

"I'm fine," I said, not very convincing. "Will you call her? She isn't answering me and I really need to talk to her?"

"About what?"

"It's nothing." I was aware that I wasn't making much sense.

"Wouldn't be about something you saw at Barbara's, would it?" He smirked as he crossed his arms.

She must have called Dominic just like I worried. He must have told Jake.

"You knew Oswald Shields," I accused him without any grandeur since it was now implied that he knew I knew.

"My mom did." His tone was trying to deflect, but the smirk was intensifying and having the opposite effect.

"Does Elyse know that?"

"Why do *you* care so much?" he asked without answering.

"Does she know?" I repeated. "Does she know her boyfriend is connected to this whole thing?"

"Jeez." He chuckled, still not answering. "You're worse than Dominic. Yeah, she knows. It's not a big deal."

I closed my eyes and took a deep breath. Was I overreacting? Elyse knew Jake had a connection to Abel Haggerty and to the arms? It didn't bother her? Jake had casually offered up that information to her but not anyone else? I had been there when they'd found out about the body being discovered, surrounded by his overeager friends. He'd said nothing. It didn't make any sense.

"No." I shook my head. "You and Dominic are sick Abel Haggerty worshippers and now I'm supposed to believe your connection to Oswald Shields is a coincidence?"

"Okay, ouch." He laughed. "But you're right about Dominic." He uncrossed his arms and slid them into his pockets. "He does know an awful lot about Abel Haggerty . . . and his *family*. He talks so much about them, you know? Can't keep anything to himself." The corners of his mouth curled. Even if Jake hadn't known my real identity this whole time, he certainly did now that Dominic had found out.

I didn't know what to say. I was in no position to keep pushing Jake about his involvement. I was alone. No one knew I was there. I had no way to defend myself, no kitchen knife slipped in a sweatshirt pocket.

I took my phone out and checked the time. He just watched me. I bobbed my head from side to side, antsy, pretending to be considering the time, pretending I hadn't picked up on what he was trying to say. "Ugh, I have a work thing. I'm supposed to be there in twenty minutes. Will you have Elyse call me as soon as she gets home?" I wasn't sure if there was any way he was going to accept my sudden flip to the casual, but I had to try something to get out of there.

"Sure . . ." he said, looking at me like I was crazy, and I was starting to feel that way. I was learning through all this that it was stressful to make assumptions about murderous psychos. If you're right, you can't trust anything they say or do; if you're wrong, you end up looking like the crazy one. I was happy to be the crazy one in that moment if it meant I could get the hell out of there.

"Thanks," I said as I headed toward the door. Once I was past him, I exhaled—a temporary consolation that he was letting me leave, not symbolic of any real relief. I still had no idea where Elyse was or if she was even alive. I had no idea the extent of Jake's involvement or Dominic's or freaking Wesley's or what I was supposed to do about it. All I could be grateful for was the opportunity to go and figure it out.

I reached for the door.

Then something struck me in the back of the head and everything went black.

FIFTY-FIVE

I STARTED TO COME TO. I didn't know how long I'd been out, but my head hurt so bad that it was hard for me to imagine opening my eyes. There was a humming that I could both hear and feel. It was smooth until it wasn't, and that's how I knew I was in a vehicle, slumped over on a bench seat.

My hands were behind my back, handcuffed together so tight I would have protested had I been conscious when it happened. I tried to adjust but quickly realized a seat belt was looped through my arms, keeping me in place. This was not good. I had to open my eyes.

I opened the left eye first. In front of me was the back of the passenger seat. I was in a van. Dominic's van.

I sucked it up and opened the other eye. It was blurry, but I endured a piercing pain in my head in order to focus, and my vision cleared.

I brought my chin to my chest so that I could see the driver's seat. Jake's profile stared ahead, eyes on the road. He wasn't gripping the steering wheel like a menacing Cruella de Vil; instead he casually rested his right wrist over the top like he was out for a Sunday drive.

He caught my motion in his periphery. "Oh, hi there," he said.

There was enough give in the seat belt for me to shift my legs onto the floor and I sat up. "Where are you taking me?"

"You'll see," he said.

"Where's Elyse?" I asked. "Did you do something to her?"

"She's fine." His answer was flippant. Did he forget he had bopped me over the head and handcuffed me to the back seat? The jig was kind of up.

"Why are you doing this?" I asked.

"Jeez," he said, "so many questions."

"You've made my life a living hell," I reminded him. "You just knocked me out and kidnapped me. I have a lot of questions."

He laughed at that. "Oh, made it a living hell, have I?"

I wasn't scared. I should have been scared, but I was too angry, too annoyed, and too defeated. I had played into everything. "Are you going to kill me?"

He didn't answer, too concerned with changing lanes to exit the highway.

"Why are you guys even doing this? Torturing me and killing me, then what?"

"First of all, there's no *you guys*," he corrected me. "Dominic has nothing to do with any of this. He really is just as pitiful as he seems. Second of all, though, I want you to think really hard about this victim narrative you've spun for yourself."

My head was pounding and my wrists were starting to chafe. I was struggling to stay on board with his self-righteousness—to follow the logic of his motivations.

"My head hurts," I mumbled.

He laughed almost maniacally at that, which I found quite rude.

"*Your* head hurts?" He hit his hand on the steering wheel, *1-2-3*. "*Your* head hurts?!"

"Yeah, you hit me in the fucking head," I reminded him.

"Marin!" he screamed, looking back at me, taking his eyes off the road for way too long.

He turned back in time to slam the brakes and narrowly avoid rear-ending the car in front of us. Once we were safely stopped, he reached up to his hair—the slicked-back black hair I used to think was so edgy. Just as Natalie had done, he pushed it away from his face, lifting the long pieces off the shaved part underneath and revealing a thick scar where no hair could grow. "*My* head fucking hurts!" he shouted.

FIFTY-SIX

T WASN'T POSSIBLE. THAT was all I could think to myself, staring at that scar right where I had landed the rock over and over again. It wasn't possible he was sitting in front of me, all grown up with cool-guy tattoos and an apartment and a life. It wasn't possible that he was anything other than a corpse, buried in a coffin, rotting away into the abyss.

"Gruesome scar, right?" He laughed. I wished he would stop laughing. It was hard to try to convince myself he wasn't completely batshit when he kept laughing like that.

"How?" I managed to ask.

"Surprise! I didn't die."

I could see that, but processing it was something wholly different. What did it mean that Cody Abbington was alive? How was Cody Abbington alive?

"I know you're thinking . . ." His face twisted, feigning bewilderment, preparing to mock me. *"But, but, but you died in the hospital."* His voice was too high-pitched, too shaky—a horrible impression, but he was pleased with it. He grinned as he transitioned back to his grandstanding. "But that's only what they said happened. You think you're the only kid they hid to protect?"

I didn't understand. They'd faked his death? For what? Witness protection? And then he'd just stewed all these years, waiting to come back and exact his revenge? Starting with chopping the arms off the two people who'd tried to help him? I'm sure James and Oswald had come from a selfless place, at least James had, but the answer to every problem couldn't be giving the kid a new identity and sending them far away to pretend nothing had happened to them. Clearly it hadn't worked.

"And you just went along with it?" I asked. "You said, *Okay, sure,* and went off and lived with a new family?"

"Here's the thing," he said. "I did have some brain damage." He ran his finger along the scar and I thought *some* damage was quite the understatement. "I didn't remember what happened. I woke up in a hospital in Maine with a lady telling me she was my mom. Turns out Oswald and her were old family friends and she was desperate for a child. She told me that I had an accident. I was ten. What was I supposed to think? That she was lying and really my whole family had been massacred two hundred miles away?"

"Not your whole family," I pointed out, and my stomach flipped at the thought of Elyse. He had sought her out, seduced her, oh my God. "Elyse. What did you do? Oh my God!" I exclaimed, repulsed.

"Calm down," he said. "It's not like that. It's just a cover."

"She knows?"

"That I'm her brother? Yes."

I leaned back in the seat. This was all too much. Elyse did know? Elyse was part of this? I had always assumed she was involved, until I hadn't, and now I didn't want her to be. "Is she . . . a part of this?"

"Don't get your panties in a bunch; it's not like that either."

"How though?" I continued with short, vague questions, unable to narrow anything down to specifics.

"I had no idea, right? The whole time—when my mom died, through my teens, later when my stepdad died—nothing. A few years ago I was experimenting with a lot of psychedelics. I'd suffered from horrible headaches my whole life—well, since someone had bashed me in the skull." He paused for effect. "Pieces started to come back. Eventually I remembered them, glimmers of their faces—my family. I couldn't place them, and the only person left to ask was good old Oswald.

"He was around a lot when I was a kid, trying to sleep with my mom before she married Mitchell, so I figured he might know something. I fed him liquor until he confessed that my mom had basically stolen me—not that anyone else wanted me. That's when he told me my real name but suggested I leave it at that. Of course I didn't listen, and that same night the internet told me all I needed to know. I had a sister who was still alive, living in Boston. Lucky for me, I had a stepbrother who lived there, so I called him up, rekindled our nonexistent bond, and moved in with him and his buddies a couple months later.

"I didn't remember *you* at first," he clarified. "I was focused on my sister and trying to remember my family. It took me a while to approach her. You can imagine how awkward it would be to tell her the truth, right?" He glared at me in the rearview mirror before accepting I wasn't going to react. He smiled and forged on.

"She took it well," he explained. "She's a lonely soul. It was weird at first, but we just needed time. Elyse and I needed a plausible reason to be spending so much time together. We were inseparable. She was really clingy—just like when we were little. No one questions it if they think you're fucking.

"One night," he continued, "she got the balls to ask me if I remembered that day, really pushed me on it. As soon as she asked if I remembered you, it all came flooding back. It unlocked everything. So thank you for that, I guess."

"You're welcome," I said, one snarky response cracking through my resolve. He grinned, and that was enough motivation not to let it happen again.

"So I went back to Oswald, this time knowing what question I really should be asking: *What the hell happened to you?* I was hoping he would tell me your new name, but he couldn't remember. Can you imagine? That priceless bit of information and he just forgot it. I suppose the specifics didn't matter much; it's not like you'd tried to kill *him*."

He waited for that jab to land, but it wasn't hard for me to resist.

"He did tell me one useful thing. He mentioned that James Calhoun had been the one who'd gotten you out of town. He'd found some boarding school in Pennsylvania to dump you in. There are quite a few boarding schools in Pennsylvania, but not too many that take in ten-year-olds."

He was so proud of himself, but I couldn't handle it anymore. "Yeah, and you went there and broke into the storage units and stole my file. I got it."

His animated posturing cracked enough for me to pick up on it. This part was important to him. He'd been waiting years to lay it all out on a platter for me—how smart he was, how stupid it made me. He'd probably practiced in the mirror. It was part of my punishment and he wasn't wrong about that. Sitting in that van, listening to him go on and on, I knew it might end up being more torturous than any physical harm he had in store for me.

- - - - -

WE WERE WELL OFF the highway now, and I knew where we were headed. The old neighborhood. It was disturbing how tragic this was—all of it, but mostly that he had planned out this grand finale, taking me right back to the origin. I'm sure he'd dreamed about how poetic it would be. He was naive to think I had an attachment to that place, that killing me there would somehow be exponentially more upsetting. The truth was, it didn't matter to me where he killed me. It only mattered that it would be over.

"Elyse is such a bleeding heart," he continued. "She likes to act like she's not, but once I told her who I was, she would have done anything for me, kept any secrets. Her sad, traumatized brother wanted to get to know her, he wanted to remember, and he wasn't ready for the world to know who he was yet. I'd seen how people who knew who she was treated her. It was all so fresh for me. I wasn't ready to be a freak yet. You can appreciate that, right?

"Honestly," he went on, "I thought she would be more ruthless. Back when we would first talk about finding you, I knew she hated you. I knew she blamed you for everything. I thought we would do it all together. But she was all talk, no action, and I worried she wasn't ready to do what really needed to be done. It's not like I was just going to shoot you in the street and be done with it. So I decided to take care of everything for her. I knew it would be better to beg for forgiveness than ask for permission."

"Does she know who I am?"

"Not yet." His delivery was ominous, but I was relieved there was still a chance she would never find out—no matter how much that chance was shrinking.

"Does she know what you did?"

"Not yet," he repeated, jaunty this time.

"And Dominic? He really knew nothing?"

"What did Dominic know . . . ?" he pondered. "Pretty much whatever I wanted him to know. See, right from the beginning, once I remembered you, before I had even figured out your new name, I used Elyse's existence to pique Dominic's interest in your father. Not that it was difficult."

He waited for my reaction, at least an acknowledgment, but I was using all my willpower to paralyze the muscles in my face and avoid giving him any satisfaction.

"He was depressed after a breakup; he's a serial monogamist, by the way, just like his mother. I told him that he was such a great writer and that he should channel his emotions into that. I suggested he write to Abel in prison. *It would make such a great book.* I thought there was a chance Abel knew where you were or what your name was. I thought there was a slimmer chance he might let something slip to Dominic."

"Why didn't you just write to him?" I asked. "Why even use Dominic?"

Jake raised an eyebrow. Pleased I was engaging again. "Well, you know Dominic. He just has that . . . I don't know what to call it . . . nonthreatening bumbling-idiot aura. Plus, if Abel recognized me, that wouldn't be ideal, now, would it? And not to pat myself on the back, but I did have some foresight about how the whole thing might play out, what I might need from that relationship with your father down the line."

He wanted me to think using Dominic had been so calculated, but I suspected it was something simpler. Talking to my father was not for the faint of heart. Especially if he had murdered your loved ones in cold blood.

"Once I found you," he continued, "I couldn't just bump into you on the street. You would have been too suspicious of me. I needed a trail you could follow; I needed you to think you were making the decisions. I knew once I left you those arms, you would think your father was involved. You would look into it and that would lead you right to Dominic. I didn't know you two would become Sherlock and Watson, but I thought you'd do some digging on him and figure out he knew Elyse. At that point, you wouldn't be able to resist getting to know all of us.

"It *was* hard to figure you out." He smiled. "I wanted to take everything from you, but how could I do that when you had nothing to take?" He chuckled like he'd told a joke instead of an astute, depressing summarization of my existence. "A guy you went on a couple dates with? I probably would have been doing you a favor to kill that dud. You're going to laugh . . ."

I was not.

"But I actually considered calling in a health code violation on that sandwich place you go to every day of your life. Absurd, I know, but I was still workshopping everything back then. It was a struggle to ascertain anything I could really use from just watching you in the shadows. Well," he scoffed, "until I realized someone else was already watching you in the shadows."

I could tell he loved delivering that turn of phrase and I hated him so much. He was the same little asshole he'd been when I'd bashed his skull in. Clearly, part of his master plan didn't involve inspiring remorse in any way.

"That girl . . ." he continued. "She was nuts. I think she might have tried to poison me with soup at one point. I didn't dare eat it—I could see there was a weird powder floating around in it—but I pretended it made me sick so she would feel bad . . . or happy, not exactly sure."

"What did she even have to do with anything?" I asked, protective of Natalie, not caring for the way he was talking about her. "You didn't have to involve her. She had no idea who you were or who I really was."

"She was a curveball," he admitted, "but she was exactly what I was looking for. Turns out you two went way back. Well, not as far back as me and you, but school chums!"

I made a point to turn my head and stare out the window as if everything he was saying wasn't devastating, made all the worse by how dumb he sounded performing for me like a total clown.

"My first instinct was to just kill her, get her out of my way. But, of course, I was curious about who she was and why she was watching you all the time. She had all these notebooks in her apartment. Crazytown. Page after page of nonsense. A real slog to get through, but then I saw her for what she was finally: someone I could *really* use."

I would have had a million questions, but I'd read her journal too, so I said nothing.

He didn't care for my simulated apathy and tried harder to get a rise out of me. "Her life was so insular, I knew I just had to penetrate her bubble. It didn't take nearly as long as I thought it might." He shook his head. "Sad, sad lady. I crafted an alter ego, moved in next door, got in her space, played house for a few weeks. One night"—he paused to snicker—"when I knew she was watching, I pretended to fall and pass out. She snuck into my house and rubbed my face. Creepy, but I knew then I had her on the hook. Once I knew she was comfortable with me, or at least fixated on me, then I spun my story and put her to work."

He glanced back at me in the rearview, but I refused to turn away from the window until I thought of something worth saying.

"But then you lost control of her," I said. "You didn't want her to do that video."

"She told you that?" he asked.

"She didn't have to." Technically that was true, but I was trying to come across more as having a gift for reading people like my father and less as caring about the semantics of her having written it in her journal instead of telling me directly.

"Look," he said. "I knew working with her had its risks. It wasn't anything I couldn't pivot around."

"Whatever you need to tell yourself," I said, finally finding something to enjoy in this conversation.

"Does it look like I've lost control of the situation?" he asked.

"Depends what your definition of *control* is."

He looked at me through the mirror. "How about who's in the handcuffs and who has the key?"

"Wow," I said. "A real mastermind."

"Stop," he said. "I know what you're doing. Just shut up and wait. You won't be so cocky once we get there."

"Can't wait," I said, going back to the window. I bookmarked that little back-and-forth. Undermining what your enemy takes great pride in can sometimes be a more effective weapon than anything you can shove into your sweatshirt pocket. "Why didn't you just kill her then?" I asked. "When she did that?"

"Meh," he said. "I still wanted to use her for this next part, but then you went and showed up."

I didn't love what he was insinuating there. If I hadn't gone to her, she would still be alive. Even if it wouldn't have been for much longer, there would have been a chance. And hats off to him; it would have been a real dagger to have no idea of Natalie's involvement until the moment he brought me back to the Abbington house and slit her throat right in front of me. It would have seemed so random, so nonsensical, so unnecessarily cruel that my brain may have exploded on the spot.

"So I had to go ahead and kill her," he said, shrugging.

I had spent my whole life callous toward life and death, but I still hated the way he was so carefree about murdering Natalie and the others. Mostly because he had gotten the better of me. Mostly because I was embarrassed.

"So this is all for revenge?" I asked, hoping he could wrap it up.

"I like to call it closure," he said, challenging the connotation.

"What kind of closure are you going to get from this? You killed . . ." I added them up on my fingers: Oswald, James, Reanne, Natalie. I paused the count. "Did you kill John?"

"What?" he scoffed. "No."

"You killed four people," I continued. "You cut up bodies and delivered me their arms. You don't need closure; you need to be in a mental hospital."

"Probably," he said. "Maybe we could get a group rate."

FIFTY-SEVEN

THE OLD ABBINGTON HOUSE looked the same as it had on Dominic's tour—abandoned, run-down, and exactly the kind of place where you would expect people to have been murdered.

Jake coasted the van into the driveway, trying to soften the impact of the rutted dirt. There were no attempts to stay hidden. Who was there to hide from? This little street was nothing more than an extension of the house, rotting until it disappeared.

He slid open the van door and I tried my best to kick at him. Even if I'd somehow managed to kick him so perfectly in the jugular that his throat collapsed and he dropped to the ground suffocating, what would I have done, starved to death in the van? Maybe I could scream loud enough that someone would hear me? Maybe Elyse would come looking for me? I wouldn't have to find out, because I barely made contact with him. He backed out of the way and waited for me to tire myself out.

When I transitioned from feeling like I was fighting back to feeling stupid, I returned my feet to the floor of the van and he climbed in and threw a bag over my head. It seemed like overkill at first, but as he got close, reaching behind me to unhook the seat belt, I felt the sudden urge to bite him. Hence the bag. I opened my mouth and got a face full of canvas, rough and a little salty on my lips.

He hooked his arms through mine and yanked me from the van. I couldn't see anything and I dropped until my feet hit the driveway. My knees almost gave out, but he hoisted me up, his hands under my armpits, until I was steady. Then he was dragging me. I shuffled to keep pace, nervous to take normal steps when I couldn't see anything in front of me.

We stopped and he separated from me, leaving only his hand resting on my forearm. I heard the grinding of rusty metal, then he jostled my body as his force lunged elsewhere and I heard what I assumed to be the door separating from the swollen frame. The hinges wailed like all the WD-40 in the world couldn't save them.

Jake guided me up a step and through the doorway. The hinges cried bloody murder again as he shut the door behind us. I knew we were inside now, but it didn't feel like it. I expected the sensation of being sealed in, but I still felt the breeze, I still heard the trees rustling.

He yanked the bag off my head and I saw why. Most of the windows inside were smashed, sharp triangles of glass ready to slice the veins of any trespassers. Dirt and leaves had made their way into the house and blown into the corners of the room. Branches from a fallen tree poked through a window to the left. It was a little like being in an abandoned Rainforest Cafe.

His phone beeped and he took it out of his pocket to check. While he typed a message, I heard the noises—inconsistent banging coming from deeper inside the house.

I looked to Jake for some kind of explanation. "Go on," he said, glancing up from his phone, encouraging me to investigate. I could tell from his pompous face that he knew very well where the noises were coming from and what was causing them.

I walked across the wood floor toward the sounds. A swinging door separated me from the next room. I reached the door, my hands still together behind my back, and leaned my shoulder into it, pushing it open.

I stepped into what used to be the kitchen. The banging stopped and in its place were voices trying to form words around rags tied across their mouths. They were on the floor, tied down—one around a supporting beam in the center of the room, the other around a thick pipe that ran through the exposed foundation.

Dominic and Porter stared at me, their eyes the same—hope for rescue rapidly fading with the realization that my hands were bound too.

I ran to Porter first, dropping to my knees with a thud, unable to brace myself.

"It's okay," I said, wishing I could reach out.

He tried to say something but it was indecipherable.

I rotated around; maybe if I could put my cuffed hands near his, I would be able to do something. It was an unrealistic dream, but when I heard the front door open again, it was motivation. Jake had stepped outside. If I could just get Porter untied . . .

Dominic said something and I turned to him, my hands still moving feverishly behind my back to try to get to Porter's ropes. If I held eye contact, maybe he would forgive me for going to Porter first. He was saying the same thing over and over. Eventually it became clear.

"Run!" Dominic was yelling, and he was right. I had to leave them. I had to go for help.

I rolled back around to my knees. Porter was shaking his head, begging me not to abandon him.

"I'm sorry," I said. "I'll be back." I stood to run, but before I could get anywhere, I heard the front door open.

"C'mon," Jake said. He was back and he wasn't alone.

It should have lit a fire under me to run, but instead I stayed. Too curious to know who was with him.

Dominic yelled again for me to go, but it was white noise to me now.

"Don't run," Jake shouted, his voice much closer to the kitchen door. "I have one more surprise."

"What's going on?" his companion asked. It was Elyse.

I stared at the door. I watched it swing open.

Jake walked through first, a shit-eating grin across his face. She followed him, seemingly oblivious to the situation, but in a split second she registered my hands behind my back, then Dominic and Porter tied up on the floor.

Her focus went immediately to her brother. "What did you do?"

He held out his hands, trying to defuse the visual, wanting her to hear him out. "I did it, Elyse. I found her. I found Marin Haggerty."

"It was you?" she asked him, not getting that he meant me and not Natalie. "*You* were the one who killed her?"

He shook his head. "No, that girl wasn't her. See—"

"Stop!" I shouted, stepping toward Jake, pleading with him not to tell Elyse. Not now. It wasn't the right time. "Please . . ."

Elyse looked at me. Trying to understand. "Why are *you* here?" she asked, but she didn't wait for my answer before turning back to her brother, desperate. "Why is *she* here?"

He went to tell her, but I cut him off. I didn't want to give him the satisfaction. "She wasn't Marin Haggerty," I admitted, bringing Elyse's attention back to me. "The woman who died—her name was Natalie Shea."

Elyse's eyes searched for Jake, looking for his confirmation. I kept talking so she would only look at me. "I knew her when I was younger . . . and I knew you too." I hesitated as long as I could. "I'm Marin Haggerty."

Jake clapped his hands together, so pleased with my admission—the smack startling us both.

Elyse backed away from me, covering her mouth as if I were rancid meat.

"I'm sorry," I said, moving toward her, wishing I could reach out, but she cowered away from me.

She turned back to Jake. Only to Jake. "You knew?" Tears formed in her eyes. Her face was pained. Each thought she tried to process led to a new grimace. "It *was* you," she said to him. "*You* killed that woman. Who even was she?"

Jake backed away, sheepish and without the cocky posturing he reserved for me. He was admitting to her what he had done without having to say it.

"And the others?" Elyse asked him. "You promised you had nothing to do with those."

"I didn't want to upset you," he said. "Let me explain." He tried to get closer.

"Get away from me!" she screamed.

Jake recoiled. "Why are you acting like this? This is what you wanted. Here she is," he said, presenting me like a game show prize. "We can finally do this . . . together."

Elyse winced. She stared at him, her face contorting as she processed. "Jake . . ." She exhaled. "I didn't want *this*." She looked at me, almost forgetting for a second who I was before aborting the sentiment. Instead, her compassion moved to Dominic and Porter. "And what about them?" she asked. "You want to hurt *them*?"

"It's not about them," he insisted. "Don't you see? We have to take them from *her*. That's the only way it's fair."

Elyse's repulsed expression returned, but this time Jake was the rancid meat. "*Fair?* It's not a contest. Nothing about what happened to us was fair, but this isn't right. You can't hurt them."

"Don't think about *them*," he demanded. "Think about *her*." He shoved his hand back in my direction, more aggressive this time. "Think about what she took from us. Our family. Our lives. These are the only people she cares about."

It wasn't true. Dominic and Porter weren't the only people I cared about. "I care about her," I said directly to him, before looking at Elyse. She lowered her eyes; she didn't want to hear it. Not from me.

"Shut up!" Jake yelled.

"Stop . . ." Elyse urged him to calm down.

"No," he said. "Don't listen to her. She's lying." He opened his jacket and slid out a knife—a real knife, like for gutting large animals, not for chopping vegetables. He shoved it in Elyse's direction. "Here, take it! I don't want to talk about it anymore."

"I don't want it," she said.

His face dropped. "Elyse . . . it's her. It's Marin Haggerty."

She softened her voice. "It's gone too far." She shook her head. "Look at what you've done. Cody, please . . ."

He cringed at the sound of his real name. He glared at her, waiting for her to change her mind, but when she didn't . . . "You don't care," he said. "Not like I do."

"That *isn't* true," she said.

"Then prove it." He held the knife out again. "Prove that you care about what happened to me."

Elyse shook her head again. "I'm not going to hurt her."

"I knew it," Jake said, tightening his grip on the knife and turning toward me.

"Wait!" Elyse lunged out to grab his arm, but before she could reach him, he hit her across the face with the butt of the handle and she fell to the ground.

He whipped back around, seemingly regretting his impulse to harm her. He dropped to his knees and reached for her.

"Is she okay?!" I asked.

"Shut up!" he yelled. "Elyse," he whispered. "Elyse, wake up."

I thrust toward him, but it was an empty threat. He stood back up before I could get anywhere close enough to harm him.

"She's breathing," he said. "She's fine." He shoved my shoulder to spin me around and take hold of the chain between my handcuffs. "Let's go," he said, slipping the knife back inside his jacket. He pushed me toward the back door. We were headed outside. Back to where it had all started.

FIFTY-EIGHT

THE BACKYARD WAS AS overgrown as the front, the grass so long it could be full of snakes or hypodermic needles. The fence was holding up well; it had a lean to it and the paint was all but gone, but it stood and provided cover from the woods behind it. I wondered which board was the loose one Elyse had watched us through.

The bones of their cheap metal swing set remained, the color of the rust matching the surface of Mars, chains hanging from the top bar, but the seats were gone, probably rotting unseen in the tall grass below.

He pushed me off what was left of the back deck and I started to resist. I dug my heels into the grass, forcing him to shove me forward in bursts.

Our destination was the swing set, and as we approached, he shoved me forward and reached into his pocket, pulling out a small key. He unlocked my left wrist, but only for a second so that he could turn me around and feed the handcuffs, behind my back, through the top triangle of one of the swing set's rusty A-frame supports. I felt the cuff around my wrist again and heard the click. He let go of me then, but I knew I wasn't going anywhere.

"There," he said, stepping in front of me. "Now, you stay here and listen while I go in and kill them. I want you to know what it's like to be stuck out here, helpless to do anything to stop what's about to happen in there."

It was so twisted, and not from his imagination. "You were awake?"

"Just enough." He smiled. "I couldn't move. I couldn't open my eyes. But I could hear them."

I did almost feel bad for him then for what he had gone through. No part of me wanted to listen to him kill Dominic and Porter. It would be worse than watching; he knew it would be worse than watching.

That was all he wanted. He wanted my reaction—to know how upset he was making me. He wanted everything that had happened to him to happen to me, as if his life were a curse and this was what it would take to break it.

Up until that point he had succeeded. He'd been patient. He had created a scenario where I'd let these people into my life. I'd broken all my rules, layered on excuses to justify why I needed to keep spending time with the three people trapped inside that house, when the reality was, I just wanted to be around them.

He'd manufactured this, drawn me out of hiding, pushed me out of my comfort zone, waited until I was in too deep. Now he could take away everyone I cared about like I had done to him. I knew what he wanted and I had to do whatever it took not to give it to him. It was the only thing left that I could control.

"Whatever, Cody," I said, rolling my eyes, suppressing every emotion I could.

I saw his jaw tighten and I knew I was onto something. I had noticed how he'd reacted to Elyse using that name.

"Don't call me that," he said.

"Why?" I asked. "It's your name."

"Cody's dead."

"Oh, grow up." I rolled my eyes again. It was my only move at the moment; hand gestures weren't an option.

He narrowed his gaze and lowered his voice. "I'm going to kill them."

"You said that already," I goaded him.

"What about Elyse?" he spit back. "I'll kill her too."

He intended for that to be a blow and it was. I couldn't tell if he was bluffing. Nothing seemed to be out of bounds, but I had to stay the course. "Okay," I said.

"Why are you being like this?!" He stomped his foot. It was jarring how juvenile it was. It took me right back to that day. That day when he was trying to kiss me and I wasn't interested and he didn't like that.

"Cody . . ."

"I said don't call me that!"

"Well, you called me Marin!" I shouted back at him. We were devolving rapidly back into the two little kids who'd fought that day in this same spot.

"Just shut up!" he yelled.

"I'm sorry, not what you were planning?" I said. "Not getting the closure you need?"

"Don't you feel anything? Don't you feel bad for what you did?"

"Do you?" I asked.

"It's your fault what I did to those people, and they deserved it." He paced in front of me.

"Cody—"

He lunged forward, pinning me against the swing set with his forearm across my chest, breathing heavily, searching for something to say that would upset me, some inkling that I was capable of feeling anything.

"Don't you see?" I said, staring at him, refusing to blink. It was critical I sold this. "One of us is pretending to be like Abel Haggerty and one of us was born and raised exactly like him. You couldn't even control Natalie," I scoffed. "Not like I could." Then I grinned through the lie. "You can kill them, all three of them, right in front of me and I won't even blink. I'll even help if you want. Would that be easier for you? I know it will probably be hard for you to kill your sister."

My insides were churning. I could have *Exorcist*-vomited, but I remained stoic. It was all I could do to take away his momentum. I had to lean into the character that I had always been afraid was genuine. The bile creeping up my throat served as further validation that it wasn't true. Unfortunately, this was not the moment to reflect on the revelation that I was nothing like my father; it was time for me to be Daddy's little girl.

"Come on," I said. "Undo the cuffs. Let's go kill her together."

"You bitch!" he screamed, jerking his arm off my chest and grabbing my throat.

I panicked. I could feel his thumbs pressing down on my larynx. I couldn't breathe. It was like an out-of-body experience, but not out of my own body. More like my life flashing before my eyes, but not really that either. They were spotty memories, memories of the people my father had strangled, the ones I had watched. I could see them, their eyes, but now I could feel it too.

Through their eyes, I saw my father's—a piercing gaze, one eye slightly askew. He might as well have been the one with his hands around my throat.

I blinked feverishly, trying to make it go away. *1-2-3-4* times I blinked until it was only Cody's eyes I could see. They were red, teary, the skin around them wrinkled—they were nothing like my father's.

Cody had had the best chance out of all of us. He'd been sent to a loving home with no memories of what had happened. Elyse and I should have been the crazy ones. We didn't stand a chance given the hands we were dealt. We'd lived with these memories our whole lives and somehow we'd managed.

I closed my eyes; it was getting foggy. I hadn't taken a breath in close to a minute and his grip was only intensifying. It was my time, I supposed. A paradoxical ending—being killed in the same spot by the boy I had supposedly killed, only I hadn't, and now it was his turn. If I somehow survived, would I wait twenty years and then start stalking him? I liked to think I would have better things to do.

All of this boiled down to a moment in time between two kids playing in the backyard. What if I had just kissed him that day? What if he hadn't been an asshole to me at school and he had been nice and when he'd tried to kiss me I'd let him? What a ridiculous thing to think about as I really started to fade away. It couldn't hurt, I thought, to mess with him one last time. I opened my eyes, made sure he saw me, not sure where else I thought he would possibly be looking, then I puckered up. *Is this what you wanted?*

His hands loosened, not so much to stop choking me, but a reaction to what he was seeing. It must have been as disturbing an image as I thought it might be. What a true psycho I would have to be to try to kiss him in that moment.

I didn't want to kiss him; I wanted to disrupt him, and when he relaxed his grip, even though it was slight, I knew I had. I reared my head back and slammed it forward. Our heads collided and his hands left my throat. I gasped for air as I watched him stumble back and drop to one knee. It gave me enough space to really kick him, straight up under the chin, in the soft spot in the center of his jaw.

He landed on his side in the tall grass, close enough for my foot to reach the side of his head. He was still, but I stomped my foot down anyway, *1-2-3* times on his temple with my heel, as hard as I could, given my restricted leverage. I wanted to keep going, to keep kicking until his skull collapsed. Then kick him again. But I stopped.

I reached down and grabbed the crossbar under my cuffed hands. It was abrasive and I accepted the fact that I was probably about to get tetanus. I yanked on the bar, ecstatic to feel the swing set budge. I released the crossbar and stretched my arms out behind me, lifting them as high as I could. I pressed myself back against the diagonal pole, my arms reaching the opposite side of the A-frame. Then I took a deep breath and sprinted forward two whole steps before the chain between my wrists crashed into the other pole and I threw my weight forward.

I seized as I sensed the swing set tipping over behind me until I remembered that was exactly what I was hoping for. I fell with it, nothing in front to catch me except Cody. I landed across his stomach. Then the pole I was attached to hit my back.

I wriggled myself out from underneath, hands still attached to each other through the enclosed triangle top of the A-frame. I inched down until my fingers were level with Cody's pockets and I pulled out the key to the handcuffs. I unlocked one and freed myself, rolling off Cody and onto the grass. It was so soft, no needles, and I lay for a second catching my breath.

I looked over at Cody. I could barely recognize him in Jake's face. He didn't have the thing like Elyse did, the recognizable ridge above her nose. Puberty had changed him more, taking the chubby kid and stretching him out into this guy. I reached over to his throat to feel for a pulse. The beat tapped my fingers and I glanced down to see he was breathing. Maybe I had kicked him right again, undone the damage I had done with the original rock against his skull.

I freed myself from the other cuff and used them to lock his hands through the A-frame. Then I slid the knife out from his jacket and threw it across the lawn. I could lie in the grass having deep thoughts about his unconscious body, but I had to be smart about it.

I finally sat up. He was helpless now. I could slit his throat. I could put my hands around his neck. I could stuff my socks down his throat. I climbed to my feet, gave one last thought to stomping on his face, then I walked away.

FIFTY-NINE

J AKE CALLOWAY, AKA CODY Abbington, aka Wesley, was charged
with four counts of first-degree murder and four counts of attempted murder. He pleaded guilty. Detective Ellison told me he had
spewed a long, rambling confession as soon as they sat him down in
the interrogation room. He explained how I was the one who'd attacked him, not my father—justification for his righteous revenge.

Cody Abbington hadn't died. I hadn't killed him. Aggravated
assault by a nine-year-old didn't have the same ring to it, and in the
midst of so many actual murders, my greatest secret disintegrated
into irrelevance. A fact that I had shaped my entire life around—
gone. Knowing everything could have been different for me, I wasn't
sure what that made me now. I was completely lost.

Jake spoke at his arraignment, another speech, this time aimed at
the cameras. He wanted to be infamous, like Abel, admired for the
lives he had taken, how he had reclaimed the narrative after his trag-
edy. He wanted it framed like a master plan he'd concocted that had
been executed flawlessly, the pinnacle of tragic manipulation. He

very much refused to acknowledge that he had been foiled in the end by a kissy face and a woman with a hard skull.

Fourteen days after Jake Calloway was processed into Edgar Valley, he was found dead in his cell—strangled. It would have been easy to wrap a sheet around his neck, hang him from a bed, and disguise it as a suicide, but his assailant hadn't gone to the trouble. Jake had been strangled by someone's bare hands.

I knew who did it and so did the rest of the world, but two corrections officers insisted they were with Abel during the entire time window. I had seen my father control one of those officers with a look and I knew his alibi meant nothing.

I couldn't stop fixating on Cody, wondering if maybe that was what he'd wanted all along, to end up in that prison, to get to Abel, to die at his hands like the rest of his family. His lawyer could have asked for a different prison. It would have been a reasonable request. I thought there must have been a reason he hadn't. Then I would hate myself for how much the idea of him maybe getting what he wanted bothered me. Then the more I spiraled, the more it felt like he *had* gotten what he wanted.

I had come a long way on paper. I wasn't a murderer after all. I was nothing like my father, and even more than knowing it, I had accepted it. I grieved for Natalie and my mother—even for James Calhoun. I had people in my life I cared about. I should have felt better, but those were just bullet points. Realizing that I could be my own person, that I didn't need to hide, and that I didn't need to hurt people—that was nice, I guess. But that's not how I had spent my thirty-year existence up to that point, and a few storybook epiphanies weren't going to reset the way I processed the world and the people in it. The frosting was pretty, but I worried the cake was still rotten.

The guys were faring better than I was. Dominic was getting his book deal—a book that didn't yet exist, but Elyse and I had both agreed to exclusive interviews and the publisher couldn't resist.

Porter got a lot of attention, mostly because he was the only one receptive to it, and he very quickly leveraged that into something more. He gained an awful lot of Instagram followers and started posting ads. I didn't know what qualified a person whose only claim to fame was almost being murdered to suggest teeth-whitening products and protein powders, but I was happy for him and his platform. He would shoot me a few texts once in a while, but I wasn't sure he needed me anymore. I wasn't sure what he thought about me, about Gwen. Or what he thought about Marin.

I sat on my couch. I'd thought everything would be so different for me now, but I was still alone and I was still battling thoughts I had hoped would dissipate.

I debated calling Elyse, but there was no way to be casual with her now. Over the past months we'd had brief conversations, never alone, always surrounded by cops or lawyers. I didn't know if she had forgiveness in her. She had hated the real me for almost twenty years. She'd gotten her brother back and now he was gone again because of me.

I could have called Dominic. He always picked up, but I didn't want to talk to him. These days, the conversations felt more like interviews.

Three dead ends.

I grabbed my phone, opened the internet browser, and stared at the search bar. Then I started typing.

Natalie Shea

She'd had no social media. Only that one video that was taken down but had lived on like all things do on the internet. There were other links though. She was one of Cody's victims after all. I read the first fifteen search results. They all listed her in the context of the bigger picture. A few described her as a mentally unstable accomplice, which I was sure they'd gotten from Cody. There was never a mention of any journals, and I had to assume Cody had taken them after he killed her.

If only people knew the truth, but I had the last journal, and I'd kept it a secret too. I told myself it was because it raised too many questions about Porter's involvement, but it was really just something I didn't want to share with the world. It was the only thing I had left of her.

I wondered what had happened to Natalie in all those years since they'd pulled her away kicking and screaming. I used to promise her that everything would be okay. Talk about broken promises.

I suddenly felt the urge to search another name.

SIXTY

_ _ _ _ _ _

HERE WERE SIX DECLAN Harrises on Facebook, but only one who lived in Pennsylvania. He had forty-two friends and his profile picture was the Monster Energy logo, which made me irrationally angry. I scrolled through his feed. His birthday was January 12. I knew this because his entire feed was four or five generic birthday messages from this year, then the year before, then the year before that, uninterrupted. Finally, there was another post from five years ago. Someone had tagged him in the background of a photo of a bonfire. It was hard to make out his face, but he was spooky skinny, looking like Slender Man in a backward hat. The photo was geotagged to a bar in Rawling, Pennsylvania. There were no recent pictures. Maybe he was dead. I would love to know the statistics on the number of people every year who wish a dead person happy birthday via Facebook.

I went to the medicine cabinet and pulled out a bottle of NyQuil. I took a generous swig, hoping for rest. Tomorrow I was going to drive to Rawling, Pennsylvania, and find out if Declan Harris was dead.

- - - - -

DECLAN WASN'T DEAD. IT took me a couple of days before someone directed me to the Bridgewood Apartments. The place was a total dump—dirty towels as curtains, trash in the bushes, living room furniture on the lawn, molding from periodic rain. It was the type of place that belonged on the outskirts of town, only it sat right in the middle, on a street behind the post office, across from a park.

I sat in my car for hours before I saw Declan. He came out of nowhere, on foot, and lay down on one of the lawn couches. I proceeded to watch him shoot up and pass out. I'd never seen someone do drugs like that in real life—the real kind, the needle kind.

Once he stopped moving, I climbed out of my car. It was full-on nighttime now, but there were enough streetlights that I could get all the way to him without having to step into the dark.

I could smell him, or the couch, once I reached the lawn. It was a urine-mildew mix that made me gag. A breeze would blow the scent away and then it would come back once the gust passed, reintroducing me to it and never quite letting me get used to it.

I walked right up to the couch and stared down at him. His face was gaunt and pitted, trying to hide behind a struggling beard. I didn't know what I was feeling. It's hard to tell what's fair for a person like that. He was an asshole when he was younger, but as far as I knew, he hadn't killed anyone. He hadn't even really hurt anyone. He was just a jerk. We were the ones who'd poisoned him.

He'd stayed in that facility with me for a year and half after Natalie left. There were lasting effects. He had some kind of issue with his kidneys and eventually he had to be taken somewhere better equipped to care for him. I had no clue what kind of man he had become. Or how much of it had to do with what we had done to him.

I didn't know why, but I started to fixate on the distance between his mouth and his nose. They seemed close together. Were they closer than normal? I put my hand to my own nose, measuring the distance to my mouth, pulling back my fingers to inspect the spacing like it was scientific research. It was normal, I guess. Maybe I was overthinking it.

I reached down, putting my thumb on the side of his nose, then my pointer finger on the other side, ready to squeeze if I was so inclined. He didn't react to my touch so I lowered my palm, confirming the distance was short enough for me to cover his mouth. I could easily pinch his nose closed and cover his mouth with the same hand.

I didn't need to be this new person, miraculously cured from all of her dark shit. He didn't look well. It would be mercy.

"Hey!" a woman's voice screeched at me.

I yanked my hand back as I turned to see her walking from the park.

"What are you doing? Get away from him!" she yelled.

I wasn't looking to get in a street fight, so I turned and ran back to my car, this time trying my best to stay out of the light.

I sped away, feeling pretty stupid. I had tried to channel every feeling of guilt and anger I had toward the universe into finding Declan, a guy I hadn't seen or thought about in years, the only bad guy I could put right in front of my face, and it had really backfired.

This concept of seeking out a single person who'd wronged you in the past, exacting revenge, and finding closure was nice on paper but completely unrealistic. I hoped in the moments before he died, as Abel strangled the life out of him, Cody realized he'd gained nothing from it either.

On my long drive home, I received a text from Dominic. Barbara had died. I had only met her once, the night I terrified the crap out of her, but it was comforting that he thought I was someone worth telling. It was a reminder that I wasn't so alone anymore. And for the first time in a long time, that wasn't a bad thing.

The wake was about an hour north of the city. The parking lot was full, but not so much that I couldn't find a spot. People were going in and out; I didn't recognize them and probably never would. I was hesitant to go inside. I didn't want to walk in alone.

At that moment, I saw Kevin get out of his car and it seemed like a sign. I jumped out of my car and hustled to cross his path.

"Kevin," I said once I was close enough to get his attention.

"Hey, Gwen." He called me Gwen and I liked it. Did I have to be Marin now? No, I could be Gwen. I was Gwen.

"It's good to see you again. C'mon," he said, guiding me toward the entrance.

"I'm late," he whispered once we were inside, patting me on the back and leaving me to join the already formed receiving line next to Megan.

Jake should have been there, standing in line with Barbara's litter of stepchildren. Two months ago and he would have been there, maybe in between Dominic and Megan. Were they in chronological order? They must have all loved her to be there, standing in formation to hug strangers.

When I got to Dominic, he was in assembly-line mode, releasing the previous hug and leaving his arms open to greet the next person—me.

"Hi," he said, blinking out of robot mode. "I'm glad you came." He enthusiastically threw his arms around me, and for a sick second I hoped people were noticing how much more important I was than them because of the intensity of the hug I received, as if somehow you could win a wake. Maybe it stemmed from my desire to belong somewhere. That seemed like a more respectable reason. I decided to go with that.

"I'm so sorry," I whispered.

He pulled back to look at me but left his hands on my shoulders. "How are you? Are you okay?"

"Yeah, stop." I shook off his concern. "Are *you* okay?"

"Yeah, we all knew it was coming." I could tell it was just something he was reciting to people.

The lady behind me coughed and we turned to see the line was backing up.

"Will you wait?" he asked. "Wait for me outside? This part will be over in like twenty."

"Yeah, sure," I said. I squeezed his hand and moved on to smile and hug Megan, Kevin, and four more people who must have lived with Barbara and Dominic at some point.

I exited the funeral home and scanned the area for a place to sit. It reminded me of the day I'd waited for Dominic outside Edgar Valley. That had really been the beginning of it all. Well, I guess getting the arm was the beginning, but that day at Edgar Valley was the beginning of everything that mattered.

A tuft of bleach-blond hair bounced across the parking lot, and when Porter noticed me, a grin exploded on his face and he started to run. He picked me up off the ground, shaking me in his arms, kissing me a million times on the cheek.

"Porter!" I yelled through my own smile. "It's a wake."

He put me down and allowed for a moment of solemn silence to acknowledge my point before taking my hand and dragging me to sit on a bench along the sidewalk. Once we were no longer technically on funeral home property, he bubbled up again.

"What the heck?" he said. "Where have you been?"

"I just needed some time."

"You're over that though, right?"

"Yeah." I smiled. "I think so."

"Good, you can't leave me again." He gave me a quick, forceful side hug and my heart grew three sizes, Grinch style.

"You seem to be doing all right," I said.

"All the followers in the world can't replace you."

"Okay, calm down," I said. It reminded me so much of before, when we used to sit together for hours in Painting Pots, talking about nonsense, his raging enthusiasm, my . . . whatever the opposite of that was. "Are you doing okay?" I asked. "Like, about the other stuff?"

"I haven't killed any cats, if that's what you're asking."

I laughed. "Sort of."

"I have a therapist. My parents agreed to pay for it. Cheaper than college. I haven't said anything about Reanne, so don't worry. There's enough I can talk about without that. I talk about you a little." He bounced his eyebrows up and down. "Only the good stuff."

"Of course," I said.

"Do you think he told anyone?" Porter asked. "About what we did to Reanne's body?"

I shrugged. "If he told the cops, they don't seem to care. How would they prove it anyway? The rantings of a dead madman? They don't even know where the body is."

"Where is the body?"

I squinted at him. "Are you wearing a wire?"

Porter's eyes bulged, the color draining from his cheeks.

"I'm kidding," I said, and he exhaled, playfully backhanding me across the arm.

We sat in silence for a moment in such a way that it seemed we could almost forget everything bad that had happened. It was short-lived. Somber reflection was never his strong suit.

"I met two of the Teen Moms at a podcast convention in Austin." He beamed.

"I don't know what any of that means," I said.

"Oh, Gwen," he said, shaking his head with his patented disappointment. "Wait, can I call you Gwen?"

"Yes."

"Not Marin?"

"No."

"Good."

I didn't know why he said good; it was probably just easier for him, but I took it as acceptance.

"Well, isn't this a sight for sore eyes," a female voice came from behind us.

We both turned and there she was.

"Elyyyyyse!" Porter screeched, jumping up and hugging her, leaving her on the ground. Apparently the airborne hug was only for me and I felt special again.

She was in her typical dark clothing—less unique in this setting—eyeliner, haunted face, all the good stuff.

"Hey," I said.

She close-mouth smiled at me and it was a tense moment.

Porter slid his eyes back and forth and read the mood. "I'm going to go in," he said. "We'll catch up later?"

"Yeah," I said.

"And you too?" he asked Elyse, and she nodded.

"Okay, wish me luck." He spun around and bounced toward the funeral home like he was about to go onstage. He really was such a light. I was glad he hadn't become a serial killer. I'd been worried there for a minute.

"Can I join you?" she asked.

"Sure," I said, scooching over, assuming she wouldn't want to invade my personal space in the same way Porter had.

She took a seat but faced forward like she wasn't fully committed to sitting with me. "Where have you been?" she asked.

"Nowhere," I said. "Just trying to clear my head."

She still didn't look at me.

"No, that's a lie," I confessed. "I ended up looking up this guy I used to know from when I was a kid in that school with Natalie."

That got her to glance over at me.

"I know," I said. "I have problems. It's just . . . I don't even know why I thought of him, but once I did . . . I don't know. I think I'm crazy."

"Did you find him?"

I nodded. "Totally strung out. Really bad drug scene there."

She went quiet again, thinking before changing subjects. "You know, Cody had the best chance out of any of us to be normal. He didn't grow up with all these dark, twisted memories like we did."

"That's what I thought!" I exclaimed, way too excited. "Sorry."

"No, it's okay. I should have known, but he really seemed fine. When they identified James Calhoun, I confronted him. Part of me did wonder, but he was really convincing. He said he had nothing to do with it, and I had to believe him. I wanted to believe him."

"Listen to me, this was not your fault—not even in the realm of being your fault." I stared at her and forced her to stare back until it started to morph into something more suggestive and I had to ruin it. "I mean, I'm the one who screwed up killing him in the first place."

She swallowed that joke hard, wincing. "Jesus."

"Sorry, that was horrible."

"Yeah," she agreed. "True though, I suppose."

"It's still all my fault," I said, "what happened to your family."

"I know," she said.

"You don't seem like you want to kill me anymore. Is that wishful thinking?"

"We'll see." She smiled before going quiet again, her focus turning to the funeral home. "Like you said, murder isn't supposed to be easy."

"I said *getting away with it* isn't supposed to be easy," I corrected her.

"Hmm." She shrugged.

At the end of the day, I guess that was the best a person like me could hope for—a thinly veiled threat to my face instead of an obvious one on my doorstep.

ACKNOWLEDGMENTS

Writing is the easiest part. Thankfully, I have amazing people to help navigate all the other stuff.

My manager and dear friend, Emma Ross, who has been with me from the beginning, and my incredible agent, Brandi Bowles. You both always believed in this book and knew it would find the right home. I am so grateful for our dynamic. I feel very lucky to have you both in my corner.

My editor, Lisa Bonvissuto, who has been so wonderful through this whole process. Thank you for pushing me through revisions that at times were difficult, but always necessary. Your enthusiasm has given me so much confidence.

I would also like to thank the team at Berkley who've worked hard to bring this book to life, including Megha Jain, Abby Graves, Anika Bates, Jin Yu, Loren Jaggers, Danielle Keir, and Sarah Oberrender.

Of course, I would be nowhere without my parents, who refused to buy me a trampoline or a pet monkey, but did buy me an electric typewriter.

And lastly, a special shout-out to my Scituate crew, who heap praises on me until my face is bright red. I may look uncomfortable, and I am, but your support means everything!